REAL
UNREAL

— ❦ —

Best American
FANTASY

Volume III

REAL UNREAL

Best American
FANTASY

Volume III

GUEST EDITOR
Kevin Brockmeier

SERIES EDITOR
Matthew Cheney

UNDERLAND PRESS
www.underlandpress.com

Underland Press
www.underlandpress.com
Portland, Oregon

Cover design by John Coulthart
Book design by Heidi Whitcomb

ISBN 978-0-9802260-8-9

Printed in the United States of America
Distributed by PGW

First Underland Press Edition: February 2010

1 3 5 7 9 10 8 6 4 2

Printed in USA

T hanks to the many publishers who sent work to us—we could not possibly achieve the variety we seek without their generosity and help.

Special thanks this year goes to our previous guest editors, Ann and Jeff VanderMeer, who volunteered as coordinators for this volume. This book would not exist without their help.

The book would also not exist without the support of our publisher, Victoria Blake, who, like the rest of us, had no idea what she was getting herself into when she agreed to take on the project, and who has worked with vigor and vision on the book's behalf.

Finally, special thanks to a number of people who helped at various crucial times: Ellen Datlow, Craig Gidney, Colleen Lindsay, Matt Staggs, Hannah Tinti, Lorrie McCullough, and Gordon van Gelder.

ACKNOWLEDGMENTS

EDITORS

Guest editor **KEVIN BROCKMEIER** is an eminent novelist and short story writer, having received three O. Henry Awards, the Chicago Tribune's Nelson Algren Award, and an Italo Calvino Short Fiction Award. His stories have been published in a wide variety of venues, including *The New Yorker, The Georgia Review, McSweeney's,* and *The Oxford American,* and have been reprinted in *Best American Short Stories, The Year's Best Fantasy & Horror,* and the first volume of *Best American Fantasy.* His novels include *The Brief History of the Dead* and *The Truth About Celia,* and his short fiction has been collected in *Things That Fall from the Sky* and *The View from the Seventh Layer.* He has also published two children's books, *City of Names* and *Grooves: A Kind of Mystery.* He lives in Little Rock, Arkansas.

Series editor **MATTHEW CHENEY** has published fiction with *One Story, Weird Tales, Failbetter.com, Web Conjunctions,* and the anthologies *Interfictions* and *Logorrhea,* among other venues. He is a columnist for *Strange Horizons* and his weblog, *The Mumpsimus,* was nominated for a World Fantasy Award. He currently lives in New Hampshire and teaches at Plymouth State University.

JEFF & ANN VANDERMEER are series co-founders. Jeff VanderMeer is a multiple-award-winning author with books published in over 20 countries. Hugo Award winner Ann VanderMeer is the fiction editor for *Weird Tales,* and co-editor with Jeff on *Best American Fantasy, Last Drink Bird Head, Fast Ships, Black Sails, Steampunk, New Weird,* and many other anthologies. This literary "power couple" (Boing Boing) has been profiled on Wired.com, the *NYT* blog, and on NPR.

TABLE OF CONTENTS

PREFACE
by Matthew Cheney

This third volume in the Best American Fantasy series continues our mission of bringing together stories from a wide variety of sources in an attempt to reveal connections, tendencies, and proclivities that might otherwise be invisible—but this volume brings a few important changes as well.

With the third volume, *Real Unreal*, we have moved to Underland Press, a new and exciting publisher that shares our interest in fantasy as a technique of writing more than a genre boundary. The move allowed us to tweak our title a little bit, too; by adding individual titles and numbering the volumes instead of identifying them by year we hope to emphasize that these anthologies are collections of stories, not yearbooks. We still seek to find work published within a single calendar year, but we make no claims of being a comprehensive representation of the world of fantasy fiction in any one year. Instead, *Best American Fantasy* offers its guest editors the opportunity to present a personal vision of what the words "best," "American," and "fantasy" mean to them.

Kevin Brockmeier graciously agreed to be our new guest editor after Ann and Jeff VanderMeer's outstanding work on the first two volumes. Kevin is a writer who represents everything we hoped *Best American Fantasy* could champion—he is equally comfortable in the communities that, for lack of a better term, we can generally identify as the worlds of genre and non-genre writing, but more importantly, he is one of the writers who reveals the complexities (and absurdities!) of such a dichotomy. Kevin has had work published not only in the first volume of *Best American Fantasy*, but also in *Best American Short Stories*, *The O. Henry Award*, and *The Year's Best Fantasy and Horror*. While finishing work on this book he was an instructor at the famed Iowa Writers' Workshop, an institution that counts many of the most prominent writers of literary realism in the last fifty years among its alumni and teachers (but also, it's worth noting, a number of previous contributors to *Best American Fantasy*, as well as Steven Erickson, author of the Malazan Book of the Fallen series of epic fantasy novels; Iowa's reality is more diverse than its reputation might suggest).

Kevin worked tirelessly to find stories, becoming consumed with the obsession that overcomes every guest editor: the desire to *read everything*. It's impossible, of course, but the passion that inspires the obsession leads to the eclectic choice of stories herein. We discovered, too, what the guest editors and I have discovered with each book in this series: as we discussed the possible stories to include, we found ourselves circling back to questions of what *best* and *American* and, especially, *fantasy* mean to us. What distinguishes fantasy from science fiction if a story is not primarily about its technology? Is a story that implies something beyond consensual reality a fantasy story or a kind of stretched realism? Will the real-world political implications of a story remain strong if it is reprinted in a book with "fantasy" in the title?

We hope each book in the series will be unique and different from its predecessors, but the ultimate goal of *Best American Fantasy* remains the same with every volume: to create a surprising and compelling collection of stories.

For guidelines on submitting material to *Best American Fantasy*, visit our blog at http://bestamericanfantasy.blogspot.com

INTRODUCTION

by Kevin Brockmeier

"Sitting under trees on or before noon is, in a number of romances, tantamount to inviting a supernatural visitation. The precise significance of a grafted tree is unclear, though notionally such a tree represents a coincidence of the natural with the unnatural."

—from a footnote to "Sir Orfeo," *Norton's Middle English Romances*, edited by Stephen H. A. Shepherd

T hough the tradition of realistic fiction is a rich and a verdant one, it is a mistake to believe that it exhibits the oldest or grandest trees in the forest of literature. Undoubtedly, realism has offered the world some of its finest chronicles of society and the family, as well its most ambitious representations of the individual mind at play with the materials of consciousness. It has attracted the talents of such extraordinary writers as Lady Murasaki and George Eliot, Tolstoy and Flaubert, Proust and Faulkner. Almost certainly, it has been the predominant mode of our time. All along, though, there has been another kind of literature stretching its limbs and putting out its leaves alongside it, one that is rooted in the magical and the otherworldly, where a deep soil of myths and creation tales has given rise to *The Epic of Gilgamesh*, to Homer and Ovid and Aristophanes, to *The Thousand and One Nights*, to *Beowulf* and *Le Morte D'Arthur*, to countless Medieval romances and morality plays, to Dante and to Shakespeare and to Goethe, to Mary Shelley and Edgar Allen Poe, Lewis Carroll and Hans Christian Andersen, H. G. Wells and Karel Capek, and to all the great fantasists of late Twentieth Century fiction: Rushdie and Borges, J. G. Ballard and Isaac Bashevis Singer, Jose Saramago and Gabriel García Márquez. Some of this literature presents itself as a violation of the ordinary, some as merely an augmentation of it. In many cases, though, it offers stories in which the branches of the ordinary and the extraordinary are so tightly intertwined that it is nearly impossible to tell them apart.

What you hold in your hands is a collection of such grafted trees: stories which take the balanced prose, complex internality, and finely gauged awareness of the human heart that's found in the best realistic fiction and join them together with the strange gymnastic possibilities of fantasy to create a single living organism. The blossoms that appear may display unexpected colors, but they are no less beautiful or vibrant for the transformation.

It was only recently, in examining the lists I keep of my fifty favorite books and movies, that I realized how suffused with fantasy my tastes really are, and how often they involve exactly this coincidence of the natural with the unnatural. Ask me for a copy of these lists and I'll happily pass them along to you. On their pages, you will find historical epics and quiet character studies brushing up against fairy tales and sci-fi apocalypses and the strange nesting boxes of magic realism and classical fabulation in one great roiling crowd. Even the most naturalistic of my favorites—novels like I Served the King of England, films like Ponette—are touched with either a religious sentiment or a clarity of perception that seems to verge on the fantastic. It appears that the conjunction of the real with the unreal, of the complications of human feeling with the whimsies and dreamlike visitations of fantasy, is an inescapable feature of my aesthetic.

Here, for instance, and apropos to this anthology, are my ten favorite fantasy stories of all time, listed in alphabetical order:

1. "Akhnilo" by James Salter

2. "Blumfeld, an Elderly Bachelor" by Franz Kafka

3. "Catskin" by Kelly Link

4. "The Dreamed" by Robert McLiam Wilson

5. "Extracts from Adam's Diary and Eve's Diary" by Mark Twain

6. "Faith and Mountains" by Augusto Monterroso

7. "From the Fifteenth District" by Mavis Gallant

8. "The Light-Years" by Italo Calvino

9. "Professor Berkowitz Stands on the Threshold" by Theodora Goss

10. "The Scalehunter's Beautiful Daughter" by Lucius Shepard

So—we have seven writers whose books are typically marketed as literary fiction, three as fantasy or science fiction; seven English-language writers and three foreign-language writers; seven men and three women; four writers who are now deceased, six who are currently living; two writers who occupy the pinpoint center of the canon, three who are slowly gravitating there, and five who, thus far, remain unjustly at the margins; two writers I know personally; one writer whose work I treasure above all others; and three writers who, to my knowledge, aside from the stories on this list, have never otherwise written outside the realist mode.

In this edition of *Best American Fantasy*, you will find the twenty finest fantasy stories I read this year. Also, inevitably, you will find a record of my own preoccupations. There are stories of the afterlife, such as Shawn Vestal's chronicle of an eternity played out beneath the weight of nostalgia, Stephen King's tender and disquieting phone call from the other world, and Ramona Ausubel's diamond-bright vision of a boat full of grandmothers floating upon a mysterious ocean—her first published piece of fiction.

There are stories in which the failings and idiosyncrasies of the human body are tipped into the fantastic, such as Ryan Boudinot's surrealist study of a town whose residents share a single heart, Paul Tremblay's beautifully vulnerable domestic chronicle of a girl with a second head, and Kuzhali Manickavel's elegant glance at the prospect of flight and the strangeness of parenthood.

There are stories that interrogate religion—Peter S. Beagle's wise, touching, and merciful tale of angelic encounter, Benjamin Rosenbaum and David Ackert's fierce reckoning with the holy and the inhumane— and stories that interrogate politics—Martin Cozza's miniaturist dose of anti-presidential venom, Thomas Glave's daring, nightmarish, yet strangely incandescent atrocity catalogue.

There are stories that turn established narrative tropes to their own ends, like John Kessel's intimate, carefully modulated collage of *Frankenstein* and *Pride and Prejudice*, Lisa Goldstein's idealist subversion of the reader's guide, Will Clarke's roughneck superhero saga, and Kellie Wells's boisterous and divinely vexed Pied Piper tale.

And there are stories in which ordinary people are confronted with the fantastic and use its mechanisms to understand their own histories, such as Deborah Schwartz's poignant examination of the way our griefs rise up to haunt us, Chris Gavaler's doorway between a forgotten childhood and an inharmonious present, Laura Kasischke's savage elegy to lost possibility, and Rebecca Makkai's teasingly yearning composer-out-of-time fable. (Makkai's story "The Briefcase," by the way, from the same issue of *The New England Review* as Chris Gavaler's, was bar none the finest non-fantasy story I read this year. Seek it out.)

There are also two stories whose status as fantasy might demand a little justification: Jeffrey Ford's unforgettable tale of scale disruption and tiny genocides, "Daltharee"—the methods of which are primarily science fictional, but the science in question, "submicroscopic differentiated cell division and growth," is so playfully unlikely that it seems to me to cross the border into fantasy—and Katie Williams's darkly comic "Serials," which profoundly violates the customs of our world, if not its rules, presenting a society that mirrors our own but is enough unlike it that I think it can rightly be considered fantastic.

As different as these stories are—as varied in their tones and approaches, as motley in their wonders—they all share one thing in common: I greeted each of them with the tingle of exhilarated discovery that is the uppermost joy of fantasy. Nearly three-quarters of them are by writers whose work I had never previously encountered (though I'm making up for lost time: Thomas Glave's *The Torturer's Wife* and Kuzhali Manickavel's *Insects Are Just Like You and Me Except Some of Them Have Wings* are every bit as good as the stories their authors contribute to this volume), and just as many are from publications I had never read before. I hope that they offer you the same sense of flourishing possibility they offered me, that feeling you get when you are sitting beneath a tree at noon and a flock of birds lifts from its branches, their tailfeathers flashing behind them like needles pulling the brightest threads.

SAFE PASSAGE

by Ramona Ausubel from *One Story*

T he grandmothers—dozens of them—find themselves at sea. They do not know how they got there. It seems to be afternoon, the glare from the sun keeps them squinting. They wander carefully, canes and orthotics, across the slippery metal deck of the ship, not built for human passage but for cargo. Huge shipping crates are stacked at bow and stern. The grandmothers do not know what it means. *Are we dead?* they ask each other. *Are we dying?* Every part of the ship is metal, great sheets and hand-sized rivets. Cranes and transverses and bulkheads and longitudinals—all metal. All painted white and now splayed with the gray stars of gull droppings.

Among the many hunched backs and stockinged legs, there is a woman named Alice who finds the nicest bench and sits down on it. The bench looks out at the horizon, that line drawn by the eye to make an ending where there is not one. Alice is a lover of views, of great expanses, and she is happy now as she has always been to look out. She thinks of her children on faraway spits of land. They have their studios and paints, their meditation cushions, their cars in need of oil changes and their grocery lists. She thinks about her one new great-granddaughter whom she has never met but who she hopes is wrapped in the gray blanket she knit.

Around Alice there are varying levels of commotion and flurry. *Does anyone have a compass? Do you know how to drive a ship? Where is my nurse? I'm from the DC area!*

There are some grandmothers who try to escape immediately. They get in a rescue craft tied to the side of the ship and sit holding their pocketbooks, waiting patiently to be lowered down to the tattered blue. Their faces become wet with wind-water but they are not lowered. Their hairdos begin to wilt, but still they do not get lowered.

There is the group of ladies whose eye makeup travels in dark tracks down cheeks; the group of proactive grandmothers who have taken scraps of paper and pens from their pocketbooks and are brainstorming a list of suggestions, diagramming these suggestions in order of popularity and feasibility. In front of Alice is the group of rememberers, recounting, as if centuries had passed, their lives. *It used to be so easy,* they remember at high volume due to a common loss of hearing, *there were lovely smooth roads, it was possible to get in the car and drive to different places where the pancakes were especially good, where the coffee was flown in from Italy.*

But even in this situation, extraordinary and new, even with the churning ocean surrounding them completely, many of the grandmothers make small talk. They compliment each other's earrings. *Are those pearls freshwater? The color reminds me of the curtains my mother bought on a trip to Bangkok where she met the princess, if you can believe that.*

Alice is joined by someone whose name she does not even listen to. The woman says, "You are from Chicago, you say. How *is* Chicago this time of year?"

"Well it's very cold on one day and then it's very warm the next day."

"And your children, what do they do?"

"I have two painters, a woodworker and a writer."

"How *interesting,*" the woman says, "mine are all lawyers. I have six."

"My father was a lawyer," Alice smiles. "It was a terrible way to grow up. I'm glad none of mine went that way."

The woman's facial muscles seem to harden but are subverted by the skin hanging soft, always, no matter how tight her smile or her frown.

"It's possible I'm dead," Alice says, looking at the differing blues of sky and water.

"I'm sorry." Though the woman is looking at Alice she seems to be most sorry for herself.

Alice nods. "Yes, I guess I might have died. Or be dying." She remembers a hospital room and behind the bed a wall of machines, each emitting a very distinct beep which would draw a different nurse with a different tool. One brought Linda with a suction pump that gathered, painfully, the mucus from Alice's lungs. One brought Kera with a new bag of liquid food to be attached to the feeding tube. The room was always half dark, permanent evening. At all times at least one of her relatives was in the room.

Uneasily, the woman comforts, "I'm sorry to hear that."

Alice nods again and stretches her legs out, covered in the skin of stockings, and wiggles her feet at the ends.

"Am I dead too, then?"

"I don't know. Did you die?" Alice asks.

"I don't remember dying."

"Well, maybe you didn't."

Under the setting sun, the ship is stained red. The deck looks like a high school cafeteria with small clusters of ladies huddled close together, constellated out over the surface. They remember to worry about things they had forgotten to worry about at first. The slippery surface is of great concern to many who fear the breaking of hips. They fret over husbands, who have been left at home with nothing in the refrigerator. Cats are likely pawing the heavy legs of couches. The couches will never survive the absence of the grandmothers. This will be the end of the couches. They talk about this. They huddle against the wind.

Some grandmothers who are quiet in the huddles do not have these things to go back to. Some have not turned off their televisions in years, not in the morning or at night. They have freezers full of food ready-packed for quick eating and the dents in the cushions where they sit all day, their faces dimming and brightening in the light, are severe. The dents do not re-puff because they do not have a chance to do so. They are always under-butt. These grandmothers nervously check their watches still set to home-time, knowing that right now, right at this moment when the sun is falling, Pat Sajak is about to welcome them, with the help of his generous audience, to Wheel! Of! Fortune! Even though they will miss this television evening, those grandmothers, the ones with no one, are not so sorry to be here at sea with so many warm bodies.

While they trade stories of survival, the proactive grandmothers who have no time for idle worrying are on a mission to find out what is inside the crates on deck. A set of bolt cutters has been discovered in the engine room. The engines were discovered there as well but were much too complicated to operate so the ship continues to float, unrumbling.

These women have been in strange situations before. "In Bermuda," someone says, fingering the gold buttons on her cardigan, "right in the middle of our perfect vacation, a hurricane hit and we had to take the little girl who sold shell jewelry into our hotel room for two straight days. Poor thing had never had a Pepsi-Cola before," she recalls. "Can you imagine?"

The fellow proactive grandmothers marvel.

Alice, meanwhile walks the edge of the boat, passing a lady whose hands are busy clenching. "Hullo," she nods to the woman, the rail-holder. The look she gets is a short, hopeful one, one that wants to see a man, any man, but a man in uniform especially. Any man in uniform with some kind of list. When she looks up to see another sagging female she deflates.

Alice has been on a lot of boats. While she runs her hand along the railing she remembers the first time and the last—love early, love late. When she was seventeen years old, after an expensive wedding at her parent's country house with none of her friends in attendance, she spent the first week as a wife on a sloop off the coast of Rhode Island. The first night, after navigating out of a very tricky harbor in a storm, her victorious husband came into the cabin where Alice was curled up. The small boat tossed in the heavy wind.

"I would rather we went back," she managed. "We're very far away from anything."

"The tide is against us. The dangerous thing would be to go back," he began, drying his glasses on a towel. She insisted, she told him she couldn't stand it out there. "Please," she said.

He put the sail back up and started the journey back. Alice, inside, did not see the work he did to take her in. She did not see the boat keel and scoop water onto his bare feet.

With the sound of the dock squeaking against the hull, they lay side by side, him reading by candlelight, her pretending to sleep with only his knots holding them steady.

In the morning she tried to be a wife. She got an egg out of the small icebox and cracked it into the pan but the yolk broke and bled. The yellow heart ran rivers over the white. She turned the heat off and left it there, dying. Alice jumped in the water in her nightgown and swam out to the small dinghy attached to the hull of their boat where she bobbed, her clothes sucked to her body.

"What are you doing?" he yelled out to her when he found her. She did not answer. He reeled her craft in until it was close enough that he could step inside. "Did you swim out?" he asked, putting his hands on her wet head. "You could have put on a bathing suit."

"I am not a good wife."

"You can learn." They sat in silence, the sound of water dripping off of her and landing in the belly of the vessel. "You stay here in your own little ship. You don't have to be anybody's wife here. I'll go make myself something to eat." He patted her and returned to his own boat, letting her rope go until she drifted back out to the maximum ten feet. The sea was a flat sheet going on until it couldn't anymore, until the sky pinned it down.

This was the beginning of a marriage that would continue into her fifties when he left for good to start another family. She is sorry that she was not the one who pressed herself up against him to keep him warm when he was dying. Instead they corresponded by mail and twice she sat on the porch swing outside his house with him and they talked about their children and their grandchildren, those lives they made together while his wife kept herself busy in the house.

Her second marriage was also over thirty years long, ending not in divorce but in his quiet death. When they met he had said, "Please, there is no reason not to marry me. I am smart and kind and I will do the dishes." This wedding, just like the first, took place at her parents' house only this time she was driven off in a golf cart instead of put on a sailboat.

They were retired for almost the entire duration and they traveled often by freighter where they were the only two paying passengers, sitting together on deck and doing the Jumble while the crew called commands to one another. Her husband couldn't see well as he got older so she'd narrate the journey for him. "On the left there is an old fishing shack. It has fallen down on one side and the porch now hangs into the water. There are vines pulling it under. Two big birds are standing on the roof."

"Are they egrets?" he wanted to know.

"No, they are great blue herons."

"Oh, I was picturing egrets."

"Well they aren't. But they *are* very nice-looking."

"I'm sure they are. I was just picturing egrets."

"Well it doesn't matter now because that shack has passed. Now we are coming to a town. There are three little girls standing in the mud in their bathing suits, waving. Do you hear them calling to us?"

"Sort of." They both listened hard, the young voices made their way over the surface of the water.

"Do they have bicycles?" he asked.

"Why would they have bicycles?"

"Or fishing poles? How did they get there?"

"They just have hands. They are only trying to say hello."

"Well hello then!" he called back. "Hello!" The two of them called together, their arms working back and forth like a pair of windshield wipers, trying to clear the view ahead.

When Alice's circumnavigation takes her around to the bow of the ship, she finds the proactive grandmothers surrounding the crates like flies. They are furious with curiosity about what is inside—what they are carrying with them on some unknown body of water. "Perhaps there are beautiful Chinese green beans or Italian leather coats," says one. "Maybe they are full of the most luxurious furs," tries someone else. "I think it will be jewels!" shrieks another, though this seems optimistic to everyone.

What they find are none of those things. When the lock springs open on the first crate and the doors too, what they see inside are rows of white. Someone pulls and to her feet fall five toilet seats. They are the padded kind, sighing under the weight of the sitter. There must be hundreds of them in there. This crate is quickly abandoned in disappointment, though Alice has put a toilet seat over her head and wears it, to everyone's enjoyment, like a necklace.

In the next crate they find child-size wooden baseball bats with the words "Sluggy Bat" written in wide cursive. This discovery interests no one except one short lady who inches a bat out of the middle and swings it, remembering playing with her sisters in the street and pleased to find that it is a nice weight for her.

Crate number three is packed with stuffed Santa Claus dolls, their beards twisted in neat knots to keep them from tangling on their journeys to the shelf. Crate number four is full—full!—of yellow roses. The grandmothers hug them in bundles to their chests, their arms pricked by the thorns. They distribute the flowers around—handing the wilting bouquets out to their fellow passengers until they all look like prom queens ready to dance their victory dance, the thorns freckling their arms with blood.

Even here, evening comes and then night. The grandmothers go inside to the galley where they make their way through the first of many cases of canned peaches, sharing a single can opener found in a drawer. They discover that the toilet seats improve the comfort of the sitter on hard benches. They begin and end card games and word games. They quiz each other on presidential trivia. They begin to slump down, exhausted.

Around them are the roses on the floor, the countertop, the cheap wood tables with names carved into them—Danny and Phoung, Rocko, the shape of a penis now covered by some blooms. Roses are worn behind ears and tucked into buttonholes. They smell as they are supposed to.

The grandmothers feel farther and farther away.

As they huddle, even under the wrap of polyester blankets taken from bunks, the work of their bodies is almost visible—the sinews of muscle responding again and again to the heart's insistence. Dozens of kerosene lanterns flicker and the grandmothers, whose eyes are falling shut but who do not want to go alone to their cabins, who fear that this might be *it* for them, begin to ask one another questions.

"Tell me the story of my life," someone asks. "Tell me what I was like when I was a baby." And they can do it. They get the details wrong— locations of birth, names of parents and siblings—but this does not matter to anyone. They chime in, answering together, bit by bit. "Your mother was so happy to meet you," someone says. "Your father brought the congratulatory tiger lilies right up to your new nose," another adds. They all close their eyes. "And you were such a good baby. You hardly ever cried." The many lips pull up into smiles. The grandmothers remember even if they don't.

"And then when I was a child?" they ask together.

"Oh, when you were a child you had hair like an angel."

"You had a sweater your mother made with a picture of a rabbit knitted in."

"You were very good in arithmetic and you would have been good at the flute too." They cannot get enough of their lives.

"The fighting was mostly over money. It wasn't about you."

"Your mother did not mean to hit you in the eye with the serving platter. You just walked into it."

"Your granddad forgave you for getting lost in Puerto Vallarta that day."

"And your sister looked beautiful in her blue dress," a husky voice adds. The grandmothers, Alice among them, see the blue dress. Some see a silk navy A-line, some see a cotton sheath belted at the waist, some see an evening dress flicker out the door and into a waiting car. They are quiet in their rememberings.

"Who is there when I die?" someone asks and they all nod to say yes, they wonder that, too. Alice clears her throat and begins, confident.

"Your children are there," she tells them. "All of them. Three of your grandchildren too. They all have their hands on your body. You can feel them letting go of warmth. It doesn't stop at the skin or at the bone, nothing can stop it. They are singing *Michael, Row the Boat Ashore*. Outside the window you can see a lake and a Ferris wheel on the edge. It is not raining outside but it looks like it might."

The grandmothers have wet eyes. They are all picturing themselves lying there with many pairs of hands covering them, more hands than possible, their bodies hidden. It is just the backs of hands familiar and radiating and with very faint pulses. In their minds, the grandmothers dissolve under those palms. They go gaseous. It is no longer necessary to maintain any particular shape.

Alice sits surrounded by the rattle of their collective breathing. These lungs are not noiseless machines anymore. In this close circle they are trading matter, molecules of one go straight into the tubes of another. Alice thinks of the ocean they are floating on, waves rolling out over the miles. And in those waves fish in schools so large they turn the ocean silver.

"We are out at sea," she says. "We should not go to bed. We should go fishing."

The faces in the dim lantern-light are uncertain.

"We are floating on top of a lot of creatures. Let's see what we catch," Alice tries to explain.

"We don't have any poles," a voice counters.

"We can make some," Alice responds. "We have no idea what might be down there!" Her voice is high and excited.

No one wants to be left alone so they pull their blankets tighter, though it isn't cold. The women set to work unraveling strings from the salt-heavy ropes, coiled like great snakes on deck. They isolate one string at a time and then tie them around the necks of some of the baseball bats. The grandmothers disperse along the railing and drop their very long lines. The lines have no hooks and no bait. Those lines on the port side, where the wind is coming from, are pasted to the hull like clinging lizards. Those lines on starboard blow out so that all together, the row of them looks like the ribcage of a whale.

The women themselves are nearly invisible but for some moonlit glowings of hair—fuzzy little white islands in the dark. The sound of the overhead ring of gulls is mostly wing-noise and an occasional vocal cry.

In the underneath, in that syrupy dark, the creatures they are trying to catch do not notice the tips of the hopeful strings. Jellies jet themselves along, not going anywhere, just moving for the sake of moving. Any fishes who can glow, glow. Some have patterns of light on their spines. Fake eyes look like real eyes for the purpose of being left alone. Sharks separate the water like curtains, currents flowing off their bared teeth.

There is always the chance of a giant squid and the great likelihood of regular squid. The octopus does not need, in the dark hours, to dispense its ink. The ink stays churning inside the cool gut of the creature, all eight arms reaching and twisting and gathering. Miniature fish congregate and suck at the bodies of bigger fish, eating the growing algae. Turtles swim the length of entire oceans in order to lay their eggs on the beach where they were born.

The ship sloshes and the grandmothers sway. They keep their lines steady, most balancing the tiny baseball bats on their laps. They hum. Their voices are crackly and uneven. Some go for television theme songs. Some fumble over old lullabies. They don't mind that their melodies do not match up; it is nice to hear the humming and to do the humming, just to make noise. To feel the throat vibrating and air in the nose.

Alice is humming a lullaby invented by her own grandmother about a small horse when she feels a tug at her line. The song dies in her chest. She is holding on with both of her hands, each one bearing a wedding ring—husband number one on her right and husband number two on her left. Her knuckles are pale hills, hunkered down, ready for anything. "Fish!" she calls. "Fish!"

The other grandmothers shriek and repeat, "Fish! Fish!" They come to her, some faster than others.

"Stand up!" one yells. "Stand up and let me help you hold that bat." Alice stands. The woman comes in from behind, threading her arms through Alice's. The handle of the bat is held now by four hands and it looks like baseball practice, like the coach will, in slow motion, move Alice's arms in a perfect swing.

Instead they walk backward, leaning away from the railing. The rope tries to resist. More grandmothers join in, taking the line and hauling the fish up. Arms tire easily. There are those who stand on the sidelines and cheer. It is a long time before the pullers come to the sea-wet part of the rope.

When the fish finally flops onto deck they are surprised to see that built into the fish's forehead is a small pole with a fleshy light at the end, a greenish bulb. "You must have come from very far down," Alice says to the fish, "to have your own lantern." The grandmothers circle up around it, everything dark except the round light, which illuminates a gnash of long sharp teeth. The heavy scales reflect the moonlight in vague arches. The fish is not content on deck. It flops its tail, slapping.

"I know that fish, that's an angler," one grandmother says.

"This fish really exists?" asks another.

"We should name it," someone ventures. "I'd like to name it Marty, after my husband." This is met with silence.

"I'd like to name it Harriet after my mother," someone else tries.

"And I'd like to name it Marcello." They add names: Bill, Mort, Jesus, Kayla, Albert, Martha, Susan, Jeanette, Anne, Ned, Hank, as if throwing pennies into a fountain. The fish flops as it takes on the names of loved ones.

"It's my fish," Alice says, "and I am going to name him Fishy. But he can have all those others as middle names." This does not meet opposition. They stand there over him and do not speak, but in all of their heads are prayers. They throw them at the scaled creature, at his round body, at his ugly face. They hope for the good ones to get what they deserve. They hope for the lost ones to get home, for the prices to go down, for more days in the back yard for everyone. Fishy's light goes a little soft and his eyes are dark liquid balls with shivers of moon inside. Alice bends down and picks the fish up. "Hello, Fishy," she says. She kisses her fingertips and touches them to its head. "I think we better throw you back now." She hobbles to the edge of the boat, tired after the long pull, while the knot of old ladies watches. She hums as she goes, returning to the lullaby about the horse. When she reaches the railing she turns back to the other grandmothers and holds Fishy up for his goodbyes.

"Goodbye!" "Goodbye, Neil!" "Goodbye, Albert!" "Goodbye, Nixon!" "Goodbye Bill!" they chant. And out he goes. He does not hit the hull but makes a very straight, very fast journey back to the water where he will continue to navigate the darkness with his green bulb. On deck some of the grandmothers kneel over the pool of water where Fishy had been. They dip their fingers in it and put it on their foreheads. They taste it, their dry old tongues bitten by the salt.

It is a warm night and though the rest of the grandmothers go inside to their claimed cabins, Alice lies down on a pile of Santas. She covers herself with her blanket. "I think tomorrow is Wednesday," she says to herself, "The garbage goes out on Wednesday." She can hear the sound of the truck, green and screeching as it devours up the trash and smashes it down. "It's the day I teach poetry, in my apartment." The day that she will not attend is laid out before her, the newspaper that she will not read lands at her doorstep. The phone, the refrigerator, the cat. She holds her own hands.

She imagines a hospital room, her four grown children surrounding her. One daughter rubs Alice's hands with lotion. "It's in and out, just like this," the daughter says, breathing to show breathing. "Go as long as you want. It can be two minutes and it can be ten years. We're going to be here, loving you."

Nervous, another daughter eats a bag of chips. Another opens a book of poems, searches for the exact right words. The nurses prepare swabs, towels. Grandchildren collect around the bedside. It is not dark in the room but it is not light either, and even the city outside whispers. There are sailboats slipping along the surface of the lake. They tack around big red buoys. The sailors' voices cannot be heard this high, this far away—the whole world between them—still their boats are part of this big view.

When a telephone in the corner rings, her only son chats with two of Alice's oldest friends before he says, "They're going to take the tubes out of her lungs. Any minute." When her son hangs up the phone he asks, "Do you have any idea how many people adore you?" And Alice smiles wide enough that her teeth, treasures in that cave, shine.

The boat is rocking, the sea stretching around her.

"Do you think this is it?" Alice asks, but there is no answer. "There are people I was hoping to see again!" she calls out to the dark. Her knees are tucked together, legs folded like wings. Below, so much water moves restlessly. Above, the air does the same.

The gulls still circle even though it is too dark to hunt. "Do you know," Alice yells to the birds above, "that I have not been swimming in ages? How do you not swim in such a great big ocean?" Soon she is tying knots along the enormous rope, every foot and a half. The knots are the size of her head. It gets harder and harder the farther she gets from the end. Her palms are sore. Each knot she ties she tries to remember a person she loves. She gets the name and the face in her mind. The Jewish boy she wasn't allowed to see, her cousin who she always got in trouble with as a girl, her brother who she loved better than others did, her mother who ended it all when she thought things were starting to get unsightly. Her two husbands whose necks she could still smell, who had left her one and then the next, alone on the turning earth. She thinks to herself, *Now I can say that I love them all. I am an old woman and no one will try to dissuade me.* All the single fibers, twisted together into ten, the ten into a hundred, the hundred into a thousand.

She drops the line over the edge, then takes her dress off. She can feel the wind moving through her loose cotton underwear as she climbs, but it is the slip that really dances. It puffs up and looks, at moments, like a wedding gown, then pastes itself to her body, every shape underneath mimicked by the fabric. The separation of her legs is defined along with the cut of her waist. The rope swings gently and Alice swings with it.

"I don't know if I can make it!" she calls up to the gulls. She is more than halfway down. Her feet slide to the next knot and her hands follow.

Alice reaches the water. When she touches the waves the salt stings. "It's cold," she says. But she wants to let go of the rope. She wants to be free of the climb so she lets herself fall in, her entire weight let loose in the water. It catches her easily and she dunks her head under. She laughs the laugh of a cold, floating person. She waves her arms and lets the yips come out of her mouth. She peers down below, trying to see, but the only things are her own feet haloed by green phosphorescence, kicking and kicking and kicking.

"Will both of my husbands be mine again?" she calls to the birds or the fish or the sky. "Can I love them again now?" She does not get her answer. Her slip rises up around her like a tutu. She looks now like a ballerina on a music box, legs bared under the high-flying skirt. The material is soft and brushes Alice's arms. She does not try to hold the slip down. Her breasts float up. All around her is the green light of stirred water.

The boat groans and leans away, then begins to slip across the smooth sea. Alice does not feel herself moving and the ship leaves no wake, yet there is much morning-bright water between them. Her rope slaps at the hull, quieter as it goes, until all she hears is the echo of a sound no longer taking place, just her ear's memory of that song. Alice is now alone, but the ocean is full and the sky is full—how plentiful the elements are! She floats on her back at the exact point of the ocean and the sky meeting, held like a prayer between two hands pressed together.

Alice dives down and spins, making a lopsided flip and emerges with her hair stuck to her face. Drops fall from her chin in a glowing chain. They fall from her hair and from her ears and from the tip of her nose. They fall from eyelashes and from the lobes of her ears. She throws her arms up in "ta-da" position, water flying off in a great celebration of sparks. The drops join back up with the whole ocean, and then disappear inside that enormous body.

UNCLE CHAIM AND AUNT RIFKE AND THE ANGEL

by Peter S. Beagle from *Strange Roads*

M y Uncle Chaim, who was a painter, was working in his studio—
as he did on every day except Shabbos—when the blue angel
showed up. I was there.

I was usually there most afternoons, dropping in on my way home from
Fiorello LaGuardia Elementary School. I was what they call a "latchkey
kid," these days. My parents both worked and traveled full-time, and
Uncle Chaim's studio had been my home base and my real playground
since I was small. I was shy and uncomfortable with other children. Uncle
Chaim didn't have any kids, and didn't know much about them, so he
talked to me like an adult when he talked at all, which suited me perfectly.
I looked through his paintings and drawings, tried some of my own, and
ate Chinese food with him in silent companionship, when he remembered
that we should probably eat. Sometimes I fell asleep on the cot. And
when his friends—who were mostly painters like himself—dropped in to
visit, I withdrew into my favorite corner and listened to their talk, and
understood what I understood. Until the blue angel came.

It was very sudden: one moment I was looking through a couple of
the comic books Uncle Chaim kept around for me, while he was trying
to catch the highlight on the tendons under his model's chin, and the
next moment there was this angel standing before him, actually *posing*,
with her arms spread out and her great wings taking up almost half
the studio. She was not blue herself—a light beige would be closer—
but she wore a blue robe that managed to look at once graceful and
grand, with a white undergarment glimmering beneath. Her face, half-
shadowed by a loose hood, looked disapproving.

I dropped the comic book and stared. No, I *gaped*, there's a difference.
Uncle Chaim said to her, "I can't see my model. If you wouldn't mind
moving just a bit?" He was grumpy when he was working, but never rude.

"*I* am your model," the angel said. "From this day forth, you will paint no one but me."

"I don't work on commission," Uncle Chaim answered. "I used to, but you have to put up with too many aggravating rich people. Now I just paint what I paint, take it to the gallery. Easier on my stomach, you know?"

His model, the wife of a fellow painter, said, "Chaim, who are you talking to?"

"Nobody, nobody, Ruthie. Just myself, same way your Jules does when he's working. Old guys get like that." To the angel, in a lower voice, he said, "Also, whatever you're doing to the light, could you not? I got some great shadows going right now." For a celestial brightness was swelling in the grubby little warehouse district studio, illuminating the warped floorboards, the wrinkled tubes of colors scattered everywhere, the canvases stacked and propped in the corners, along with several ancient rickety easels. It scared me, but not Uncle Chaim. He said. "So you're an angel, fine, that's terrific. Now give me back my shadows."

The room darkened obediently. "*Thank* you. Now about *moving* . . ." He made a brushing-away gesture with the hand holding the little glass of Scotch.

The model said, "Chaim, you're worrying me."

"What, I'm seventy-six years old, I'm not entitled to a hallucination now and then? I'm seeing an angel, you're not—this is no big deal. I just want it should move out of the way, let me work." The angel, in response, spread her wings even wider, and Uncle Chaim snapped, "Oh, for God's sake, shoo!"

"It is for God's sake that I am here," the angel announced majestically. "The Lord—Yahweh—I Am That I Am—has sent me down to be your muse." She inclined her head a trifle, by way of accepting the worship and wonder she expected.

From Uncle Chaim, she didn't get it, unless very nearly dropping his glass of Scotch counts as a compliment. "A muse?" he snorted. "I don't need a muse—I got models!"

"That's it," Ruthie said. "I'm calling Jules, I'll make him come over and sit with you." She put on her coat, picked up her purse, and headed for the door, saying over her shoulder, "Same time Thursday? If you're still here?"

"I got more models than I know what to do with," Uncle Chaim told the blue angel. "Men, women, old, young—even a cat, there's one lady always brings her cat, what am I going to do?" He heard the door slam, realized that Ruthie was gone, and sighed irritably, taking a larger swallow of whiskey than he usually allowed himself. "Now she's upset, she thinks she's my mother anyway, she'll send Jules with chicken soup and an enema." He narrowed his eyes at the angel. "And what's this, how I'm only going to be painting you from now on? Like Velázquez stuck painting royal Hapsburg imbeciles over and over? Some hope you've got! Listen, you go back and tell,"—he hesitated just a trifle—"tell whoever sent you that Chaim Malakoff is too old not to paint what he likes, when he likes, and for who he likes. You got all that? We're clear?"

It was surely no way to speak to an angel; but as Uncle Chaim used to warn me about everyone, from neighborhood bullies to my fourth-grade teacher, who hit people, "You give the bastards an inch, they'll walk all over you. From me they get *bupkes*, *nichevo*, nothing. Not an inch." I got beaten up more than once in those days, saying that to the wrong people.

And the blue angel was definitely one of them. The entire room suddenly filled with her: with the wings spreading higher than the ceiling, wider than the walls, yet somehow not touching so much as a stick of charcoal; with the aroma almost too impossibly haunting to be borne; with the vast, unutterable beauty that a thousand medieval and Renaissance artists had somehow not gone mad (for the most part) trying to ambush on canvas or trap in stone. In that moment, Uncle Chaim confided later, he didn't know whether to pity or envy Muslims their ancient ban on depictions of the human body.

"I thought maybe I should kneel, what would it hurt? But then I thought, *what would it hurt?* It'd hurt my left knee, the one had the arthritis twenty years, that's what it would hurt." So he only shrugged a little and told her, "I could manage a sitting on Monday. Somebody cancelled, I got the whole morning free."

"Now," the angel said. Her air of distinct disapproval had become one of authority. The difference was slight but notable.

"*Now*," Uncle Chaim mimicked her. "All right, already—Ruthie left early, so why not?" He moved the unfinished portrait over to another easel, and carefully selected a blank canvas from several propped against a wall. "I got to clean off a couple of brushes here, we'll start. You want to take off that thing, whatever, on your head?" Even I knew perfectly well that it was a halo, but Uncle Chaim always told me that you had to start with people as you meant to go on.

"You will require a larger surface," the angel instructed him. "I am not to be represented in miniature."

Uncle Chaim raised one eyebrow (an ability I envied him to the point of practicing—futilely—in the bathroom mirror for hours, until my parents banged on the door, certain I was up to the worst kind of no good). "No, huh? Good enough for the Persians, good enough for Holbein and Hilliard and Sam Cooper, but not for you? So okay, so we'll try this one . . ." Rummaging in a corner, he fetched out his biggest canvas, dusted it off, eyed it critically—"Don't even remember what I'm doing with anything this size, must have been saving it for you"—and finally set it up on the empty easel, turning it away from the angel. "Okay, Malakoff's rules. Nobody—*nobody*—looks at my painting till I'm done. Not angels, not Adonai, not my nephew over there in the corner, that's David, Duvidl—not even my wife. Nobody. Understood?"

The angel nodded, almost imperceptibly. With surprising meekness, she asked, "Where shall I sit?"

"Not a lot of choices," Uncle Chaim grunted, lifting a brush from a jar of turpentine. "Over there's okay, where Ruthie was sitting—or maybe by the big window. The window would be good, we've lost the shadows already. Take the red chair, I'll fix the color later."

But sitting down is not a natural act for an angel: they stand or they fly; check any Renaissance painting. The great wings inevitably get crumpled, the halo always winds up distinctly askew; and there is simply no way, even for Uncle Chaim, to ask an angel to cross her legs or to hook one over the arm of the chair. In the end they compromised, and the blue angel rose up to pose in the window, holding herself there effortlessly, with her wings not stirring at all. Uncle Chaim, settling in to work—brushes cleaned and Scotch replenished—could not refrain from remarking, "I always imagined you guys sort of hovered. Like hummingbirds."

"We fly only by the Will of God," the angel replied. "If Yahweh, praised be His name,"—I could actually *hear* the capital letters— "withdrew that mighty Will from us, we would fall from the sky on the instant, every single one."

"Doesn't bear thinking about," Uncle Chaim muttered. "Raining angels all over everywhere—falling on people's heads, tying up traffic—"

The angel looked first startled and then notably shocked. "I was speaking of *our* sky," she explained haughtily, "the sky of Paradise, which compares to yours as gold to lead, tapestry to tissue, heavenly choirs to the bellowing of feeding hogs—"

"All *right* already, I get the picture." Uncle Chaim cocked an eye at her, poised up there in the window with no visible means of support, and then back at his canvas. "I was going to ask you about being an angel, what it's like, but if you're going to talk about us like that— badmouthing the *sky*, for God's sake, the whole *planet*."

The angel did not answer him immediately, and when she did, she appeared considerably abashed and spoke very quietly, almost like a scolded schoolgirl. "You are right. It is His sky, His world, and I shame my Lord, my fellows and my breeding by speaking slightingly of any part of it." In a lower voice, she added, as though speaking only to herself, "Perhaps that is why I am here."

Uncle Chaim was covering the canvas with a thin layer of very light blue, to give the painting an undertone. Without looking up, he said, "What, you got sent down here like a punishment? You talked back, you didn't take out the garbage? I could believe it. Your boy Yahweh, he always did have a short fuse."

"I was told only that I was to come to you and be your model and your muse," the angel answered. She pushed her hood back from her face, revealing hair that was not bright gold, as so often painted, but of a color resembling the night sky when it pales into dawn. "Angels do not ask questions."

"Mmm." Uncle Chaim sipped thoughtfully at his Scotch. "Well, one did, anyway, you believe the story."

The angel did not reply, but she looked at him as though he had uttered some unimaginable obscenity. Uncle Chaim shrugged and continued preparing the ground for the portrait. Neither one said anything for some time and it was the angel who spoke first. She said, a trifle hesitantly, "I have never been a muse before."

"Never had one," Uncle Chaim replied sourly. "Did just fine."

"I do not know what the duties of a muse would be," the angel confessed. "You will need to advise me."

"What?" Uncle Chaim put down his brush. "Okay now, wait a minute. *I* got to tell you how to get into my hair, order me around, probably tell me how I'm not painting you right? Forget it, lady—you figure it out for yourself, I'm working here."

But the blue angel looked confused and unhappy, which is no more natural for an angel than sitting down. Uncle Chaim scratched his head and said, more gently, "What do I know? I guess you're supposed to stimulate my creativity, something like that. Give me ideas, visions, make me see things, think about things I've never thought about." After a pause, he added, "Frankly, Goya pretty much has that effect on me already. Goya and Matisse. So that's covered, the stimulation— maybe you could just tell them, *him* about that . . ."

Seeing the expression on the angel's marble-smooth face, he let the sentence trail away. Rabbi Shulevitz, who cut his blonde hair close and wore shorts when he watered his lawn, once told me that angels are supposed to express God's emotions and desires, without being troubled by any of their own. "Like a number of other heavenly dictates," he murmured when my mother was out of the room, "that one has never quite functioned as I'm sure it was intended."

They were still working in the studio when my mother called and ordered me home. The angel had required no rest or food at all, while Uncle Chaim had actually been drinking his Scotch instead of sipping it (I never once saw him drunk, but I'm not sure that I ever saw him entirely sober), and needed more bathroom breaks than usual. Daylight gone, and his precarious array of 60-watt bulbs proving increasingly unsatisfactory, he looked briefly at the portrait, covered it, and said to the angel, "Well, *that* stinks, but we'll do better tomorrow. What time you want to start?"

The angel floated down from the window to stand before him. Uncle Chaim was a small man, dark and balding, but he already knew that the angel altered her height when they faced each other, so as not to overwhelm him completely. She said, "I will be here when you are."

20

Uncle Chaim misunderstood. He assured her that if she had no other place to sleep but the studio, it wouldn't be the first time a model or a friend had spent the night on that trundle bed in the far corner. "Only no peeking at the picture, okay? On your honor as a muse."

The blue angel looked for a moment as though she were going to smile, but she didn't. "I will not sleep here, or anywhere on this earth," she said. "But you will find me waiting when you come."

"Oh," Uncle Chaim said. "Right. Of course. Fine. But don't change your clothes, okay? Absolutely no changing." The angel nodded.

When Uncle Chaim got home that night, my Aunt Rifke told my mother on the phone at some length, he was in a state that simply did not register on her long-practiced seismograph of her husband's moods. "He comes in, he's telling jokes, he eats up everything on the table, we snuggle up, watch a little TV, I can figure the work went well today. He doesn't talk, he's not hungry, he goes to bed early, tosses and tumbles around all night . . . okay, not so good. Thirty-seven years with a person, wait, you'll find out." Aunt Rifke had been Uncle Chaim's model until they married, and his agent, accountant, and road manager ever since.

But the night he returned from beginning his portrait of the angel brought Aunt Rifke a husband she barely recognized. "Not up, not down, not happy, not *not* happy, just . . . *dazed*, I guess that's the best word. He'd start to eat something, then he'd forget about it, wander around the apartment—couldn't sit still, couldn't keep his mind on anything, had trouble even finishing a sentence. One sentence. I tell you, it scared me. I couldn't keep from wondering, *is this how it begins?* A man starts acting strange, one day to the next, you think about things like that, you know?" Talking about it, even long past the moment's terror, tears still started in her eyes.

Uncle Chaim did tell her that he had been visited by an angel who demanded that he paint her portrait. *That* Aunt Rifke had no trouble believing, thirty-seven years of marriage to an artist having inured her to certain revelations. Her main concern was how painting an angel might affect Uncle Chaim's working hours, and his daily conduct. "Like actors, you know, Duvidl? They *become* the people they're doing, I've seen it over and over." Also, blasphemous as it might sound, she wondered how much the angel would be paying, and in what currency. "And saying we'll get a big credit in the next world is not funny, Chaim. *Not* funny."

Uncle Chaim urged Rifke to come to the studio the very next day to meet his new model for herself. Strangely, that lady, whom I'd known all my life as a legendary repository of other people's lives, stories, and secrets, flatly refused to take him up on the offer. "I got nothing to wear, not for meeting an angel in. Besides, what would we talk about? No, you just give her my best, I'll make some *rugelach*." And she never wavered from that position, except once.

The blue angel was indeed waiting when Uncle Chaim arrived in the studio early the next morning. She had even made coffee in his ancient glass percolator, and was offended when he informed her that it was as thin as rain and tasted like used dishwater. "Where I come from, no one ever *makes* coffee," she returned fire. "We command it."

"That's what's wrong with this crap," Uncle Chaim answered her. "Coffee's like art, you don't order coffee around." He waved the angel aside and set about a second pot, which came out strong enough to widen the angel's eyes when she sipped it. Uncle Chaim teased her— "Don't get stuff like *that* in the Green Pastures, huh?"—and confided that he made much better coffee than Aunt Rifke. "Not her fault. Woman was raised on decaf, what can you expect? Cooks like an angel, though."

The angel either missed the joke or ignored it. She began to resume her pose in the window, but Uncle Chaim stopped her. "Later, later, the sun's not right. Just stand where you are, I want to do some work on the head." As I remember, he never used the personal possessive in referring to his models' bodies: it was invariably "turn the face a little," "relax the shoulder," "move the foot to the left." Amateurs often resented it; professionals tended to find it liberating. Uncle Chaim didn't much care either way.

For himself, he was grateful that the angel proved capable of holding a pose indefinitely, without complaining, asking for a break, or needing the toilet. What he found distracting was her steadily emerging interest in talking and asking questions. As requested, her expression never changed and her lips hardly moved; indeed, there were times when he would have sworn he was hearing her only in his mind. Enough of her queries had to do with his work, with how he did what he was doing, that he finally demanded point-blank, "All those angels, seraphs, cherubim, centuries of them—all those Virgins and Assumptions and whatnot—and you've never once been painted? Not one time?"

"I have never set foot on earth before," the angel confessed. "Not until I was sent to you."

"Sent to me. Directly. Special Delivery, Chaim Shlomovitch Malakoff—one angel, totally inexperienced at modeling. Or anything else, got anything to do with human life." The angel nodded, somewhat shyly. Uncle Chaim spoke only one word. "*Why?*"

"I am only eleven thousand, seven hundred and twenty-two years old," the angel said, with a slight but distinct suggestion of resentment in her voice. "No one tells me a *thing*."

Uncle Chaim was silent for some time, squinting at her face from different angles and distances, even closing one eye from time to time. Finally he grumbled, more than half to himself, "I got a very bad feeling that we're both supposed to learn something from this. Bad, bad feeling." He filled the little glass for the first time that day, and went back to work.

But if there was to be any learning involved in their near-daily meetings in the studio, it appeared to be entirely on her part. She was ravenously curious about human life on the blue-green ball of damp dirt that she had observed so distantly for so long, and her constant questioning reminded a weary Uncle Chaim—as he informed me more than once—of me at the age of four. Except that an angel cannot be bought off, even temporarily, with strawberry ice cream, or threatened with loss of a bedtime story if she can't learn to take "I don't *know*!" for an answer. At times he pretended not to hear her; on other occasions, he would make up some patently ridiculous explanation that a grandchild would have laughed to scorn, but that the angel took so seriously that he was guiltily certain he was bound to be struck by lightning. Only the lightning never came, and the tactic usually did buy him a few moments' peace—until the next question.

Once he said to her, in some desperation, "You're an angel, you're supposed to know everything about human beings. Listen, I'll take you out to Bleecker, MacDougal, Washington Square, you can look at the books, magazines, TV, the classes, the beads and crystals . . . it's all about how to get in touch with angels. Real ones, real angels, never mind that stuff about the angel inside you. Everybody wants some of that angel wisdom, and they want it bad, and they want it right now. We'll take an afternoon off, I'll show you."

The blue angel said simply, "The streets and the shops have nothing to show me, nothing to teach. You do."

"No," Uncle Chaim said. "No, no, no, no, *no*. I'm a painter—that's all, that's it, that's what I know. Painting. But you, you sit at the right hand of God—"

"He doesn't have hands," the angel interrupted. "And nobody exactly *sits*—"

"The point I'm making, you're the one who ought to be answering questions. About the universe, and about Darwin, and how everything really happened, and what is it with God and shellfish, and the whole business with the milk and the meat—*those* kinds of questions. I mean, I should be asking them, I know that, only I'm working right now."

It was almost impossible to judge the angel's emotions from the expressions of her chillingly beautiful porcelain face; but as far as Uncle Chaim could tell, she looked sad. She said, "I also am what I am. We angels—as you call us—we are messengers, minions, lackeys, knowing only what we are told, what we are ordered to do. A few of the Oldest, the ones who were there at the Beginning—Michael, Gabriel, Raphael—*they* have names, thoughts, histories, choices, powers. The rest of us, we tremble, we *hide* when we see them passing by. We think, *if those are angels, we must be something else altogether,* but we can never find a better word for ourselves."

She looked straight at Uncle Chaim—he noticed in some surprise that in a certain light her eyes were not nearly as blue as he had been painting them, but closer to a dark sea-green—and he looked away from an anguish that he had never seen before, and did not know how to paint. He said, "So okay, you're a low-class angel, a heavenly grunt, like they say now. So how come they picked you to be my muse? Got to mean *something*, no? Right?"

The angel did not answer his question, nor did she speak much for the rest of the day. Uncle Chaim posed her in several positions, but the unwonted sadness in her eyes depressed him past even Laphroaig's ability to ameliorate. He quit work early, allowing the angel—as he would never have permitted Aunt Rifke or me—to potter around the studio, putting it to rights according to her inexpert notions, organizing brushes, oils, watercolors, pastels and pencils, fixatives, rolls of canvas, bottles of tempera and turpentine, even dusty chunks of rabbit-skin glue, according to size. As he told his friend Jules Sidelsky, meeting for their traditional weekly lunch at a Ukrainian restaurant on Second Avenue, where the two of them spoke only Russian, "Maybe God could figure where things are anymore. Me, I just shut my eyes and pray."

Jules was large and fat, like Diego Rivera, and I thought of him as a sort of uncle too, because he and Ruthie always remembered my birthday, just like Uncle Chaim and Aunt Rifke. Jules did not believe in angels, but he knew that Uncle Chaim didn't necessarily believe in them either, just because he had one in his studio every day. He asked seriously, "That helps? The praying?" Uncle Chaim gave him a look, and Jules dropped the subject. "So what's she like? I mean, as a model? You like painting her?"

Uncle Chaim held his hand out, palm down, and wobbled it gently from side to side. "What's not to like? She'll hold any pose absolutely forever—you could leave her all night, morning I guarantee she wouldn't have moved a muscle. No whining, no bellyaching—listen, she'd make Cinderella look like the witch in that movie, the green one. In my life I never worked with anybody gave me less *tsuris.*"

"So what's with—?" and Jules mimicked his fluttering hand. "I'm waiting for the *but*, Chaim."

Uncle Chaim was still for a while, neither answering nor appearing to notice the steaming *varyniki* that the waitress had just set down before him. Finally he grumbled, "She's an angel, what can I tell you? Go reason with an angel." He found himself vaguely angry with Jules, for no reason that made any sense. He went on, "She's got it in her head she's supposed to be my muse. It's not the most comfortable thing sometimes, all right?"

25

Perhaps due to their shared childhood on Tenth Avenue, Jules did not laugh, but it was plainly a near thing. He said, mildly enough, "Matisse had muses. Rodin, up to here with muses. Picasso about had to give them serial numbers—I think he married them just to keep them straight in his head. You, me . . . I don't see it, Chaim. We're not muse types, you know? Never were, not in all our lives. Also, Rifke would kill you dead. Deader."

"What, I don't know that? Anyway, it's not what you're thinking." He grinned suddenly, in spite of himself. "She's not that kind of girl, you ought to be ashamed. It's just she wants to help, to inspire, that's what muses do. I don't mind her messing around with *my* mess in the studio—I mean, yeah, I mind it, but I can live with it. But the other day,"—he paused briefly, taking a long breath—"the other day she wanted to give me a haircut. A haircut. It's all right, go ahead."

For Jules was definitely laughing this time, spluttering tea through his nose, so that he turned a bright cerise as other diners stared at them. "A haircut," he managed to get out, when he could speak at all clearly. "An angel gave you a haircut."

"No, she didn't *give* me a haircut," Uncle Chaim snapped back crossly. "She wanted to, she offered—and then, when I said *no, thanks*, after awhile she said she could play music for me while I worked. I usually have the news on, and she doesn't like it, I can tell. Well, it wouldn't make much sense to her, would it? Hardly does to me anymore."

"So she's going to be posing *and* playing music? What, on her harp? That's true, the harp business?"

"No, she just said she could command the music. The way they do with coffee." Jules stared at him. "Well, I don't know—I guess it's like some heavenly Muzak or something. Anyway, I told her no, and I'm sorry I told you anything. Eat, forget it, okay?"

But Jules was not to be put off so easily. He dug down into his *galushki poltavski* for a little time, and then looked up and said with his mouth full, "Tell me one thing, then I'll drop it. Would you say she was beautiful?"

"She's an angel," Uncle Chaim said.

"That's not what I asked. Angels are all supposed to be beautiful, right? Beyond words, beyond description, the works. So?" He smiled serenely at Uncle Chaim over his folded hands.

Uncle Chaim took so long to answer him that Jules actually waved a hand directly in front of his eyes. "Hello? Earth to Malakoff—this is your wakeup call. You in there, Chaim?"

"I'm there, I'm there, stop with the kid stuff." Uncle Chaim flicked his own fingers dismissively at his friend's hand. "Jules, all I can tell you, I never saw anyone looked like her before. Maybe that's beauty all by itself, maybe it's just novelty. Some days she looks eleven thousand years old, like she says—some days . . . some days she could be younger than Duvidl, she could be the first child in the world, first one ever." He shook his head helplessly. "I don't *know*, Jules. I wish I could ask Rembrandt or somebody. Vermeer. Vermeer would know."

Strangely, of the small corps of visitors to the studio—old painters like himself and Jules, gallery owners, art brokers, friends from the neighborhood—I seemed to be the only one who ever saw the blue angel as anything other than one of his unsought acolytes, perfectly happy to stretch canvases, make sandwiches and occasionally pose, all for the gift of a growled thanks and the privilege of covertly studying him at work. My memory is that I regarded her as a nice-looking older lady with wings, but not my type at all, I having just discovered Alice Faye. Lauren Bacall, Lizabeth Scott, and Lena Horne came a bit later in my development.

I knew she was an angel. I also knew better than to tell any of my own friends about her: we were a cynical lot, who regularly got thrown out of movie theaters for cheering on the Wolf Man and booing Shirley Temple and Bobby Breen. But I was shy with the angel, and—I guess—she with me, so I can't honestly say I remember much either in the way of conversation or revelation. Though I am still haunted by one particular moment when I asked her, straight out, "Up there, in heaven—do you ever see Jesus? Jesus Christ, I mean." We were hardly an observant family, any of us, but it still felt strange and a bit dangerous to say the name.

The blue angel turned from cleaning off a palette knife and looked directly at me, really for the first time since we had been introduced. I noticed that the color of her wings seemed to change from moment to moment, rippling constantly through a supple spectrum different from any I knew; and that I had no words either for her hair color, or for her smell. She said, "No, I have never seen him."

"Oh," I said, vaguely disappointed, Jewish or not. "Well—uh—what about his mother? The—the Virgin?" Funny, I remember that *that* seemed more daringly wicked than saying the other name out loud. I wonder why that should have been.

"No," the angel answered. "Nor,"—heading me off—"have I ever seen God. You are closer to God now, as you stand there, than I have ever been."

"That doesn't make any sense," I said. She kept looking at me, but did not reply. I said, "I mean, you're an angel. Angels live with God, don't they?"

She shook her head. In that moment—and just for that moment— her richly empty face showed me a sadness that I don't think a human face could ever have contained. "Angels live alone. If we were with God, we would not be angels." She turned away, and I thought she had finished speaking. But then she looked back quite suddenly to say, in a voice that did not sound like her voice at all, being lower than the sound I knew, and almost masculine in texture, "*Dark and dark and dark . . . so empty . . . so dark . . .*"

It frightened me deeply, that one broken sentence, though I couldn't have said why: it was just so dislocating, so completely out of place— even the rhythm of those few words sounded more like the hesitant English of our old Latvian rabbi than that of Uncle Chaim's muse. He didn't hear it, and I didn't tell him about it, because I thought it must be me, that I was making it up, or I'd heard it wrong. I was accustomed to thinking like that when I was a boy.

"She's got like a dimmer switch," Uncle Chaim explained to Aunt Rifke; they were putting freshly washed sheets on the guest bed at the time, because I was staying the night to interview them for my Immigrant Experience class project. "Dial it one way, you wouldn't notice her if she were running naked down Madison Avenue at high noon, flapping her wings and waving a gun. Two guns. Turn that dial back the other way, all the way . . . well, thank God she wouldn't ever do that, because she'd likely set the studio on fire. You think I'm joking. I'm not joking."

"No, Chaim, I know you're not joking." Rifke silently undid and remade both of his attempts at hospital corners, as she always did. She said, "What I want to know is, just where's that dial set when you're painting her? And I'd think a bit about that answer, if I were you." Rifke's favorite cousin Harvey, a career social worker, had recently abandoned wife and children to run off with a beautiful young dope dealer, and Rifke was feeling more than slightly edgy.

Uncle Chaim did think about it, and replied, "About a third, I'd say. Maybe half, once or twice, no more. I remember, I had to ask her a couple times, turn it down, please—go work when somebody's *glowing* six feet away from you. I mean, the moon takes up a lot of space, a little studio like mine. Bad enough with the wings."

Rifke tucked in the last corner, smoothed the sheet tight, faced him across the bed and said, "You're never going to finish this one, are you? Thirty-seven years, I know all the signs. You'll do it over and over, you'll frame it, you'll hang it, you'll say, *okay, that's it, I'm done*—but you won't be done, you'll just start the whole thing again, only maybe a different style, a brighter palette, a bigger canvas, a smaller canvas. But you'll never get it the way it's in your head, not for you." She smacked the pillows fluffy and tossed them back on the bed. "Don't even bother arguing with me, Malakoff. Not when I'm right."

"So am I arguing? Does it look like I'm arguing?" Uncle Chaim rarely drank at home, but on this occasion he walked into the kitchen, filled a glass from the dusty bottle of *grappa*, and turned back to his wife. He said very quietly, "Crazy to think I could get an angel right. Who could paint an angel?"

Aunt Rifke came to him then and put her hands on his shoulders. "My crazy old man, that's who," she answered him. "Nobody else. God would know."

And my Uncle Chaim blushed for the first time in many years. I didn't see this, but Aunt Rifke told me.

Of course, she was quite right about that painting, or any of the many, many others he made of the blue angel. He was never satisfied with any of them, not a one. There was always *something* wrong, something missing, something there but *not* there, glimpsed but gone. "Like that Chinese monkey trying to grab the moon in the water," Uncle Chaim said to me once. "That's me, a Chinese monkey."

Not that you could say he suffered financially from working with only one model, as the angel had commanded. The failed portraits that he lugged down to the gallery handling his paintings sold almost instantly to museums, private collectors, and corporations decorating their lobbies and meeting rooms, under such generic titles as *Angel in the Window*, *Blue Wings*, *Angel with Wineglass*, and *Midnight Angel*. Aunt Rifke banked the money, and Uncle Chaim endured the unveilings and the receptions as best he could—without ever looking at the paintings themselves—and then shuffled back to his studio to start over. The angel was always waiting.

I was doing my homework in the studio when Jules Sidelsky visited at last, lured there by other reasons than art, beauty, or deity. The blue angel hadn't given up the notion of acting as Uncle Chaim's muse, but never seemed able to take it much beyond making a tuna salad sandwich, or a pot of coffee (at which, to be fair, she had become quite skilled), summoning music, or reciting the lost works of legendary or forgotten poets while he worked. He tried to discourage this habit; but he did learn a number of Shakespeare's unpublished sonnets, and was able to write down for Jules three poems that drowned with Shelley off the Livorno coast. "Also, your boy Pushkin, his wife destroyed a mess of his stuff right after his death. My girl's got it all by heart, you believe that?"

Pushkin did it. If the great Russian had been declared a saint, Jules would have reported for instruction to the Patriarch of Moscow on the following day. As it was, he came down to Uncle Chaim's studio instead, and was at last introduced to the blue angel, who was as gracious as Jules did his bewildered best to be. She spent the afternoon declaiming Pushkin's vanished verse to him in the original, while hovering tirelessly upside down, just above the crossbar of a second easel. Uncle Chaim thought he might be entering a surrealist phase.

Leaving, Jules caught Uncle Chaim's arm and dragged him out his door into the hot, bustling Village streets, once his dearest subject before the coming of the blue angel. Uncle Chaim, knowing his purpose, said, "So now you see? Now you see?"

"I see." Jules's voice was dark and flat, and almost without expression. "I see you got an angel there, all right. No question in the world about that." The grip on Uncle Chaim's arm tightened. Jules said, "You have to get rid of her."

"*What?* What are you *talking* about? Just finally doing the most important work of my life, and you want me . . . ?" Uncle Chaim's eyes narrowed and he pulled forcefully away from his friend. "What is it with you and my models? You got like this once before, when I was painting that Puerto Rican guy, the teacher, with the big nose, and you just couldn't stand it, you remember? Said I'd stolen him, wouldn't speak to me for weeks, *weeks*, you remember?"

"Chaim, that's not true—"

"And so now I've got this angel, it's the same thing—worse, with the Pushkin and all—"

"Chaim, damn it, I wouldn't care if she were Pushkin's sister, they played Monopoly together—"

Uncle Chaim's voice abruptly grew calmer; the top of his head stopped sweating and lost its crimson tinge. "I'm sorry, I'm sorry, Jules. It's not I don't understand, I've been the same way about other people's models." He patted the other's shoulder awkwardly. "Look, I tell you what, anytime you want, you come on over, we'll work together. How about that?"

Poor Jules must have been completely staggered by all this. On the one hand he knew—I mean, even *I* knew—that Uncle Chaim never invited other artists to share space with him, let alone a model; on the other, the sudden change can only have sharpened his anxiety about his old friend's state of mind. He said, "Chaim, I'm just trying to tell you, whatever's going on, it isn't good for you. Not her fault, not your fault. People and angels aren't supposed to hang out together—we aren't built for it, and neither are they. She really needs to go back where she belongs."

"She can't. Absolutely not." Uncle Chaim was shaking his head, and kept on shaking it. "She got *sent* here, Jules, she got sent to *me*—"

"By whom? You ever ask yourself that?" They stared at each other. Jules said, very carefully, "No, not by the Devil. I don't believe in the Devil any more than I believe in God, although he always gets the good lines. But it's a free country, and I *can* believe in angels without swallowing all the rest of it, if I want to." He paused, and took a gentler hold on Uncle Chaim's arm. "And I can also imagine that angels might not be exactly what we think they are. That an angel might lie and still

31

be an angel. That an angel might be selfish—jealous, even. That an angel might just be a little bit out of her head."

In a very pale and quiet voice, Uncle Chaim said, "You're talking about a fallen angel, aren't you?"

"I don't know what I'm talking about," Jules answered. "That's the God's truth." Both of them smiled wearily, but neither one laughed. Jules said, "I'm dead serious, Chaim. For your sake, your sanity, she needs to go."

"And for my sake, she can't." Uncle Chaim was plainly too exhausted for either pretense or bluster, but there was no give in him. He said, "*Landsmann*, it doesn't matter. You could be right, you could be wrong, I'm telling you, it doesn't matter. There's no one else I want to paint anymore—there's no one else I *can* paint, Jules, that's just how it is. Go home now." He refused to say another word.

In the months that followed, Uncle Chaim became steadily more silent, more reclusive, more closed off from everything that did not directly involve the current portrait of the blue angel. By autumn, he was no longer meeting Jules for lunch at the Ukrainian restaurant; he could rarely be induced to appear at his own openings, or anyone else's; he frequently spent the night at his studio, sleeping briefly in his chair, when he slept at all. It had been understood between Uncle Chaim and me since I was three that I had the run of the place at any time; and while it was still true, I felt far less comfortable there than I was accustomed, and left it more and more to him and the strange lady with the wings.

When an exasperated—and increasingly frightened—Aunt Rifke would challenge him, "You've turned into Red Skelton, painting nothing but clowns on velvet—Margaret Keane, all those big-eyed war orphans," he only shrugged and replied, when he even bothered to respond, "You were the one who told me I could paint an angel. Change your mind?"

Whatever she truly thought, it was not in Aunt Rifke to say such a thing to him directly. Her only recourse was to mumble something like, "Even Leonardo gave up on drawing cats," or "You've done the best anybody could ever do—let it go now, let *her* go." Her own theory, differing somewhat from Jules's, was that it was as much Uncle Chaim's obsession as his model's possible madness that was holding the angel to earth. "Like Ella and Sam," she said to me, referring to the perpetually quarrelling parents of my favorite cousin Arthur. "Locked together, like some kind of punishment machine. Thirty years they hate each other, cats and dogs, but they're so scared of being alone, if one of them died,"—she snapped her fingers—"the other one would be gone in a week. Like that. Okay, so not exactly like that, but like that." Aunt Rifke wasn't getting a lot of sleep either just then.

She confessed to me—it astonishes me to this day—that she prayed more than once herself, during the worst times. Even in my family, which still runs to atheists, agnostics, and cranky anarchists, Aunt Rifke's unbelief was regarded as the standard by which all other blasphemy had to be judged, and set against which it invariably paled. The idea of a prayer from her lips was, on the one hand, fascinating—how would Aunt Rifke conceivably address a Supreme Being?—and more than a little alarming as well. Supplication was not in her vocabulary, let alone her repertoire. Command was.

I didn't ask her what she had prayed for. I did ask, trying to make her laugh, if she had commenced by saying, "To Whom it may concern . . ." She slapped my hand lightly. "Don't talk fresh, just because you're in fifth grade, sixth grade, whatever. Of course I didn't say that, an old Socialist Worker like me. I started off like you'd talk to some kid's mother on the phone, I said, 'It's time for your little girl to go home, we're going to be having dinner. You better call her in now, it's getting dark.' Like that, polite. But not fancy."

"And you got an answer?" Her face clouded, but she made no reply. "You didn't get an answer? Bad connection?" I honestly wasn't being fresh: this was my story too, somehow, all the way back, from the beginning, and I had to know where we were in it. "Come *on*, Aunt Rifke."

"I got an answer." The words came slowly, and cut off abruptly, though she seemed to want to say something more. Instead, she got up and went to the stove, all my aunts' traditional *querencia* in times of emotional stress. Without turning her head, she said in a curiously dull tone, "*You* go home now. Your mother'll yell at me."

My mother worried about my grades and my taste in friends, not about me; but I had never seen Aunt Rifke quite like this, and I knew better than to push her any further. So I went on home.

33

From that day, however, I made a new point of stopping by the studio literally every day—except Shabbos, naturally—even if only for a few minutes, just to let Uncle Chaim know that someone besides Aunt Rifke was concerned about him. Of course, obviously, a whole lot of other people would have been, from family to gallery owners to friends like Jules and Ruthie; but I was ten years old, and feeling like my uncle's only guardian, and a private detective to boot. A guardian against *what*? An angel? Detecting *what*? A portrait? I couldn't have said for a minute, but a ten-year-old boy with a sense of mission definitely qualifies as a dangerous flying object.

Uncle Chaim didn't talk to me anymore while he was working, and I really missed that. To this day, almost everything I know about painting—about *being* a painter, every day, all day—I learned from him, grumbled out of the side of his mouth as he sized a canvas, touched up a troublesome corner, or stood back, scratching his head, to reconsider a composition or a subject's expression, or simply to study the stoop of a shadow. Now he worked in bleak near-total silence; and since the blue angel never spoke unless addressed directly, the studio had become a far less inviting place than my three-year-old self had found it. Yet I felt that Uncle Chaim still liked having me there, even if he didn't say anything, so I kept going, but it was an effort some days, mission or no mission.

His only conversation was with the angel—Uncle Chaim always chatted with his models; paradoxically, he felt that it helped them to concentrate—and while I honestly wasn't trying to eavesdrop (except sometimes), I couldn't help overhearing their talk. Uncle Chaim would ask the angel to lift a wing slightly, or to alter her stance somewhat: as I've said, sitting remained uncomfortable and unnatural for her, but she had finally been able to manage a sort of semi-recumbent posture, which made her look curiously vulnerable, almost like a tired child after an adult party, playing at being her mother, with the grownups all asleep upstairs. I can close my eyes today and see her so.

One winter afternoon, having come tired, and stayed late, I was half-asleep on a padded rocker in a far corner when I heard Uncle Chaim saying, "You ever think that maybe we might both be dead, you and me?"

"We angels do not die," the blue angel responded. "It is not in us to die."

"I told you, lift your chin," Uncle Chaim grunted. "Well, it's built into *us*, believe me, it's mostly what we do from day one." He looked up at her from the easel. "But I'm trying to get you into a painting, and I'll never be able to do it, but it doesn't matter, got to keep trying. The head a *little* bit to the left—no, that's too much, I said a *little*." He put down his brush and walked over to the angel, taking her chin in his hand. He said, "And you . . . whatever you're after, you're not going to get that right, either, are you? So it's like we're stuck here together—and if we *were* dead, maybe this is hell. Would we know? You ever think about things like that?"

"No." The angel said nothing further for a long time, and I was dozing off again when I heard her speak. "You would not speak so lightly of hell if you had seen it. I have seen it. It is not what you think."

"*Nu?*" Uncle Chaim's voice could raise an eyebrow itself. "So what's it like?"

"*Cold.*" The words were almost inaudible. "So cold . . . so lonely . . . so *empty*. God is not there . . . no one is there. No one, no one, no one . . . no one . . ."

It was that voice, that other voice that I had heard once before, and I have never again been as frightened as I was by the murmuring terror in her words. I actually grabbed my books and got up to leave, already framing some sort of gotta-go to Uncle Chaim, but just then Aunt Rifke walked into the studio for the first time, with Rabbi Shulevitz trailing behind her, so I stayed where I was. I don't know a thing about ten-year-olds today; but in those times one of the major functions of adults was to supply drama and mystery to our lives, and we took such things where we found them.

Rabbi Stuart Shulevitz was the nearest thing my family had to an actual regular rabbi. He was Reform, of course, which meant that he had no beard, played the guitar, performed Bat Mitzvahs and interfaith marriages, invited local priests and imams to lead the Passover ritual, and put up perpetually with all the jokes told, even by his own congregation, about young, beardless, terminally tolerant Reform rabbis. Uncle Chaim, who allowed Aunt Rifke to drag him to *shul* twice a year, on the High Holidays, regarded him as being somewhere between a mild head cold and mouse droppings in the pantry. But Aunt

Rifke always defended Rabbi Shulevitz, saying, "He's smarter than he looks, and anyway he can't help being blonde. Also, he smells good."

Uncle Chaim and I had to concede the point. Rabbi Shulevitz's immediate predecessor, a huge, hairy, bespectacled man from Riga, had smelled mainly of rancid hair oil and cheap peach schnapps. And he couldn't sing "Red River Valley," either.

Aunt Rifke was generally a placid-appearing, *hamishe* sort of woman, but now her plump face was set in lines that would have told even an angel that she meant business. The blue angel froze in position in a different way than she usually held still as required by the pose. Her strange eyes seemed almost to change their shape, widening in the center and somehow *lifting* at the corners, as though to echo her wings. She stood at near-attention, silently regarding Aunt Rifke and the rabbi.

Uncle Chaim never stopped painting. Over his shoulder he said, "Rifke, what do you want? I'll be home when I'm home."

"So who's rushing you?" Aunt Rifke snapped back. "We didn't come about you. We came the rabbi should take a look at your *model* here." The word burst from her mouth trailing blue smoke.

"What look? I'm working, I'm going to lose the light in ten, fifteen minutes. Sorry, Rabbi, I got no time. Come back next week, you could say a *barucha* for the whole studio. Goodbye, Rifke."

But my eyes were on the rabbi, and on the angel, as he slowly approached her, paying no heed to the quarreling voices of Uncle Chaim and Aunt Rifke. Blonde or not, "Red River Valley" or not, he was still magic in my sight, the official representative of a power as real as my disbelief. On the other hand, the angel could fly. The Chassidic wonder-*rebbes* of my parents' Eastern Europe could fly up to heaven and share the Shabbos meal with God, when they chose. Reform rabbis couldn't fly.

As Rabbi Shulevitz neared her, the blue angel became larger and more stately, and there was now a certain menacing aspect to her divine radiance, which set me shrinking into a corner, half-concealed by a dusty drape. But the rabbi came on.

"Come no closer," the angel warned him. Her voice sounded deeper, and slightly distorted, like a phonograph record when the Victrola hasn't been wound tight enough. "It is not for mortals to lay hands on the Lord's servant and messenger."

"I'm not touching you," Rabbi Shulevitz answered mildly. "I just want to look in your eyes. An angel can't object to that, surely."

"The full blaze of an angel's eyes would leave you ashes, impudent man." Even I could hear the undertone of anxiety in her voice.

"That is foolishness." The rabbi's tone continued gentle, almost playful. "My friend Chaim paints your eyes full of compassion, of sorrow for the world and all its creatures, every one. Only turn those eyes to me for a minute, for a very little minute, where's the harm?"

Obediently he stayed where he was, taking off his hat to reveal the black *yarmulke* underneath. Behind him, Aunt Rifke made as though to take Uncle Chaim's arm, but he shrugged her away, never taking his own eyes from Rabbi Shulevitz and the blue angel. His face was very pale. The glass of Scotch in his left hand, plainly as forgotten as the brush in his right, was beginning to slosh over the rim with his trembling, and I was distracted with fascination, waiting for him to drop it. So I wasn't quite present, you might say, when the rabbi's eyes looked into the eyes of the blue angel.

But I heard the rabbi gasp, and I saw him stagger backwards a couple of steps, with his arm up in front of his eyes. And I saw the angel turning away, instantly; the whole encounter couldn't have lasted more than five seconds, if that much. And if Rabbi Shulevitz looked stunned and frightened—which he did—there is no word that I know to describe the expression on the angel's face. No words.

Rabbi Shulevitz spoke to Aunt Rifke in Hebrew, which I didn't know, and she answered him in swift, fierce Yiddish, which I did, but only insofar as it pertained to things my parents felt were best kept hidden from me, such as money problems, family gossip, and sex. So I missed most of her words, but I caught anyway three of them. One was *shofar*, which is the ram's horn blown at sundown on the High Holidays, and about which I already knew two good dirty jokes. The second was *minyan*, the number of adult Jews needed to form a prayer circle on special occasions. Reform *minyanim* include women, which Aunt Rifke always told me I'd come to appreciate in a couple of years. She was right.

The third word was *dybbuk*.

I knew the word, and I didn't know it. If you'd asked me its meaning, I would have answered that it meant some kind of bogey, like the Invisible Man, or just maybe the Mummy. But I learned the real meaning fast, because Rabbi Shulevitz had taken off his glasses and was wiping his forehead, and whispering, "No. No. Ich vershtaye nicht . . ."

Uncle Chaim was complaining, "What the hell *is* this? See now, we've lost the light already, I *told* you." No one—me included—was paying any attention.

Aunt Rifke—who was never entirely sure that Rabbi Shulevitz *really* understood Yiddish—burst into English. "It's a *dybbuk*, what's not to understand? There's a *dybbuk* in that woman, you've got to get rid of it! You get a *minyan* together, right now, you get rid of it! Exorcise!"

Why on earth did she want the rabbi to start doing pushups or jumping-jacks in this moment? I was still puzzling over that when he said, "That woman, as you call her, is an angel. You cannot . . . Rifke, you do not exorcise an angel." He was trembling—I could see that—but his voice was steady and firm.

"You do when it's possessed!" Aunt Rifke looked utterly exasperated with everybody. "I don't know how it could happen, but Chaim's angel's got a *dybbuk* in her," —she whirled on her husband—"which is why she makes you just keep painting her and painting her, day and night. You finish—really finish, it's done, over—she might have to go back out where it's not so nice for a *dybbuk*, you know about that? Look at her!" and she pointed an orange-nailed finger straight in the blue angel's face. "*She* hears me, *she* knows what I'm talking about. You know what I'm talking, don't you, Miss Angel? Or I should say, Mister *Dybbuk*? You tell me, okay?"

I had never seen Aunt Rifke like this; she might have been possessed herself. Rabbi Shulevitz was trying to calm her, while Uncle Chaim fumed at the intruders disturbing his model. To my eyes, the angel looked more than disturbed—she looked as terrified as a cat I'd seen backed against a railing by a couple of dogs, strays, with no one to call them away from tearing her to pieces. I was anxious for her, but much more so for my aunt and uncle, truly expecting them to be struck by lightning, or turned to salt, or something on that order. I was scared for the rabbi as well, but I figured he could take care of himself. Maybe even with Aunt Rifke.

"A *dybbuk* cannot possibly possess an angel," the rabbi was saying. "Believe me, I majored in Ashkenazic folklore—wrote my thesis on Lilith, as a matter of fact—and there are no accounts, no legends, not so much as a single *bubbemeise* of such a thing. *Dybbuks* are wandering spirits, some of them good, some malicious, but all houseless in the universe. They cannot enter heaven, and Gehenna won't have them, so they take refuge within the first human being they can reach, like any parasite. But an angel? Inconceivable, take my word. Inconceivable."

"In the mind of God," the blue angel said, "nothing is inconceivable."

Strangely, we hardly heard her; she had almost been forgotten in the dispute over her possession. But her voice was that other voice—I could see Uncle Chaim's eyes widen as he caught the difference. That voice said now, "She is right. I am a *dybbuk*."

In the sudden absolute silence, Aunt Rifke, serenely complacent, said, "Told you."

I heard myself say, "Is she bad? I thought she was an angel."

Uncle Chaim said impatiently, "What? She's a model."

Rabbi Shulevitz put his glasses back on, his eyes soft with pity behind the heavy lenses. I expected him to point at the angel, like Aunt Rifke, and thunder out stern and stately Hebrew maledictions, but he only said, "Poor thing, poor thing. Poor creature."

Through the angel's mouth, the *dybbuk* said, "Rabbi, go away. Let me alone, let me be. I am warning you."

I could not take my eyes off her. I don't know whether I was more fascinated by what she was saying, and the adults having to deal with its mystery, or by the fact that all the time I had known her as Uncle Chaim's winged and haloed model, someone else was using her the way I played with my little puppet theater at home—moving her, making up things for her to say, perhaps even putting her away at night when the studio was empty. Already it was as though I had never heard her strange, shy voice asking a child's endless questions about the world, but only this grownup voice, speaking to Rabbi Shulevitz. "You cannot force me to leave her."

"I don't want to force you to do anything," the rabbi said gently. "I want to help you."

I wish I had never heard the laughter that answered him. I was too young to hear something like that, if anyone could ever be old enough.

I cried out and doubled up around myself, hugging my stomach, although what I felt was worse than the worst bellyache I had ever wakened with in the night. Aunt Rifke came and put her arms around me, trying to soothe me, murmuring, half in English, half in Yiddish, "Shh, shh, it's all right, *der rebbe* will make it all right. He's helping the angel, he's getting rid of that thing inside her, like a doctor. Wait, wait, you'll see, it'll be all right." But I went on crying, because I had been visited by a monstrous grief not my own, and I was only ten.

The *dybbuk* said, "If you wish to help me, Rabbi, leave me alone. I will not go into the dark again."

Rabbi Shulevitz wiped his forehead. He asked, his tone still gentle and wondering, "What did you do to become . . . what you are? Do you remember?"

The *dybbuk* did not answer him for a long time. Nobody spoke, except for Uncle Chaim muttering unhappily to himself, "Who needs this? Try to get your work done, it turns into a *ferkockte* party. Who needs it?" Aunt Rifke shushed him, but she reached for his arm, and this time he let her take it.

The rabbi said, "You are a Jew."

"I was. Now I am nothing."

"No, you are still a Jew. You must know that we do not practice exorcism, not as others do. We heal, we try to heal both the person possessed and the one possessing. But you must tell me what you have done. Why you cannot find peace."

The change in Rabbi Shulevitz astonished me as much as the difference between Uncle Chaim's blue angel and the spirit that inhabited her and spoke through her. He didn't even look like the crew-cut, blue-eyed, guitar-playing, basketball-playing (well, he tried) college-student-dressing young man whose idea of a good time was getting people to sit in a circle and sing "So Long, It's Been Good to Know You" or "Dreidel, Dreidel, Dreidel" together. There was a power of his own inhabiting him, and clearly the *dybbuk* recognized it. It said slowly, "You cannot help me. You cannot heal."

"Well, we don't know that, do we?" Rabbi Shulevitz said brightly. "So, a bargain. You tell me what holds you here, and I will tell you, honestly, what I can do for you. *Honestly.*"

Again the *dybbuk* was slow to reply. Aunt Rifke said hotly, "What is this? What *help*? We're here to expel, to get rid of a demon that's taken over one of God's angels, if that's what she really is, and enchanted my husband so it's all he can paint, all he can think about painting. Who's talking about *helping* a demon?"

"The rabbi is," I said, and they all turned as though they'd forgotten I was there. I gulped and stumbled along, feeling like I might throw up. I said, "I don't think it's a demon, but even if it is, it's given Uncle Chaim a chance to paint a real angel, and everybody loves the paintings, and they buy them, which we wouldn't have had them to sell if the—the *thing*—hadn't made her stay in Uncle Chaim's studio." I ran out of breath, gas, and show-business ambitions all at pretty much the same time, and sat down, grateful that I had neither puked nor started to cry. I was still grandly capable of both back then.

Aunt Rifke looked at me in a way I didn't recall her ever doing before. She didn't say anything, but her arm tightened around me. Rabbi Shulevitz said quietly, "Thank you, David." He turned back to face the angel. In the same voice, he said, "Please. Tell me."

When the *dybbuk* spoke again, the words came one by one—two by two, at most. "A girl . . . There was a girl . . . a young woman . . ."

"*Ai*, how not?" Aunt Rifke's sigh was resigned, but not angry or mocking, just as Uncle Chaim's "*Shah*, Rifkela" was neither a dismissal nor an order. The rabbi, in turn, gestured them to silence.

"She wanted us to marry," the *dybbuk* said. "I did too. But there was time. There was a world . . . there was my work . . . there were things to see . . . to taste and smell and do and *be* . . . It could wait a little. She could wait . . ."

"Uh-huh. Of course. You could *die* waiting around for some damn man!"

"*Shah*, Rifkela!"

"But this one did not wait around," Rabbi Shulevitz said to the *dybbuk*. "She did not wait for you, am I right?"

"She married another man," came the reply, and it seemed to my ten-year-old imagination that every tortured syllable came away tinged with blood. "They had been married for two years when he beat her to death."

It was my Uncle Chaim who gasped in shock. I don't think anyone else made a sound.

The *dybbuk* said, "She sent me a message. I came as fast as I could. I *did* come," though no one had challenged his statement. "But it was too late."

This time we were the ones who did not speak for a long time. Rabbi Shulevitz finally asked, "What did you do?"

"I looked for him. I meant to kill him, but he killed himself before I found him. So I was too late again."

"What happened then?" That was me, once more to my own surprise. "When you didn't get to kill him?"

"I lived. I wanted to die, but I lived."

From Aunt Rifke—how not? "You ever got married?"

"No. I lived alone, and I grew old and died. That is all."

"Excuse me, but that is *not* all." The rabbi's voice had suddenly, startlingly, turned probing, almost harsh. "That is only the beginning." Everyone looked at him. The rabbi said, "So, after you died, what did happen? Where did you go?"

There was no answer. Rabbi Shulevitz repeated the question. The *dybbuk* responded finally, "You have said it yourself. Houseless in the universe I am, and how should it be otherwise? The woman I loved died because I did not love her enough—what greater sin is there than that? Even her murderer had the courage to atone, but I dared not offer my own life in payment for hers. I chose to live, and living on has been my punishment, in death as well as in life. To wander back and forth in a cold you cannot know, shunned by heaven, scorned by purgatory . . . do you wonder that I sought shelter where I could, even in an angel? God himself would have to come and cast me out again, Rabbi—you never can."

I became aware that my aunt and uncle had drawn close around me, as though expecting something dangerous and possibly explosive to happen. Rabbi Shulevitz took off his glasses again, ran his hand through his crew cut, stared at the glasses as though he had never seen them before, and put them back on.

"You are right," he said to the *dybbuk*. "I'm a rabbi, not a *rebbe*—no Solomonic wisdom, no magical powers, just a degree from a second-

class seminary in Metuchen, New Jersey. You wouldn't know it." He
drew a deep breath and moved a few steps closer to the blue angel. He
said, "But this *gornisht* rabbi knows anyway that you would never have
been allowed this refuge if God had not taken pity on you. You must
know this, surely?" The *dybbuk* did not answer. Rabbi Shulevitz said,
"And if God pities you, might you not have a little pity on yourself? A
little forgiveness?"

"Forgiveness . . ." Now it was the *dybbuk* who whispered. "Forgiveness
may be God's business. It is not mine."

"Forgiveness is everyone's business. Even the dead. On this earth or
under it, there is no peace without forgiveness." The rabbi reached out
then, to touch the blue angel comfortingly. She did not react, but he
winced and drew his hand back instantly, blowing hard on his fingers,
hitting them against his leg. Even I could see that they had turned
white with cold.

"You need not fear for her," the *dybbuk* said. "Angels feel neither cold
nor heat. You have touched where I have been."

Rabbi Shulevitz shook his head. He said, "I touched you. I touched
your shame and your grief—as raw today, I know, as on the day your
love died. But the cold . . . the cold is yours. The loneliness, the
endless guilt over what you should have done, the endless turning
to and fro in empty darkness . . . none of that comes from God.
You must believe me, my friend." He paused, still flexing his frozen
fingers. "And you must come forth from God's angel now. For her
sake and your own."

The *dybbuk* did not respond. Aunt Rifke said, far more sympathetically
than she had before, "You need a *minyan*, I could make some calls.
We'd be careful, we wouldn't hurt it."

Uncle Chaim looked from her to the rabbi, then back to the blue
angel. He opened his mouth to say something, but didn't.

The rabbi said, "You have suffered enough at your own hands. It is
time for you to surrender your pain." When there was still no reply, he
asked, "Are you afraid to be without it? Is that your real fear?"

"It has been my only friend!" the *dybbuk* answered at last. "Even God
cannot understand what I have done so well as my pain does. Without
the pain, there is only me."

"There is heaven," Rabbi Shulevitz said. "Heaven is waiting for you. Heaven has been waiting a long, long time."

"*I am waiting for me!*" It burst out of the *dybbuk* in a long wail of purest terror, the kind you only hear from small children trapped in a nightmare. "You want me to abandon the one sanctuary I have ever found, where I can huddle warm in the consciousness of an angel and sometimes—for a little—even forget the thing I am. You want me to be naked to myself again, and I am telling you *no, not ever, not ever, not ever.* Do what you must, Rabbi, and I will do the only thing I can." It paused, and then added, somewhat stiffly, "Thank you for your efforts. You are a good man."

Rabbi Shulevitz looked genuinely embarrassed. He also looked weary, frustrated, and older than he had been when he first recognized the possession of Uncle Chaim's angel. Looking vaguely around at us, he said, "I don't know—maybe it *will* take a *minyan*. I don't want to, but we can't just . . ." His voice trailed away sadly, too defeated even to finish the sentence.

Or maybe he didn't finish because that was when I stepped forward, pulling away from my aunt and uncle, and said, "He can come with me, if he wants. He can come and live in me. Like with the angel."

Uncle Chaim said, "*What?*" and Aunt Rifke said, "*No!*" and Rabbi Shulevitz said, "*David!*" He turned and grabbed me by the shoulders, and I could feel him wanting to shake me, but he didn't. He seemed to be having trouble breathing. He said, "David, you don't know what you're saying."

"Yes, I do," I said. "He's scared, he's so scared. I know about scared."

Aunt Rifke crouched down beside me, peering hard into my face. "David, you're ten years old, you're a little boy. This one, he could be a thousand years, he's been hiding from God in an angel's body. How could you know what he's feeling?"

I said, "Aunt Rifke, I go to school. I wake up every morning, and right away I think about the boys waiting to beat me up because I'm small, or because I'm Jewish, or because they just don't like my face, the way I look at them. Every day I want to stay home and read, and listen to the radio, and play my All-Star Baseball game, but I get dressed and I eat breakfast, and I walk to school. And every day I have to think how I'm going to get through recess, get through gym class, get home without running into Jay Taffer, George DiLucca. Billy Kronish. I know all about not wanting to go outside."

Nobody said anything. The rabbi tried several times, but it was Uncle Chaim who finally said loudly, "I got to teach you to box. A little Archie Moore, a little Willie Pep, we'll take care of those *mamzers*." He looked ready to give me my first lesson right there.

When the *dybbuk* spoke again, its voice was somehow different: quiet, slow, wondering. It said, "Boy, you would do that?" I didn't speak, but I nodded.

Aunt Rifke said, "Your mother would *kill* me! She's hated me since I married Chaim."

The *dybbuk* said, "Boy, if I come . . . outside, I cannot go back. Do you understand that?"

"Yes," I said. "I understand."

But I was shaking. I tried to imagine what it would be like to have someone living inside me, like a baby, or a tapeworm. I was fascinated by tapeworms that year. Only this would be a spirit, not an actual physical thing—that wouldn't be so bad, would it? It might even be company, in a way, almost like being a comic-book superhero and having a secret identity. I wondered whether the angel had even known the *dybbuk* was in her, as quiet as he had been until he spoke to Rabbi Shulevitz. Who, at the moment, was repeating over and over, "No, I can't permit this. This is *wrong*, this can't be allowed. No." He began to mutter prayers in Hebrew.

Aunt Rifke was saying, "I don't care, I'm calling some people from the *shul*, I'm getting some people down here right *away*!" Uncle Chaim was gripping my shoulder so hard it hurt, but he didn't say anything. But there was really no one in the room except the *dybbuk* and me. When I think about it, when I remember, that's all I see.

I remember being thirsty, terribly thirsty, because my throat and my mouth were so dry. I pulled away from Uncle Chaim and Aunt Rifke, and I moved past Rabbi Shulevitz, and I croaked out to the *dybbuk*, "Come on, then. You can come out of the angel, it's safe, it's okay." I remember thinking that it was like trying to talk a cat down out of a tree, and I almost giggled.

I never saw him actually leave the blue angel. I don't think anyone did. He was simply standing right in front of me, tall enough that I had to look up to meet his eyes. Maybe he wasn't a thousand years old, but Aunt Rifke hadn't missed by much. It wasn't his clothes that told me—he wore a white turban that looked almost square, a dark red vest sort of thing, and white trousers under a gray robe that came all the way to the ground—it was the eyes. If blackness is the absence of light, then those were the blackest eyes I'll ever see, because there was no light in those eyes, and no smallest possibility of light ever. You couldn't call them sad: *sad* at least knows what *joy* is, and grieves at being exiled from joy. However old he really was, those eyes were a thousand years past sad.

"Sephardi," Rabbi Shulevitz murmured. "Of course he'd be Sephardi."

Aunt Rifke said, "You can see through him. Right through."

In fact he seemed to come and go: near-solid one moment, cobweb and smoke the next. His face was lean and dark, and must have been a proud face once. Now it was just weary, unspeakably weary—even a ten-year-old could see that. The lines down his cheeks and around the eyes and mouth made me think of desert pictures I'd seen, where the earth gets so dry that it pulls apart, cracks and pulls away from itself. He looked like that.

But he smiled at me. No, he smiled *into* me, and just as I've never seen eyes like his again, I've never seen a smile as beautiful. Maybe it couldn't reach his eyes, but it must have reached mine, because I can still see it. He said softly, "Thank you. You are a kind boy. I promise you, I will not take up much room."

I braced myself. The only invasive procedures I'd had any experience with then were my twice-monthly allergy shots and the time our doctor had to lance an infected finger that had swollen to twice its size. Would possession be anything like that? Would it make a difference if you were sort of inviting the possession, not being ambushed and taken over, like in *Invasion of the Body Snatchers*? I didn't mean to close my eyes, but I did.

Then I heard the voice of the blue angel.

"There is no need." It sounded like the voice I knew, but the *breath* in it was different—I don't know how else to put it. I could say it sounded stronger, or clearer, or maybe more musical; but it was the breath, the free breath. Or maybe that isn't right either, I can't tell you—I'm not even certain whether angels breathe, and I knew an angel once. There it is.

"Manassa, there is no need," she said again. I turned to look at her then, when she called the *dybbuk* by his name, and she was smiling herself, for the first time. It wasn't like his; it was a faraway smile at something I couldn't see, but it was real, and I heard Uncle Chaim catch his breath. To no one in particular, he said, "*Now* she smiles. Never once, I could never once get her to smile."

"Listen," the blue angel said. I didn't hear anything but my uncle grumbling, and Rabbi Shulevitz's continued Hebrew prayers. But the *dybbuk*—Manassa—lifted his head, and the endlessly black eyes widened, just a little.

The angel said again, "Listen," and this time I did hear something, and so did everyone else. It was music, definitely music, but too faint with distance for me to make anything out of it. But Aunt Rifke, who loved more kinds of music than you'd think, put her hand to her mouth and whispered, "*Oh.*"

"Manassa, listen," the angel said for the third time, and the two of them looked at each other as the music grew stronger and clearer. I can't describe it properly: it wasn't harps and psalteries—whatever a psaltery is, maybe you use it singing psalms—and it wasn't a choir of soaring heavenly voices, either. It was almost a little scary, the way you feel when you hear the wild geese passing over in the autumn night. It made me think of that poem of Tennyson's, with that line about *the horns of Elfland faintly blowing.* We'd been studying it in school.

"It is your welcome, Manassa," the blue angel said. "The gates are open for you. They were always open."

But the *dybbuk* backed away, suddenly whimpering. "I cannot! I am afraid! They will see!"

The angel took his hand. "They see now, as they saw you then. Come with me, I will take you there."

The *dybbuk* looked around, just this side of panicking. He even tugged a bit at the blue angel's hand, but she would not let him go. Finally he sighed very deeply—lord, you could feel the dust of the tombs in that sigh, and the wind between the stars—and nodded to her. He said, "I will go with you."

The blue angel turned to look at all of us, but mostly at Uncle Chaim. She said to him, "You are a better painter than I was a muse. And you taught me a great deal about other things than painting. I will tell Rembrandt."

Aunt Rifke said, a little hesitantly, "I was maybe rude. I'm sorry." The angel smiled at her.

Rabbi Shulevitz said, "Only when I saw you did I realize that I had never believed in angels."

"Continue not to," the angel replied. "We rather prefer it, to tell you the truth. We work better that way."

Then she and the *dybbuk* both looked at me, and I didn't feel even ten years old; more like four or so. I threw my arms around Aunt Rifke and buried my face in her skirt. She patted my head—at least I guess it was her, I didn't actually see her. I heard the blue angel say in Yiddish, "*Sei gesund*, Chaim's Duvidl. You were always courteous to me. Be well."

I looked up in time to meet the old, old eyes of the *dybbuk*. He said, "In a thousand years, no one has ever offered me freely what you did." He said something else, too, but it wasn't in either Hebrew or Yiddish, and I didn't understand.

The blue angel spread her splendid, shimmering wings one last time, filling the studio—as, for a moment, the mean winter sky outside seemed to flare with a sunset hope that could not have been. Then she and Manassa, the *dybbuk*, were gone, vanished instantly, which makes me think that the wings aren't really for flying. I don't know what other purpose they could serve, except they did seem somehow to enfold us all and hold us close. But maybe they're just really decorative. I'll never know now.

Uncle Chaim blew out his breath in one long, exasperated sigh. He said to Aunt Rifke, "I never did get her right. You know that."

I was trying to hear the music, but Aunt Rifke was busy hugging me, and kissing me all over my face, and telling me not ever, *ever* to do such a thing again, what was I thinking? But she smiled up at Uncle Chaim and answered him, "Well, she got *you* right, that's what matters."

Uncle Chaim blinked at her. Aunt Rifke said, "She's probably telling Rembrandt about you right now. Maybe Vermeer, too."

"You think so?" Uncle Chaim looked doubtful at first, but then he shrugged and began to smile himself. "Could be."

I asked Rabbi Shulevitz, "He said something to me, the *dybbuk,* just at the end. I didn't understand."

The rabbi put his arm around me. "He was speaking in old Ladino, the language of the Sephardim. He said, '*I will not forget you.*'" His smile was a little shaky, and I could feel him trembling himself, with everything over. "I think you have a friend in heaven, David. Extraordinary Duvidl."

The music was gone. We stood together in the studio, and although there were four of us, it felt as empty as the winter street beyond the window where the blue angel had posed so often. A taxi took the corner too fast, and almost hit a truck; a cloud bank was pearly with the moon's muffled light. A group of young women crossed the street, singing. I could feel everyone wanting to move away, but nobody did, and nobody spoke, until Uncle Chaim finally said, "Rabbi, you got time for a sitting tomorrow? Don't wear that suit."

CARDIOLOGY

by Ryan Boudinot from *Five Chapters*

———————⌘———————

Years ago there was a town not far from here where nobody had their own heart. They shared one gigantic heart located in a former water purification plant near the center of town. When enlivened by physical activity, the heart beat more rapidly, sending its blood to the neighborhoods, rattling silverware on restaurant tables, shaking portraits off walls, tickling bare feet on cobblestones with its vibrations.

The townspeople were connected to the heart by a vast system of valves and pipes distributed throughout the town. The streets boasted five or six blood hydrants for every one fire hydrant. Every home came equipped with as many blood outlets as electrical outlets. Nobody could travel very far beyond the reach of these outlets and hydrants, as they were tethered to them by sturdy surgical tubing that came in a variety of fashion colors. These tubes snaked through alleys and parks, under doors, up ladders, and down stairwells. One never left the house without at least 20 feet of tubing and a portable placenta which they kept in purses, also in fashion colors. Children walking to school became adept at quickly refilling their placentas from one hydrant to the next. Some kids even developed elaborate games around the tube transferral process, choosing sides, cruelly leaving "captured" children tethered to hydrants with little hope of rescue. There was an etiquette to removing the tubes from one's chest and replacing them with a new pair. To travel without a pair of clamps with which to momentarily cease the flow of blood while switching to new tubes was considered a faux pas. To drip blood on a table cloth or a friend's shoes was also bad form, but tolerated. Everyone carried a travel-size packet of absorbent wipes and was an expert at removing bloodstains from carpet.

The blood moved slower at the edges of town, where the senior citizens lived. One widower named Ike lived in a one-bedroom place with a garden full of untended perennials that his wife had planted before she died five years previous. Every Sunday, Ike's grandson Magnus visited to make him dinner and watch a video together. While they ate, Ike would tell Magnus stories about when he worked in the vast, subterranean plant where they maintained the heart. Ike had belonged to the department that monitored the left ventricle.

"We stuffed our ears with cotton down there 'cause of the thudding, but my hearing still went to hell," Ike said, "Night shifts were the worst. We'd get a sudden increase of flow on account of everyone making love. I was there during the murmurs of '03, the Great Aneurysm of '08. The very life of this community was in our hands. I just thank God we never had to use the paddles to get that ticker started again."

One Sunday night after a dinner of macaroni and cheese, salad, and bread, with coffee ice cream for dessert, Magnus set up the video, *Beverly Hills Cop*, and sat beside his grandfather on the sofa. The tubes snaked out from between the buttons of their shirts, one tube delivering blood to their bodies, the other one sending it into the wall and back to the center of town. The slow flow always made Magnus feel sleepy at his grandfather's house, and it took some effort to stay awake during the video. During the part of the film where Eddie Murphy stuffs bananas into the tailpipe of a car, Magnus suddenly heard a loud hissing. Ike's vein tube had come loose from his chest and was squirting bright red blood all over the lampshade and a paint-by-numbers portrait of Jesus that hung on the wall. It wasn't the first time Ike's tubes had come loose, and Magnus knew what to do. He quickly clamped the tubes, opened his grandfather's stained shirt, and located the two hair-ringed orifices in his chest. After reinserting the tubes and making sure they were secure, Magnus wiped down the mess with bleach on a rag.

Frustrated that his movie had been interrupted by his grandfather's incontinence, Magnus threw down his rag and said, "I hate this place! Why can't we live somewhere like Beverly Hills? Why can't we have palm trees and funny police officers? I want to be able to walk down the street without worrying about whether the next blood hydrant is already being used. Why can't I walk freely wherever I want? How come I have to live in this stupid town with everyone sucking blood from the same stupid heart?"

Ike didn't say anything for a moment and immediately Magnus feared that he had offended his grandfather. After all, the man had devoted himself to the heart for sixty years, had scraped fat from inside its chambers, had watched friends die in horrible diastolic accidents. As long as Magnus had been alive he had associated Ike so closely with the giant cardiac muscle that maligning the heart was akin to maligning his own family.

As Ike's circulation picked back up, he sighed and made his mouth into an expression that in better light might have been a smile. "Of course, if you want to get out of this town, you'll have to create your own heart."

Magnus laughed. The suggestion was absurd. But quickly he saw that his grandfather was not joking; in fact he had adopted an expression of the utmost gravity.

"There is a man who can help you," Ike said, "His name is Gatton. You can find him in the tumor farm deep beneath the plant. Tell him that you come to claim my payment for what happened during the blood poisoning of '99. He'll know what you're talking about. He can supply you with a handmade heart and you will be able to get out of town."

"But they'll know I don't belong there as soon as I get to the plant. How will I even make it to the tumor farm?"

"You'll wear my old uniform, and have my key card. It should still work. They never deactivated it when I left."

The rest of the movie passed unmemorably through Magnus' eyes. He tried to imagine the tumor farm, where the polyp trees grew, where they sent the convicts to work. He'd heard horrible things about the place, workers inadvertently fused to tumors, unable to escape, eventually becoming one with the cancerous cells, packs of rats who feasted on the growths and cysts, developing mutations that gave them five sets of legs, horns, wings.

Nonetheless, Magnus took the cake box that contained his grandfather's uniform and badge home with him and spent the next few weeks avoiding making a decision about whether he was going to pursue acquiring his own heart. One afternoon on his way home from school Magnus became entangled in the tubes of a girl named Carly, with whom he shared a fifth period AP calculus class. They had never spoken to each other in school, but here on an elm-lined lane, trapped in a knot of surgical tubing, they had no way to avoid each other. As they slowly moved their bodies in such a way as to disentangle the tubes without disconnecting them, they started talking about their plans for the following year.

"After graduation I think I'm going to spend a week fishing, then look for a job," Magnus said, "What about you?"

"I hate this place," Carly said, "I want to go to a big college thousands of miles away from here."

"But you'll have to be connected to your placenta the whole time, and get regular blood transfusions, and those aren't reliable for more than a few days at a time," Magnus said.

"That's what they tell us anyway," Carly said, "I don't care. If I die out there it'll be better than staying in this place where people think you're crazy for liking plaid pants."

"I might know another way," Magnus said, then revealed to Carly everything his grandfather had told him about the tumor farm and portable hearts.

"Magnus, you have to go! This could be your chance out of this place."

"I'm afraid to go down there," Magnus said sheepishly.

Carly's cell phone rang. It was one of those new phones with the camera attached, and over Carly's shoulder Magnus could see the scrunched up face of Carly's mother, inquiring as to when she planned to come home for dinner.

Carly and Magnus parted ways, with Magnus continuing toward the center of town. With every tube transfer he felt the flow grow stronger, as though he were wandering upstream into the tumultuous rapids of a river. Every fourth house or so was replaced by a coffee shop or book store, then the houses began inching closer together, blocks interrupted by restaurants, then apartment buildings, and finally no place to live at all, just businesses with lit-up signs and wares on display. Men and women conducted conversations on hands-free phones, speaking into buds dangling from their ears, weaving from hydrant to hydrant, intersections turning into cats' cradles of tubing that miraculously resolved with every light change. Magnus rarely made it this far into town, and he couldn't tell if it was his own excitement or his proximity to the gigantic, energy-giving organ that made him feel as though he was being hit in the chest with a fire hose. He stopped and leaned against the front of a bagel shop. When the owner told him to get lost, he turned into an alley, hurrying past a couple junkies shooting up directly into their vein tubes. Luckily, the detoxification department would scrub the drugs from the blood when it returned to the plant.

Magnus changed into his grandfather's uniform behind a dumpster. It was clearly too big for him. How would anyone be fooled? He'd be found out, tossed into jail, left to die of lethal dis-attachment on death row. Then he imagined the swaying palms of Beverly Hills, the witty people in turtlenecks, and it was enough to propel him forward, onto the sidewalk, toward the decrepit former cathedral that served as the plant's main point of entrance.

The cathedral's exterior was all sooty stone and busted stained glass windows. One of its spires had crumbled long after the god worshipped here had been forgotten. Workers in uniforms like Ike's hurried in and out of the opening where the doors used to be, trailing tubes, great red ropes of speeding blood. Magnus fell into a mass of workers on their way to their shifts. Inside the cathedral, the workers branched off toward various banks of escalators marked with different departments: Aorta, Left Ventricle, Right Ventricle, Pulmonary Vessels, Mitral Valve. There didn't appear to be any sign for the tumor farm, so Magnus headed toward the elevator leading to the Left Ventricle, where his grandfather had worked.

"Hey, hold it a minute there, son." A security officer of some sort grabbed Magnus by the shoulder. He had a big, blonde mustache and wore the heart-shaped insignia of the plant on his chest, with all the chambers highlighted in green to indicate he had full access. "You're obviously new here. You can't go in with these wimpy surgical tubes, they can't stand the pressure. You'll need to go to the Bypass office and get some new ones. And whoever issued you this uniform, they must have been in a real retro mood. Let them know you're going to need new duds."

"Where is the Bypass office?" Magnus said.

"Man, you are green. Up there." The officer pointed to a point high above the floor, a kind of balcony just out of reach of the pipe organ. Magnus took the appropriately labeled elevator and exited into an office overlooking the throng of workers below. Administrative types wearing shirts and ties hurried about, making photocopies, faxing spreadsheets. A woman at a broad, ebony desk motioned for Magnus to have a seat, telling him she'd be with him after she completed an email. A minute or two later she turned and said, "So. First day. We're glad you're here, Magnus. We've been looking forward to your arrival since your grandfather retired. You'll find that around here he's a real legend. You'll need new tubes, a new uniform, a real ID card." Magnus plugged into a nearby outlet that sent blood coursing so powerfully into his body that he felt he could climb a mountain, and filled out some paperwork.

That day Magnus was put to work in the outskirts of the vast underground operation, monitoring flow to and from the poorer neighborhoods. Someday, his shift supervisor, Jim, told him, he could work his way up from these dank, subterranean passages to work on an actual valve, maybe even the Purkinje fibers. His grandfather had started out at the bottom of the totem pole, repairing capillaries. Through hard work he had become one of the most respected valvemen this operation had ever had the honor of employing.

For the first weeks of his employment, Magnus walked for miles under the city, pressing his stethoscope against the pipes through which oxygenated blood flowed, noting changes in pressure in his palm computer, and calling in the repair crew whenever he detected a leak. Magnus learned to locate leaks by following rats and other misshapen vermin who could smell the blood before any human. One morning Magnus followed a gaggle of rats down several flights of stairs and came upon an entrance to the tumor farm. The space was as big as a stadium, the floor, walls, and ceiling high overhead covered in strange fleshy forms that almost resembled trees. The floor was rubbery down here, and occasionally viscous fluids squirted up from underfoot like clams spitting on a beach. While the handbook had assured Magnus that nothing in the tumor farm was contagious, the place still put him ill at ease. He swept his Maglite across the trembling mounds of flesh, each grotesque growth fueled by the same blood that beat quickly in his own body.

"You lost, kid?" said a man perched on a tumor in the vague shape of a couch. He wore the insignia of his department on his dirty jumpsuit next to his name, Kyle, and a cap drawn low over his eyes. He picked his fingernails with a knife. Magnus hurriedly introduced himself and explained he had come here following rats, but this didn't provoke any change in the bored expression fixed on Kyle's face.

"I'm looking for someone named Gatton, who worked with my grandfather Ike. My grandfather said Gatton could help me."

Kyle nodded and motioned for Magnus to follow him. They wound their way through a forest of abnormal growths. "We keep this tumor farm for a reason, case you hadn't figured out by now," Kyle said, "For years we been trying to develop individual hearts for folks to carry around in they own chests, not bein' dependent on the big thumper up there in the cave. Down here's where the cardiac scientists cultivate materials and toss their failed experiments. When the breakthrough comes we'll be turning this place into a giant factory of hearts, with the people coming in one end empty-chested and leaving the other with independent tickers allowing them to not have to hook up to the blood hydrants every goddamn day. Then we can destroy that big muscle that keeps us all enslaved to the ebb and flow."

They found a slippery staircase and made their way down deep enough for Magnus to have to pop his ears. Finally the stairs opened into an echoing chamber more vast than the tumor farm, and reeking of blood. As Magnus's eyes adjusted he came to understand that he was standing on the bank of an underground river of blood, too wide to see across to the other shore.

"They'll come soon enough," Kyle said, taking off his hat, wiping his brow. As if lying in wait, the sounds of a vessel came across the flowing plasma, ringing with percussion and horns. From the dark emerged a craft about forty feet long. At first Magnus thought the people crowded on its deck were men in armored suits, but slowly they revealed themselves to be birds the size of humans, standing upright, some of them wearing jeweled clothes or helmets, squawking hideously with their long beaks.

"I wasn't supposed to see this place yet," Magnus said, though the words seemed as foreign in his mouth as the creatures manifest before him. He couldn't help feeling that some sealed repository of knowledge had been opened within his mind, some place that had existed prior to his birth, now revealed on the path his curiosity had so dangerously compelled him to follow. The bird-beings in their craft raised a great squawking din of horns and drums upon seeing him standing petrified on the shore, a sound panicked and angry, and this was enough to frighten Magnus back up the stairs to the tumor farm, into the labyrinth of vessel-lined halls, and out an exit into the night of a town he no longer understood.

Magnus tried to cleanse himself of the disturbing scene he had witnessed by throwing himself into his routines. That night was movie night with his grandfather. He chose a video at the video store and walked across the park in the middle of town with it tucked under his arm, a bag of burritos from his favorite taqueria in the other. He decided the only way to relieve his fear of the bird-creatures on the river of blood was to convince himself that they had been a hallucination. By the time he reached his grandfather's house he decided that he must have been working too hard these past few weeks and suffered a fatigue-related mental lapse. This idea comforted him, more so than the possibility that there existed beneath his feet an underground blood river navigated by alien forms.

If he had peeked in the windows when he arrived at his grandfather's the house, Magnus would have certainly noticed something awfully wrong about the place. But instead he instinctively grabbed the doorknob and entered without knocking as was his habit. Instead of being met with Ike's friendly hello, a wall of blood swept Magnus off the porch, depositing him in the gnarled rose bushes in the front lawn. He'd heard of this problem before but never seen it. A leak that slowly fills an entire house. Waves of the red stuff rolled out to the street. Inside he found the entire place awash in blood, covering every surface, saturating every permeable material. He rushed to his grandfather's bedroom, where he found the drowned body still in bed, unrecognizable, covered in all this mess. Crying, he carried the body from the house.

After the ambulance arrived, leisurely, with its sirens off, Magnus sat in the blood-soaked front lawn watching nightcrawlers emerge from the tunnels hidden beneath the grass. Some police officers may have spoken to him, he couldn't be sure. As the light faded and the seizure crew exited the house, Magnus felt a hand on his shoulder and looked up to see Carly in her plaid pants, holding a suitcase.

"It's time to leave this place," Carly said.

"I think there's only one way to leave this place," Magnus said, "And it's underground. At least until they start manufacturing individual hearts."

Carly opened her suitcase, moved aside some shirts and showed him the two mechanical hearts inside. They were made of bright yellow plastic, like waterproof electronic equipment.

THE PENTECOSTAL HOME FOR FLYING CHILDREN

by Will Clarke from *The Oxford American*

In 1984, Shreveport, Louisiana was experiencing a woeful lack of economic growth, turbulent race relations, and a rash of flying teenagers. The airborne bastards were the offspring of The Redbird—a handsome alien half-breed who had once graced the cover of *LIFE* magazine for rescuing Chicago from The Stalinizer—a radioactive cosmonaut who could shoot lasers from his mouth.

Unfortunately, The Redbird didn't possess the necessary might to be a major league super hero. In the world of super powers, flight was pretty much table stakes. Who couldn't fly? Flying was just the delivery method, a mode of transportation for real super powers like invincibility, colossal strength, or energy blasts. You couldn't very well fly a super villain to death. Without invincibility and super strength how could you ever stop a nuclear missile? Sure, The Redbird looked pretty up there doing loopty-loops in the sky wearing those bright red tights, but other than marshalling 4th of July parades, he really wasn't much use in America's fight against super evil. So The Redbird was relegated to working in the super hero farm leagues. He was banished from New York and assigned to Shreveport.

Our town welcomed The Redbird with more than open arms. Everyone loved the idea that we had our very own super hero to look after us. We didn't care if all he could do was fly. That was more than any of us could do. In fact, The Redbird united our city with hope. We loved this alien half-breed with his magic red hair and his black mask, and this love we had for him overflowed from our hearts and spread to one another. Redbird-mania transcended racial lines and mended our violent histories with one another. The Redbird allowed us to see the good in everyone—black white rich or poor. The Redbird's reign ushered in a golden age for Shreveport. We became a city known for our brotherly love and dream-like prosperity.

However, as the years passed, it became apparent that The Redbird had moved to Shreveport for less than savory reasons. Turns out The Redbird came to our town not just for the easy work, but for our chronically bored housewives, our prodigal daughters, and our all too easily seduced Baptist Ladies Prayer Circle.

By the time we figured out that The Redbird was turning us all into pillars of salt, he up and flew away—leaving his lovers' hearts ragged, his red-headed babies abandoned, and our city unprotected.

———— ⌘ ————

The Pentecostal Home for Flying Children was founded by Pauline Pritchard, a barren Pentecostal woman with gray hair so long that it hung to her ankles when she took it down at night. One day while eating a dipped cone at Dairy Queen, Pauline Pritchard heard a terrible mewling coming from the restaurant's dumpsters. So she walked over to the trash, still licking her ice cream, thinking it was perhaps the screams of feral cats mating, but the sounds were loud enough and human enough to press her concern.

When Pauline opened the dumpster lid, she dropped her ice cream cone and screamed. There among the greasy wrappers and the industrial-sized mayonnaise jars was a naked baby boy with red locks that danced and shined liked the fire of the Pentecost. The baby was crying just as loud as Pauline was now screaming. Then something happened that took Pauline's screams away: the wailing infant began to float like a soap bubble out of the trash bin, drifting into the air above Pauline's considerable mound of gray hair.

Pauline quickly removed the pale brown cardigan that she had just bought at TG&Y and she began using the sweater as a net, flinging it at the airborne infant. Pauline flung and jumped, jumped and flung. Until finally, she cast the makeshift net upon the infant and pulled him into her arms. She swaddled the child in the synthetic wool of her new sweater and she held him close to her breast.

The baby squalled.

And Pauline wept.

Pauline Pritchard hugged the baby tight, and she ran as fast as her ankle-length skirt would let her.

"The good Lord has answered my prayers just like He answered Sarah and Abraham's." Pauline pulled her makeshift blanket away from the baby's face to show her husband the redhead that she had just found.

"We should call the police." Jeffery Pritchard put his finger into the baby's tender fist and shook it ever so gently. "Someone's probably missing this little fella."

"They left him in the Dumpster, Jeffery."

"It's the right thing to do."

"Jesus gave him to me."

"All I'm saying is that you can't just up and take a baby."

"I didn't take him."

"Then what do you call it?

"I found him like Pharaoh's daughter found Moses in the basket."

If you had ever dared to ask Pauline Pritchard if she was submissive to her husband as it says to be in Ephesians, she would have been wildly indignant that you would have even asked such a question.

"My husband is my master," Pauline would have said without a whiff of irony. And Jeffery would have agreed.

"I wear the pants around here!" he would have barked.

While Jeffery Pritchard may have worn the well-starched pants in that marriage, it was Pauline who brandished the fiery iron. In short, Jeffery Pritchard never called the police and Pauline named the boy Zaccheus.

One night when Pauline was washing Zaccheus in the kitchen sink, she was given a word of faith—a message straight from the Holy Ghost. Pauline hosed off the baby with the vegetable sprayer, and ran into the garage where her husband Jeffery was repairing the lawnmower.

"The Lord! He spoke to me!" Pauline held the dripping baby to her chest.

"Calm down, woman. You'll drop the baby."

"He said we should open our home to all The Redbird's babies!"

"Well," Jeffery looked into the engine filter and shook it. "Then I guess we better get busy."

Being a man of exuberant faith, Jeffery Pritchard painted a sign and hung it on his front porch that very night. The sign alerted the broken-hearted harlots of Shreveport that The Pentecostal Home for Flying Children was now open for business and ready to receive their newborn sins.

From that point on, the Pritchard's doorbell rang at all hours of the night and day. Every time they unfastened the seven locks and seven bolts on their big blue front door, there stood a shorn-haired Baptist woman, a painted Methodist, a pants-wearing Presbyterian, a cleavage-baring Catholic, an ankle-flaunting Lutheran, a drunk Episcopalian, a teenage Pentecostal, a divorced Jewess, a lock-jawed Seventh-Day Adventist, a black-eyed Mormon—all holding crying babies or struggling toddlers in their arms.

Sister Pauline gathered up the flying babies from their mothers. Despite Pauline's warmth and grace, there was often very little said in the exchange. Sometimes the women would tell Pauline the child's name. Sometimes they would be weeping so hard that Pauline had to pry the child from the mother's arms, and then politely shut the door. Each handoff was painful both for the mother and for Pauline. Because now that Pauline's heart was full of babies, she could feel the sting of these women's tears as if they were her own.

Pauline's husband and master, Jeffery, had wanted to splash the weeping mothers with holy water and cleanse them with prayer, but Pauline broke with her code of wifely obedience.

"Don't you say a word to them, Jeffery."

"They brought it on themselves, fornicating and carrying on like that." He mixed a flask of holy water imported all the way from Galilee with a bucket of tap water.

"Maybe so. But that's between them and the Lord and their husbands."

"A little splash would do them good."

"Don't, Jeffery. I'm asking you, don't."

As the flying babies filled the Pritchard house, Pauline rejoiced in the squalling, the feeding, and the diapers. Her house was blessed with chubby red-headed babies everywhere just as the Lord had promised. As The Redbird babies grew, they learned how to walk and talk, and of course, fly. This made keeping them out of harm's way almost impossible, but somehow the Pritchards managed to do it.

Their biggest problem was when the children slept. The babies would float out of their beds while dreaming and sometimes fall to the floor in a start. Once a red-haired babe drifted out of an open second-story window, but luckily for him, he landed on the boughs of the Pritchards' magnolia tree where Jeffery found him sleeping the next morning.

Flying babies were a much bigger problem to take care of than any of us would have ever imagined. And soon the babies were all over the place, bumping their noggins, busting their lips, knocking out their teeth, and breaking every little delicate thing that Pauline had ever loved.

But Pauline Pritchard was a faithful and industrious woman who loved the Lord and those wayward children. She would sit in her rocker on the front porch of her enormous old home, speaking in tongues and crocheting for the babies. She would pour her prayers into pink and baby-blue tethers that she fastened to the children's ankles and bedposts to keep them from floating away in the night. During the day Pauline would gather up the babies by their tethers and carry them around like a bunch of squirming balloons. It was a site to behold and eventually a now-famous photo of Pauline and her tethered babies made the cover of *The Shreveport Times*.

To remedy the bumps and bruises of the babies' midair collisions, Pauline had Jeffery staple-gun goose down pillows to the ceilings of their house. She also used donated quilts as wallpaper and she glued down bushels of disregarded stuffed animals to cushion the floors. Pauline Pritchard amazed us with her maternal ingenuity, and there was a time there that we almost admired her for it.

The real mystery for most of us was how Pauline got all those flying babies potty trained. We can all remember a time when the Pentecostal Home reeked of piss and poo. The stains were everywhere: on the pillowed ceilings, the stuffed-animal floors, the padded walls, and the tattered yarn restraints. Bits of who-knows-what were forever caught in Pauline's hair and the stains were eternally splattered all over Jeffery's coveralls. How Pauline and Jeffery Pritchard took care of all those crying, pooping, suckling, slobbering, flying babies was surely a miracle of God's own hand—at least that's what Pauline told everyone.

Apparently, she had made some kind of blood covenant with God, and that's why she was able to take care of all those flying babies like she did. It's also why she re-Christened the children with Biblical names of famous sinners like Cane, Bathsheba, and Lot. Pauline gave the children the most unwanted names in the Bible to forever remind them that they too had been born unwanted, and that the only way to make their lives right with God was by washing away the sins of their parents.

While it was disconcerting for most of us to call a three-year-old girl in pigtails, Jezebel, and her adorable baby brother, Onan, we did appreciate Pauline and Jeffery Pritchard's hard work. By taking in The Redbird bastards, the Pritchards allowed our families to heal. The Pentecostal Home for Flying Children offered so many of us a certain kind of grace. So we all pulled together and everyone did what they could to help out. Some of us made cash donations to the cause while others donated canned foods and clothes. It wasn't cheap keeping all those flying children clothed and fed. Eventually we had to resort to sending our own kids out to sell popcorn and candy bars door-to-door while our churches raised money with weekly Bingo nights, cakewalks, and car washes. We did what we had to do to keep the lights on at The Home. We did it because we had to, because we had to keep our mistakes in a place where we could live with them.

From the moment that Pauline had wrapped Zaccheus Redbird in her sweater, he had clung very closely to her heart. Though Pauline would have denied it, everyone knew that this child was her favorite. She was often heard around town telling the boy that one day he "would bring the devil to his knees." Pauline Pritchard saw something special in Zaccheus, something that the other Redbirds didn't have, and that is why she named the boy for a redeemed tax collector instead of a whoremaster or a sodomite. It's also why she kept all his baby teeth in the jingle-jangledy lockets that she wore on her wrists despite her religion's strict rules against jewelry.

Now that Zaccheus, or Zac, as his classmates called him, had entered high school, he was living proof that Pentecostalism could redeem even the most wretched among us. Zac, though he was quite obviously The Redbird's son, refused to fly. Which, to Pauline, proved that Zac had somehow conquered his father's wicked ways.

Zac refused to indulge in any sort of pride that would put him above the rest of us or do anything that might seem cruel. Instead he did as he was told: he sold Gideon Bibles in front of K&B Drugs to raise money for The Home, he took care of Sister Pauline when she lost her leg to the diabetes, he troubled over scripture and his schoolwork in equal measure. He wasn't just respectful of everyone he met, he was kind—effortlessly kind in the way that one would imagine that Jesus must have been to lepers and thieves and the like. And because of this, we all thought that Zaccheus Redbird was the biggest weirdo we had ever met.

"Baby oil and iodine works way better than Crisco," Tamara Cooksey admonished her fellow cheerleaders. Then to prove her point, she hiked up her cheerleading skirt, pulled down the left side of her bright yellow bloomers, and revealed a stripe of fluorescent-white skin on her otherwise mahogany hip. "See, look at that tan line."

Tamara Cooksey was Shreveport's version of Christy Brinkley. She was blonde and famous. Tamara's double-decker smile and her savage tan were sure signs of hope for our hard-luck town. After all, she had sprung up from all the chaos and shame brought upon us in the '70s, just as pure and radiant as a lotus bloom growing from a pile of dung. She was one of the best things that Shreveport had going for it in an otherwise very grim time in our history.

Tamara Cooksey had dedicated her life to tanning and cheerleading. When she wasn't practicing her pom-pom routines, she was laying out, making sure that she was the darkest girl with the blondest hair in all of Shreveport. You could always tell when she was sunbathing because there, high above the Cookseys' ranch-style house, would be a flock of circling teenage boys. The boys from the Pentecostal Home would fly over Tamara Cooksey, as she lay there all greased up and glistening in her string bikini. They would shout stupid teenage-boy things like, "Look-see, look-see, it's sexy Tamara Cooksey!"

Some days the boys would hoot and holler. Other days, they'd just fly in circles, with one or two diving to take a closer look. Sometimes they would shout things that were profound if not a little odd, like, "The seed of God is within all of us!"

Other times, they'd shout profane and disturbing things, like, "Hey, Tamara Cooksey! Suck it!"

A number of the boys, the gentler ones, tried to shower Tamara with rose petals. They were crestfallen when the wind carried the flurry of velvet-red petals into the backyard of Tamara's neighbors instead of bathing her in their beauty.

One petal, however, did drift down to her, and it landed on her belly button. This made Tamara laugh. So the next day, in an effort to thrill Tamara Cooksey even more, the boys stole thousands of Hershey's kisses and poured them on her as she laid out. The silver kisses pelted her, bringing huge, red welts to her perfect tan skin. Tamara had to cover her head with her beach towel and run inside to escape the chocolate hailstorm.

Afraid that they might have hurt their earthbound crush, the boys never showered her with anything ever again. Instead they settled on circling high above, as she would lie there, glistening and sweating, in the midst of her father's tomato garden.

It was Mr. Cooksey's tomato plants that kept The Redbird brothers far away from Tamara. The boys knew that all Redbird children were deathly allergic to any plant in the nightshade family—tomatoes, bell peppers, eggplants, even potatoes. The mere fumes given off by the leaves and stalks of a nightshade could drop a Redbird child from the sky and kill them. So the boys flew high above Mr. Cooksey's tomato garden and rode the thermals as they spied on his sylphy daughter with stolen binoculars and deer rifle scopes. Like the rest of Shreveport, The Redbirds had to admire Tamara Cooksey from afar.

———— ⌇ ————

"Why don't you ever fly?"

"I don't want to talk about it."

"Your brothers landed on my roof today."

"I'm sorry. They shouldn't do that."

"Don't apologize. I think they're funny."

———— ⌇ ————

Why and how Tamara Cooksey fell so hard for Zaccheus Redbird was not public knowledge. Tamara, for once in her life, was keeping her mouth shut, which was odd, because usually Tamara was a one-girl power station broadcasting Tamara Cooksey's ever-fascinating, always-scintillating life 24 hours a day.

Typically, Tamara Cooksey held court in the cafeteria where she would report on the most intimate and minute details of her teenage life: the brutal frequency of her menstrual cramps, the adorable iced cookies that she made for the JV football team, her need to make herself throw up after her mother made her eat meatloaf, the kind of toilet paper she used to vandalize Lacey Monroe's house, the number of lipsticks she had filched from Selber's Department store. But when Tamara's friends would ask her about Zac, she would only wink and say, "Nunya."

Eventually her friends grew weary of this response and they mounted a full-fledged interrogation with Tamara's best friend, Holly Ferguson, leading the charge.

"Oh, come on, Tam. Don't be a whore. Tell us about you and Zac." Holly said one day in the locker room after a pep rally.

"I already told you. Nunya. Nunya business."

"What's the matter? Are you embarrassed to be dating one of those Pentecostal flying retards or something?"

"Embarrassed?"

"Yeah, embarrassed."

"Holly, I'm not the one stomping around out there with my big white thunder thighs and cellulite. So, no, I'm not embarrassed."

There are words that can never be taken back or forgiven. For Holly Ferguson, "thunder thighs" and "cellulite" were three of those words. From that day forward, she never spoke to Tamara Cooksey again.

So that left the rest of Shreveport to pry where we shouldn't be prying, to figure out how someone like Tamara Cooksey ended up with someone like Zaccheus Redbird. 10,000 notes were passed back and forth in Civics and Algebra classes. 242 malicious theories were whispered by concerned mothers at PTA meetings. 777 phone calls were placed by the cheerleaders alone. Zac and Tamara's secret romance became the impolite topic to broach at potluck suppers and church picnics all over town.

———— ❧ ————

"I. Love. You."

"Shhh, my dad will hear you."

"I don't care."

"You'll care when he comes in here and shoots your pecker off."

———— ❧ ————

The now famous phrase, "beat you like a red-headed stepchild," was actually coined in Shreveport. It was, of course, referring to The Redbird children, and Jeffery and Pauline's tough-love efforts to set them on the straight and narrow. Jeffery never spared the rod to spoil the child. He'd take his belt off and whip their little hides as red as their hair if he had to. And not a day went by that Pauline Pritchard wasn't seen chasing one of the flying children down the street with a flyswatter, and when she finally caught the offending brat, she would beat the devil out of the child. Some hippies actually protested the Pritchards' public whippings of the flying children. The hippies made signs and picketed The Pentecostal Home. They sang folk songs and shouted, "Free the Baby Birds!" Nobody paid them much attention though so the hippies eventually took their free-loving, no-deodorant-wearing ways down to New Orleans.

Now history has proven that those hippies were bigger idiots than we initially thought. In fact, the Pritchards were perhaps not strict enough with their Redbird charges as Jeffery Pritchard met a dubious end in June of 1985 when he supposedly fell from the roof of The Pentecostal Home and broke his thick neck.

The Pritchards had dedicated their lives to putting the fear of God into those Redbird bastards, but foster parents can only do so much. Once most of The Redbirds reached their teenage years, their alien blood somehow trumped their strict upbringing—the lone exception being good-hearted Zaccheus.

The problem with most of the flying children was that you never knew what one of them would do. They were constantly pulling pranks. The boys' favorite stunt was to fly up behind people, grabbing their victims underneath the armpits and taking them fast and high into the sky. All the while their victims would be kicking and screaming, terrified that they would fall to their death. The Redbirds would then drop their victims into a swimming pool or a shallow lake. The little bastards laughed maniacally like this life-threatening attack was just one big joke. Many of their victims reported that their flying attackers smelled of Pabst Blue Ribbon and marijuana.

The Redbird girls were actually worse than their brothers. They had no shame. They would strip down naked and fly all over town, through grocery stores, church services, weddings, even funerals. With their long, red Pentecostal hair, they thought of themselves as flying Lady Godivas, but they were no better than common strippers and prostitutes to most of us. The girls were notorious for floating in front of our teenage sons' windows, knocking at the glass and giggling. When the boys would unlatch the windows to let them in, The Redbird girls would fly away. This kind of teasing was meant to drive our sons crazy, and it did. Oh, how it did.

It was during one of these stunts that Bobby Tyler discovered the full power of the nightshades. One night, Salome Redbird was hovering by his teenage son's window, pressing her breasts up against the glass, torturing his son like the devil's own succubus. Bobby grabbed the closest thing he could find to throw at the tramp. He grabbed a rotting tomato.

"Get!" He hummed the tomato at the girl, hitting her square in the chest. The tomato exploded into a fury of seeds and juice, killing the girl and crashing her into his wife's pink azaleas below.

Our town had run out of patience for those flying freaks, and now that Pauline had the diabetes and Jeffery was dead, something had to be done. Those scurrilous Redbirds were using The Pentecostal Home for Flying Children as a haven for their misdeeds and their liquor-sloshing parties. Meanwhile crazy old Pauline Pritchard, with her one good leg, stayed locked away in her room, watching Oral Roberts and Pat Robertson, ignoring her duties to us and her promises to God.

It was finally time to rid our city of this scourge. So we planted gardens full of red, yellow, and green peppers. We grew tomatoes of every variety: Big Boys, Yellow Brandywines, Cherokee Purples—you name it. There were over 50 varieties of eggplants growing all over our fair city. Our lady-folk kept tomato sandwiches in their purses and we all kept handfuls of new potatoes in the glove compartments of our cars, just in case.

Eventually, The Redbirds got the message, and interestingly enough, none of them thought it was very funny to fly naked through the funerals for their own brothers and sisters. We, the mere mortals of Shreveport, had finally taught The Redbird bastards a lesson: Don't mess with good people.

———— ⊗ ————

"I wanna run away."
"Tamara."
"I'm serious."
"I can't."
"They're going to kill you."
"Trust me, they won't."

The Nightshade Retaliation Program was the city-sponsored initiative for "growing and throwing" nightshade vegetables at Redbird delinquents. State laws were even amended to clear any citizen of murder charges if they had to resort to throwing a nightshade in self-defense. This program was hugely successful. It only took five nightshade throwings for all The Redbirds to pick up and fly away from Shreveport—well, all except for one, Zaccheus, who was so kind and mannerly that most of us forgot that he even was a Redbird.

However, the terror that The Redbirds had raged over our town for all those years had obviously affected the tender minds of our own teenagers and many of our kids had a hard time turning the other cheek here, which would explain why they had such hard time with the last Redbird dating Captain Shreve's head cheerleader, no matter how nice he was or how much he refused to fly—which would also explain why our otherwise very Christian kids left eggplants and death threats in Zaccheus Redbird's locker.

On August 13th, 1986, Zaccheus Redbird was with Tamara Cooksey, holding hands at the Circle K on Youree Drive. They were both drinking Icees and smiling when Holly "Thunder Thighs" Ferguson snuck up behind them.

Holly Ferguson held her breath and lobbed a Hazel Mae yellow tomato at Zaccheus Redbird's head. The golden fruit splattered against Zac's skull and ran down his neck in yellow gobs of seed and slime.

That's when the holy kindness of Zaccheus Redbird must have curdled into biblical vengeance because he exploded into hundreds of redbirds—cardinals to be exact. Tamara screamed and covered her face while Holly Ferguson dropped to the ground, scared that the birds would scratch out her eyes for what she had just done, but the screeching flock of cardinals flew past her. They flew high into the sky, multiplying with each flap of their wings until the flock was in the millions.

The skies turned red and our blood turned white. Millions upon millions of redbirds pecked and ravaged our tomatoes, peppers, and eggplants. They even pulled up our potato plants and flew away with them. It was like a plague of the Old Testament kind.

After tearing our gardens and yards apart, the waves of cardinals once again darkened our skies, but this time they blanketed our homes, our parks, and our cars in oceans of horrible splatters. By nightfall, they had nearly destroyed our town.

Now that there wasn't a single nightshade vegetable left in Shreveport, we waited under our beds with our guns loaded and our doors bolted. We waited for The Redbird Children to return and take their revenge on us. We waited for weeks, but they never came.

Some people say that they saw the cardinals swarm together that night and reform into Zaccheus Redbird, and it was a reborn Zaccheus who stole Tamara Cooksey from us. Others say that the cardinals landed on the Cookseys' front lawn, and when Tamara went outside to see them, to say goodbye to what was left of Zac, the birds tore her to pieces, and flew away with her remains in their tiny yellow talons. Some people swear that Holly Ferguson, a half-eaten box of Ding-Dongs, and a piano wire were somehow involved in Tamara Cooksey's disappearance. Somewhere between the gossip, the legends, and the lies is the truth, but we won't go looking for it now. It flew away with The Redbirds.

FOR A RUTHLESS CRITICISM OF EVERYTHING EXISTING

by Martin Cozza from *Pindeldyboz*

The President came over for lunch. He ate the grilled cheese I gave him in big, blind chomps and left bent arcs of crust on the plate. He didn't talk, or even look at me. I didn't want him here. Other people forced me to let him come.

First they bought all the ground and air around my house. Then they bought a path for him straight through my front door, across my living room and into the kitchen. They bought one of my kitchen chairs for him and two square feet of my kitchen table. Nobody knows who they are, and nobody knows who they bought it all from. It wasn't from me.

On his way out the President defaced my family pictures with a very fancy-looking pen. He slashed right through the picture of my mother in her bathrobe, but the slash started to heal itself right away, and by the time he reached the door my mother herself was in the room, brushing dirt from her hair and holding her stilled heart in her hand. She presented it to him, her face bronze and scornful, but he didn't even know to be scared.

DALTHAREE

by Jeffrey Ford from *The Del Rey Book of Science Fiction and Fantasy*

———————⟨⟨⟩⟩———————

You've heard of bottled cities, no doubt—society writ miniscule and delicate beyond reason: toothpick-spired towns, streets no thicker than thread, pinprick faces of the citizenry peering from office windows smaller than sequins. Hustle, politics, fervor, struggle, capitulation, wrapped in a crystal firmament, stoppered at the top to keep reality both in and out. Those microscopic lives, striking glass at the edge of things, believed themselves gigantic, their dilemmas universal.

Our research suggested that Daltharee had many multi-storied buildings carved right into its hillsides. Surrounding the city there was a forest with lakes and streams and all of it was contained within a dome, like a dinner beneath the lid of a serving dish. When the inhabitants of Daltharee looked up they were prepared to not see the heavens. They knew that the light above, their Day, was generated by a machine, which they oiled and cared for. The stars that shone every sixteen hours when Day left darkness behind were simple bulbs regularly changed by a man in a hot air balloon.

They were convinced that the domed city floated upon an iceberg, which it actually did. There was one door in the wall of the dome at the end of a certain path through the forest. When opened, it led out onto the ice. The surface of the iceberg extended the margin of one of their miles all around the enclosure. Blinding snows fell, winds constantly roared in a perpetual blizzard. Their belief was that Daltharee drifted upon the oceans of an otherwise frozen world. They prayed for the end of eternal winter, so they might reclaim the continents.

And all of this: their delusions, the city, the dome, the iceberg, the two quarts of water it floated upon, were contained within an old gallon glass milk bottle, plugged at the top with a tattered handkerchief and painted dark blue. When I'd put my ear to the glass, I heard, like the ocean in a seashell, fierce gales blowing.

Daltharee was not the product of a shrinking ray as many of these pint-size metropolises are. And please, there was no magic involved. In fact, once past the early stages of its birth it was more organically grown than shaped by artifice. Often, in the origin stories of these diminutive places, there's a deranged scientist lurking in the wings. Here, too, we have the notorious Mando Paige, the inventor of sub-microscopic differentiated cell division and growth. What I'm referring to was Paige's technique for producing super-miniature human cells. From the instant of their atomic origin, these parcels of life were beset by enzymatic reaction and electric stunting the way tree roots are tortured over time to create a bonsai. Paige shaped human life in the form of tiny individuals. They landscaped and built the city, laid roads, and lurched in a sleep-walking stupor induced by their creator.

Once the city in the dome was completed, Paige introduced more of the crumb-sized citizenry through the door that opened onto the iceberg. Just before closing that door, he set off a device that played an A flat for approximately ten seconds, a pre-ordained spur to consciousness, which brought them all awake to their lives in Daltharee. Seeding the water in the gallon bottle with crystal ions, he soon after introduced a chemical mixture that formed a slick, unmelting ice-like platform beneath the floating dome. He then introduced into the atmosphere fenathol nitrate, silver iodite, anamidian betheldine, to initiate the frigid wind and falling snow. When all was well within the dome, when the iceberg had sufficiently grown, when winter ruled, he plugged the gallon bottle with an old handkerchief. That closed system of winter, with just the slightest amount of air allowed in through the cloth, was sustainable forever, feeding wind to snow and snow to cold to claustrophobia and back again in an infinite loop. The Daltthareens made up the story about a frozen world to satisfy the unknown. Paige manufactured three more of these cities, each wholly different from the others, before laws were passed about the imprisonment of humanity, no matter how minute or unaware. He was eventually, himself, imprisoned for his crimes.

We searched for a method to study life inside the dome but were afraid to disturb its delicate nature, unsure whether simply removing the handkerchief would upset a brittle balance between inner and outer universes. It was suggested that a very long, exceedingly thin probe that had the ability to twist and turn by computational command could be shimmied in between the edge of the bottle opening and the cloth of the handkerchief. This probe, like the ones physicians used in the twentieth and twenty-first centuries to read the hieroglyphics of the bowel, would be fitted out with both a camera and a microphone. The device was adequate for those cities that didn't have the extra added boundary of a dome, but even in them, how incongruous, a giant metal snake just out of the blue, slithering through one's reality. The inhabitants of these enclosed worlds were exceedingly small but not stupid.

In the end it was my invention that won the day—a voice-activated transmitter the size of two atoms was introduced into the bottle. We had to wait for it to work its way from the blizzard atmosphere, through the dome's air filtration system, and into the city. Then we had to wait for it to come in contact with a voice. At any point a thousand things could have gone wrong, but one day, six months later, who knows how many years that would be in Dalthareen time, the machine transmitted and my receiver picked up conversations from the domed city. Here's an early one we managed to record that had some interesting elements:

"I'm not doing that now. Please, give me some room . . ." she said.

There is a long pause filled with the faint sound of a utensil clinking a plate.

"I was out in the forest the other day," he said.

"Why?" she asked.

"I'm not sure," he told her.

"What do you do out there?" she asked.

"I'm in this club," he said. "We got together to try to find the door in the wall of the dome."

"How did that go?" she asked.

"We knew it was there and we found it," he said. "Just like in the old stories . . ."

"Blizzard?"

"You can't believe it," he said.

"Did you go out in it?"

"Yes, and when I stepped back into the dome, I could feel a piece of the storm stuck inside me."

"What's that supposed to mean?" she said.

"I don't know."

"How did it get inside you?" she asked.

"Through my ears," he said.

"Does it hurt?"

"I was different when I came back in."

"Stronger?"

"No, more something else."

"Can you say?"

"I've had dreams."

"So what," she said. "I had a dream the other night that I was out on the Grand Conciliation Balcony, dressed for the odd jibbery when all of a sudden a little twisher rumbles up and whispers to me the words—'Elemental Potency.' What do you think it means? I can't get the phrase out of my head."

"It's nonsense," he said.

"Why aren't *your* dreams nonsense?"

"They are," he said. "The other night I had this dream about a theory. I can't remember if I saw it in the pages of a dream magazine or someone spoke it or it just jumped into my sleeping head. I've never dreamt about a theory before. Have you?"

"No," she said.

"It was about living in the dome. The theory was that since the dome is closed things that happen in the dome only affect other things in the dome. Because the size of Daltharee is as we believe so miniscule compared to the rest of the larger world, the repercussions of the acts you engage in in the dome will have a higher possibility of intersecting each other. If you think of something you do throughout the day as an act, each act begins a chain reaction of mitigating energy in all directions. The will of your own energy, dispersed through myriad acts within only a morning will beam, refract, and reflect off the beams of others' acts and the walls of the closed system, barreling into each other and causing sparks at those locations where your essence meets itself. In those instances, at those specific locations, your will is greater than the will of the dome. What I was then told was that a person could learn a way to act at a given hour—a quick series of six moves that send out so many ultimately crisscrossing intentions of will that it creates a power mesh capable in its transformative strength of bending reality to whim."

"You're crazy," she said.

There is a slight pause here, the sound of wind blowing in the trees.

"Hey, what ever happened to your aunt?" he asked.

"They got it out of her."

"Amazing," he said. "Close call . . ."

"She always seemed fine too," she said. "But swallowing a knitting needle? That's not right."

"She doesn't even knit, does she?"

"No," she said.

"Good thing she didn't have to pass it," he said. "Think about the intersecting beams of will resulting from that act."

She laughed. "I heard the last pigeon died yesterday."

"Yeah?"

"They found it in the park, on the lawn amidst the Moth trees."

"In all honesty, I did that," he said. "You know, not directly, but just by the acts I went through yesterday morning. I got out of bed, had breakfast, got dressed, you know . . . like that. I was certain that by midday that bird would be dead."

"Why'd you kill it?" she asked.

There's a pause in the conversation here filled up by the sound of machinery in the distance just beneath that of the wind in the trees.

"Having felt what I felt outside the dome, I considered it a mercy," he said.

"Interesting . . ." she said. "I've gotta get going. It looks like rain."

"Will you call me?" he asked.

"Eventually, of course," she said.

"I know," he said. "I know."

Funny thing about Paige, he found religion in the latter years of his life. After serving out his sentence, he renounced his crackpot Science and retreated to a one room apartment in an old boarding house on the edge of the great desert. He courted an elderly woman there, a Mrs. Trucy. I thought he'd been long gone when we finally contacted him. After a solid fifteen years of recording conversations, it became evident that the domed city was failing—the economy, the natural habitat, were both in disarray. A strange illness had sprung up amid the population, an unrelenting, fatal insomnia that took a dozen of them to Death each week. Nine months without a single wink of sleep. The conversations we recorded then were full of anguish and hallucination.

Basically, we asked Paige what he might do to save his own created world. He came to work for us and studied the problem full time. He was old then, wrinkles and flyaway hair in strange, ever-shifting formations atop his scalp, eyeglasses with one ear loop. Every time he'd make a mistake on a calculation or a technique, he'd swallow a thumbtack. When I asked if the practice helped him concentrate he told me, "No."

Eventually, on a Saturday morning when no one was at the lab but himself and an uninterested security guard, he broke into the vault that held the shrinking ray. He started the device up, aimed it at the glass milk bottle containing Daltharee, and then sat on top of the bottle, wearing a parachute. The ray discharged, shrinking him. He fell in among the gigantic folds of the handkerchief. Apparently he managed to work his way down past the end of the material and leap into the blizzard, out over the dome of the city. No one was there to see him slowly descend, dangerously buffeted by the insane winds. No one noticed him slip through the door in the dome.

Conversations came back to us eventually containing his name. Apparently he'd told them the true nature of the dome and the bottle it resided inside of. And then after some more time passed, there came word that he was creating another domed city inside a gallon milk bottle from the city of Daltharee. *Where would it end?*, we wondered, but it was not a thought we enjoyed pursuing as it ran in a loop, recrossing itself, reiterating its original energy in ever-diminishing reproductions of ourselves. Perhaps it was the thought of it that made my assistant accidentally drop the milk bottle one afternoon. It exploded into a million dark blue shards, dirt and dome and tiny trees spread across the floor. We considered studying its remains, but instead, with a shiver, I swept it into a pile and then into the furnace.

A year later, Mrs. Trucy came looking for Mando. She insisted upon knowing what had become of him. We told her that the law did not require us to tell her, and then she pulled a marriage certificate out of her purse. I was there with the Research General at the time, and I saw him go pale as a ghost upon seeing that paper. He told her Mando had died in an experiment of his own devising. The wrinkles of her gray face torqued to a twist and sitting beneath her pure silver hair, her head looked like a metal screw. Three tears squeezed out from the corners of her eyes. If Mando died performing an experiment, we could not be held responsible. We would, though, have to produce the body for her as proof that he'd perished. The Research General told her we were conducting a complete investigation of the tragedy and would contact her in six weeks with the results and the physical proof—in other words, Mando's corpse.

My having shoveled Daltharee into the trash without searching for survivors or mounting even a cursory rescue effort was cause for imprisonment. My superior, the Research General, having had my callous act take place on his watch was also liable. After three nerve racking days, I conceived of a way for us to save ourselves. In fact it was so simple it astounded me that neither one of us, scientific minds though we be, didn't leap to the concept earlier. Using Mando's own process for creating diminutive humanity, we took his DNA from our genetic files, put it through a chemical bath to begin the growth process, and then tortured the cells into tininess. We had to use radical enzymes to speed the process up given we only had six weeks. By the end of week five we had a living, breathing Mando Paige, trapped under a drinking glass in our office. He was dressed in a little orange jumpsuit, wore black boots, and was in the prime of his youth. We studied his attempts to escape his prison with a jeweler's loupe inserted into each eye. We thought we could rely on the air simply running out in the glass and him suffocating.

Days passed and Paige hung on. Each day I'd spy on his meager existence and wonder what he must be thinking. When the time came and he wasn't dead, I killed him with a cigarette. I brought the glass to the very edge of the table, bent a plastic drinking straw that I shoved the longer end of up into the glass, and then caught it fairly tightly against the table edge. As for the part that stuck out, I lit a cigarette, inhaled deeply and then blew the smoke up into the glass. I gave him five lung-fulls. The oxygen displacement was too much, of course.

Mrs. Trucy accepted our story and the magnified view of her lover's diminutive body. We told her how he bravely took the shrinking ray for the sake of Science. She remarked that he looked younger than when he was full sized and alive, and the Research General told her, "As you shrink, wrinkles have a tendency to evaporate." We went to the funeral out in the desert near her home. It was a blazingly hot day. She'd had his remains placed into a thimble with some tape across the top, and this she buried in the red sand.

Later, as the sun set, the Research General and I ate dinner at a ramshackle restaurant along a dusty road right outside of Mateos. He had the pig knuckle with sauerkraut and I had the chicken croquettes with orange gravy that tasted brown.

"I'm so relieved that asshole's finally dead," whispered the Research General.

"There's dead and there's dead," I told him.

"Let's not make this complicated," he said. "I know he's out there in some smaller version of reality, he could be filling all available space with smaller and smaller reproductions of himself, choking the ass of the universe with pages and pages of Mando Paige. I don't give a fuck as long as he's not here."

"He is here," I said, and then they brought the martinis and the conversation evaporated into reminiscence.

That night as I stood out beneath the desert sky having a smoke, I had a sense that the cumulative beams generated by the repercussions of my actions over time, harboring my inherent will, had reached some far-flung boundary and were about to turn back on me. In my uncomfortable bed at the Hacienda Motel, I tossed and turned, drifting in and out of sleep. It was then that I had a vision of the shrinking ray, its sparkling blue emission bouncing off a mirror set at an angle. The beam then travels a short distance to another mirror with which it collides and reflects. The second mirror is positioned so that it sends the ray back at its own original source. The beam strikes and mixes with itself only a few inches past the nozzle of the machine's barrel. And then I see it in my mind—when a shrinking ray is trained upon itself, its diminutive-making properties are cancelled twice and as it is a fact that when two negatives are multiplied they make a positive, this process makes things bigger. As soon as the concept was upon me, I was filled with excitement and couldn't wait to get back to the lab the next day to work out the math and realize an experiment.

It was fifteen years later, the Research General had long been fired, when Mando Paige stepped out of the spot where the shrinking ray's beam crossed itself. He was blue and yellow and red and his hair was curly. I stood within feet of him and he smiled at me. I, of course, couldn't let him go—not due to any law but my own urge to finish the job I'd started at the outset. As he stepped back toward the ray, I turned it off, and he was trapped, for the moment, in our moment. I called for my assistants to surround him, and I sent one to my office for the revolver I kept in my bottom drawer. He told me that one speck of his saliva contained four million Daltharees. "When I fart," he said, "I set forth Armadas." I shot him and the four assistants and then automatically acid-washed the lab to destroy the Dalthareen plague and evidence of murder. No one suspected a thing.

I found a few cities sprouting beneath my fingernails last week. There were already rows of domes growing behind my ears. My blood no doubt is the manufacture of cities, flowing silver through my veins. Crowds behind my eyes, commerce in my joints. Each idea I have is a domed city that grows and opens like a flower. I want to tell you about cities and cities and cities named Daltharee.

IS

by Chris Gavaler from *New England Review*

The door that Is found at the back of the closet, the morning it was raining and the backyard was mud and she had nowhere to play, only came as high as her new tooth. Is thought the door would have reached to the bright gold button between her mother's breasts, or the pale bottom button on her father's belly, if one of them had been behind the vacuum cleaner in the back of the hall closet instead of her, but they were not and probably could not since no one but Is could stand with the shelf of board games and woollens and broken umbrellas over her head, and anyway, on Is the door came to her tooth. It was a new tooth, a jagged white bump with an empty space below it. She asked her mother about the door.

"There's a door in the back of the coat closet."

"It goes to the basement," her mother said. Her mother was sitting on a kitchen stool and leaning over so that her nose almost touched the nose reflected in the metal counter. She was holding the pieces of her glasses in the palm of one hand and a tiny screwdriver in the fingers of the other. The dishwasher was humming.

"What's it doing in the back of the closet?"

"Renovations," her mother said. "The people who lived here before us moved everything around, the walls and doors and things." She leaned even closer when the screwdriver began to turn in her fingers. Is watched and sucked her lip into the empty space below her new tooth, which was something that she did often now and not because she wanted to.

"Why would they move the walls?"

"They were renovators."

Is went back to the coat closet after finding her flashlight in the toy box in her room. It was only a play flashlight because when she turned the switch in one direction it glowed green and when she turned it in the other it glowed red, but when she didn't turn it at all, as she was not turning it now, the flashlight glowed white like a real flashlight. The walls of the closet glowed white too. So did the door. Is could see now that there was a knob on the door but it was not a doorknob. It was small and made of wood and did not turn—like the knob on the cabinet in the living room that Is was not supposed to open but sometimes did. There was nothing inside the cabinet except wires and plugs and CD cases, so nothing had come of her opening it. She wondered if anything would come of her opening this door, if she did open this door, which she hadn't yet, and not just because it was locked. The lock was only a metal sliding pin that brightened the nearer she held the light. She asked her father about it.

"Why would they put a lock on the door in the back of the coat closet?"

"Who?" her father asked. "You mean the door that goes to the basement?"

Her father was sitting on the toilet lid with his yellow towel knotted around his stomach. His foot was curled on his lap with the sole turned up so he could dig at his wart with the fingernail clippers. It was not a normal wart. Her father had told her that instead of growing out of the skin, his wart grew into the skin, and weekend mornings he picked and rubbed and gouged at it and made it bleed.

"Why would they put a lock on a door to the basement? What's down there?"

"Cold air," said her father. The air in the bathroom was heavy and wet and hard to breathe. Is stayed by the door.

"Cold air can't open doors," she said.

"Not if the door is locked." Her father eased his foot from his lap and tried to straighten his leg but his leg had been bent too long and made his face wrinkle and twitch. "Ow," he said. "Ow ow ow."

"Can I go down there?"

"You have been down there. You know the door out back by the garden? That's how we get the bikes in and out."

"Can I go down there now?"

"Not now," he said. "It's raining."

Is closed the bathroom door and walked downstairs to find her mother. Her mother was lying on the living room couch with an enormous book on her knees. Her left eye looked small and flat behind the lens of her glasses. The other lens was missing. Her cheek was pinching that eye closed.

"Did they move all the walls?"

Except for the twitch of the closed eye and the flutter of the open one, her mother did not move. Then her hand rose from the page, paused, began to droop, stopped, and unfurled a finger. "Just that one." She was pointing at the kitchen.

Is looked at the wall behind the sink. The kitchen window hung there, with smeary green branches bobbing in the gray glass squares. White cabinets hung on each side. The cabinets went up almost all the way to the ceiling and came down almost all the way to the counter, so it was not much of a wall. It was blue because her father had painted it blue a long time ago. All the walls in the kitchen were blue, a strip of blue above the cabinets and a strip of blue below the cabinets. Is turned to her mother.

"Which one?"

Her mother's closed eyelid twitched.

"The one that's not there."

Is looked again. There were three walls in the kitchen, and all three of them were, as far as she could tell, definitely there. She tried to look for other walls, but all she could see were counters and archways and cabinets. The green smears were still bobbing. The dishwasher was still humming. Is looked down.

The rows of the kitchen floorboards ended at her toes. She lifted her blue sneaker and saw where the rows of the living room floorboards began at the heel of her other sneaker. Those floorboards were different. They were shorter and lighter and thinner and did not line up with the long dark wide boards. Is walked through the open space between the kitchen and the living room all the time, and she had known the two floors were different, but she had never asked why. Is did not ask why about most things that she noticed because there were so many things to notice and if she asked why about all of them, or even half of them—why is orange juice yellow, why is her room a square and her parents' a rectangle, why is thirteen called thirteen and not threeteen or ten-three since twenty-three isn't called three-twenty or thirtweenty—she would have to ask why all the time, and that would get annoying and not just for her.

"But what," asked Is, "do walls have to do with the closet?"

Her mother's book flopped face down onto her stomach.

"You used to be able to get down to the basement from the kitchen, but when they took out the wall and moved the counters, they closed off the door, so then they had to cut another door somewhere else so you could go down there if you really had to."

"Why would you have to?"

"You wouldn't really. We never do."

"Did they?"

"Who?"

"The renovators."

"I doubt it."

"Can I?"

"I wish you wouldn't."

Is looked at the ceiling where the top of the missing wall hung like a long narrow upside down stump. She wondered if walls had roots, because she knew that roots could be a problem, like the ones her parents said had broken the pipes and made the toilets and sinks not work. The pipes were under the house and in the basement and in the walls. Is tried to imagine other walls that might also not be there anymore, but couldn't.

"Did the wall go upstairs?"

Her mother turned a page.

"Upstairs is your room. You're standing under your mirror."

Is looked at the ceiling again. The tiny hairs on the skin of her arms all stood and fluttered at once. My room, she thought. And then she climbed the stairs two at a time while pushing down on her knees with both hands. Of course she had known that her bedroom was upstairs and that the downstairs was downstairs, but otherwise the two spaces were unrelated, like the backyard and the front yard. You got to them through different doors.

She stood in her bedroom and turned carefully on the heel of one foot, staring at each wall, each window, each corner, realizing that another wall, another window, another corner of the living room was directly beneath them. Her mother was lying on the couch below her bed. Is was standing above the coffee table. She felt suspended. She felt weightless.

She stopped turning when she noticed her father standing in her open door. He was dressed now. His hair was fluffy and hard to look at because of the light from the hall window behind him.

"Want to come on some errands?"

"Where?"

"Bakery, oil change, cash machine," he said. "Not in that order."

"No, thank you," said Is. "Can I go in the basement when it stops raining?"

Her father started down the steps. He was limping. "Do you have to?" he asked. "It's messy down there." Is watched through the slats of the banister until the top of his head bobbed and vanished below the angle of the landing.

She was still standing in the middle of her room, pushing the tip of her tongue into the space below her new tooth, when she noticed herself standing in her mirror. The mirror hung above her dresser from a nail her father hammered into the wall after he painted her room peach. The room in the mirror was peach too. It was not really a room—Is never imagined that she could climb through the glass like the girl in that story that her mother was reading to her every night after dinner. It was a reflection, something her father said was so completely opposite of itself that it was identical again. Is looked at her reflection, at her yellow hair and zigzaggy part, at her fresh blue sneakers and worn-pink socks, her sweater, her jeans, the circle of her face, the tiny black dots squinting to see herself in them. She did not believe that this was what she looked like from the outside, though she did not disbelieve it either. It just was not something that concerned her. The house was much more interesting.

When she stepped into the hall, she was trying to imagine the ceiling of the coat closet under her feet, but instead she noticed a spot of blood on the wood by her door. No, it was two spots, tiny and dark and far apart. She looked for a third, where her father's stride would have smeared the next, and there it was. She stared at it, her tongue pushing in and out and in.

When Is arrived downstairs, her mother's book was drooped on the arm of the couch, a white crease down its black spine. Her mother was not there. Is opened the closet and reached for her coat. She did not look where the little door's hinges hung behind her mother's plastic-draped coat, where the handle of the vacuum almost touched the knob that did not turn. Is knew she should not go down that way, that she would have to go outside and in through the garden door. The door in the back of the closet had been made for emergencies, in case of a fire or an earthquake or if someone was trapped inside the house and needed to escape without anyone knowing. Using the door when it was not an emergency was dangerous. It might make something bad happen.

Is was nearly to the back door, with her coat half-buttoned and umbrella unsnapped, when a splinter of light caught her eye. The lens from her mother's glasses rested on the counter. The lens was moving, rocking slightly on its curved and almost invisible back. A screw the size of an insect's leg rested beside it. Is touched her cheek to the chill of the counter to watch it vibrate. Then she turned to go outside.

The rain seemed light, a mist, but the roof of her umbrella rattled with taps as Is opened it over her head. She looked for her shadow, for any shadows, but the lawn was flat and gray-green. Her boots were gray-yellow. Her father's car was gone from the driveway.

She stopped at the garden door, which was not a very good door at all. The siding was torn and wedged around the top of the frame, plus the wood at the hinges was soft. The bottom panel had fallen out too. But it was the same sort of paneled door that opened into her bedroom, into all of the rooms inside. When she tugged at the knob, it was cold and wet. She used both of her hands before the siding twanged and the wood let go.

The cement steps and the shelves lining the entrance were cluttered with rags and gardening gloves, a hand rake, faded seed packets, a torn bag of lawn fertilizer. The air smelled of moss and lawn mower oil. Is lowered her foot onto the first step. Spilled seeds shifted and crushed under her soles as she stared into the black of the basement. The space was shapeless but for a high shelf of a window, shallow and dirt-smeared, squinting from a far wall, and the crook of the ceiling, and a few pipes branching down like tree limbs. Is was breathing through her mouth.

Something squatted near the door, trying to glitter in the half light. She recognized the rust-spotted curve of her old tricycle's handlebars when she reached the bottom step. Her old baby pool leaned behind it, half-propped on a brick column, but it was not her baby pool anymore, not with the tear down the plastic center and the globs of dried cement from her father using it as a giant mixing bowl for fixing the cracks in the driveway. She had forgotten that. Summer was so long ago. Soon the bikes and the sleds emerged from the twilight, plus the grime green outline of her old kitchenette, the pretend sink, the pretend oven, the pretend stove. She had outgrown those too.

There was more in the black beyond the web of pipes spooling from the furnace and water heater. A metal pull cord dangled beside a bare bulb, but Is could not reach it. She raised her hand, not to try to pull it but to see the distance she would have to grow—a foot, two feet? Her fingers wiggled before she dropped back to her heels.

It was the staircase she was looking for anyway. It was wooden and the first step groaned. She touched the banister, and a shadow of dust swept into the air and thinned. She could not see even an outline of the top steps or the walls boxing them. It was black and her legs and feet vanished as she climbed. She should have brought her flashlight, but it was too late to go back. Her fingertips traced the cinder blocks and then the wooden joints and then the chipped plaster. She was breathing something other than air, something thicker, or thinner, dust-heavy or frost-burnt. She sneezed, fumbled for her balance, and sneezed again.

She found the kitchen door first, the old one, the lost one. It was the size of a real door, with a real knob and hinges down low and probably way up if she could have reached. The knob did not turn. It did not rattle. It was not a door anymore. The other side was a wall. It was blue. The toaster oven and the fruit bowl sat on the other side. This side was a door but that side was a wall. Is started to wonder what that meant exactly, but then her fingers were searching again. More plaster, more cracks and flakes and black-thick air, and then she found it. The little door to her left. She could touch the top of the frame. She could glide her hands around the prickly edges. She could push both palms against the center of the wood and hear the metal locking pin clack in place.

Is pushed. But the lock did not clack. The door moved. A splinter of light framed it now. She had pushed and the door had begun to open. Something in her stomach or her lungs or the long thin hollows of her bones emptied. She withdrew her hands, all ten fingertips at once. This was not the same door. If she opened it any further and looked into the coat closet, she understood that it would not be the same coat closet, and that the hallway and the living room arch outside of the closet would be different too, the whole house would be a different house, and so the windows and everything she could look at through the windows, the whole outside would be a different outside. She knew that if she had gone into the basement through the door in the back of the closet that she would have gone into a basement just like this basement but different from this basement, that this basement could only be reached through the garden door, and that the other basement, the one that belonged to the other house, that basement could only be reached through the little door in front of her now.

It did not matter which direction she stepped through. The other world was always on the other side. The other world might be so much like her own that she might not notice the difference. The other house might be the same, or almost the same, and there would be an almost-the-same mother and her almost-the-same father. They might not see that Is was not their Is but only an Is very much like her. They might never know the difference. They might live for years and years together and never know that anything had changed, that they all had become entirely other people. All she had to do was step through.

Isabelle remembers pushing the door. She remembers the scrape of the jamb against her shin as she crawled over the half-step into the closet. She even remembers the velvety give of the coats as she wove toward the glowing hallway, but after that the moments sift back into the shadowless gray of other memories. Of her entire childhood, this is the one day, the shard of a single morning that she retains with any clarity, with a crystalline precision that still pulses twenty years later. The rest is vague and borderless. Had she started first grade yet, or was that the following year? There are the school pictures, the scrapbooks of evidence, the stories her mother still loves to repeat. It wasn't till almost middle school that her father moved out. Isabelle didn't understand the chronology until much later, the first affair, the second, the trial separation, the third affair, the divorce. Her mother spared her none of the details. Her father died seven years after that, of prostate cancer, a fact that piqued her mother's new and darker sense of humor. Isabelle was relieved when she remarried.

Isabelle is engaged now too, or possibly. She fudged the detail so that her mother wouldn't say anything about her and her boyfriend sharing the new bed in her old room, the guest room. They met during their first year of graduate school, before Isabelle dropped out. Second-year scholarships were awarded competitively, and she wasn't really even sure if she cared all that much about a degree anyway. Her boyfriend has a post-doc lined up now, and Isabelle is going to have to move out west with him, where there are probably just as many high school teaching jobs for her as there would be anywhere else she could go, if that's what she ends up wanting to do with her life. She doesn't like to think about that right now. She doesn't even like thinking about having to fly, the way the plane will lift through a wall of clouds and hours later dip down somewhere else, and the whole while she's sweating in a cushioned chair waiting for her prescription to kick in, to lull her away.

The trip home has felt awkward and obligatory. Her boyfriend insisted that he didn't mind coming, but he sulked during the drive down, and he spends hours by himself at his laptop at the small desk in Isabelle's old room. It's a child's desk, but it wasn't Isabelle's. She doesn't know where it came from. The walls in there are yellow now. Her mother hired painters and had all the upstairs redone the year her stepfather moved in. They rehung the dresser mirror sideways, longways, because someone told her mother it suited the shape of the room better. Isabelle doesn't glance at the mirror, doesn't register it, when she comes to kiss the crown of her boyfriend's head on her way downstairs to help her mother with the next meal. Her mother talks and talks about almost nothing at all and Isabelle nods and asks questions during the pauses and feels grateful that her mother isn't asking her questions. Isabelle's stomach hurts, and she imagines that it is her father's tumors growing like roots from her intestines, but she knows it's just her diet. Her boyfriend says she's too anxious and thin.

After dinner, Isabelle makes a pot of decaf and everyone watches a movie on television before going to bed. She brushes her teeth at the bathroom mirror where she brushed her teeth for years and years. She still uses the same toothpaste, only she buys it herself now, it and the upscale whitening brand that her boyfriend writes on the shopping list. She watches the motion of her hand in the mirror, the rigorous blur of the red toothbrush, and though her gaze pauses on her face, rests eye to eye with her pale reflection, she doesn't register anything, and she doesn't retain the drift of her thoughts when she steps away.

She and her boyfriend have sex, on the carpet because the bed groans and Isabelle can't begin to relax otherwise. After intercourse her boyfriend always insists on giving her a clitoral orgasm which he brags about to their mutual friends during raucous dinner parties. When Isabelle returns from inside her faraway body to the room and him again, she leans her naked back against the dresser's bottom drawer and tells him her favorite childhood memory. She describes the morning, the rain in the window, the creak of the steps, the dank of the basement, all of the details that she has told and retold to herself for years. He claims that he has never heard the story before, that this is the first time she has ever told him this story, but Isabelle doesn't believe that. He must have forgotten. She must have told him before.

"You know that's not a real memory, right? You dreamed it or embellished it or something."

"What do you mean?"

"That stuff with your dad? Come on. The wart. That's obviously his cancer. Your subconscious is projecting backward."

"The cancer was in his intestines, not his foot."

"Exactly. His *foot*. He *walked* out on your family. And the errands? He was leaving the house to go meet his girlfriend."

"That wasn't—that was years later."

"It's symbolism, Isabelle. The blood, it's almost Christ-like, with the fingernail clipper. Only the wart regenerates, so it's more like, like Sisyphus getting his liver gouged out every day. You're punishing him for what he did to your family."

"You mean Prometheus."

"Whatever. And your mother turning a *blind eye*. Come on, how much more obvious can it get? Look at the way you describe her ignoring you. You always say she was like that growing up."

"I never said my mother ignored me. She read to me constantly."

"C. S. Lewis, right? The door is totally derivative. I can't believe you don't—"

"The door is real, go look in the coat closet right now. And she never read any of those books to me."

"You know the story. It's cultural literacy. Plus the closet, and the basement, you can't get more loaded than that. And, oh my God, the missing walls. You spent, what, like a year in therapy, talking about your mother not having appropriate barriers after the divorce. You went into this memory with her, right, with your therapist? I don't know how she kept a straight face. She must have been cracking up inside."

Isabelle stands and leaves to pee. She doesn't slap on the hall or bathroom light, even after she stubs her toe on the bathroom door. She sits in the glow of the moon and street lamp through the window and watches her shadowy self not blinking from deep inside the mirror.

When she pads back to her room, her boyfriend is in the bed. His voice is deep and slow and he spoons his hips against hers, pulling her tighter with his arm. He's sorry, he says, he didn't mean anything. It's possible that all those things could have happened exactly the way that she remembers them. After a long pause, he says something else, but it's not words anymore. Isabelle listens to his breathing. The yellow curtains are luminous. She is wide awake.

The bed groans as she stands, and her boyfriend's hand flops to the mattress and doesn't move. Isabelle pulls her jeans on, wrestles her arms into a sweater, and shuts the door behind her. Her mother and stepfather's door is sealed too. There's no light underneath it, no sounds. She avoids the loudest steps as she creeps downstairs barefoot. The air feels different in the dark, thinner and chillier, and she goes to the closet to get another layer. That's what she tells herself. She's just getting a jacket. She runs her hand over the sleeves, wool, denim, polyester, wool again, before parting the mass at its center. It's the same closet, but it is a different vacuum handle protruding from the back, a new leaf to the dining room table leaning along the side, and the clear plastic bins on the top shelf hold the winter things so much better.

Isabelle ducks her head and crinkles dry-cleaning bags as she pushes into the web of fabrics. Her hand finds the rear wall. It's right there. For a moment she thinks she did make it up, that there was never room enough to explore here, to play with a flashlight on a rainy morning, but then her hand touches wood. Here's the edge of the frame. Here's the indented panel. And there, as her fingers grope lower, she's found the knob and the tiny bolt. The metal is cold and she thinks she can almost see it in the black. She thinks it is almost glowing. She can't help sliding it or enjoying the dull clink of its release. At first the door resists her push, and a panicked cold surges through her. Have they sealed it? Are there nails or plaster or brick on the other side? But then it gives against her hip, and Isabelle tilts into the well beyond.

She catches herself and is already feeling her way down in the dark. The staircase is invisible under her feet. Each wooden step catches her weight before vanishing again. The cement floor is there too, gritty and cold and comforting. She considers pulling the light cord, but she can't reach it and there's no need. She can see the handles of her tricycle. There's the baby pool, blue and tall and round. The same seeds and grassy smells fill the steps to the garden. She climbs them and shoves at the rotting door, which twangs open. Outside the air is gray-blue. Her bare face and hands bristle to it. She is running through the grass which is sunken and marshy from the day of rain. Is feels the wet through the toes of her sneakers. Her socks soak it in.

She doesn't look at the car in the driveway. She steps to the back door and sets her hand on the cool knob. It won't turn. She tries it both ways, but it must be locked. She wonders why doorknobs can be turned in either direction, left or right, and why it doesn't make any difference. For everything else, faucets and knobs on radios and ovens, it's the difference between on and off. But doorknobs open either way. Unless the door is locked, like this one. Is looks at the window, but it's too dark to see in. She can only make out the outline of her reflection. It could be someone else, someone her height and shape but not her necessarily, a different girl.

Her tiny palms slap at the glass. It shakes and warps, but it does not break. When the light bursts in her face, she rears back, blinded, but aware of the knob turning inside the circle of her fingers. The door is opening. There are voices. Oh my God, they say, Is, they say, Is, Is, are you alright? Isabelle, are you all right? She wants to be lifted up. She wants the ground to fall away, and then only their hands, her mother's hair, the prickling of her father's cheek. She wants to be carried inside. Where were you? How did you get outside? Is can't see yet. She can't breathe. Her tears catch in the plush of her mother's bathrobe. The fingers pressing the width of her back are her father's. She doesn't answer. She doesn't speak at all, as she is drawn into the warm bright air of the house again.

THE TORTURER'S WIFE
by Thomas Glave from *The Kenyon Review*

*B*ut *in the earlier days*, these deadwomen are saying (sitting in a circle, in a muddy field far from any homes or people, long after dark)—*in the earlier days, she truly had not known. No. Of course not*, they say. *A young laughing girl like that, as she had been when she first came to* Him, He *to her? And what a figure she'd had!* one woman says, sighing out of what remains of her face. *A gorgeous young thing she was back then, even while falling in love with* Him. *What do you mean "even while"?* asks another. (The Lost Whore Without Arms, they call her. She is remembering now the feelings on her fingers of rings. Her fingers, like her arms, now somewhere at the bottom of the sea.) *Especially while, you mean to say. Oh yes, well,* He *had that effect on her. On every woman*, another says, known among them as the One Who Never Stops Sobbing. (And it is true—since her death twenty-nine days ago, she hasn't. Sobbing now and still wearing the necklace of blood that He had given her.) *On every woman who survived* His *attentions, you mean*, says an old, toothless one, bent over to the point that what remains of her forehead touches the ground before her. *Yes, and the same for every man* He *favored also*, laughs another. They all laugh. And laugh some more. But they soon grow quiet, knowing that they will not be here long—for they are dead, after all, just a bunch of deadwomen with scars over their rotting flesh and amputations in a few places. If this is a dream— and tonight it is, once again, as always, her bluewashed dream of them—who can stand to gaze upon them for long?

In complete darkness, they sit in a circle, in this muddy field that changes color minute to minute from brown to black to blue-blackbrown.

Those who still have complete faces try, from time to time, to look at each other.

Soon, all of them will feel a terrible, stabbing pain in their breasts (in what remains of their breasts, for a few). The pain will sear their decaying flesh to consume them utterly. The flames will come then— bright orange licks that will roast them unto blackest ash. They will scream, will feel unimaginable pain—worse than the pain that, in one of the secret underground places, had finally killed them. But how can they know that the flames that will finally incinerate them will, at least in this dream, be the rage of the dreamer? How can any of them know how much she, even while suffering their deaths and obliteration, hates them? *So many dying and deadwomen beneath a naked light bulb suspended far beneath the ground. The women who are gathered there now in complete darkness, sitting in that circle.*

The women who try from time to time—those who still have complete faces—to look at each other.

Being a witness is never easy, one of them thinks.

They return frequently. (She tosses on the pillow. Lying next to Him. Listening, in the deepest passages of her dream, to the sounds of His breathing next to her. He is there. Do the deadwomen now watching her chest rise and fall, and her tossing, quail before the sight of Him?) Frequently, among many other voices. Yes.

She truly had not known. Hadn't known, when, younger, still a laughing glowing creature, about all those secret rooms. Twisted limbs. Eyelids

100

sewn shut. Lighted cigarettes pressed into—but oh my God, I can't take anymore, one of them screams out. (She tosses on the pillow. He breathes. She registers His breathing. She tosses. Where, right now, can there be a place for her hands?) *And so the laughing glowing creature she had been had soon disappeared over the years, hadn't she, as the knowledge slowly, inevitably, became more, more . . . more* inescapable, *she herself came to think on the heels of all those increasingly thick-blue-dreamed nights, those hours lying beside Him . . . hours filled with listening to Him breathe. In. Out. Wondering what it would be like to hear Him breathe no longer. In, out.* The words once known only by deadwomen and deadmen (and who knew how many deadchildren) had finally been carried into her nights even by the things she had trusted for so long: the reliable evening breezes, seasonal rains, and the spreading sea that she had so long believed to be her friend. But at last even the sea had betrayed her—reviled her, when, on that afternoon not so long ago, in an hour when she had sought its caresses against her tender skin, it had thrown out to her from its depths that sightless chorus of mermaids. Those voices obsessed with

"falling,"

they had sung, gazing directly at her out of those sightless eyes,

"from planes."

But do not blame her, one of the deadwomen beseeches the others, even as she begins, with them, to feel the first fire licking at her flesh. *For who can know exactly what she will do when, soon enough, that rainfall of most secret parts clatters, in moonlight, upon her roof? How will she feel about the sea then?*

And about Him, the others murmur as the flames, in the field and beyond it, begin to roast their flesh—

And So Once Again Hating (But Really Fearing) Moonlight.
With Difficult Breathing, and Skulls

Yes, it is true. She abhors the moonlight.

Lying next to Him, breathing in His nightscents and the sweat glistening on the back of His neck, she does her best to close her eyes against it.

It frightens me, she thinks, *the way it shines so brightly, insistently, on skulls.*

(*The skulls that return every night,* she dare not think.)

It terrifies me, she thinks, *the way it exposes all those skeletons out there in the garden—in the garden,* she thinks, *where all those skulls are or soon will be. Out there,* she tries so desperately not to think, *where I know all those hands lie waiting. Waiting—*

(But tonight is still weeks away from the time she will send the maid out there to sweep up that most unbearable rainfall of hands.)

It is hard to breathe, she thinks, lying next to Him.

I'm afraid to breathe, she thinks. *Afraid to breathe in too much of Him, all of those things that made me so wild when I was a young girl. Oh God,* she thinks—

Afraid to see His face in the faces of my children.
  Our children.
  (His)

The moonlight, she knows, reveals skulls. Gleaming. Grinning. Skulls of bodies dumped "somewhere out there," she thinks, "in the secret places that everyone pretends don't exist." The moonlight reveals "teeth," she thinks (but trying so hard right now not to breathe Him in), "knocked out by truncheons. Scattered like dice. And fingernails," she thinks (but how can she bear to think of *that?*), "—that the men, working down there, in all those secret rooms everyone says don't exist, wrenched out. With pliers," she thinks, screwing shut her eyes, clenching her fists.

Moonlight, she thinks, listening for the clattering of the first skull's teeth outside, surely, in the front garden. One of them will soon come. One of them always, in the dream-hours, comes. Hangs. Hovers. *Moonlight*, she thinks, *reveals too much. Like the most vulnerable kind of face*, she thinks, *capable of hiding nothing.*

Song (But from a Chorus of Mermaids). The Madwoman, in Flight

But now here: of an afternoon in a place that she will insist is part of another dream, although today she actually is here: a long narrow beach of sand and salt, salt and all that water, that so-enormous water she had once (but why?) believed to be her "friend" and somehow "protector"—pulling her legs down. *Down.* It is here, in what she has managed to convince herself is this afternoon's dream, that she will refuse to see them. Refuse to see the women whom she had seen long ago in the bluegreengray waters of so many other dreams. The same women whose bodies, this afternoon, will shortly surface and surface again from beneath that sea's curling waves. She is here, alone (and so happy for once to be alone—out in the sunlight so much is easier)—on this beach: not the dirtier, more dangerous public beach accessible to all, but this private one where she and people like her can come without care to bathe, laugh; to delight in the unexpected pleasures of an afternoon. A beach surveilled, sometimes unobtrusively, by His uniformed men. A place where women, women like herself, even alone, can feel safe: no catcalls, no ogling, nor (but she will not think of it) anything worse. It is an unlikely day even for someone like her, a woman of relative leisure, to visit the beach: a weekday. But only two hours ago or so she had ventured forth from His house (their house) so high up above the city, to "escape," *yes, it had definitely been an escape*, down to the beach to bathe in this surf that, as she will later recall (though right now still completely unsuspecting), had, on her arrival, so blithely licked its lips, and beckoned her with those soothing if slightly odd refrains of *Return Come Return*. She lies on her back now on the blanket she has brought, feeling something sublime; feeling actually vaguely "happy," she thinks; noting the freewheeling dives and swoops of seabirds as, her eyes just barely closed against the moody in-and-out sun, she recalls the faces of her children: the faces she will see again in only a few hours. And so in this repose she is at peace, she thinks: *I am at peace, I am nobody. I am alone . . .*

Who will ever know exactly how she knew to sit up so abruptly in the next moment as she did? If the sky had any idea, it discloses nothing now to the sand and the water so far below. It continues to gaze down at her with a blank, impassive face. Gazes down at her as she jerks to her feet with a cry, because she *does see them,* she thinks, *but how can they be here?* All those women out there, in the surf. Out there looking directly at her but as if they are blind. All of them, rising up out of the waves and standing. Standing there. Dripping. Naked. Sightless. Clutching their breasts, she sees: clutching the places where their breasts should be. Crying. No, singing. A tuneless song. A chorus of blind mermaids singing

"About the planes," they sing,
"the planes, so full of us, and counting,

laden with bodies and counting,
drugged bodies and counting,
bodies dying, unmoving,
parts twitching, soon to rest
as they lifted off and *up*, the pilots,
with us all inside and counting,
took off to bank sharply out over the sea,
always at night, the darkest hours,
the time when (yes, it is true) some were pulled—
pulled out,
out
from their homes,
blindfolded,
gagged,
manacled and bound,
along with others to whom that all had happened long ago,
then loaded into the (yes, into the planes)
(counting)
the fingers of a few officers on board even then
diddling
more than a few of our
cunts,

drugged cunts,
deeply asleep, unspeaking cunts,
unanswering-back cunts,
officers' cocks dipping into drugged flesh for one last
(yes, with all of us)
before they took their final count and
dumped us,
pitched all of us, some still living,
still breathing (though drugged),
into the so-far-below sea.
The planes, the planes," they sing,
"and us falling beneath the waves.
So far down beneath the waves.
Those waves—"

105

But then her absolute refusal. Refusal to admit, before their sightless eyes, clasped hands, and all of their wounds, that a scream at last explodes out of her; impels her feet beneath her; provides her with the speed with which she hurtles so fast so far from them from the song from the waves from the soldiers guarding the sands the redsun redsun redred beach. Away from all of them still standing there naked sightless but seeing her somehow (yes, she knows it) and holding each other's hands above the curling returning waves *Oh all that foam* as she flies, as she: *Because no*, she insists, flying, *No. I never saw them.* As she had screamed and screams now. *In the beach in the dream but today. No,* she insists now (*what is the way out—?*). *I was never there.*

Her eyes tightly closed. Screwed shut. Locked. Because of course some of the mermaids hadn't washed up headless. Handless. Headless and handless to elude dental records, fingerprint tracing. How very clever, she dare not think. How impossibly clever of Him, His cover-ups. *How invincible* (but she is not thinking this, she tells herself) *the machetes of His soldier minions.* Ah, but the sun. How it still shines, she sees: now yellow, not red. How the trees flare green, gold. How the day—in dreams, in actuality—still beckons. Life, she thinks, then mouthing the word, "Life": something perhaps still possible, as—not entirely to her surprise—she runs. Feels herself running. Still. And faster still. Racing—

Later, gathered in market squares beneath retreating light, or plaiting their children's hair while daydreaming about the whirr and secrecy of hummingbirds, assorted watchers in the small town that is not far from that sea (a place soothed in twilight hours by the sea, by its crooning, those same curling sighing waves and their perpetual call of *Return, come, stay*) will recount to each other in hushed tones that afternoon's vision they all had shared: that sight of the madwoman racing through their midst, screaming what had sounded to them not like a scream but a toneless song. *Like a song of long ago*, one of them will say. *Long ago, no*, will say another. *As new as the last hour's whispers.* A song without tone of deadwomen standing before her there and still so red, she had screamed, in the surf. A chorus of dead mermaids baring before her and the waning afternoon the evidence of their lacerated breasts. A chorus singing of what had happened to them in secret hours of blindfolds and handcuffs and (of course, she had guessed: interrogations), and most of all what had been done to them as they had lain drugged in the planes—*the planes*, she had screamed, running. What had been done to them that *He*, only *He*, she had cried out, could have arranged. Out of the sky, into the sea, to form a redchorus of once-were-women, with missing parts. Once-were-women with too much shame, she had screamed to the retreating sky, or none at all.

The Country Itself. But Also She

As a place of beauty? But unparalleled, of course. A place of dark, lean-flanked mountains with sturdy shoulders, more than willing to accept the sea's reliable fawning at their feet. A country busy with trees, birds: birds of which there are many thousands, even millions, all of which (perhaps having received news of the excesses of the evening patrols) make certain to sequester themselves after dark.

Beauty and majesty in this place in every type of flower, every sort of butterfly, and in the most fantastically designed insects known to inhabit the sphere. Lushness in rolling hillocks everywhere, and meadows only too pleased to preen beneath the sun that adores their wide-open bellies. A guaranteed rainy season, and—for at least the past two hundred years— none of the devastating betrayals of volcanoes. Nor those of earthquakes. Broad fields ripe with crops whisked quickly enough to the teeming capital, and a surfeit of cracked hands only too willing to work them. Better roads than ever before. Telephone service in almost every village.

And freedom—for the country is, certainly, a free one. So free, so filled with so many choices (flee or remain; survive or die; remember or forget; laugh loudly in daylight, or sob in deepest darkness until a fearsome pounding at the door, accompanied by the growling of waiting

Jeeps and the clicking of long rifles). So many choices that none of the citizens need even believe in freedom, and in fact are encouraged by those presiding not to do so. Why entertain the need to believe in it, this thing called "freedom," when it so clearly abounds? the citizens are asked. You might as well believe in air, they are told, or in light; you might as well believe in the passing of time, as if such belief would make any significant difference. You need not *believe* you are alive when you so clearly are. Do snakes *believe* that they possess skins, fish *believe* that they sport fins? Does the sea *believe* in its perpetual embrace of the shore?

Similarly, those presiding remind the nation, one need not believe in things that simply are not true, and which, here, have obviously never been true: that in this, our beloved and gorgeous country, extrajudicial executions are regularly carried out in secret; that innocent people are kidnapped nightly from their homes, to emerge from other places some time later as assorted hands, legs, feet, and arms in small black plastic bags; that more than fifty secret mass graves litter the country, especially the lowland rural areas and the more remote mountainsides in the north; that the most promising soldiers in the nation's sleek army were trained abroad in an infamous school in the most ingenious practices of "detainment" and "innocuous interrogation"; that the very young children of those allegedly kidnapped people—infants and toddlers, mostly—have occasionally been sold on a so-called black market as "orphans" to childless couples; and that He—known in most quarters simply as He—in His splendid uniform, an official of elevated rank just below our cherished President, is, with our President and so many lieutenants, commanders, generals, and soldiers, "behind" it all. "Behind" that which, of course, never occurs.

He: as everyone knows, of magnificent shape and height. Promoted to his rank only five years ago, at a still-useful age, after sixteen sterling years in the illustrious armed forces. (No, of course He hadn't worked for the secret police during those years. How could He have done, when—remind yourself now, please—such a thing has never existed?) He: blessed with a house of enviable design and size, flanked by an Elysian garden, well situated in the palatial suburbs high above the teeming capital, with that ever-matchless view of the boundless sea. Blessed too with His children: two adorable dumplings, who, naturally enough, resemble Him, and whom, laughing heartily, He bounces frequently enough on His knees; and blessed most noticeably with His superb wife—known by many as She, but more commonly, among many, by her actual name. A lovely name. A name that brings to mind swaying bluebells, lilacs, and the scent of roses glancing off lithe trellises in sultry-houred afternoons. She who had first encountered Him in her earlier days when still a young laughing thing. Encountered Him as a girl at that time bedazzled by His beauty and His force—as, shortly thereafter, He, gazing upon her, swiftly enchanted by the lively glow she had invariably brought in those times to dulled faces and dim corners alike, had felt rapidly genuflect within Him that thing, that indefinable whatever-thing, that, so tripped unawares within Him, compelled Him whenever in her presence in the time that followed those first gazes, and for years after, to adopt both before and beside her (at embassy parties, at so many required functions of state) the precise adoring position: a sometime (though subtle) bowing of the head, an occasional lowering of the hands, and an always murmuring of her name, followed in His deepest mind by the word "She," He had thought, by the word "Mine," He had thought, and always by

Exactly. By the word "Yes."

He who had had built for them and the children they would soon bring forth that enormous house so far up above the city. She who, on His magnificent uniformed arm, lifted high in one easy swing by Him and carried across the threshold, had moved into it with Him and a flock of servants ready for her (surely) imperious command. He who, on so many nights and even during the days, had steadily risen and fallen above her there; had panted and, in earnest desire, conjured her face beneath Him; had imagined the conquering and plundering of continents as—though she had not, at the time, felt so—He had in fact conquered her; subdued something in her; quelled her, of course—but had also somehow tenderly come to know some most indefinable and secret part of her, a part not easily given to surrender. He marveling all the while as she had lain beneath Him at what had so unquestionably become, without significant contest, truly His. Spoils. Endless riches. A fertile plain for the planting of much seed, and seed planted again. She who, as He had labored and panted, risen and fallen, had gazed up at Him and clung to Him, her arms about His broad back, in adoration, fulfillment, absolute wonder.

She who had not, at that time, turned her face to the wall in darkness and pondered the flesh of deadmen. No, nor feared the power of moonlight to bear witness.

She who, at that time, had had no fear of skulls or stones raining down upon their (His) roof.

Nor had she felt anything then about what she had not yet discovered: all those other deadwomen who had begun to infiltrate her dreams.

She who, like Him, had always appeared to love the gorgeous, spreading country so completely free it need not concern itself with freedom. The same she who, lovely to the eye as she had appeared during those early years, rapidly began to fade sometime in the last . . . but who can remember, in a place where remembering is anyway never wise? Sometime in the last whenever. Began to fade, as if, plagued by unfortunate dreams, she became, at first, slightly—ever so slightly—haggard; then, over time, more so. More thin about the mouth, some thought, and darker than ever in those depthless eyes. Oh, those eyes. And legs. Yes, even now. Even now such overall form. A body still capable of outdressing every other woman in the nation. A being still capable, despite a fuller knowledge of who exactly, in the nation's long history, He has been and continues to be, of grace. Elegance. Style, in spite of all those things brought to her by gradually more insistent dreams, whispers, voices *out there*: secret underground chambers, and blistered testicles set afire before the next round of shouts and punches beneath the naked, dangling light bulb. Ah, yes, some of the citizens had long murmured and sighed, for years, a model of *haute couture*. Utter aplomb. She.

Garden, Morning Sun; Keeping at Bay Thoughts of Killed Children

But then let her have it: this most secret, nourished hatred. For it is now, after all these years, what she most reliably possesses. What she possesses as, from day to day, pondering her impossible thoughts, she meanders the spreading garden of that house; as she envies the ignorance, simple destinies, of birds. What she possesses aside from her children, who remain—like everything else—part of Him.

Allow her this private, cherished, solitary time in the beckoning garden. He far off in the teeming city at work ("or something," she thinks, feeling the grimace).

Allow her to feel the sun's soft nuzzle along her exposed shoulders, the breeze from the far-off sea carrying to her today the scents merely of sea, not of a redchorus of ruined mermaids.

Allow her, as she strolls, to register that great relief: the relief that comes when, gradually cajoled (seduced) by the sun, she is unable to think. Unable to recall deep-throated dreams. The relief a sojourn that she knows will not last.

Allow her not to summon the very late night, or the very early morning, when she just might—yes, just possibly—murder her children. Murder them perhaps because "they so resemble Him," she thinks, and because she also fears "what they might become," she thinks, "carrying His blood." (She will not dare, right now, to look down at her hands.) What they might become "as they grow," she thinks, "and as they—" —but she cannot finish that thought. *What they might finally have in them*, she thinks, especially the boy, who just might (but who really can ever know these things? Who can ever—) —"just might have all of *that* in him from *Him*," she thinks, shuddering-nearly-trembling in the sun. "All of *that* in him," she thinks, "my God. And so much more."

Her head hurts. Too much to think. Too much sun. And no, she thinks, *no*: she has not, absolutely not, lost her mind.

———— ❧ ————

("But even now," she tells the deadman lover who visits her regularly in the hidden room of her most desperate hours, the deadman whose face she can never forget—the deadman who wraps her securely and warmly in what remains of his arms: what the soldiers, before running over his prone body with their Jeep, had permitted to remain of his arms, "— even now, sometimes, I really do. I want to—"

"To kill them," he says, stroking her face with a decayed wrist. "Your children. The two of them. Yes. I know."

"I want to kill them not because I don't love them," she says, pulling so hard on his withered cock—pulling on it a way she could never have dared do to Him— "because, in truth, I do love them. They are my—"

"They are your—" Pressing ruined lips to her throat.

"My most precious—"

"Your most beautiful—"

"Yes," she whispers, squeezing his mutilated testicles against her belly, "my most precious beautiful gorgeous things."

"Except for the flowers in your garden," he whispers, massaging her breasts.

"Except for . . . yes, but they are the flowers in my garden. They remain so."

"They always will be."

"Oh, yes," she says, moving down to kiss his withered cock. "For all time."

Years later, the walls of that hidden room of her most desperate hours, the walls of that room filled with the stench of a decaying deadman and the misery of a still-beautiful woman, will still remember: recall how, in that next moment, she rose up to climb onto and sit on the shimmering tip of her deadlover's cock. It was there, swaying backward and forward, that she began telling him, through all those tears, what he already knew: how

They are her children,	"Yes, mine,
But to have to see, every day,	"Always,
His face in theirs,	"Can you imagine the horror,
His laughing in theirs,	"Oh my God, as if I,
And His smile, those teeth,	"Close your mouth, children, don't smile, I sometimes tell them,

So that she does sometimes, yes, "Of course,
Want to obliterate them, "Eradicate them,
Wipe clean from the earth's face "Annihilate them,
His finest creations,
And kill myself too, "Yes, rip open my own throat,
For how frightening it is—is it not? "Of course it is,
That they, her most precious "Might grow up to be a something
somethings, like Him,

And that their Father,
in addition to all else, "Yes, all else,
Betrayed me, lied to me, with so "Lied to you, yes, and to others,
many others,
And then there are also the moments
of perversity, "Of course there are,
Moments when she thinks, "When I think,
Ah, and now how will You feel, "To come home and find Your
children dismembered,
Your boy's little mushroom, "Yes, ripped out and stuffed down
his throat,
Your daughter's budding breasts, "Carved. Sliced. Forced down into
her deepest part,
All because, like those others, "All those nameless others,
they would not tell, "They would not tell,
they would not "Oh no. To the soldiers. Tell."

*She weeps out the tale to him once again: the confession, rocking back
and forth on his cock: grateful to be able to tell him again what she has
told him so many times before: grateful to be able to tell someone—even a
deadman who, she knows, by the time she comes (if indeed she comes this
time), by the time she looks down fully from her rocking and crying, will be
gone, gone again: I am bereft, she is bereft, I wanted to murder my children
unable to bear the thought of His face growing in theirs, I could not stand
the idea that one day they and the boy especially might grow to become
like Him and oh my God to bring about more redchoruses of mermaids
thrown out of planes into the sea and so many daughters incinerated (but*

113

first raped) and so many sons raped and carved up their remains fed to the pigs the goats the dogs the:

> but I cannot bear it but he the deadman who always came to me in that hidden room kept every time my hand from striking them down slicing open their throats shooting them in the head as they slept shooting them with the pistol He keeps in the house in that room in that cabinet for our "protection" and: no she thinks I did not kill them I will never kill them I will

—she thinks, coming; gasping: holding onto the hips that already are no longer there; holding fast to the cock that has already vanished beneath her and the thighs that already are no more, as the walls of that room that does not quite exist will remember many years from now, as she sobs, sobbing, looking down now to see without doubt that he who on so many afternoons like this one, through so many dreams like this one (but not quite a dream), provided her with both pleasure and comfort even in the midst of his remorseless decay: he who, as so many times before, is "gone," she thinks, slowly sliding down off the mound of her conjure, to lie there once more alone and finger herself in the sorrow that flushed through her coming: "gone," she thinks, "the way he must have gone when His men came and took him away from wherever it was, and took his wife, too, and children . . . the grandparents survived because he had long before sent them into hiding abroad. Gone," she thinks, fingering where a deadman's cock had just rubbed against what He had always half-playfully called her "rose" (ridiculous, she had always thought, what a ridiculous term for a part of the body that was), "and who knows," she thinks, lying there so alone in the room that is now slowly becoming another one, one of light and billowing curtains into which she knows the children she has not killed will soon race, shouting, with news of school and the day, "who knows," she wonders, turning her face away from the billowing curtains and back to her fleeting entertainments of death, "who knows when, if ever, he will come again?"

Parties; a Smile; Astonishment Regarding the Body that is Not Hers

But how could she not despise them? All those stupid laughing women? The women so brightly attired in silver. In gold and diamonds. The women whose hands, at the last shining party, had fluttered like the sparrows' wings that have never, not ever, come to comfort her. Fluttered as their mouths sipped red wine, champagne (imported from "the continent"), and asked in those so bright voices how she was doing these days, darling, and doesn't she look di*vine*? Divine, darling, and how jealous we all are of you looking so splendid, so lovely with that gorgeous uh huh absolutely *beau*tiful husband of yours. Yes, my dear, you know He is. And in that uniform . . . a few epaulets make all the difference, don't they . . . in the position He's in at his age, and so tall, so grand, well . . . you can only imagine the things He'll be doing in this country in another five years . . . But then wait. For how could they not have seen? Seen the rage and contempt in her eyes, and the loathing, even though her hands, her very own hands, also had reached for this tray or that one of champagne flutes carried about with perfect balance by the ever-silent white-jacketed, white-gloved waiters . . . how could they all not have sensed that her whinnying laughter was merely a response to their own? Could they, none of them, not see how much she abhorred Him? "My dear, they look *so* good together—" (yes, well, they always had), "and before you know it, she'll be carrying another one." "Of course, with a man as virile as Him, and that body of hers . . ." "*Made* in Paris, my dear, as if she just stepped off the Champs-Elysées, like nothing you would ever see in this country, except at one of our parties, of course . . ."

They had never known. Her smile, so well held in place by the accustomed muscles, had revealed nothing, hidden everything. "But who *is* that woman, standing next to you, smiling like that?"—so she, not quite awake, sitting half-upright in bed, had asked Him one morning on glancing at that photo—God, not another one!— on one of the newspaper's pages.

— Who,— He had half-absently responded. (He had already dressed and inspected Himself, but something had momentarily distracted Him: a button missing, God forbid, from His uniform; a bit of lint on the cuff.) — Why, you, darling,—He told her, laughing, looking down at the photo over her shoulder, — Who else? What an odd sense of humor you have sometimes, my sweet.— Bending down His towering form to kiss her. To press His freshly shaven face close to hers. (She had caught the scent of shaving cream: lime, one He liked and had reminded her earlier that morning to make sure and remind one of the house staff to pick up that week; something so *masculine*, she'd thought, not quite permitting her lower lip to curl and disclose the clenched teeth prepared, given the right circumstances, to snarl.)

Me? The word formed without form in her mind. Me?

She looked carefully at the newspaper. Blinked. Then, in the photograph before her, regarded her own smiling, if glazed, face. Blinked again, then thought . . . but what she thought she could hardly say. For her thoughts just then formed not words, but colors.

She felt His mouth touch her skin as, still utterly dazed, she sat on the bed amid rumpled sheets and a comforter, her mouth half-open in that way He had always, even from the very beginning, found so "adorable," He'd once told a lieutenant. "Just like her, you know? Always so in her own little world, and still so innocent." Her mouth had hung half-open, suggesting in her face the beginning of the slightly stupid look she had habitually, when taken unawares by it before unexpected mirrors, despised; and her brain—well, "frazzled" had been the only word she'd been able to summon in those moments to describe, accurately, the sensation: "I am frazzled," she'd thought, "to see myself smiling that way, in that dress that looks so ridiculous, at some embassy party or the other, holding onto His arm as He puts His face next to mine (bending down as always) to plant a kiss on my cheek."

Even with that half-dazed expression still on her face (one of the maids would soon come in to make up the bed and tidy up the scattered nightclothes), she had been pondering— though far behind her veiled eyes— knives. Knives, of course. One or many, right there, in her smooth though trembling hands: hands awake or dreaming or (as was so often the case) someplace restively in between. Any large shining knife that, securely grasped, would complete the necessary task as He slept beside her; as, between shiftings, twitchings, rapid eye movements, occasional teeth-grinding, he called out to the darkness or murmured indecipherable things, memories not yet revealed. She envisioned His naked back, so smooth and broad, hairless, as He slept; or, better yet, His chest. His chest into which she. Into which she would. His chest into which she now feels trembling at the thought: trembling over the danger, utter cruelty, *daring*, of the thought. She feels that swift leap of her eyebrows that means *I have transformed*, she thinks, *no longer she but* She . . . but, feeling the slow trembling now quaking throughout her, the trembling that could so easily (*but pretend it isn't so*) carve up her children and rip to shreds the entire world's living fabric, she drops it. Drops the knife that is not there in her hand. Banishes it. Banishes all of them—butcher, cleaver, bread knife. Banishes them to the place where dead lovers disappear, where deadwomen and skulls do not, at least not so insistently, call her name. She is startled, of course, when He whom, in this reverie, she had long ago left behind, walks up to her still sitting there on the bed with her mouth half-open ("So innocent! Always in her own little world"), and pats her on the head, does something like kiss her on the head; says something now like

—Goodbye—

and

—*Have a lovely day, I'll see you later tonight*—

as she sees and feels herself lift a hand, an all at once weary and fragile hand, in adieu: adieu, my love, her hands seems to say. The illusion must go on, she knows, like her condemnation: it must continue.

She sits there for some time. ("Not now," she tersely tells the maid who puts her head around the door to inquire if Madame is finished, if she may tidy the room, "in five minutes, please.") She visits, once more, rooms that do not quite exist. Inhales in them the forlorn scents of dead lovers. Deadmen who, in the very worst of times, can always be relied on to make ghostly love to her on creaking beds wrenched out of blue (but, thank God, not red) dreams. Some time later—only minutes later, possibly, or hours—she understands the truth. The truth as to "What I know now," she says in a room that is not quite there. "The simple fact that I am not living in my own body. So that when He kissed me," she says out loud, "or kissed that woman who had my face and was smiling in the newspaper photo as she held that glittering champagne flute, I was completely unaware of it because I wasn't there. That wasn't my body," she tells the room that gazes so dully back at her, "nor was it my face, or my mind behind those eyes so full of laughter in the photo. That's why, for so many years now (and who can count them?), I have never felt Him when He has touched me, because He hasn't touched me. No, not me.

"Them," she thinks, feeling the knives once again in her hands, "His face so close to theirs, underground beneath a naked light bulb, and the sound of other men's laughter. But not me.

"I live in dreams," she tells the not-there room. "In those dreams (though I would prefer that most of them were different) is where my body, my truest body, truly begins.

"And as for this," she tells the room, looking down at the body covered in pajamas, "well, I don't know.

"I do not know who *she* belongs to or even—sometimes, yes, sometimes—what her truest name will finally be."

<hr />

A Rainfall of Hands, a Nineteen-Day Sweep

MAID:

"Well, yes. She did. It's been nineteen days now, and she did ask me on that day, or, no, *commanded* me, to . . . but wait. I want you to listen. I mean listen carefully. Because—well, because I would never say a word against her. I still love her with all my heart. Oh yes, I do. I've been with her and the Sir fifteen years, right from the time they got married. (Such a gorgeous bride she was, and He!—He looked so handsome in His uniform! So happy!) And, well, never in all that time until now—never in all that time did she ask me to do anything so, so—

"So *outrageous*. That's the word. Outrageous, unbelievable, what you see me doing now. Right here. Always. Alone. In tears.

" 'Come here,' she called to me that morning. And, well, no . . . in truth, she didn't look so good that day. She didn't look like herself. I mean, you know the Madame! She was always made up so beautifully, with her hair just so—everything just so . . . like a true . . . I don't know, majesty, she always was. Perfect, I mean. And the loveliest dresses, and shoes . . . yes, even at eight o'clock in the morning, always when the Sir was ready to leave for the city and the children were packed and ready to be driven by the chauffeur to school . . . But that day, well—

"No, I don't want to say it, but . . . well, it's true. She did look as if she hadn't slept in days. Deep, deep rings under her eyes, there were, and her beautiful skin looking so . . . I don't know. So sickish, sickly, as if she really was sick. And—well, you know, she really was . . . was *swaying* a little bit. Looking a little unsteady on her feet. But her eyes were bright enough— almost as if she had fever, or something . . . And so she called me. When she called I always went quick. Why wouldn't I? I loved her. She was the Madame. She . . . yes, I loved her. I still do. With all my heart.

'Yes, Madame?'

"She was shaking. I saw that as soon as I got up close to her. But in sickness or health, well—far be it from me to say anything to her, except what I tried to say, which was only:

'Madame, is anything—'

'I want you to sweep up all those hands outside. Every single one of them, in the garden and on the walkways. There are even some in the—in the *pool*,' she said in that shaking voice, as she covered her face for a minute. Standing there before me, swaying, and looking more sickly than ever. Looking like she was about to be ill.

"I—well, no, I didn't think I'd heard her right. Hands? *Hands?* You mean like *people's* hands? I thought. But I must have misheard her. She must've said 'ants,' or—

'Why are you standing there looking at me like that?' she said. Her voice louder. And more—I don't know, like it had a—a pistol in it? Something. Something about to snap, or crack, or—

'Madame?' I said. Staring at her.

'I *said*'—she took one big deep breath then, as if she didn't want to repeat in any way what she had just told me to do.

'I. Told. You. To go. To go sweep up. To go sweep up those—those *hands*,' she said, truly beginning to shake then. That was when—yes, I'm sure of it—I began to get—to get really scared—

'Madame –'

'There are *thous*ands and thousands and *thousands* of hands in the garden!' she began to scream, moving closer to me and stretching out her own hands toward me as if she intended to (but she couldn't have, no; not the Madame. No!) hit me. Hit me! And I—

'Hands all over the place,' she shouted, pulling me over to the hallway window. 'Look! Down there! Don't you see them?'

'Madame, I—'

'Burnt hands. Severed hands. Melted. Hands stuck all over with cigarettes. With lighted cigarettes stuck *into* them. With their fingers broken at the knuckles. And with—oh my God, but how could He— how could anyone have—

'With their *fingernails* pulled out,' she whispered. Putting her own hands up to her face then and covering it. Shaking, her hands. I remember. Trembling.

'Oh yes.' Very quietly. So quietly, she said that. 'Smashed by the hammers they use in that place. By the *wrenches* —' She covered her face again. 'They all fell down last night in the rainstorm.' Talking through the fingers covering her face. 'A rainstorm of hands clattering all over the roof and keeping me up all night. Some of them are already—look, girl, don't you see?—are already becoming, becoming—

'Becoming skeletal,' she whispered. 'Down there.

'But no,' she finished, turning away from the window and wrapping her arms about her shoulders and squeezing, squeezing herself that way as she began to rock back and forth: standing there in the morning sun streaming in from the window. The same sun that was shining over the garden below, where there were—I'm telling you honestly—*where there were no hands*. Only the forward lawn and the hedges and all the flowers she had always loved so much. And the marble statues. And the pool.

'No,' she said, still turned away and rocking herself, 'not this. Not a rainfall of hands. Anything but this. Even the skeletons reaching to me out of the dreams I could take, up to a point. Even the deadmen who wanted me to do all those things to them as they told me one more time what He and His men had done to them I could take up to a point. But not this. Not hands. Not here. Not in this house. Not where my children—my children . . . *live*. No. *No*,' she said, and—

"She was moaning. Groaning. Sounding as if she needed so desperately to—to sob, cry out loud. But no sobs came. None that I saw.

"I . . . well, I was so terrified I couldn't . . . no, honestly, I just couldn't move. I couldn't . . .

"That was when—well, when I just went up right behind her and tried to—tried to, to just—

"To touch her. Hold her. Put my arms around her and say, Madame. Madame, please. Madame, it's all right, Madame. Whatever's bothering you, it's—it's all right, Madame, all right. You don't have to worry, Madame, I wanted to say—yes, so much! I wanted so much to say I'll take care of everything, Madame. You won't have to worry about anything. Haven't I and the others always taken care of everything since you and the Sir brought us here? You just rest now. Yes, rest, Madame. We all love you so much, I wanted so much to say, if only you would let me, let us—

"But that was when she did it. The moment my hands touched her, she jumped back from me and—

"Yes. She did. Struck me. Struck *me*, who had always loved her. Who had *worshipped* her. Who had sung songs to her children at night, through so many long afternoons, and comforted them and kept them company when she and the Sir were out at one of those parties. I'm telling you. She. Struck. Me.

'Don't you—don't *you* ever put your hands on me like that again,' she said. Or no, she *hissed* it. Hissed it like a garden snake, or . . . and looked at me. Kept on looking at me that way.

'Do you hear?' she hissed once more. Shaking as if she might break into pieces right there in front of me. Her eyes so bright, as if with fever.

'Don't *any* of you ever touch me again. Not you, nor *Him*. Especially not *Him*.'

'Madame, I—'

"But she had already turned away and, with her shoulders so caved in that way, in a way I had never ever seen in her before, slowly shuffled—she, the Madame, shuffled!—down the hallway, back toward her and the Sir's bedroom.

'Just make sure that you get *every last one* of those hands cleaned up,' she called back, without looking back over the sunken shoulders. 'Do you hear?'

'Madame, if you –'

'Don't stop until you've cleared away every single last one. Otherwise . . . '—but her voice became even more faint then, like the whisper of—

Yes, I thought. *My God*, I thought. Like the whisper of a ghost.

'Madame . . . ' I tried calling once more. But she was gone. Mumbling, whispering, then nothing. She was gone.

"What could I do? This is the only place I've ever known aside from my home. Both of my parents and my two brothers—that's right, and my grandmother—are all dead. In the countryside, that's right. Well, the northern mountains, really. My parents were taken away one night by some men in a Jeep, after word reached the government about some kind of 'uprising' in our town. Uniforms? No, in that time they didn't always wear uniforms. Only the soldiers did . . . The soldiers, three of them bearing enormous rifles, came for my brother much later, and my grandmother . . . I was a very small child then. On the night they came for my parents, I had been sent to sleep in the house of a woman who lived down the road, not far from where the forests begin. Everyone in town heard about what happened to my parents—well, of course, they weren't the first—and someone— no, I still don't know who, though I think it might have been the woman's young nephew—hid me underneath some dirty clothes in a basket. The next day, they both sent me across to the other side of the country to live with some of her people, who themselves vanished one night a few years later . . . she herself is still alive . . . and her nephew. Don't get involved in politics, everyone always told us. You never know who you might be talking to, or—

"And so I did. Of course. I had no choice, did I? I followed her instructions. Followed them with a broom in my hand, while weeping all the while in my most secret place for the Madame I once had known. That one. The one who had laughed and told stories and jokes to her children, and had always looked so happy when her husband, in those earlier years, had come home to her . . . both of them so young together and lovely . . .

"And every few days—well . . . I wish it wasn't true. I *wish*. But it is. She comes out from her bedroom looking more exhausted than ever. She walks out to the garden, past the marble fountains, and asks me: 'How are you getting on?' 'Fine, Madame,' I say, 'just fine.' But I'm not fine at all. I never let her see how now I'm almost always crying. 'Ah, well,' she says, not quite looking at me but at something else, something that you'd think she sees in the garden there, from the way she frowns and then shudders, then closes, so tightly, her eyes. 'You missed one there, and one there, too,' she always says, pointing over to the manicured hydrangeas, or beneath the huge crouching pines. 'Yes, Madame,' I always say, turning my face away from her, and continuing.

"I don't know if the children have noticed, God save them. No, really, I don't know. Or the Sir. I don't know what they would say if they did. The angels. The precious little dumplings. A boy and a girl. They smile, and tease me: 'You're sweeping so much!' they say, 'like forever!' 'Like forever' is what it feels like, I can tell you. But mostly I—I miss her. The way she used to laugh. I want *her* back. Not the ghost. Not the—the *thing* that she became. That she still is.

"And so . . . well, now you know all of it. Now you know why you see me here in the garden perpetually crying, holding this broom in my hand. Holding it and sweeping up the hands she's so convinced are scattered everywhere about here. '*Decaying,*' she sometimes screams out at me. '*Curling,*' she sometimes screams, 'with their fingers broken at the knuckles. And the—the fingernails . . . pulled . . . no, *wrenched*—'

"And so that's why. Why I've been here all this time. Sweeping without end. Holding this broom and moving it back and forth, back and forth across the grass and beneath the trees, for these past nineteen days. Every day now. Always. Yes. Alone. In tears."

<hr />

A Clattering; Transformations; the Sea

In years to come, before all of the events recounted herein are completely forgotten, another voice living or dead (or somewhere in between) will rise up out of the spreading sea and tell it: tell the truth about how it was the strange deluge of that night and no other that would finally propel her. Propel her into flight as soon as, so very late that final night, she awakened out of the sleep that as usual had been plagued with "dreams"—so came the word to her, abruptly, where, on that bed next to Him, she had lain perfectly motionless for hours, eyes wide open and fists and jaw clenched: "Will I never ever be free," she had wondered, those staring eyes focused on the dark ceiling, "of all these choking dreams?" Never be free, the ticking silence whispered back to her, aware of her shallow breaths, but nothing even in all those shadows and those that had come before could have prepared her for what happened next: the sound of clattering, outside, on the roof just above. A clattering as of insistent heavy rain which that night was not rain at all, but rather a rainfall of mutilated "vaginas," she knew instantly on hearing them. "Vaginas that, right now, this very minute, are raining down on the roof, in the very same way that all those hands did only weeks ago—hands, and now vaginas, filling up the garden."

It took her only a moment to spring, half-clothed, from her bed, to peer with that expression on her face out into the moonwhite garden. And so yes, she thought, believing the evidence of her eyes; for there, below, across the moonlit grounds, were indeed a scattering of "vaginas," she thought, "without question vaginas, nothing more nor less." Hundreds of them. "No, thousands," she thought, gripping the windowsill and not yet daring to glance back through the shadows at Him asleep. Vaginas everywhere. And, in long curling rivulets from where each one fell onto the grass with a thud, redness. Redness everywhere beneath the moonlight. Vaginas that had been "slashed out," one of the shadow-voices that always came to her in those hours whispered into her deepest ear just then, "and tossed into secret places. Secret graves. Or burnt. Chopped out," another voice among the shadows whispered to her. Vaginas clattering down out of the sky and filling the moonlit night; but how much more did her face change and change again when she began to see that, unmistakably, there could be no mistaking it, every single vagina falling out of the sky all at once changed upon its hitting the grass of her garden? Changed without any effort at all, to a face?—or, rather, changed from simply a vagina fallen from the sky to a vagina fallen and with a face at its very center. A face with eyes, lips, mouth; a face with a nose that surely, she thought just then, could scent her very blood; as those eyes, all those watching eyes and growing as more plummeted down onto the *house and into the garden, gazed upon her "like the ruined mermaids," she thought, "except that these faces can see."*

Staring down at them for one minute or two but no more, she soon apprehended that more than one of them, red and wet as they appeared in that without-mercy moonlight, began to mouth her name—to call her name as the sea might have done on a distant afternoon, with refrains of Come. Return. Come. *She watched them upon the grass as more continued to fall, thudding upon the grass between those already moving, shining, glowing. Moving like spiders, some growing (but extremely quickly) the short, dark, bent limbs of spiders; clambering over each other, or tearing with the small teeth in their small mouths at the dewsoaked grass. A few of them scurried over the ground to devour unsuspecting night insects. But more than a few lay still—panting, gasping, as if in that moment, in all moments yet to come, nothing more for them could be possible. As if everything possible had ended long ago.*

But then now, here, is especially what the voice either living or dead (or somewhere in between) will recall when, years later, it rises up out of the sea and recounts the events of this night: how, in this very moment, she sees and feels her body moving directly toward Him, still sleeping. Finally. Sees and feels herself moving toward Him as, amid the clattering outside and all those noises down on the garden grass, she feels within the hand that is somehow astonishingly her own the thing, the cold, hard, sharp, shining thing that cannot possibly be in it, she tells herself: the thing that, in regard to Him, she has dreamt of one day or night holding and using over and over again—the thing that cannot possibly now be in this hand that is somehow mine, she thinks, for how could something like this ever happen? Yet she feels it, that thing, ready and sharp in her amazingly not-trembling hand, and her hand knows it. Grips it. It had always been there somewhere, hidden not far from where, looking through the darkness at Him sleeping, she now stands. Holding it, she moves closer to Him. Looks, briefly, at Him. Then looks around in the darkness. (But does not, will not, turn to look over her shoulder out the window at what continues to fall from the sky out there.) Looks at Him sleeping again; then moves closer, as the noises outside rise.

Rise, as she, now standing over the sleeping Him and watched only by the lengthening shadows, sees with her very own eyes what happens next. Standing in the shadows, she sees that woman who so incredibly resembles her raise a hand, the hand holding that long, sharp, shining thing, and plunge it into Him. Once. Twice. Three times. Then her ears hear that noise. A gurgled cry. She sees: those arms, flailing. Grasping, uselessly, the air. Then the head above the arms turned, jerking, its eyes all at once widely, terribly open. How is it that her eyes suddenly know the danger of looking at those eyes? She looks at them. Into them. (But she is not there, she thinks all at once. No, though she feels herself standing there, utterly still, watching with her face also utterly still, she knows that she cannot possibly be there.) She sees how the woman looks steadily down at Him with that expression on her utterly still face, unflinching, not moving, as she herself, watching and feeling that thing pressing so hard against her hand and feeling her face still so completely still, does not flinch. Does not flinch despite His violent cry, despite His useless arms. Despite all that coughing, spitting. The gurgling of a throat engorged. She sees Him grab out wildly again at the air and attempt, jerking with that terrible gurgling sound, to sit up in the bed with that look in His eyes, that look, as she watches the woman again plunge the thing into Him. Plunge it. Twist it. Pull it out. Plunge it again. And again. Now, deep beneath His left armpit. Now, just below His collarbone. Now, in spite of the gurgling and His wild hands reaching, grasping, directly into His navel. At one point the thing, shining, gleaming, gripped so tightly, she feels it, the other woman feels it, the thing gripped so tightly in the hand that simply cannot, no, of course not, be her own—at one point it accidentally runs right through one of His hands, ripping open His palm, but by the time He can even manage to get out a small gasp (the sound of bubbles churning louder in His throat), she, that other woman, has run it, that thing, directly into His throat. Stained, wet, but still so sharp and shining, it emerges on the other side of His neck. Now, His form falling heavily back on the bed, His eyes do not close, but He ceases, all at once, to thrash. He lies there, unmoving. She watches, and feels her hands. Watches also the other woman who, standing exactly as she does and wearing that expression that is no expression, watches her.

All movement stilled, but for what continues to happen outside.

How warm her hands feel, she thinks. Warm and wet, as if she had recently dipped them in a summer sea. The sea. But how cold, too. There is coldness there. Somewhere.

She watches the other woman look down at Him as she feels herself looking down at Him. Then, when the woman turns away, away back into the shadows, she feels herself do the same.

But she has not forgotten the voices outside that continue to call. That continue to grow. Louder. More of them than before.

She feels her body moving. Down the hall. Down the stairs. Through darkness, though not yet through (toward) light.

The voice that will rise in a future time from the sea and recount this entire night will remember how, now, she stops outside the boy's room. Stops, and gazes with that expression that is no expression at that other woman, reappeared, who gazes back at her. Who now soundlessly opens the door to the boy's room as she feels her own hand on the doorknob, as they both walk into the room.

No, she cannot possibly be here. Of course not. But how long this dream is. And how wet.

There are voices, so many: inside her, outside of her, and out there, in the garden. Voices begging her now please, not to do it. Begging her to leave him, leave him, please. The boy. The precious sleeping little boy. Please. Do not. You cannot. Do that. No. But why are they all begging me, that smallest voice within her asks, when I am not the one doing any of this? Why do they not beg her, she wonders, that woman now standing over his bed, holding that thing in her hand and preparing to do to him what she just finished doing to Him? And ah, sighs the night, it is anyway much too late for begging of any kind, isn't it? Much too late for Do Not, No, You Cannot. The future voice that will recount these events will remember all that useless begging, and know that, as the vaginas continue to plummet outside and transform to faces on the dewsoaked grass, it is too late: for her, and for all of them.

Now standing completely still, she gazes silently upon her sleeping boychild for not long at all—for barely a minute, if that. Gazes, remembering His face in his. His blood coursing through his. The boychild, the seed of His loins. Bloodfury. Bloodrage. Vicious. She gazes, before watching what happens next: that other woman, the one with her exact face and even her hands, bending over him swiftly, drawing so quietly across his throat the shiny thing still held so tightly in her hand. Watching, she feels it in her own hand; feels her grip tighten on it as she (no, no, the other woman, the one who is doing all this) draws it across his throat; feels her hand pull away as the other woman pulls her hand away. In the small, soft place where the boy would have screamed and now cannot runs only wetness, warmth: "On my hands—no, on that other woman's hands—and on him," she thinks, looking neither to the right nor the left. Looking not at that other woman she feels looking back at her. Then looking down to see him looking up at her. Seeing his eyes widen, then dim so rapidly. Hearing his last muffled attempts to speak. Noting that he, like Him, cannot speak, for the choking. Watching him grab briefly, very briefly, at the air—at her—before, shortly, his arms, incapable, fall back upon him; then become still.

She is so relieved knowing that she cannot possibly be here. So happy that the boychild, before those movements of his arms, did not call her what he always calls her. That word, that most now unbearable word.

"The voices outside," she thinks. "Rising."

"Yes," she hears the other woman say.

"And all the vaginas," she thinks, "still falling. By now there must be millions of them on the lawn, throughout the garden, all transformed into faces. Millions of them."

"Of course," she hears the other woman say.

And the enveloping night, knowing what will happen next, pleading: Do not. Please. No more.

But the girlchild has His face and blood too, she thinks, turning to that other woman, who nods back at her. (Later, on her way to the sea, she will recall how strange it was to see a face so like her own nodding back at her.) The girlchild who—one day, like all of them—will grow up to be a woman. A laughing crying woman. A woman, but with His flesh and face.

And so she does. Must, she thinks. With the sleeping girl also. The girl, who, immediately on feeling that thing slicing into the warmth of her throat, awakens to look up and see the woman standing and looking down at her that way: looking down at the girl as though she is not looking at her but rather watching someone else do what her own hands, holding that thing, just did, then did again. The girl feels herself drowning in the warmth that is entirely her own. This is what she, girlchild, knows in the final quiet place where such things are ultimately known: that all that spreading warmth and wetness are entirely hers. That warmth, spreading its broad creeping shawl over everything. Sinking into the deep water that she all at once feels sucking at her feet and the entire bed. The deep water that for her will be of all time *and utter silence, through which she manages to get out only one word: the awful, unbearable word the boychild had not murmured, that they both had always used when talking to the woman standing over her. That word, mouthed before falling asleep and not long after waking. Mouthed, shrieked, or whispered in all moments of affection, weariness, need. It is the last word she hears herself say before, understanding nothing of what all this means and why those hands above all others did that thing to her throat, she sees the woman standing over her swoop down like a great tall thing. A tree. A great tall tree, though slim, holding to its chest a pillow. A pillow, as, between all that warmth still spreading outward over the bed, spreading, the small head now pressed firmly beneath the lowered pillow attempts to fight, push upward, though feebly, for the first few seconds; then finally goes limp. Its tongue, pressing against the small teeth within, suddenly loses all sense of purpose, as its eyes, rolling back, confirm beneath the pillow for the darkness what the night and the voices outside already know.*

"And now," the woman holding the pillow in place thinks, "He is no more. Here," she thinks, "in both of their faces, He is finally gone. All of them are gone."

She looks through the darkness over at the other woman who, as always, looks back at her. The woman: crying, she sees. Sobbing, her shoulders shaking softly, but with that strange light across her face; sobbing, her face lit that way, standing there holding a pillow bearing the stains of so much warmth released. It is then that she feels in her own hands the thick thing that is the, the—yes, that, clutched; as she feels that movement in her shoulders. As she feels the wetness on her own face.

Now, she tells the other woman, but without speaking the actual words, go. Go away, she tells her, and do not ever come back.

Go, she repeats without speaking when the woman makes no move but simply continues to stare at her, her face shining wet.

I mean it, she tells that staring face. Get out of here. And don't ever come back.

Weeping, still clutching the stained pillow, the woman slowly moves out of her sight into the shadows. Slowly out toward all the voices out there. Then, all at once, more quickly out into the night. "Yes, vanished," she thinks. Gone.

In this hour, while the moon-filled night still fills its belly on the dreams of the restless living and the dead (and those somewhere in between), let it be known throughout every corner of the mountain-filled country that there will come a time when all of the events recounted herein will, by even the most steadfast, be completely forgotten. Yet let it also be known that long before that dire time, on a future moonful night, a voice shall rise up out of the yawning sea and recall it: recall how, on this night, with all those shadows licking so closely at her heels and her hands in that unspeakable condition— her hands holding still some of the warmth of Him, and of the boychild and the girl—and with her back so impossibly straight, her face so unmoving, her eyes staring straight ahead (yet still seeing somewhere else that other woman, watching her with that face), she walked in the first moment of her waking (for a kind of waking it certainly was) directly out of the house. Walked, and did not—no, not even once—turn back. Moved casually and cleanly out into the garden to find herself, in that moment somehow not trembling, among the thousandfold vaginas that had almost entirely transformed to those enormous mongrel-spiders, littering that always-impeccable garden— scuttling in every direction across it as their open mouths, tearing at the dew-damp grass, continued to move and stretch from side to side. It was then, in the precise hour of the heavy moon's beginning its slow crawl back down into the sea, that she began her own walk toward that water: quite like a sleepwalker, some of the shadows would later attest. Like someone in the deepest and most irretrievable of dreams. Toward the black stretching water, past the sleeping houses and the faithful late-hour patrols always accountable to His command but that night evidently lost for all time in a thick (though useless) dream of their own, or simply stone-drunk on the job; for, though armed with their submachine guns and rifles and ready for a fight with any hapless late passer-by who might be up to some evil business against the magnificent nation's peace and order, they noticed neither her nor that grotesque parade of spider-vaginas crawling, some mutely and all with their mouths wide open, at her heels. "She was without question walking toward the sea," the night observed, wrapping its slinky arms more closely about her as it continued to whisper profanities over those skulking mountains.

Yet here is where some of the shadows that witnessed the next moments became confused. For, upon her reaching the shore in the company of all the strange creatures following her, did she in fact step out into those dark waters, into the arms of the blind mermaids who—according to some watchers— rose up just then out of the churning waves to surround her? The sightless *mermaids who, singing their tuneless forever song, then descended beneath the waves with her, their unseeing faces to the last all turned up toward the lowering night sky, to be seen no more? Their arms all about her, pulling her down between them as, her face also turned unseeingly upward, she— evidently willingly—went down with them? Went down stretching out at the very end her hands still bearing the evidence of what that other woman, the woman who had borne her exact face, had done? Or, as others later insisted, did she in fact rise above and walk on those waters out into the dark? Walk, followed by those innumerable strange, spider-like creatures, farther out, still farther, until no trace whatsoever could be seen of her or them from land by those who, improbably in those last moments of the final moon, convinced themselves and others that they actually had seen her—had fully witnessed her journey?*

But now here is all that any of those who remain—remain amidst occasional rainfalls of severed hands and other parts, including tattered vaginas—are willing to commit to memory: that by and by the night, in collusion with the heavy moon, shrugged, snapped shut its eyes, and lowered its weary head against the retreating shore. By and by, as the sun edged up out of the sea and daylight stuttered in, the news spiraled and rose, then charged, of a woman known to many somehow gone missing—vanished, voices began to murmur, then repeated in loud whispers (but not too loud), with God only knew how much of Him and two others on her hands.

The boychild and the girl—but the maid, yet condemned to sweeping up the garden where the torrent of vaginas had plummeted only the night before, would be the one to find them. All of them.

And the funerals. In the next days to come first for those three. For all of them a monarchical procession of state wreathed through with weeping cascades of flowers, during which actual human weeping was both expected and required; then, not long afterward, ceremonies for the several who had worked directly beneath Him and who for expediency's sake, on rapid orders from high above, had been quickly "detained," accused, and summarily secretly shot. For she could not possibly be connected with any of it in the public memory in any way, the higher voices had insisted; whatever had actually happened, it remained critical that she not be linked to it in any way—for obvious reasons, one of them had muttered to a comrade-skeptic, you know what He meant to this country, to everything—why do you even need to ask?

More funerals would be held over the next several weeks for those who continued, as many had all along, to struggle, cry out, and ultimately succumb, red-mouthed, to terrible dreams.

And the final rainfall, about which that future voice, ascended out of the sea, will tell? It will happen. On the tenth day after the last of these events, the entire country will be nearly overcome by a literal deluge of assorted parts: throats, fingertips, and the smooth undersides of chins. The storm will continue for an uncountable cycle of dreams, well into the time of the new He appointed to replace Him; well into the time of unfathomable dark water and a returning chorus of blind mermaids staring sightlessly, heads bent impossibly back and open-mouthed, so far beneath the waves. Well beyond even the memories of this recounting and the echoes of the sea-voice that will tell it all and tell it again, until the inevitable time when the faces and flesh of the living and the dead recalled herein will, by even the most steadfast, long have been forgotten.

READER'S GUIDE

by Lisa Goldstein from *Fantasy & Science Fiction*

———————⟲⟳———————

1 How does Mary Bainbridge, the author of *Winter Swan*, let us know that Donny is unhappy? Is it significant that the novel takes place in winter?

2. In what ways does Bainbridge contrast Donny with the other farmers?

3. Do you think everyone else in this town is really as cheerful as Bainbridge shows them to be? What kinds of problems might they be hiding: bankruptcy, blackmail, adultery, madness, murder? Do you think Mr. and Mrs. Conway, who own the farm down the road, are really brother and sister?

4. What is the significance of the single swan on the lake? The swan's mate has died; what does he have in common with Donny?

5. Why did Bainbridge set *Winter Swan* at the beginning of the twentieth century? If the story was set in the present, which characters would have cell phones? Which ones would have iPods? Rewrite Donny's love letter to Mrs. Thompson as a text message.

6. How would the story be different if the characters were lemurs?

7. How many times does Bainbridge call Great-aunt Gracie "quaint"? Did you think she really was quaint? What words would you use to describe her? How important is it for a writer to have a large vocabulary, or at least a good thesaurus?

8. There are other symbols in *Winter Swan* besides the single swan: for example, Donny gets lost in the woods to symbolize the fact that he's lost his way in life; the farmer Ephraim, who disapproves of Mrs.

Thompson dating so soon after she lost her husband, is colorblind—
that is, he sees things in black and white. What other symbols are
there? Do these symbols seem heavy-handed to you? Do you think
they might seem heavy-handed to Donny as well?

9. What about all the coincidences? Isn't it strange that whenever
Donny goes to the lake Mrs. Thompson is there too?

10. Are these symbols and coincidences so obvious that Donny might
come to suspect that he's in a story?

11. If he does realize he's in a story, what can he do about it?

12. On the other hand, strange coincidences do happen all the time.
What coincidences have you experienced? Go to the nearest lake in
your town and wait on the shore for ten minutes. Did you meet your
true love? (If there is no lake near where you live, find something with
the word "lake" in it—Lakeshore Avenue, for example, or Lake Dry
Cleaners.)

13. Why do you think love stories are so popular? Did you fall in love
with Donny and/or Mrs. Thompson?

14. Do you think people really spend this much time thinking about
how much milk they have to buy, the way Donny does, or what they
should get their great-aunt for her birthday, like Mrs. Thompson?
Aren't people, in the privacy of their own thoughts, more interesting,
more complex, than this? What are some interesting thoughts you
have had, thoughts you have never shared with anyone? Do you think
Donny and Mrs. Thompson might be aliens?

15. What other kinds of stories are popular, besides love stories? Why
are stories important? People in every culture, in every time, have
told stories—do you think there might be a great Library of Story
somewhere, where all possible permutations of every possible story
might exist?

16. Do you think that writers should always write with passion, to the utmost of their ability? What should happen to writers who don't, who use clichéd plots, cardboard characters, lifeless prose? If there is a Library of Story, do you think there might be a Lord of Story, a Muse who grants access to the great stories, the ones that are told again and again? Would this Muse see and judge the stories that people write? Might he punish lazy authors by, for example, writing Reader's Guides like this one, and causing them to appear in every copy of their novel?

17. To be honest, I'm not the Lord of Story. I'm his acolyte. I'm that kid who spent all his time reading, who read instead of paying attention in class, who hid in the school library instead of playing games with the other boys at recess. Even as a child I felt that there had to be a Lord of Story, someone who kept these stories and gave them to the writers he thought were worthy of them, and when I was twenty-eight I walked away from my job and set out to find him.

I'm a reader, not a writer, but I worked as hard at my quest as any of the great writers; I kept to my task, I answered the riddles I was asked, and even when I lost faith I continued on my journey. And some time later (how much later it was I don't know—I had lost all track of time) I found myself before the Lord of Story, and I knelt and asked him if I might become his acolyte.

He put me to work in his Library, as a Shelver. Every day I go to the room where I left off shelving the night before; every day I take up the cart that's waiting for me there, filled with books. I walk from room to room with my cart, five up and to the left, five down and to the right, shelving the books according to the code on their spine. The bookcases are all of dark red wood, but there are subtle differences in each room: sometimes tables of the same red wood; sometimes fat comfortable chairs in the corners, beneath old dark portraits of a man or a woman reading a book; sometimes a fireplace filled with fragrant branches. The lamps all cast a gentle glow when I turn them on, though some of them are electric, some gas, some a technology I don't recognize, with a faceted crystal the size of my thumbnail beneath the shade. The floors and walls are made of wood or stone or marble, but there are soft carpets in every room that hush my footsteps when I walk.

The Lord of Story taught me his shelving system, but that was all; he said nothing else about his realm. But I've had years to think about the Library, and when I meet other Shelvers we share our speculations. (Different Shelvers seem to have different patterns, like chess pieces, some moving diagonally through the Library, some in straight rows, and we meet at various points). I think that the shelves are infinite, or at least I've never reached the end of them, row upon row of bookcases, room after room opening out one after the other. And it seems to me that the books that are checked out return to us changed, more substantial; the paper seems thicker, the print darker. I think that these books were once possibilities of story, but that now they exist in the world, given by the Lord of Story to writers who have reached the Library somehow. And sometimes when I'm shelving, a book will appear in my cart from nowhere—a book that, I think, some writer has returned at just that moment, that has just now become a reality where it was once only a possibility.

Maybe my life sounds dull to you; as for me, though, it's all I could ever want. Because when my shelving is done for the day I can read any of the books on the shelves, the ones that have already been written and the ones that have yet to be discovered. I read stories you have never dreamed of—though someone, somewhere, may dream of them one day, and give them to the world.

I talk about these books with the other Shelvers—and here no one makes fun of me for reading, the way they used to in my life before, because here everyone is like me. Sometimes one of us will recommend a book, but we have both been traveling for so long, moving toward each other from places so far away, that the book's code will usually be unknown to the other Shelver, from a room so far distant that it would take months or even years to get there.

We discuss books, as I said, and we discuss the Library, but we also talk about the Lord of Story, who walks through these rooms and has a word for everyone he passes. Other Shelvers have come across him once or even several times, but I've never seen him in all the long years I have been working here, not since that first time, and sometimes I wonder why that is.

But I should ask a question; this is a Reader's Guide, after all. Have you ever read a book from the Library of Story? Was it a good story, dazzling, wonderful, a true story? Write this story down, and send it out into the world—and if it appears there I or one of the other Shelvers will know it, we will see that it has changed when it comes back to us to shelve.

18. I asked if the story you found here was a good one. Very few of them here are, I'm afraid. There are infinite ways of telling a tale, but only rarely do all the elements coalesce, only rarely is everything perfect, the characters engaging, the setting sharply drawn, the action compelling. Sometimes I think that the Library itself generates these books, stirring together an infinite number of people and places and events, and it is only chance that creates a good story. Or maybe the Library sleeps; maybe these are its dreams. Maybe there is another Library, reached somehow by this Library . . . But no, my mind cannot encompass it.

I've read a lot of good books here, but I've also read a lot I disliked, and some I hated; I do nothing but read and work, after all. I can forget the mediocre ones, but a truly bad book makes me angry. If the stories here are infinite then the good stories are infinite as well (another thing impossible to imagine, but one of the Shelvers convinced me that it is true), and writers shouldn't be so lazy that they take down the first book they find.

Winter Swan is one of those wretched stories—boring, poorly constructed, filled with easy choices and sloppy writing and false emotion. And yet with just a little more work, just a bit of reaching to a shelf above or to the left or right, Mary Bainbridge might have found some very fine stories indeed. Here's one, a tale about a woman who turns into a werewolf, and who comes to enjoy being part of a pack of wolves, the camaraderie and the closeness—and who begins, slowly and reluctantly, to fall in love with one of the wolves of the pack. Or this one, about a man who dials Information and finds himself enamored of the mechanical voice that gives out the phone numbers.

A while ago I discovered a way to add my own writing to the books in the Library, and I began to insert these Reader's Guides whenever I found a book that I thought needed one. Doing this helps me get rid of my anger— at least for a while, until I come across another dreadful story.

A Shelver I talked to once said that the Lord of Story wouldn't be pleased by my sarcasm, that our work here is holy, and should be treated with reverence. But of course I know that. No one feels that more than I do, as I walk through the sacred silence of these rooms. It is because I have been entrusted with this task that I hate these stories, which profane the art of storytelling more than anything I can do. Anyway, how could that Shelver possibly know the likes and dislikes of the Lord of Story? She has never seen him after her first time, any more than I have; I made sure to ask her.

Sometimes, though, I worry that she might be right. Maybe the Lord of Story is unhappy with me, maybe that's why I never see him. On the other hand, by Gutenberg, he must have given me these powers for a reason. This is the only power I have found so far, though, this and one other—sometimes I can see the writers who come to the Library. They are barely more than outlines, wraiths, looking through the shelves, reaching out their transparent hands for a book.

19. And here—look at this piece of writing: "Donny's heart leapt into his mouth, and he felt as though he had jumped out of his skin." That's a lot of hopping around for just one sentence—first the heart, then Donny himself. Do they go off in separate directions, do you think? Or do they jump together, leaving the skin behind?

Mary Bainbridge would say—in fact I can almost hear her saying it—that the first is a metaphor, and the second a simile. (Or would she? Does she know the difference?) Perhaps they are, Ms. B, but they are also clichés, phrases that have been used so often they have lost their meaning.

There you are, Ms. B. I thought I sensed you. You're looking for another story, Caxton help us. What about this one, over here? A man and a woman crash their cars; they argue over whose fault it was and go to court and end up falling in love.

Her hand is hovering over it—but no, she's shaking her head. Too simple, she says, too cute. Can it be that she's actually learned something from *Winter Swan*? It was her first novel, after all. She even seems to feel something of the nature of this place—look at her expression as she studies the shelves, a strange combination of awe and humility and excitement. And greed, too—she wants to be the one who tells these stories, and to be known for telling them. I've seen that greed before, on the faces of other writers.

20. Was that other Shelver right, have I been too harsh with the writers who come here? Should I help her?

But holy Manutius—"His heart leapt into his mouth"? How does he eat with—

It's exaggeration, you idiot, she says. Hyperbole.

Do you know what does it? It's that she pronounces "hyperbole" with three syllables instead of four. "Hyperbowl," as though it's some relative of the Superbowl. She reads books about creative writing, obviously, but she doesn't seem to have anyone to talk to. She's never had any of those passionate arguments that are so important to the beginning writer, never stayed up until three o'clock in the morning talking about books that have changed her life. Maybe she lives in a small town, maybe all her conversations are about how much milk to buy, or what to get her great-aunt for her birthday. And yet she perseveres, almost blindly. She perseveres, and she tries to learn from her mistakes. That's no small thing. Just that one mispronunciation, and my heart is shaken with pity and admiration.

All right then, Ms. B. Here's a story about werewolves, about a woman who—No, you're not interested in werewolves, I can see that. This shelf seems to be all love stories, though, of a sort—I'm sure we can find something here for you. There's one, way up at the top there—no, don't give up, you can reach it. It's about a woman who finds herself falling in love with a man who is almost completely superficial. Does he change? Does she? Does she leave him? Not as predictable as Donny and Mrs. Thompson, are they?

21. Do you hear that? A voice, someone calling me. It sounds like . . . it is, it's the Lord of Story. I leave Ms. B and hurry through the rooms, books blurring past me on either side. The voice grows louder.

Finally I reach the room where he's standing. He's a tall man, with a cloak that I thought at first was black but later realized is covered in writing—writing that changes constantly, that moves as he moves. A hood covers his face, mostly, but from what little I can see his skin is as dark as his cloak.

You passed the first test, he says. I'm giving you new work now, advancing you from Shelving to Information.

He turns. He opens a door that had not been there a minute ago—and as it closes behind him it fades once more into the wall.

What does he mean? He explained my first job, how to read the codes on the spines, but what does someone who works in Information do? I barely know this place myself.

Well, I help people, I suppose. People like Ms. B. I guide them to the books they're looking for. But that—wouldn't that make me a sort of Muse?

I stand there, transfixed. A Muse, like the Lord of Story himself. Am I ready for a task that huge, that consequential? But he thought I was.

22. Ms. B is saying something, asking me a question. I force myself out of my trance—my job is to help her, after all. No, I'm afraid I can't say where I'll be when you finish the story, Ms. B. One of these rooms somewhere. Yes, of course you can come look for me. I hope you will.

23. Do you think you'll read the story Ms. B writes next? Why or why not?

SEARCH CONTINUES FOR ELDERLY MAN

by Laura Kasischke from *Fantasy & Science Fiction*

———◆———

There was a child on the porch, a boy. He had a dog on a leash. The boy and the dog looked up at me. The boy was smiling. The dog was panting as if it had been running. I said, "Yes?"

"Mr. Rentz?"

"Yes?" I said.

"Don't you remember us?" the boy asked.

Behind him, a tractor rumbled by on the gravel road. A cloud of dust rose behind the tractor. A young farmer in a white T-shirt took one hand off the wheel and waved. I lifted my hand to wave back, but the farmer had only glanced in my direction for a second, less than a second, before rumbling away.

"*What?*" I said, leaning down to the boy.

Of course, I'd heard what he'd said, my hearing was perfect, but I'd already forgotten what it was I'd heard. The dog—some kind of terrier—had begun to wag its tail, whining excitedly on its leash, as if it were anticipating something from me, as if it expected me to open the door.

"I just asked," the boy said, looking a bit amused, "if you remembered us."

"Oh," I said.

Behind the boy, on the other side of the gravel road, there was a young girl running barelegged, leaping through the field. She had a handful of clover, or something blurred and purple, and she was shrieking. I watched her for a few moments, and then, as if she'd slipped into a hole in the earth, both she and her shrieks were gone.

I looked back down at the boy and his dog. *Yes*, I thought, there was certainly something familiar here. The boy's chipped front tooth. But also that dog.

"We were in the neighborhood," the boy said, "and we remembered your house, and wondered if you wanted to come out, if you could come out and play."

I snorted a little, of course. *Come out and play.* I supposed this was supposed to bring it all back—those childhood years, those carefree summer days! I supposed this boy was supposed to be some hallucinated version of me. I supposed that dog was supposed to be my dog, way back when, and here was Death at my door, beckoning me outside "to play," and I was supposed to step out there and follow the boy into the field, and maybe later he'd get me to take his hand, and we'd find ourselves back at my mother's table with a big ham at the center and all my dead relatives would be shiny-eyed and happy to see me, and in a startling epiphanic moment of ambivalence and ecstasy I'd suddenly understand that the boy, who was me, was dead. But I'd never had a dog.

And my mother had packed me up by the age of four and sent me to live with Aunt Elizabeth, who was an all-out drunk. The kind of drunk who'd manage to get dinner on the table every few nights, and then would stumble into the table and knock it all onto the floor, then chase me and that girl, Francine, and that other orphan, whose name I'm not sure I ever even knew, around with a broken bottle screaming that she was going to kill us all. When Uncle Ernest would get home, he'd sock her in the mouth, and we'd all go salvage whatever we could from the floor for supper. If there was ever a dog, it would have run off.

"I'm busy," I said to the boy, and the dog sat down then, as if on cue, on its haunches. The boy narrowed his eyes. Yes, there was certainly something sinister about the kid. Anyone could see that, even a confused old man. I knew right away that he wouldn't be taking no for an answer.

"That's too bad," the boy said. His voice was lower this time around. Overhead, a plane came barreling out of a cloud, crashing in only seconds somewhere over the horizon, never making a sound. He hooked a thumb in his belt buckle as if he might yank his pants down. As if he was planning to take a piss or a shit right there on my stoop. The little dog curled his lip a bit, like he was thinking about growling.

"Now, look," I said. "I do know you. I know all about you, and you can stand out here on my stoop all day and do whatever foul thing you can think up to do, but I'm not coming out . . ." and then I added, sarcastically, *"to play,"* so he'd know I wasn't quite the sentimental old doddering fool he'd taken me for.

He frowned. And then he shrugged. He started to turn around. "Fine," he said. "Have it your way."

He headed back down the steps. The dog turned to follow him.

I couldn't help it. I'd been expecting trouble. All my life, there it had been, every time I opened the god-damned door. First Aunt Elizabeth, of course. And then the disastrous marriage. Anne with hands like claws within two years of the honeymoon, twisted up like a crabapple tree in the rollaway bed, the whole house smelling of death, and still a hundred chores dawn to dusk to be done. And the children. A limb now and then. A shovel brought down accidentally on some neighbor kid's head. "You just wait a minute you little bastard," I said.

He turned around, slowly, and this time he had a whole new face. The face of an angel! His voice was as sweet as a girl's. The dog had cocked its head, sweetly. And then it vanished. Just a blank space on a limp leash. The angel said, "Yes, Mr. Rentz? Yes?"

It was hard not to give right in. But I knew what this was about. I hadn't avoided this encounter for eighty years just to walk straight into its booby-trap now. I hadn't forgotten the way Duke and Erma had signed over that insurance policy to their son just before the thing in the ravine. Duke with his foot in a coyote trap and a plastic bag over his face. Erma . . . and them making it look like a rape, but nobody would have raped poor crippled Erma. The devil, maybe.

No. Not even the devil.

I took a step backward. I raised up both fists. I said, "I know you know I can fight. I know you've fought me before. And you remember what happened then."

"Oh, Mr. Rentz." He said it as if he were tired of this particular fight. *Yes, yes, yes.* Those nurses with their pockets full of pills. Those prostitutes down on Division Avenue, tapping on the window of your car. I'd fallen for this once or twice, but whoever that poor fellow was, I was not him any more. The farmer on the tractor came chugging by again, but he came from the same direction he'd come from the last time. They couldn't even get this part right. They were just running the same film twice. Trying to save money, I supposed, thinking an old man wouldn't notice. This time, when he waved, I didn't bother to raise my hand.

The boy seemed to be trying to stifle a laugh.

I'd always had a bad temper.

Of course, it made me mad.

And then the girl again. The clover, the bare legs, the hole. I was shaking. It was like that copy of the copy of the copy of the letter my mother had written to me, dug up out of the trunk by my daughter, which she'd mailed off to everybody and their cousin before she thought to bring it over to me. *Daddy, I found this in the attic, and I thought you'd want a copy.*

And my own mother's handwriting, like a retarded child's.

And she couldn't even spell the name of the month.

Which was February.

And something about when I get you back I'm going to get you that little dog.

That little dog.

It was back. But it was behind me. It was smiling up at me from my own rug. And then it was on the couch. And then it was under the coffee table. Pissing on the leg of it. Taking a crap on the carpet. Then lunging in my direction. Then snapping at my heels. Then tearing at the cuffs of my trousers with its teeth. *Get outta here, get outta here.* I was kicking at it, and the girl was screaming, *Help help, someone get him offa me.* But I didn't care about that. I was going to have her if it was the last thing I ever had. My pants were down around my ankles, and I was sure as hell going to stick it inside her, and then some fat woman in white stepped out into the waiting room and said, only her eyebrow twitching a little, *I'm sorry to tell ya the baby has died.* I shrugged. I said, *D'ya tell my wife?*

Soon enough, I'd stumbled out the door, just as I'm sure they'd planned it. The dog sobered up and started whining to be petted. The little boy said, "I *knew* you'd come out to play, Mr. Rentz. I knew it! I knew it!" The tractor and the farmer and the little girl, as if someone up there just kept hitting *rewind rewind.* That girl stood up and I could see my seed trickling down her thigh. I stifled a laugh, chuckling behind my hand, *How stupid do you think I am?*

Well, that's how stupid I am.

And then I heard the door slam behind me.

And then the boy turned to look at me with those big serious eyes and said, "I'm sorry to have had to mislead you, Mr. Rentz."

And I said, "Oh, kid, forget it. I understand."

And we shuffled off into the dust, the two of us—the beautiful boy I might have been and the dog I might have had—in search of the old lost man I had become.

PRIDE AND PROMETHEUS

by John Kessel from *Fantasy & Science Fiction*

H ad both her mother and her sister Kitty not insisted upon it,
Miss Mary Bennet, whose interest in Nature did not extend to
the Nature of Society, would not have attended the ball in Grosvenor
Square. This was Kitty's season. Mrs. Bennet had despaired of Mary
long ago, but still bore hopes for her younger sister, and so had set
her determined mind on putting Kitty in the way of Robert Sidney of
Detling Manor, who possessed a fortune of six thousand pounds a year,
and was likely to be at that evening's festivities. Being obliged by her
unmarried state to live with her parents, and the whims of Mrs. Bennet
being what they were, although there was no earthly reason for Mary
to be there, there was no good excuse for her absence.

So it was that Mary found herself in the ballroom of the great house,
trussed up in a silk dress with her hair piled high, bedecked with her
sister's jewels. She was neither a beauty, like her older and happily
married sister Jane, nor witty, like her older and happily married sister
Elizabeth, nor flirtatious, like her younger and less happily married sister
Lydia. Awkward and nearsighted, she had never cut an attractive figure,
and as she had aged she had come to see herself as others saw her. Every
time Mrs. Bennet told her to stand up straight, she felt despair. Mary
had seen how Jane and Elizabeth had made good lives for themselves by
finding appropriate mates. But there was no air of grace or mystery about
Mary, and no man ever looked upon her with admiration.

Kitty's card was full, and she had already contrived to dance once with
the distinguished Mr. Sidney, than whom Mary could not imagine a being
more tedious. Hectically glowing, Kitty was certain that this was the
season she would get a husband. Mary, in contrast, sat with her mother
and her Aunt Gardiner, whose good sense was Mary's only respite from
her mother's silliness. After the third minuet Kitty came flying over.

"Catch your breath, Kitty!" Mrs. Bennet said. "Must you rush about like this? Who is that young man you danced with? Remember, we are here to smile on Mr. Sidney, not on some stranger. Did I see him arrive with the Lord Mayor?"

"How can I tell you what you saw, Mother?"

"Don't be impertinent."

"Yes. He is an acquaintance of the mayor. He's from Switzerland! Mr. Clerval, on holiday."

The tall, fair-haired Clerval stood with a darker, brooding young man, both impeccably dressed in dove gray breeches, black jackets, and waistcoats, with white tie and gloves.

"Switzerland! I would not have you marry any Dutchman—though 'tis said their merchants are uncommonly wealthy. And who is that gentleman with whom he speaks?"

"I don't know, Mother—but I can find out."

Mrs. Bennet's curiosity was soon to be relieved, as the two men crossed the drawing room to the sisters and their chaperones.

"Henry Clerval, madame," the fair-haired man said, "and this is my good friend Mr. Victor Frankenstein."

Mr. Frankenstein bowed but said nothing. He had the darkest eyes that Mary had ever encountered, and an air of being there only on obligation. Whether this was because he was as uncomfortable in these social situations as she, Mary could not tell, but his diffident air intrigued her. She fancied his reserve might bespeak sadness rather than pride. His manners were faultless, as was his command of English, though he spoke with a slight French accent. When he asked Mary to dance she suspected he did so only at the urging of Mr. Clerval; on the floor, once the orchestra of pianoforte, violin, and cello struck up the quadrille, he moved with some grace but no trace of a smile.

At the end of the dance, Frankenstein asked whether Mary would like some refreshment, and they crossed from the crowded ballroom to the sitting room, where he procured for her a cup of negus. Mary felt obliged to make some conversation before she should retreat to the safety of her wallflower's chair.

"What brings you to England, Mr. Frankenstein?"

"I come to meet with certain natural philosophers here in London, and in Oxford—students of magnetism."

"Oh! Then have you met Professor Langdon, of the Royal Society?"

Frankenstein looked at her as if seeing her for the first time. "How is it that you are acquainted with Professor Langdon?"

"I am not personally acquainted with him, but I am, in my small way, an enthusiast of the sciences. You are a natural philosopher?"

"I confess that I can no longer countenance the subject. But yes, I did study with Mr. Krempe and Mr. Waldman in Ingolstadt."

"You no longer countenance the subject, yet you seek out Professor Langdon."

A shadow swept over Mr. Frankenstein's handsome face. "It is unsupportable to me, yet pursue it I must."

"A paradox."

"A paradox that I am unable to explain, Miss Bennet."

All this said in a voice heavy with despair. Mary watched his sober black eyes, and replied, "The heart has its reasons of which reason knows nothing."

For the second time that evening he gave her a look that suggested an understanding. Frankenstein sipped from his cup, then spoke: "Avoid any pastime, Miss Bennet, that takes you out of the normal course of human contact. If the study to which you apply yourself has a tendency to weaken your affections, and to destroy your taste for simple pleasures, then that study is certainly unlawful."

The purport of this extraordinary speech Mary was unable to fathom. "Surely there is no harm in seeking knowledge."

Mr. Frankenstein smiled. "Henry has been urging me to go out into London society; had I known that I might meet such a thoughtful person as yourself I would have taken him up on it long 'ere now."

He took her hand. "But I spy your aunt at the door," he said. "No doubt she has been dispatched to protect you. If you will, please let me return you to your mother. I must thank you for the dance, and even more for your conversation, Miss Bennet. In the midst of a foreign land, you have brought me a moment of sympathy."

And again Mary sat beside her mother and aunt as she had half an hour before. She was nonplussed. It was not seemly for a stranger to speak so much from the heart to a woman he had never previously met, yet she could not find it in herself to condemn him. Rather, she felt her own failure in not keeping him longer.

A cold March rain was falling when, after midnight, they left the ball. They waited under the portico while the coachman brought round the carriage. Kitty began coughing. As they stood there in the chill night, Mary noticed a hooded man, of enormous size, standing in the shadows at the corner of the lane. Full in the downpour, unmoving, he watched the town house and its partiers without coming closer or going away, as if this observation were all his intention in life. Mary shivered.

In the carriage back to Aunt Gardiner's home near Belgravia, Mrs. Bennet insisted that Kitty take the lap robe against the chill. "Stop coughing, Kitty. Have a care for my poor nerves." She added, "They should never have put the supper at the end of that long hallway. The young ladies, flushed from the dance, had to walk all that cold way."

Kitty drew a ragged breath and leaned over to Mary. "I have never seen you so taken with a man, Mary. What did that Swiss gentleman say to you?"

"We spoke of natural philosophy."

"Did he say nothing of the reasons he came to England?" Aunt Gardiner asked.

"That was his reason."

"That's not so!" said Kitty. "He came to forget his grief! His little brother William was murdered, not six months ago, by the family maid!"

"How terrible!" said Aunt Gardiner.

Mrs. Bennet asked in open astonishment, "Could this be true?"

"I have it from Lucy Copeland, the Lord Mayor's daughter," Kitty replied. "Who heard it from Mr. Clerval himself. And there is more! He is engaged to be married—to his cousin. Yet he has abandoned her, left her in Switzerland and come here instead."

"Did he say anything to you about these matters?" Mrs. Bennet asked Mary.

Kitty interrupted. "Mother, he's not going to tell the family secrets to strangers, let alone reveal his betrothal at a dance."

Mary wondered at these revelations. Perhaps they explained Mr. Frankenstein's odd manner. But could they explain his interest in her? "A man should be what he seems," she said.

Kitty snorted, and it became a cough.

"Mark me, girls," said Mrs. Bennet, "that engagement is a match that he does not want. I wonder what fortune he would bring to a marriage?"

In the days that followed, Kitty's cough became a full-blown catarrh, and it was decided against her protest that, the city air being unhealthy, they should cut short their season and return to Meryton. Mr. Sidney was undoubtedly unaware of his narrow escape. Mary could not honestly say that she regretted leaving, though the memory of her half hour with Mr. Frankenstein gave her as much regret at losing the chance of further commerce with him as she had ever felt from her acquaintance with a man.

Within a week Kitty was feeling better, and repining bitterly their remove from London. In truth, she was only two years younger than Mary and had made none of the mental accommodations to approaching spinsterhood that her older sister had attempted. Mr. Bennet retreated to his study, emerging only at mealtimes to cast sardonic comments about Mrs. Bennet and Kitty's marital campaigns. Perhaps, Mrs. Bennet said, they might invite Mr. Sidney to visit Longbourn when Parliament adjourned. Mary escaped these discussions by practicing the pianoforte and, as the advancing spring brought warm weather, taking walks in the countryside, where she would stop beneath an oak and read, indulging her passion for Goethe and German philosophy. When she tried to engage her father in speculation, he warned her, "I am afraid, my dear, that your understanding is too dependent on books and not enough on experience of the world. Beware, Mary. Too much learning makes a woman monstrous."

What experience of the world had they ever allowed her? Rebuffed, Mary wrote to Elizabeth about the abrupt end of Kitty's latest assault on marriage, and her subsequent ill temper, and Elizabeth wrote back inviting her two younger sisters to come visit Pemberley.

Mary was overjoyed to have the opportunity to escape her mother and see something more of Derbyshire, and Kitty seemed equally willing. Mrs. Bennet was not persuaded when Elizabeth suggested that nearby Matlock and its baths might be good for Kitty's health (no man would marry a sickly girl), but she was persuaded by Kitty's observation that, though it could in no way rival London, Matlock did attract a finer society than sleepy Meryton, and thus offered opportunities for meeting eligible young men of property. So in the second week of May, Mr. and Mrs. Bennet tearfully loaded their last unmarried daughters into a coach for the long drive to Derbyshire. Mrs. Bennet's tears were shed because their absence would deprive Kitty and Mary of her attentions, Mr. Bennet's for the fact that their absence would assure him of Mrs. Bennet's.

The two girls were as ever delighted by the grace and luxury of Pemberley, Mr. Darcy's ancestral estate. Darcy was kindness itself, and the servants attentive, if, at the instruction of Elizabeth, less indulgent of Kitty's whims and more careful of her health than the thoroughly cowed servants at home. Lizzy saw that Kitty got enough sleep, and the three sisters took long walks in the grounds of the estate. Kitty's health improved, and Mary's spirits rose. Mary enjoyed the company of Lizzy and Darcy's eight-year-old son William, who was attempting to teach her and Darcy's younger sister Georgiana to fish. Georgiana pined after her betrothed, Captain Broadbent, who was away on crown business in the Caribbean, but after they had been there a week, Jane and her husband Mr. Bingley came for an extended visit from their own estate thirty miles away, and so four of the five Bennet sisters were reunited. They spent many cordial afternoons and evenings. Both Mary and Georgiana were accomplished at the pianoforte, though Mary had come to realize that her sisters tolerated more than enjoyed her playing. The reunion of Lizzy and Jane meant even more time devoted to Kitty's improvement, with specific attention to her marital prospects, and left Mary feeling invisible. Still, on occasion she would join them and drive into Lambton or Matlock to shop and socialize, and every week during the summer a ball was held in the assembly room of the Old Bath Hotel, with its beeswax polished floor and splendid chandeliers.

On one such excursion to Matlock, Georgiana stopped at the milliner's while Kitty pursued some business at the butcher's shop—Mary wondered at her sudden interest in Pemberley's domestic affairs—and Mary took William to the museum and circulating library, which contained celebrated cabinets of natural history. William had told her of certain antiquities unearthed in the excavation for a new hotel and recently added to the collection.

The streets, hotels, and inns of Matlock bustled with travelers there to take the waters. Newly wedded couples leaned on one another's arms, whispering secrets that no doubt concerned the alpine scenery. A crew of workmen was breaking up the cobblestone street in front of the hall, swinging pickaxes in the bright sun. Inside she and Will retreated to the cool quiet of the public exhibition room.

Among the visitors to the museum Mary spied a slender, well-dressed man at one of the display cases, examining the artifacts contained there. As she drew near, Mary recognized him. "Mr. Frankenstein!"

The tall European looked up, startled. "Ah—Miss Bennet?"

She was pleased that he remembered. "Yes. How good to see you."

"And this young man is?"

"My nephew, William."

At the mention of this name, Frankenstein's expression darkened. He closed his eyes. "Are you not well?" Mary asked.

He looked at her again. "Forgive me. These antiquities call to mind sad associations. Give me a moment."

"Certainly," she said. William ran off to see the hall's steam clock. Mary turned and examined the contents of the neighboring cabinet.

Beneath the glass was a collection of bones that had been unearthed in the local lead mines. The card lettered beside them read: Bones, resembling those of a fish, made of limestone.

Eventually Frankenstein came to stand beside her. "How is it that you are come to Matlock?" he inquired.

"My sister Elizabeth is married to Mr. Fitzwilliam Darcy, of Pemberley. Kitty and I are here on a visit. Have you come to take the waters?"

"Clerval and I are on our way to Scotland, where he will stay with friends, while I pursue . . . certain investigations. We rest here a week. The topography of the valley reminds me of my home in Switzerland."

"I have heard it said so," she replied. Frankenstein seemed to have regained his composure, but Mary wondered still at what had awakened his grief. "You have an interest in these relics?" she asked, indicating the cabinets.

"Some, perhaps. I find it remarkable to see a young lady take an interest in such arcana." Mary detected no trace of mockery in his voice.

"Indeed, I do," she said, indulging her enthusiasm. "Professor Erasmus Darwin has written of the source of these bones:

"Organic life beneath the shoreless waves
Was born and nurs'd in ocean's pearly caves;
First forms minute, unseen by spheric glass,
Move on the mud, or pierce the watery mass;
These, as successive generations bloom,
New powers acquire and larger limbs assume;
Whence countless groups of vegetation spring,
And breathing realms of fin and feet and wing.

"People say this offers proof of the great flood. Do you think, Mr. Frankenstein, that Matlock could once have been under the sea? They say these are creatures that have not existed since the time of Noah."

"Far older than the flood, I'll warrant. I do not think that these bones were originally made of stone. Some process has transformed them. Anatomically, they are more like those of a lizard than a fish."

"You have studied anatomy?"

Mr. Frankenstein tapped his fingers upon the glass of the case. "Three years gone by it was one of my passions. I no longer pursue such matters."

"And yet, sir, you met with men of science in London."

"Ah—yes, I did. I am surprised that you remember a brief conversation, more than two months ago."

"I have a good memory."

"As evidenced by your quoting Professor Darwin. I might expect a woman such as yourself to take more interest in art than science."

"Oh, you may rest assured that I have read my share of novels. And even more, in my youth, of sermons. Elizabeth is wont to tease me for a great moralizer. 'Evil is easy,' I tell her, 'and has infinite forms.'"

Frankenstein did not answer. Finally he said, "Would that the world had no need of moralizers."

Mary recalled his warning against science from their London meeting. "Come, Mr. Frankenstein. There is no evil in studying God's handiwork."

"A God-fearing Christian might take exception to Professor Darwin's assertion that life began in the sea, no matter how poetically stated." His voice became distant. "Can a living soul be created without the hand of God?"

"It is my feeling that the hand of God is everywhere present." Mary gestured toward the cabinet. "Even in the bones of this stony fish."

"Then you have more faith than I, Miss Bennet—or more innocence."

Mary blushed. She was not used to bantering in this way with a gentleman. In her experience, handsome and accomplished men took no interest in her, and such conversations as she had engaged in offered little of substance other than the weather, clothes, and town gossip. Yet she saw that she had touched Frankenstein, and felt something akin to triumph.

They were interrupted by the appearance of Georgiana and Kitty, entering with Henry Clerval. "There you are!" said Kitty. "You see, Mr. Clerval, I told you we would find Mary poring over these heaps of bones!"

"And it is no surprise to find my friend here as well," said Clerval.

Mary felt quite deflated. The party moved out of the town hall and in splendid sunlight along the North Parade. Kitty proposed, and the visitors acceded to, a stroll on the so-called Lover's Walk beside the river. As they walked along the gorge, vast ramparts of limestone rock, clothed with yew trees, elms, and limes, rose up on either side of the river. William ran ahead, and Kitty, Georgiana, and Clerval followed, leaving Frankenstein and Mary behind. Eventually they came in sight of the High Tor, a sheer cliff rearing its brow on the east bank of the Derwent. The lower part was covered with small trees and foliage. Massive boulders that had fallen from the cliff broke the riverbed below into foaming rapids. The noise of the waters left Mary and Frankenstein, apart from the others, as isolated as if they had been in a separate room. Frankenstein spent a long time gazing at the scenery. Mary's mind raced, seeking some way to recapture the mood of their conversation in the town hall.

"How this reminds me of my home," he said. "Henry and I would climb such cliffs as this, chase goats around the meadows and play at pirates. Father would walk me though the woods and name every tree and flower. I once saw a lightning bolt shiver an old oak to splinters."

"Whenever I come here," Mary blurted out, "I realize how small I am, and how great time is. We are here for only seconds, and then we are gone, and these rocks, this river, will long survive us. And through it all we are alone."

Frankenstein turned toward her. "Surely you are not so lonely. You have your family, your sisters. Your mother and father."

"One can be alone in a room of people. Kitty mocks me for my 'heaps of bones.'"

"A person may marry."

"I am twenty-eight years old, sir. I am no man's vision of a lover or wife."

What had come over her, to say this aloud, for the first time in her life? Yet what did it matter what she said to this foreigner? There was no point in letting some hope for sympathy delude her into greater hopes. They had danced a single dance in London, and now they spent an afternoon together; soon he would leave England, marry his cousin, and Mary would never see him again. She deserved Kitty's mockery.

Frankenstein took some time before answering, during which Mary was acutely aware of the sound of the waters, and of the sight of Georgiana, William, and Clerval playing in the grass by the river bank, while Kitty stood pensive some distance away.

"Miss Bennet, I am sorry if I have made light of your situation. But your fine qualities should be apparent to anyone who took the trouble truly to make your acquaintance. Your knowledge of matters of science only adds to my admiration."

"You needn't flatter me," said Mary. "I am unused to it."

"I do not flatter," Frankenstein replied. "I speak my own mind."

William came running up. "Aunt Mary! This would an excellent place to fish! We should come here with Father!"

"That's a good idea, Will."

Frankenstein turned to the others. "We must return to the hotel, Henry," he told Clerval. "I need to see that new glassware properly packed before shipping it ahead."

"Very well."

"Glassware?" Georgiana asked.

Clerval chuckled. "Victor has been purchasing equipment at every stop along our tour—glassware, bottles of chemicals, lead and copper disks. The coachmen threaten to leave us behind if he does not ship these things separately."

Kitty argued in vain, but the party walked back to Matlock. The women and William met the carriage to take them back to Pemberley. "I hope I see you again, Miss Bennet," Frankenstein said. Had she been more accustomed to reading the emotions of others she would have ventured that his expression held sincere interest—even longing.

On the way back to Pemberley William prattled with Georgiana, Kitty, subdued for once, leaned back with her eyes closed, while Mary puzzled over every moment of the afternoon. The fundamental sympathy she had felt with Frankenstein in their brief London encounter had only been reinforced. His sudden dark moods, his silences, bespoke some burden he carried. Mary was almost convinced that her mother was right—that Frankenstein did not love his cousin, and that he was here in England fleeing from her. How could this second meeting with him be chance? Fate had brought them together.

At dinner that evening, Kitty told Darcy and Elizabeth about their encounter with the handsome Swiss tourists. Later, Mary took Lizzy aside and asked her to invite Clerval and Frankenstein to dinner.

"This is new!" said Lizzy. "I expected this from Kitty, but not you. You have never before asked to have a young man come to Pemberley."

"I have never met someone quite like Mr. Frankenstein," Mary replied.

———— ·⚬· ————

"Have you taken the Matlock waters?" Mary asked Clerval, who was seated opposite her at the dinner table. "People in the parish say that a dip in the hot springs could raise the dead."

"I confess that I have not," Clerval said. "Victor does not believe in their healing powers."

Mary turned to Frankenstein, hoping to draw him into discussion of the matter, but the startled expression on his face silenced her.

The table, covered with a blinding white damask tablecloth, glittered with silver and crystal. A large epergne, studded with lit beeswax candles, dominated its center. In addition to the family members, and in order to even the number of guests and balance female with male, Darcy and Elizabeth had invited the vicar, Mr. Chatsworth. Completing the dinner party were Bingley and Jane, Georgiana, and Kitty.

The footmen brought soup, followed by claret, turbot with lobster and Dutch sauce, oyster pâté, lamb cutlets with asparagus, peas, a fricandeau a l'oseille, venison, stewed beef à la jardinière, with various salads, beetroot, French and English mustard. Two ices, cherry water and pineapple cream, and a chocolate cream with strawberries. Champagne flowed throughout the dinner, and Madeira afterward.

Darcy inquired of Mr. Clerval's business in England, and Clerval told of his meetings with men of business in London, and his interest in India. He had even begun the study of the language, and for their entertainment spoke a few sentences in Hindi. Darcy told of his visit to Geneva a decade ago. Clerval spoke charmingly of the differences in manners between the Swiss and the English, with witty preference for English habits, except, he said, in the matter of boiled meats. Georgiana asked about women's dress on the continent. Elizabeth allowed as how, if they could keep him safe, it would be good for William's education to tour the continent. Kitty, who usually dominated the table with bright talk and jokes, was unaccustomedly quiet. The Vicar spoke amusingly of his travels in Italy.

Through all of this, Frankenstein offered little in the way of response or comment. Mary had put such hopes on this dinner, and now she feared she had misread him. His voice warmed but once, when he spoke of his father, a counselor and syndic, renowned for his integrity. Only on inquiry would he speak of his years in Ingolstadt.

"And what did you study in the university?" Bingley asked.

"Matters of no interest," Frankenstein replied.

An uncomfortable silence followed. Clerval gently explained, "My friend devoted himself so single-mindedly to the study of natural philosophy that his health failed. I was fortunately able to bring him back to us, but it was a near thing."

"For which I will ever be grateful to you," Frankenstein mumbled.

Lizzy attempted to change the subject. "Reverend Chatsworth, what news is there of the parish?"

The vicar, unaccustomed to such volume and variety of drink, was in his cups, his face flushed and his voice rising to pulpit volume. "Well, I hope the ladies will not take it amiss," he boomed, "if I tell about a curious incident that occurred last night!"

"Pray do."

"So, then—last night I was troubled with sleeplessness—I think it was the trout I ate for supper, it was not right—Mrs. Croft vowed she had purchased it just that afternoon, but I wonder if perhaps it might have been from the previous day's catch. Be that as it may, lying awake some time after midnight, I thought I heard a scraping out my bedroom window—the weather has been so fine of late that I sleep with my window open. It is my opinion, Mr. Clerval, that nothing aids the lungs more than fresh air, and I believe that is the opinion of the best continental thinkers, is it not? The air is exceedingly fresh in the alpine meadows, I am told?"

"Only in those meadows where the cows have not been feeding."

"The cows? Oh, yes, the cows—ha, ha!—very good! The cows, indeed! So, where was I? Ah, yes. I rose from my bed and looked out the window, and what did I spy but a light in the churchyard. I threw on my robe and slippers and hurried out to see what might be the matter.

"As I approached the churchyard I saw a dark figure wielding a spade. His back was to me, silhouetted by a lamp which rested beside Nancy Brown's grave. Poor Nancy, dead not a week now, so young, only seventeen."

"A man?" said Kitty.

The vicar's round face grew serious. "You may imagine my shock. 'Halloo!' I shouted. At that the man dropped his spade, seized the lantern and dashed 'round the back of the church. By the time I had reached the corner he was out of sight. Back at the grave I saw that he had been on a fair way to unearthing poor Nancy's coffin!"

"My goodness!" said Jane.

"Defiling a grave?" asked Bingley. "I am astonished."

Darcy said nothing, but his look demonstrated that he was not pleased by the vicar bringing such an uncouth matter to his dinner table. Frankenstein, sitting next to Mary, put down his knife and took a long draught of Madeira.

The vicar lowered his voice. He was clearly enjoying himself. "I can only speculate on what motive this man might have had. Could it have been some lover of hers, overcome with grief?"

"No man is so faithful," Kitty said.

"My dear vicar," said Lizzy. "You have read too many of Mrs. Radcliffe's novels."

Darcy leaned back in his chair. "Gypsies have been seen in the woods about the quarry. It was no doubt their work. They were seeking jewelry."

"Jewelry?" the vicar said. "The Browns had barely enough money to see her decently buried."

"Which proves that whoever did this was not a local man."

Clerval spoke. "At home, fresh graves are sometimes defiled by men providing cadavers to doctors. Was there not a spate of such grave robbings in Ingolstadt, Victor?"

Frankenstein put down his glass. "Yes," he said. "Some anatomists, in seeking knowledge, will abandon all human scruple."

"I do not think that is likely to be the cause in this instance," Darcy observed. "Here there is no university, no medical school. Doctor Phillips, in Lambton, is no transgressor of civilized rules."

"He is scarcely a transgressor of his own threshold," said Lizzy. "One must call him a day in advance to get him to leave his parlor."

"Rest assured, there are such men," said Frankenstein. "I have known them. My illness, as Henry has described to you, was in some way my spirit's rebellion against the understanding that the pursuit of knowledge will lead some men into mortal peril."

Here was Mary's chance to impress Frankenstein. "Surely there is a nobility in risking one's life to advance the claims of one's race. With how many things are we upon the brink of becoming acquainted, if cowardice or carelessness did not restrain our inquiries?"

"Then I thank God for cowardice and carelessness, Miss Bennet," Frankenstein said, "One's life, perhaps, is worth risking, but not one's soul."

"True enough. But I believe that science may demand our relaxing the strictures of common society."

"We have never heard this tone from you, Mary," Jane said.

Darcy interjected, "You are becoming quite modern, sister. What strictures are you prepared to abandon for us tonight?" His voice was full of the gentle condescension with which he treated Mary at all times.

How she wished to surprise them! How she longed to show Darcy and Lizzy, with their perfect marriage and perfect lives, that she was not the simple old maid they thought her. "Anatomists in London have obtained the court's permission to dissect the bodies of criminals after execution. Is it unjust to use the body of a murderer, who has already forfeited his own life, to save the lives of the innocent?"

"My uncle, who is on the bench, has spoken of such cases," Bingley said.

"Not only that," Mary added. "Have you heard of the experiments of the Italian scientist Aldini? Last summer in London at the Royal College of Surgeons he used a powerful battery to animate portions of the body of a hanged man. According to the *Times*, the spectators genuinely believed that the body was about to come to life!"

"Mary, please!" said Lizzy.

"You need to spend less time on your horrid books," Kitty laughed. "No suitor is going to want to talk with you about dead bodies."

And so Kitty was on their side, too. Her mockery only made Mary more determined to force Frankenstein to speak. "What do you say, sir? Will you come to my defense?"

Frankenstein carefully folded his napkin and set it beside his plate. "Such attempts are not motivated by bravery, or even curiosity, but by ambition. The pursuit of knowledge can become a vice deadly as any of the more common sins. Worse still, because even the most noble of natures are susceptible to such temptations. None but he who has experienced them can conceive of the enticements of science."

The vicar raised his glass. "Mr. Frankenstein, truer words have never been spoken. The man who defiled poor Nancy's grave has placed himself beyond the mercy of a forgiving God."

Mary felt charged with contradictory emotions. "You have experienced such enticements, Mr. Frankenstein?"

"Sadly, I have."

"But surely there is no sin that is beyond the reach of God's mercy? 'To know all is to forgive all.'"

The vicar turned to her. "My child, what know you of sin?"

"Very little, Mr. Chatsworth, except of idleness. Yet I feel that even a wicked person can have the veil lifted from his eyes."

Frankenstein looked at her. "Here I must agree with Miss Bennet. I have to believe that even the most corrupted nature is susceptible to grace. If I did not think this were possible, I could not live."

"Enough of this talk," insisted Darcy. "Vicar, I suggest you mind your parishioners, including those in the churchyard, more carefully. But now I, for one, am eager to hear Miss Georgiana play the pianoforte. And perhaps Miss Mary and Miss Catherine will join her. We must uphold the accomplishments of English maidenhood before our foreign guests."

<hr>

On Kitty's insistence, the next morning, despite lowering clouds and a chill in the air that spoke more of March than late May, she and Mary took a walk along the river.

They walked along the stream that ran from the estate toward the Derwent. Kitty remained silent. Mary's thoughts turned to the wholly unsatisfying dinner of the previous night. The conversation in the parlor had gone no better than dinner. Mary had played the piano ill, showing herself to poor advantage next to the accomplished Georgiana. Under Jane and Lizzy's gaze she felt the folly of her intemperate speech at the table. Frankenstein said next to nothing to her for the rest of the evening; he almost seemed wary of being in her presence.

She was wondering how he was spending this morning when, suddenly turning her face from Mary, Kitty burst into tears.

Mary touched her arm. "Whatever is the matter, Kitty?"

"Do you believe what you said last night?"

"What did I say?"

"That there is no sin beyond the reach of God's mercy?"

"Of course I do! Why would you ask?"

"Because I have committed such a sin!" She covered her eyes with her hand. "Oh, no, I mustn't speak of it!"

Mary refrained from pointing out that, having made such a provocative admission, Kitty could hardly remain silent—and undoubtedly had no intention of doing so. But Kitty's intentions were not always transparent to Mary.

After some coaxing and a further walk along the stream, Kitty was prepared finally to unburden herself. It seemed that, from the previous summer she had maintained a secret admiration for a local man from Matlock, Robert Piggot, son of the butcher. Though his family was quite prosperous and he stood to inherit the family business, he was in no way a gentleman, and Kitty had vowed never to let her affections overwhelm her sense.

But, upon their recent return to Pemberley, she had encountered Robert on her first visit to town, and she had been secretly meeting with him when she went into Matlock on the pretext of shopping. Worse still, the couple had allowed their passion to get the better of them, and Kitty had given way to carnal love.

The two sisters sat on a fallen tree in the woods as Kitty poured out her tale. "I want so much to marry him." Her tears flowed readily. "I do not want to be alone, I don't want to die an old maid! And Lydia—Lydia told me about—about the act of love, how wonderful it was, how good Wickham makes her feel. She boasted of it! And I said, why should vain Lydia have this, and me have nothing, to waste my youth in conversation and embroidery, in listening to Mother prattle and Father throw heavy sighs. Father thinks me a fool, unlikely ever to find a husband. And now he's right!" Kitty burst into wailing again. "He's right! No man shall ever have me!" Her tears ended in a fit of coughing.

"Oh, Kitty," Mary said.

"When Darcy spoke of English maidenhood last night, it was all I could do to keep from bursting into tears. You must get Father to agree to let me marry Robert."

"Has he asked you to marry him?"

"He shall. He must. You don't know how fine a man he is. Despite the fact that he is in trade, he has the gentlest manners. I don't care if he is not well born."

Mary embraced Kitty. Kitty alternated between sobs and fits of coughing. Above them the thunder rumbled, and the wind rustled the trees. Mary felt Kitty's shivering body. She needed to calm her, to get her back to the house. How frail, how slender her sister was.

She did not know what to say. Once Mary would have self-righteously condemned Kitty. But much that Kitty said was the content of her own mind, and Kitty's fear of dying alone was her own fear. As she searched for some answer, Mary heard the sound of a torrent of rain hitting the canopy of foliage above them. "You have been foolish," Mary said, holding her. "But it may not be so bad."

Kitty trembled in her arms, and spoke into Mary's shoulder. "But will you ever care for me again? What if Father should turn me out? What will I do then?"

The rain was falling through now, coming down hard. Mary felt her hair getting soaked. "Calm yourself. Father would do no such thing. I shall never forsake you. Jane would not, nor Lizzy."

"What if I should have a child!"

Mary pulled Kitty's shawl over her head. She looked past Kitty's shoulder to the dark woods. Something moved there. "You shan't have a child."

"You can't know! I may!"

The woods had become dark with the rain. Mary could not make out what lurked there. "Come, let us go back. You must compose yourself. We shall speak with Lizzy and Jane. They will know—"

Just then a flash of lightning lit the forest, and Mary saw, beneath the trees not ten feet from them, the giant figure of a man. The lightning illuminated a face of monstrous ugliness: long, thick, tangled black hair; yellow skin the texture of dried leather; black eyes sunken deep beneath heavy brows. Worst of all, an expression hideous in its cold, inexpressible hunger. All glimpsed in a split second; then the light fell to shadow.

Mary gasped, and pulled Kitty toward her. A great peal of thunder rolled across the sky.

Kitty stopped crying. "What is it?"

"We must go. Now." Mary seized Kitty by the arm. The rain pelted down on them, and the forest path was already turning to mud.

Mary pulled her toward the house, Kitty complaining. Mary could hear nothing over the drumming of the rain. But when she looked over her shoulder, she caught a glimpse of the brutish figure, keeping to the trees, but swiftly, silently moving along behind them.

"Why must we run?" Kitty gasped.

"Because we are being followed!"

"By whom?"

"I don't know!"

Behind them, Mary thought she heard the man croak out some words: "Halt! Bitter!"

They had not reached the edge of the woods when figures appeared ahead of them, coming from Pemberley. "Miss Bennet! Mary! Kitty!"

The figures resolved themselves into Darcy and Mr. Frankenstein. Darcy carried a cloak, which he threw over them. "Are you all right?" Frankenstein asked.

"Thank you!" Mary gasped. "A man. He's there," she pointed, "following us."

Frankenstein took a few steps beyond them down the path.

"Who was it?" Darcy asked.

"Some brute. Hideously ugly," Mary said.

Frankenstein came back. "No one is there."

"We saw him!"

Another lighting flash, and crack of thunder. "It is very dark, and we are in a storm," Frankenstein said.

"Come, we must get you back to the house," Darcy said. "You are wet to the bone."

The men helped them back to Pemberley, trying their best to keep the rain off the sisters.

Darcy went off to find Bingley and Clerval, who had taken the opposite direction in their search. Lizzy saw that Mary and Kitty were made dry and warm. Kitty's cough worsened, and Lizzy insisted she must be put to bed. Mary sat with Kitty, whispered a promise to keep her secret, and waited until she slept. Then she went down to meet the others in the parlor.

"This chill shall do her no good," Jane said. She chided Mary for wandering off in such threatening weather. "I thought you had developed more sense, Mary. Mr. Frankenstein insisted he help to find you, when he realized you had gone out into the woods."

"I am sorry," Mary said. "You are right." She was distracted by Kitty's plight, wondering what she might do. If Kitty were indeed with child, there would be no helping her.

Mary recounted her story of the man in the woods. Darcy said he had seen no one, but allowed that someone might have been there. Frankenstein, rather than engage in the speculation, stood at the tall windows staring across the lawn through the rain toward the tree line.

"This intruder was some local poacher, or perhaps one of those gypsies," said Darcy. "When the rain ends I shall have Mr. Mowbray take some men to check the grounds. We shall also inform the constable."

"I hope this foul weather will induce you to stay with us a few more days, Mr. Frankenstein," Lizzy ventured. "You have no pressing business in Matlock, do you?"

"No. But we were to travel north by the end of this week."

"Surely we might stay a while longer, Victor," said Clerval. "Your research can wait for you in Scotland."

Frankenstein struggled with his answer. "I don't think we should prevail on these good people any more."

"Nonsense," said Darcy. "We are fortunate for your company."

"Thank you," Frankenstein said uncertainly. But when the conversation moved elsewhere, Mary noticed him once again staring out the window. She moved to sit beside him. On an impulse, she said to him, *sotto voce*, "Did you know this man we came upon in the woods?"

"I saw no one. Even if someone was there, how should I know some English vagabond?"

"I do not think he was English. When he called after us, it was in German. Was this one of your countrymen?"

A look of impatience crossed Frankenstein's face, and he lowered his eyes. "Miss Bennet, I do not wish to contradict you, but you are mistaken. I saw no one in the woods."

Kitty developed a fever, and did not leave her bed for the rest of the day. Mary sat with her, trying, without bringing up the subject of Robert Piggot, to quiet her.

It was still raining when Mary retired, to a separate bedroom from the one she normally shared with Kitty. Late that night, Mary was wakened by the opening of her bedroom door. She thought it might be Lizzy to tell her something about Kitty. But it was not Lizzy.

Rather than call out, she watched silently as a dark figure entered and closed the door behind. The remains of her fire threw faint light on the man as he approached her. "Miss Bennet," he called softly.

Her heart was in her throat. "Yes, Mr. Frankenstein."

"Please do not take alarm. I must speak with you." He took two sudden steps toward her bed. His handsome face was agitated. No man, in any circumstances remotely resembling these, had ever broached her bedside. Yet the racing of her heart was not entirely a matter of fear.

"This, sir, is hardly the place for polite conversation," she said. "Following on your denial of what I saw this afternoon, you are fortunate that I do not wake the servants and have you thrown out of Pemberley."

"You are right to chide me. My conscience chides me more than you ever could, and should I be thrown from your family's gracious company it would be less than I deserve. And I am afraid that nothing I have to say to you tonight shall qualify as polite conversation." His manner was greatly changed; there was a sound of desperation in his whisper. He wanted something from her, and he wanted it a great deal.

Curious, despite herself, Mary drew on her robe and lit a candle. She made him sit in one of the chairs by the fire and poked the coals into life. When she had settled herself in the other, she said, "Go on."

"Miss Bennet, please do not toy with me. You know why I am here."

"Know, sir? What do I know?"

He leaned forward, earnestly, hands clasped and elbows on his knees. "I come to beg you to keep silent. The gravest consequences would follow your revealing my secret."

"Silent?"

"About—about the man you saw."

"You *do* know him!"

"Your mockery at dinner convinced me that, after hearing the vicar's story, you suspected. Raising the dead, you said to Clerval—and then your tale of Professor Aldini. Do not deny it."

"I don't pretend to know what you are talking about."

Frankenstein stood from his chair and began to pace the floor before the hearth. "Please! I saw the look of reproach in your eyes when we found you in the forest. I am trying to make right what I put wrong. But I will never be able to do so if you tell." To Mary's astonishment, she saw, in the firelight, that his eyes glistened with tears.

"Tell me what you did."

And with that the story burst out of him. He told her how, after his mother's death, he longed to conquer death itself, how he had studied chemistry at the university, how he had uncovered the secret of life. How, emboldened and driven on by his solitary obsession, he had created a man from the corpses he had stolen from graveyards and purchased from resurrection men. How he had succeeded, through his science, in bestowing it with life.

Mary did not know what to say to this astonishing tale. It was the raving of a lunatic—but there was the man she had seen in the woods. And the earnestness with which Frankenstein spoke, his tears and desperate whispers, gave every proof that, at least in his mind, he had done these things. He told of his revulsion at his accomplishment, how he had abandoned the creature, hoping it would die, and how the creature had, in revenge, killed his brother William and caused his family's ward Justine to be blamed for the crime.

"But why did you not intervene in Justine's trial?"

"No one should have believed me."

"Yet I am to believe you now?"

Frankenstein's voice was choked. "You have seen the brute. You know that these things are possible. Lives are at stake. I come to you in remorse and penitence, asking only that you keep this secret." He fell to his knees, threw his head into her lap, and clutched at the sides of her gown.

Frankenstein was wholly mistaken in what she knew; he was a man who did not see things clearly. Yet if his story were true, it was no wonder that his judgment was disordered. And here he lay, trembling against her, a boy seeking forgiveness. No man had ever come to her in such need.

She tried to keep her senses. "Certainly the creature I saw was frightening, but to my eyes he appeared more wretched than menacing."

Frankenstein lifted his head. "Here I must warn you—his wretchedness is mere mask. Do not let your sympathy for him cause you ever to trust his nature. He is the vilest creature that has ever walked this earth. He has no soul."

"Why then not invoke the authorities, catch him, and bring him to justice?"

"He cannot be so easily caught. He is inhumanly strong, resourceful, and intelligent. If you should ever be so unlucky as to speak with him, I warn you not to listen to what he says, for he is immensely articulate and satanically persuasive."

"All the more reason to see him apprehended!"

"I am convinced that he can be dealt with only by myself." Frankenstein's eyes pleaded with her. "Miss Bennet—Mary—you must understand. He is in some ways my son. I gave him life. His mind is fixed on me."

"And, it seems, yours on him."

Frankenstein looked surprised. "Do you wonder that is so?"

"Why does he follow you? Does he intend you harm?"

"He has vowed to glut the maw of death with my remaining loved ones, unless I make him happy." He rested his head again in her lap.

Mary was touched, scandalized, and in some obscure way aroused. She felt his trembling body, instinct with life. Tentatively, she rested her hand on his head. She stroked his hair. He was weeping. She realized that he was a physical being, a living animal, that would eventually, too soon, die. And all that was true of him was true of herself. How strange, frightening, and sad. Yet in this moment she felt herself wonderfully alive.

"I'll keep your secret," she said.

He hugged her skirts. In the candle's light, she noted the way his thick, dark hair curled away from his brow.

"I cannot tell you," he said softly, "what a relief it is to share my burden with another soul, and to have her accept me. I have been so completely alone. I cannot thank you enough."

He rose, kissed her forehead, and was gone.

Mary paced her room, trying to grasp what had just happened. A man who had conquered death? A monster created from corpses?

Such things did not happen, certainly not in her world, not even in the world of the novels she read. She climbed into bed and tried to sleep, but could not. The creature had vowed to kill all whom Frankenstein loved. Mary remembered the weight of his head upon her lap.

The room felt stiflingly hot. She got up, stripped off her nightgown, and climbed back between the sheets, where she lay naked, listening to the rain on the window.

———— ❦ ————

Kitty's fever worsened in the night, and before dawn Darcy sent to Lambton for the doctor. Lizzy dispatched an urgent letter to Mr. and Mrs. Bennet, and the sisters sat by Kitty's bedside through the morning, changing cold compresses from her brow while Kitty labored to breathe.

When Mary left the sick room, Frankenstein approached her. His desperation of the previous night was gone. "How fares your sister?"

"I fear she is gravely ill."

"She is in some danger?"

Mary could only nod.

He touched her shoulder, lowered his voice. "I will pray for her, Miss Bennet. I cannot thank you enough for the sympathy you showed me last night. I have never told anyone—"

Just then Clerval approached them. He greeted Mary, inquired after Kitty's condition, then suggested to Frankenstein that they return to their hotel in Matlock rather than add any burden to the household and family. Frankenstein agreed. Before Mary could say another word to him in private, the visitors were gone.

Doctor Phillips arrived soon after Clerval and Frankenstein left. He measured Kitty's pulse, felt her forehead, examined her urine. He administered some medicines, and came away shaking his head. Should the fever continue, he said, they must bleed her.

Given how much thought she had spent on Frankenstein through the night, and how little she had devoted to Kitty, Mary's conscience tormented her. She spent the day in her sister's room. That night, after Jane had retired and Lizzy fallen asleep in her chair, she still sat up, holding Kitty's fevered hand. She had matters to consider. Was Kitty indeed with child, and if so, should she tell the doctor? Yet even as she sat by Kitty's bedside, Mary's mind cast back to the feeling of Frankenstein's lips on her forehead.

In the middle of the night, Kitty woke, bringing Mary from her doze. Kitty tried to lift her head from the pillow, but could not. "Mary," she whispered. "You must send for Robert. We must be married immediately."

Mary looked across the room at Lizzy. She was still asleep.

"Promise me," Kitty said. Her eyes were large and dark.

"I promise," Mary said.

"Prepare my wedding dress," Kitty said. "But don't tell Lizzy."

Lizzy awoke then. She came to the bedside and felt Kitty's forehead. "She's burning up. Get Dr. Phillips."

Mary sought out the doctor, and then, while he went to Kitty's room, pondered what to do. Kitty clearly was not in her right mind. Her request ran contrary to both sense and propriety. If Mary sent one of the footmen to Matlock for Robert, even if she swore her messenger to silence, the matter would soon be the talk of the servants, and probably the town.

It was the sort of dilemma that Mary would have had no trouble settling, to everyone's moral edification, when she was sixteen. She hurried to her room and took out paper and pen:

> I write to inform you that one you love, residing at Pemberley House, is gravely ill. She urgently requests your presence. Simple human kindness, which from her description of you I do not doubt you possess, let alone the duty incumbent upon you owing to the compact that you have made with her through your actions, assure me that we shall see you here before the night is through.
>
> —Miss Mary Bennet

She sealed the letter and sought out one of the footmen, whom she dispatched immediately with the instruction to put the letter into the hand of Robert Piggot, son of the Matlock butcher.

Dr. Phillips bled Kitty, with no improvement. She did not regain consciousness through the night. Mary waited. The footman returned, alone, at six in the morning. He assured Mary that he had ridden to the Piggot home and given the letter directly to Robert. Mary thanked him.

Robert did not come. At eight in the morning Darcy sent for the priest. At nine-thirty Kitty died.

———— ❧ ————

On the evening of the day of Kitty's passing, Mr. and Mrs. Bennet arrived, and a day later Lydia and Wickham—it was the first time Darcy had allowed Wickham to cross the threshold of Pemberley since they had become brothers by marriage. In the midst of her mourning family, Mary felt lost. Jane and Lizzy supported each other in their grief. Darcy and Bingley exchanged quiet, sober conversation. Wickham and Lydia, who had grown fat with her three children, could not pass a word between them without sniping, but in their folly they were completely united.

Mrs. Bennet was beyond consoling, and the volume and intensity of her mourning was exceeded only by the degree to which she sought to control every detail of Kitty's funeral. There ensued a long debate over where Kitty should be buried. When it was pointed out that their cousin Mr. Collins would eventually inherit the house back in Hertfordshire, Mrs. Bennet fell into despair: who, when she was gone, would tend to her poor Kitty's grave? Mr. Bennet suggested that Kitty be laid to rest in the churchyard at Lambton, a short distance from Pemberley, where she might also be visited by Jane and Bingley. But when Mr. Darcy offered the family vault at Pemberley, the matter was quickly settled to the satisfaction of both tender hearts and vanity.

Though it was no surprise to Mary, it was still a burden for her to witness that even in the gravest passage of their lives, her sisters and parents showed themselves to be exactly what they were. And yet, paradoxically, this did not harden her heart toward them. The family was together as they had not been for many years, and she realized that they should never be in the future except on the occasion of further losses. Her father was grayer and quieter than she had ever seen him, and on the day of the funeral even her mother put aside her sobbing and exclamations long enough to show a face of profound grief, and a burden of age that Mary had never before noticed.

The night after Kitty was laid to rest, Mary sat up late with Jane and Lizzy and Lydia. They drank Madeira and Lydia told many silly stories of the days she and Kitty had spent in flirtations with the regiment. Mary climbed into her bed late that night, her head swimming with wine, laughter, and tears. She lay awake, the moonlight shining on the counterpane through the opened window, air carrying the smell of fresh earth and the rustle of trees above the lake. She drifted into a dreamless sleep. At some point in the night she was half awakened by the barking of the dogs in the kennel. But consciousness soon faded and she fell away.

In the morning it was discovered that the vault had been broken into and Kitty's body stolen from her grave.

———— ⌁ ————

Mary told the stable master that Mrs. Bennet had asked her to go to the apothecary in Lambton, and had him prepare the gig for her. Then, while the house was in turmoil and Mrs. Bennet being attended by the rest of the family, she drove off to Matlock. The master had given her the best horse in Darcy's stable; the creature was equable and quick, and despite her inexperience driving, Mary was able to reach Matlock in an hour. All the time, despite the splendid summer morning and the picturesque prospects which the valley of the Derwent continually unfolded before her, she could not keep her mind from whirling through a series of distressing images—among them the sight of Frankenstein's creature as she had seen him in the woods.

When she reached Matlock she hurried to the Old Bath Hotel and inquired after Frankenstein. The concierge told her that he had not seen Mr. Frankenstein since dinner the previous evening, but that Mr. Clerval had told him that morning that the gentlemen would leave Matlock later that day. She left a note asking Frankenstein, should he return, to meet her at the inn, then went to the butcher shop.

Mary had been there once before, with Lizzy, some years earlier. The shop was busy with servants purchasing joints of mutton and ham for the evening meal. Behind the counter Mr. Piggot senior was busy at his cutting board, but helping one of the women with a package was a tall young man with thick brown curls and green eyes. He flirted with the house servant as he shouldered her purchase, wrapped in brown paper, onto her cart.

On the way back into the shop, he spotted Mary standing unattended. He studied her for a moment before approaching. "May I help you, miss?"

"I believe you knew my sister."

His grin vanished. "You are Miss Mary Bennet."

"I am."

The young man studied his boots. "I am so sorry what happened to Miss Catherine."

Not so sorry as to bring you to her bedside before she died, Mary thought. She bit back a reproach and said, "We did not see you at the service. I thought perhaps the nature of your relationship might have encouraged you to grieve in private, at her graveside. Have you been there?"

He looked even more uncomfortable. "No. I had to work. My father—"

Mary had seen enough already to measure his depth. He was not a man to defile a grave, in grief or otherwise. The distance between this small-town lothario—handsome, careless, insensitive—and the hero Kitty had praised, only deepened Mary's compassion for her lost sister. How desperate she must have been. How pathetic.

As Robert Piggot continued to stumble through his explanation, Mary turned and departed.

She went back to the inn where she had left the gig. The barkeep led her into a small ladies' parlor separated from the tap room by a glass partition. She ordered tea, and through a latticed window watched the people come and go in the street and courtyard, the draymen with their Percherons and carts, the passengers waiting for the next van to Manchester, and inside, the idlers sitting at tables with pints of ale. In the sunlit street a young bootblack accosted travelers, most of whom ignored him. All of these people alive, completely unaware of Mary or her lost sister. Mary ought to be back with their mother, though the thought turned her heart cold. How could Kitty have left her alone? She felt herself near despair.

She was watching through the window as two draymen struggled to load a large square trunk onto their cart when the man directing them came from around the team of horses, and she saw it was Frankenstein. She rose immediately and went out into the inn yard. She was at his shoulder before he noticed her. "Miss Bennet!"

"Mr. Frankenstein. I am so glad that I found you. I feared that you had already left Matlock. May we speak somewhere in private?"

He looked momentarily discommoded. "Yes, of course," he said. To the draymen he said. "When you've finished loading my equipment, wait here."

"This is not a good place to converse," Frankenstein told her. "I saw a churchyard nearby. Let us retire there."

He walked Mary down the street to the St. Giles Churchyard. They walked through the rectory garden. In the distance, beams of afternoon sunlight shone through a cathedral of clouds above the Heights of Abraham. "Do you know what has happened?" she asked.

"I have heard reports, quite awful, of the death of your sister. I intended to write you, conveying my condolences, at my earliest opportunity. You have my deepest sympathies."

"Your creature! That monster you created—"

"I asked you to keep him a secret."

"I have kept my promise—so far. But it has stolen Kitty's body."

He stood there, hands behind his back, clear eyes fixed on her. "You find me astonished. What draws you to this extraordinary conclusion?"

She was hurt by his diffidence. Was this the same man who had wept in her bedroom? "Who else might do such a thing?"

"But why? This creature's enmity is reserved for me alone. Others feel its ire only to the extent that they are dear to me."

"You came to plead with me that night because you feared I knew he was responsible for defiling that town girl's grave. Why was he watching Kitty and me in the forest? Surely this is no coincidence."

"If, indeed, the creature has stolen your sister's body, it can be for no reason I can fathom, or that any God-fearing person ought to pursue. You know I am determined to see this monster banished from the world of men. You may rest assured that I will not cease until I have seen this accomplished. It is best for you and your family to turn your thoughts to other matters." He touched a strand of ivy growing up the side of the garden wall, and plucked off a green leaf, which he twirled in his fingers.

She could not understand him. She knew him to be a man of sensibility, to have a heart capable of feeling. His denials opened a possibility that she had tried to keep herself from considering. "Sir, I am not satisfied. It seems to me that you are keeping something from me. You told me of the great grief you felt at the loss of your mother, how it moved you to your researches. If, as you say, you have uncovered the secret of life, might you—have you taken it upon yourself to restore Kitty? Perhaps a fear of failure, or of the horror that many would feel at your trespassing against God's will, underlies your secrecy. If so, please do not keep the truth from me. I am not a girl."

He let the leaf fall from his fingers. He took her shoulders, and looked directly into her eyes. "I am sorry, Mary. To restore your sister is not in my power. The soulless creature I brought to life bears no relation to the man from whose body I fashioned him. Your sister has gone on to her reward. Nothing—nothing I can do would bring her back."

"So you know nothing about the theft of her corpse?"

"On that score, I can offer no consolation to you or your family."

"My mother, my father—they are inconsolable."

"Then they must content themselves with memories of your sister as she lived. As I must do with my dear, lost brother William, and the traduced and dishonored Justine. Come, let us go back to the inn."

Mary burst into tears. He held her to him and she wept on his breast. Eventually she gathered herself and allowed him to take her arm, and they slowly walked back down to the main street of Matlock and the inn. She knew that when they reached it, Frankenstein would go. The warmth of his hand on hers almost made her beg him to stay, or better still, to take her with him.

They came to the busy courtyard. The dray stood off to the side, and Mary saw the cartmen were in the taproom. Frankenstein, agitated, upbraided them. "I thought I told you to keep those trunks out of the sun."

The older of the two men put down his pint and stood, "Sorry, Gov'nor. We'll see to it directly."

"Do so now."

As Frankenstein spoke the evening coach drew up before the inn and prepared for departure. "You and Mr. Clerval leave today?" Mary asked.

"Yes. As soon as Henry arrives from the Old Bath, we take the coach to the Lake District. And thence to Scotland."

"They say it is very beautiful there."

"I am afraid that its beauty will be lost on me. I carry the burden of my great crime, not to be laid down until I have made things right."

She felt that she would burst if she did not speak her heart to him. "Victor. Will I ever see you again?"

He avoided her gaze. "I am afraid, Miss Bennet, that this is unlikely. My mind is set on banishing that vile creature from the world of men. Only then can I hope to return home and marry my betrothed Elizabeth."

Mary looked away from him. A young mother was adjusting her son's collar before putting him on the coach. "Ah, yes. You are affianced. I had almost forgotten."

Frankenstein pressed her hand. "Miss Bennet, you must forgive me the liberties I have taken with you. You have given me more of friendship than I deserve. I wish you to find the companion you seek, and to live your days in happiness. But now, I must go."

"God be with you, Mr. Frankenstein." She twisted her gloved fingers into a knot.

He bowed deeply, and hurried to have a few more words with the draymen. Henry Clerval arrived just as the men climbed to their cart and drove the baggage away. Clerval, surprised at seeing Mary, greeted her warmly. He expressed his great sorrow at the loss of her sister, and begged her to convey his condolences to the rest of her family. Ten minutes later the two men climbed aboard the coach and it left the inn, disappearing down the Matlock high street.

Mary stood in the inn yard. She did not feel she could bear to go back to Pemberley and face her family, the histrionics of her mother. Instead she re-entered the inn and made the barkeep seat her in the ladies' parlor and bring her a bottle of port.

———✥———

The sun declined and shadows stretched over the inn yard. The evening papers arrived from Nottingham. The yard boy lit the lamps.

Still, Mary would not leave. Outside on the pavements, the bootblack sat in the growing darkness with his arms draped over his knees and head on his breast. She listened to the hoofs of the occasional horse striking the cobbles. The innkeeper was solicitous. When she asked for a second bottle, he hesitated, and wondered if he might send for someone from her family to take her home.

"You do not know my family," she said.

"Yes, miss. I only thought—"

"Another port. Then leave me alone."

"Yes, Miss." He went away. She was determined to become intoxicated. How many times had she piously warned against young women behaving as she did now? *Virtue is her own reward.* She had an apothegm for every occasion, and had tediously produced them in place of thought. *Show me a liar, and I'll show thee a thief. Marry in haste, repent at leisure. Men should be what they seem.*

She did not fool herself into thinking that her current misbehavior would make any difference. Perhaps Bingley or Darcy had been dispatched to find her in Lambton. But within an hour or two she would return to Pemberley, where her mother would scold her for giving them an anxious evening, and Lizzy would caution her about the risk to her reputation. Lydia might even ask her, not believing it possible, if she had an assignation with some man. The loss of Kitty would overshadow Mary's indiscretion, pitiful as it had been. Soon all would be as it had been, except Mary would be alive and Kitty dead. But even that would fade. The shadow of Kitty's death would hang over the family for some time, but she doubted that anything of significance would change.

As she lingered over her glass, she looked up and noticed, in the now empty taproom, a man sitting at the table farthest from the lamps. A huge man, wearing rough clothes, his face hooded and in shadow. Mary rose, left the parlor for the taproom, and crossed toward him. On the table in front of him was a tankard of ale and a few coppers.

He looked up, and the faint light from the ceiling lamp caught his black eyes, sunken beneath heavy brows. He was hideously ugly. "May I sit with you?" she asked. She felt slightly dizzy.

"You may sit where you wish." The voice was deep, but swallowed, unable to project. It was almost a whisper.

Trembling only slightly, she sat. His wrists and hands, resting on the table, stuck out past the ragged sleeves of his coat. His skin was yellowish brown, and the fingernails livid white. He did not move. "You have some business with me?"

"I have the most appalling business." Mary tried to look him in the eyes, but her gaze kept slipping. "I want to know why you defiled my sister's grave, why you have stolen her body, and what you have done with her."

"Better you should ask Victor. Did he not explain all to you?"

"Mr. Frankenstein explained who—what—you are. He did not know what had become of my sister."

The thin lips twitched in a sardonic smile. "Poor Victor. He has got things all topsy-turvy. Victor does not know what I am. He is incapable of knowing, no matter the labors I have undertaken to school him. But he does know what became, and is to become, of your sister." The creature tucked the thick black hair behind his ear, a sudden unconscious gesture that made him seem completely human for the first time. He pulled the hood further forward to hide his face.

"So tell me."

"Which answer do you want? Who I am, or what happened to your sister?"

"First, tell me what happened to—to Kitty."

"Victor broke into the vault and stole her away. He took the utmost care not to damage her. He washed her fair body in diluted carbolic acid, and replaced her blood with a chemical admixture of his own devising. Folded up, she fit neatly within a cedar trunk sealed with pitch, and is at present being shipped to Scotland. You witnessed her departure from this courtyard an hour ago."

Mary's senses rebelled. She covered her face with her hands. The creature sat silent. Finally, without raising her head, she managed, "Victor warned me that you were a liar. Why should I believe you?"

"You have no reason to believe me."

"*You* took her!"

"Though I would not have scrupled to do so, I did not. Miss Bennet, I do not deny I have an interest in this matter. Victor did as I have told you at my bidding."

"At your bidding? Why?"

"Kitty—or not so much Kitty, as her remains—is to become my wife."

"Your wife! This is insupportable! Monstrous!"

"Monstrous." Suddenly, with preternatural quickness, his hand flashed out and grabbed Mary's wrist.

Mary thought to call for help, but the bar was empty and she had driven the innkeeper away. Yet his grip was not harsh. His hand was warm, instinct with life. "Look at me," he said. With his other hand he pushed back his hood.

She took a deep breath. She looked.

His noble forehead, high cheekbones, strong chin, and wide-set eyes might have made him handsome, despite the scars and dry yellow skin, were it not for his expression. His ugliness was not a matter of lack of proportion—or rather, the lack of proportion was not in his features. Like his swallowed voice, his face was submerged, as if everything was hidden, revealed only in the eyes, the twitch of a cheek or lip. Every minute motion showed extraordinary animation. Hectic sickliness, but energy. This was a creature who had never learned to associate with civilized company, who had been thrust into adulthood with the passions of a wounded boy. Fear, self-disgust, anger. Desire.

The force of longing and rage in that face made her shrink. "Let me go," she whispered.

He let go her wrist. With bitter satisfaction, he said, "You see. If what I demand is insupportable, that is only because your kind has done nothing to support me. Once, I falsely hoped to meet with beings, who, pardoning my outward form, would love me for the excellent qualities which I was capable of bringing forth. Now I am completely alone. More than any starving man on a deserted isle, I am cast away. I have no brother, sister, parents. I have only Victor who, like so many fathers, recoiled from me the moment I first drew breath. And so, I have commanded him to make of your sister my wife, or he and all he loves will die at my hand."

"No. I cannot believe he would commit this abomination."

"He has no choice. He is my slave."

"His conscience could not support it, even at the cost of his life."

"You give him too much credit. You all do. He does not think. I have not seen him act other than according to impulse for the last three years. That is all I see in any of you."

Mary drew back, trying to make some sense of this horror. Her sister, to be brought to life, only to be given to this fiend. But would it be her sister, or another agitated, hungry thing like this?

She still retained some scraps of skepticism. The creature's manner did not bespeak the isolation which he claimed. "I am astonished at your grasp of language," Mary said. "You could not know so much without teachers."

"Oh, I have had many teachers." The creature's mutter was rueful. "You might say that, since first my eyes opened, mankind has been all my study. I have much yet to learn. There are certain words whose meaning has never been proved to me by experience. For example: *Happy.* Victor is to make me happy. Do you think he can do it?"

Mary thought of Frankenstein. Could he satisfy this creature? "I do not think it is in the power of any other person to make one happy."

"You jest with me. Every creature has its mate, save me. I have none."

She recoiled at his self-pity. Her fear faded. "You put too much upon having a mate."

"Why? You know nothing of what I have endured."

"You think that having a female of your own kind will ensure that she will accept you?" Mary laughed. "Wait until you are rejected, for the most trivial of reasons, by one you are sure has been made for you."

A shadow crossed the creature's face. "That will not happen."

"It happens more often than not."

"The female that Victor creates shall find no other mate than me."

"That has never prevented rejection. Or if you should be accepted, then you may truly begin to learn."

"Learn what?"

"You will learn to ask a new question: Which is worse, to be alone, or to be wretchedly mismatched?" Like Lydia and Wickham, Mary thought. Like Collins and his poor wife Charlotte. Like her parents.

The creature's face spasmed with conflicting emotions. His voice gained volume. "Do not sport with me. I am not your toy."

"No. You only seek a toy of your own."

The creature was not, apparently, accustomed to mockery. "You must not say these things!" He lurched upward, awkwardly, so suddenly that he upended the table. The tankard of beer skidded across the top and spilled on Mary, and she fell back.

At that moment the innkeeper entered the barroom with two other men. They saw the tableau and rushed forward. "Here! Let her be!" he shouted. One of the other men grabbed the creature by the arm. With a roar the creature flung him aside like an old coat. His hood fell back. The men stared in horror at his face. The creature's eyes met Mary's, and with inhuman speed he whirled and ran out the door.

The men gathered themselves together. The one whom the creature had thrown aside had a broken arm. The innkeeper helped Mary to her feet. "Are you all right, miss?"

Mary felt dizzy. Was she all right? What did that mean?

"I believe so," she said.

When Mary returned to Pemberley, late that night, she found the house in an uproar over her absence. Bingley and Darcy both had been to Lambton, and had searched the road and the woods along it throughout the afternoon and evening. Mrs. Bennet had taken to bed with the conviction that she had lost two daughters in a single week. Wickham condemned Mary's poor judgment, Lydia sprang to Mary's defense, and this soon became a row over Wickham's lack of an income and Lydia's mismanagement of their children. Mr. Bennett closed himself up in the library.

Mary told them only that she had been to Matlock. She offered no explanation, no apology. Around the town the story of her conflict with the strange giant in the inn was spoken of for some time, along with rumors of Robert Piggot the butcher's son, and the mystery of Kitty's defiled grave—but as Mary was not a local, and nothing of consequence followed, the talk soon passed away.

That winter, Mary came upon the following story in the Nottingham newspaper.

GHASTLY EVENTS IN SCOTLAND

Our northern correspondent files the following report.
In early November, the body of a young foreigner, Mr. Henry Clerval of Geneva, Switzerland, was found

upon the beach near the far northern town of Thurso. The body, still warm, bore marks of strangulation. A second foreigner, Mr. Victor Frankstone, was taken into custody, charged with the murder, and held for two months. Upon investigation, the magistrate Mr. Kirwan determined that Mr. Frankstone was in the Orkney Islands at the time of the killing. The accused was released in the custody of his father, and is assumed to have returned to his home on the continent.

A month after the disposition of these matters, a basket, weighted with stones and containing the body of a young woman, washed up in the estuary of the River Thurso. The identity of the woman is unknown, and her murderer undiscovered, but it is speculated that the unfortunate may have died at the hands of the same person or persons who murdered Mr. Clerval. The woman was given Christian burial in the Thurso Presbyterian churchyard.

The village has been shaken by these events, and prays God to deliver it from evil.

Oh, Victor, Mary thought. She remembered the pressure of his hand, through her dressing gown, upon her thigh. Now he had returned to Switzerland, there, presumably, to marry his Elizabeth. She hoped that he would be more honest with his wife than he had been with her, but the fate of Clerval did not bode well. And the creature still had no mate.

She clipped the newspaper report and slipped it into the drawer of her writing table, where she kept her copy of Samuel Galton's *The Natural History of Birds, Intended for the Amusement and Instruction of Children*, and the *Juvenile Anecdotes* of Priscilla Wakefield, and a Dudley locust made of stone, and a paper fan from the first ball she had ever attended, and a dried wreath of flowers that had been thrown to her, when she was nine years old, from the top of a tree by one of the town boys playing near Meryton common.

After the death of her parents, Mary lived with Lizzy and Darcy at Pemberley for the remainder of her days. Under a pen name, she pursued a career as a writer of philosophical speculations, and sent many letters to the London newspapers. Aunt Mary, as she was called at home, was known for her kindness to William, and to his wife and children. The children teased Mary for her nearsightedness, her books, and her piano. But for a woman whose experience of the world was so slender, and whose soul it seemed had never been touched by any passion, she came at last to be respected for her understanding, her self possession, and her wise counsel on matters of the heart.

THE *NEW YORK TIMES* AT SPECIAL BARGAIN RATES

by Stephen King from *Fantasy & Science Fiction*

She's fresh out of the shower when the phone begins to ring, but although the house is still full of relatives—she can hear them downstairs, it seems they will never go away, it seems she never had so many—no one picks up. Nor does the answering machine, as James programmed it to do after the fifth ring.

Anne goes to the extension on the bed-table, wrapping a towel around herself, her wet hair thwacking unpleasantly on the back of her neck and bare shoulders. She picks it up, she says hello, and then he says her name. It's James. They had thirty years together, and one word is all she needs. He says *Annie* like no one else, always did.

For a moment she can't speak or even breathe. He has caught her on the exhale and her lungs feel as flat as sheets of paper. Then, as he says her name again (sounding uncharacteristically hesitant and unsure of himself), the strength slips from her legs. They turn to sand and she sits on the bed, the towel falling off her, her wet bottom dampening the sheet beneath her. If the bed hadn't been there, she would have gone to the floor.

Her teeth click together and that starts her breathing again.

"James? Where *are* you? *What happened?*" In her normal voice, this might have come out sounding shrewish—a mother scolding her wayward eleven-year-old who's come late to the supper-table yet again—but now it emerges in a kind of horrified growl. The murmuring relatives below her are, after all, planning his funeral.

James chuckles. It is a bewildered sound. "Well, I tell you what," he says. "I don't exactly know where I am."

Her first confused thought is that he must have missed the plane in London, even though he called her from Heathrow not long before it took off. Then a clearer idea comes: although both the *Times* and the TV news say there were no survivors, there was at least one. Her husband crawled from the wreckage of the burning plane (and the burning apartment building the plane hit, don't forget that, twenty-four more dead on the ground and the number apt to rise before the world moved on to the next tragedy) and has been wandering around Brooklyn ever since, in a state of shock.

"Jimmy, are you all right? Are you . . . are you burned?" The truth of what that would mean occurs after the question, thumping down with the heavy weight of a dropped book on a bare foot, and she begins to cry. "Are you in the hospital?"

"Hush," he says, and at his old kindness—and at that old word, just one small piece of their marriage's furniture—she begins to cry harder. "Honey, hush."

"But I don't *understand!*"

"I'm all right," he says. "Most of us are."

"Most—? There are *others?*"

"Not the pilot," he says. "He's not so good. Or maybe it's the co-pilot. He keeps screaming, 'We're going down, there's no power, oh my God.' Also 'This isn't my fault, don't let them blame it on me.' He says that, too."

She's cold all over. "Who is this really? Why are you being so horrible? I just lost my husband, you asshole!"

"Honey—"

"Don't call me that!" There's a clear strand of mucus hanging from one of her nostrils. She wipes it away with the back of her hand and then flings it into the wherever, a thing she hasn't done since she was a child. "Listen, mister — I'm going to star-sixty-nine this call and the police will come and slam your ass . . . your ignorant, unfeeling *ass.* . . ."

But she can go no further. It's his voice. There's no denying it. The way the call rang right through—no pick-up downstairs, no answering machine—suggests this call was just for her. And . . . *honey, hush.* Like in the old Carl Perkins song.

He has remained quiet, as if letting her work these things through for herself. But before she can speak again, there's a beep on the line.

"James? *Jimmy?* Are you still there?"

"Yeah, but I can't talk long. I was trying to call you when we went down, and I guess that's the only reason I was able to get through at all. Lots of others have been trying, we're lousy with cell phones, but no luck." That beep again. "Only now my phone's almost out of juice."

"Jimmy, did you know?" This idea has been the hardest and most terrible part for her—that he might have known, if only for an endless minute or two. Others might picture burned bodies or dismembered heads with grinning teeth; even light-fingered first responders filching wedding rings and diamond ear-clips, but what has robbed Annie Driscoll's sleep is the image of Jimmy looking out his window as the streets and cars and the brown apartment buildings of Brooklyn swell closer. The useless masks flopping down like the corpses of small yellow animals. The overhead bins popping open, carry-ons starting to fly, someone's Norelco razor rolling up the tilted aisle.

"Did you know you were going down?"

"Not really," he says. "Everything seemed all right until the very end—maybe the last thirty seconds. Although it's hard to keep track of time in situations like that, I always think."

Situations like that. And even more telling: *I always think.* As if he has been aboard half a dozen crashing 767s instead of just the one.

"In any case," he goes on, "I was just calling to say we'd be early, so be sure to get the FedEx man out of bed before I got there."

Her absurd attraction for the FedEx man has been a joke between them for years. She begins to cry again. His cell utters another of those beeps, as if scolding her for it.

"I think I died just a second or two before it rang the first time. I think that's why I was able to get through to you. But this thing's gonna give up the ghost pretty soon."

He chuckles as if this is funny. She supposes that in a way it is. She may see the humor in it herself, eventually. *Give me ten years or so,* she thinks.

Then, in that just-talking-to-myself voice she knows so well: "Why didn't I put the tiresome motherfucker on charge last night? Just forgot, that's all. Just forgot."

"James . . . honey . . . the plane crashed two days ago."

A pause. Mercifully with no beep to fill it. Then: "Really? Mrs. Corey *said* time was funny here. Some of us agreed, some of us disagreed. I was a disagreer, but looks like she was right."

"Hearts?" Annie asks. She feels now as if she is floating outside and slightly above her plump damp middle-aged body, but she hasn't forgotten Jimmy's old habits. On a long flight he was always looking for a game. Cribbage or canasta would do, but hearts was his true love.

"Hearts," he agrees. The phone beeps, as if seconding that.

"Jimmy . . ." She hesitates long enough to ask herself if this is information she really wants, then plunges with that question still unanswered. "Where *are* you, exactly?"

"Looks like Grand Central Station," he says. "Only bigger. And emptier. As if it wasn't really Grand Central at all but only . . . mmm . . . a movie set of Grand Central. Do you know what I'm trying to say?"

"I . . . I think so . . ."

"There certainly aren't any trains . . . and we can't hear any in the distance . . . but there are doors going everywhere. Oh, and there's an escalator, but it's broken. All dusty, and some of the treads are gone." He pauses, and when he speaks again he does so in a lower voice, as if afraid of being overheard. "People are leaving. Some climbed the escalator—I saw them—but most are using the doors. I guess I'll have to leave, too. For one thing, there's nothing to eat. There's a candy machine, but that's broken, too."

"Are you . . . honey, are you hungry?"

"A little. Mostly what I'd like is some water. I'd *kill* for a cold bottle of Dasani."

Annie looks guiltily down at her own legs, still beaded with water. She imagines him licking off those beads and is horrified to feel a sexual stirring.

"I'm all right, though," he adds hastily. "For now, anyway. But there's no sense staying here. Only . . ."

"What? What, Jimmy?"

"I don't know which door to use."

Another beep.

"I wish I knew which one Mrs. Corey took. She's got my damn cards."

"Are you . . ." She wipes her face with the towel she wore out of the shower; then she was fresh, now she's all tears and snot. "Are you scared?"

"Scared?" he asks thoughtfully. "No. A little worried, that's all. Mostly about which door to use."

Find your way home, she almost says. *Find the right door and find your way home.* But if he did, would she want to see him? A ghost might be all right, but what if she opened the door on a smoking cinder with red eyes and the remains of jeans (he always traveled in jeans) melted into his legs? And what if Mrs. Corey was with him, his baked deck of cards in one twisted hand?

Beep.

"I don't need to tell you to be careful about the FedEx man anymore," he says. "If you really want him, he's all yours."

She shocks herself by laughing.

"But I did want to say I love you—"

"Oh honey I love you t—"

"—and not to let the McCormack kid do the gutters this fall, he works hard but he's a risk-taker, last year he almost broke his fucking neck. And don't go to the bakery anymore on Sundays. Something's going to happen there, and I know it's going to be on a Sunday, but I don't know which Sunday. Time really *is* funny here."

The McCormack kid he's talking about must be the son of the guy who used to be their caretaker in Vermont . . . only they sold that place ten years ago, and the kid must be in his mid-twenties by now. And the bakery? She supposes he's talking about Zoltan's, but what on *Earth*—

Beep.

"Some of the people here were on the ground, I guess. That's very tough, because they don't have a clue how they got here. And the pilot keeps screaming. Or maybe it's the co-pilot. I think he's going to be here for quite a while. He just wanders around. He's very confused."

The beeps are coming closer together now.

"I have to go, Annie. I can't stay here, and the phone's going to shit the bed any second now, anyway." Once more in that I'm-scolding-myself voice (impossible to believe she will never hear it again after today; impossible *not* to believe), he mutters, "It would have been so simple just to . . . well, never mind. I love you, sweetheart."

"Wait! Don't go!"

"I c—"

"I love you, too! Don't go!"

But he already has. In her ear there is only black silence.

She sits there with the dead phone to her ear for a minute or more, then breaks the connection. The non-connection. When she opens the line again and gets a perfectly normal dial tone, she touches star-sixty-nine after all. According to the robot who answers her page, the last incoming call was at nine o'clock that morning. She knows who that one was: her sister Nell, calling from New Mexico. Nell called to tell Annie that her plane had been delayed and she wouldn't be in until tonight. Nell told her to be strong.

All the relatives who live at a distance—James's, Annie's—flew in. Apparently they feel that James used up all the family's Destruction Points, at least for the time being.

There is no record of an incoming call at—she glances at the bedside clock and sees it's now 3:17 P.M.—at about ten past three, on the third afternoon of her widowhood.

Someone raps briefly on the door and her brother calls, "Anne? Annie?"

"Dressing!" she calls back. Her voice sounds like she's been crying, but unfortunately, no one in this house would find that strange. "Privacy, please!"

"You okay?" he calls through the door. "We thought we heard you talking. And Ellie thought she heard you call out."

"Fine!" she calls, then wipes her face again with the towel. "Down in a few!"

"Okay. Take your time." Pause. "We're here for you." Then he clumps away.

"Beep," she whispers, then covers her mouth to hold in laughter that is some emotion even more complicated than grief trying to find the only way out it has. "Beep, beep. Beep, beep, beep." She lies back on the bed, laughing, and above her cupped hands her eyes are large and awash with tears that overspill down her cheeks and run all the way to her ears. "Beep-fucking-beepity-beep."

She laughs for quite a while, then dresses and goes downstairs to be with her relatives, who have come to mingle their grief with hers. Only they feel apart from her, because he didn't call any of them. He called her. For better or worse, he called her.

———————⪦⪧———————

During the autumn of that year, with the blackened remains of the apartment building the jet crashed into still closed off from the rest of the world by yellow police tape (although the taggers have been inside, one leaving a spray-painted message reading CRISPY CRITTERS LAND HERE), Annie receives the sort of e-blast computer-addicts like to send to a wide circle of acquaintances. This one comes from Gert Fisher, the town librarian in Tilton, Vermont. When Annie and James summered there, Annie used to volunteer at the library, and although the two women never got on especially well, Gert has included Annie in her quarterly updates ever since. They are usually not very interesting, but halfway through the weddings, funerals, and 4-H winners in this one, Annie comes across a bit of news that makes her catch her breath. Jason McCormack, the son of old Hughie McCormack, was killed in an accident on Labor Day. He fell from the roof of a summer cottage while cleaning the gutters and broke his neck.

"He was only doing a favor for his dad, who as you may remember had a stroke the year before last," Gert wrote before going on to how it rained on the library's end-of-summer lawn sale, and how disappointed they all were.

Gert doesn't say in her three-page compendium of breaking news, but Annie is quite sure Jason fell from the roof of what used to be their cottage. In fact, she is positive.

Five years after the death of her husband (and the death of Jason McCormack not long after), Annie remarries. And although they relocate to Boca Raton, she gets back to the old neighborhood often. Craig, the new husband, is only semi-retired, and his business takes him to New York every three or four months. Annie almost always goes with him, because she still has family in Brooklyn and on Long Island. More than she knows what to do with, it sometimes seems. But she loves them with that exasperated affection that seems to belong, she thinks, only to people in their fifties and sixties. She never forgets how they drew together for her after James's plane went down, and made the best cushion for her that they could. So she wouldn't crash, too.

When she and Craig go back to New York, they fly. About this she never has a qualm, but she stops going to Zoltan's Family Bakery on Sundays when she's home, even though their raisin bagels are, she is sure, served in heaven's waiting room. She goes to Froger's instead. She is actually there, buying doughnuts (the doughnuts are at least passable), when she hears the blast. She hears it clearly even though Zoltan's is eleven blocks away. LP gas explosion. Four killed, including the woman who always passed Annie her bagels with the top of the bag rolled down, saying, "Keep it that way until you get home or you lose the freshness."

People stand on the sidewalks, looking east toward the sound of the explosion and the rising smoke, shading their eyes with their hands. Annie hurries past them, not looking. She doesn't want to see a plume of rising smoke after a big bang; she thinks of James enough as it is, especially on the nights when she can't sleep. When she gets home she can hear the phone ringing inside. Either everyone has gone down the block to where the local school is having a sidewalk art sale, or no one can hear that ringing phone. Except for her, that is. And by the time she gets her key turned in the lock, the ringing has stopped.

Sarah, the only one of her sisters who never married, *is* there, it turns out, but there is no need to ask her why she didn't answer the phone; Sarah Bernicke, the one-time disco queen, is in the kitchen with the Village People turned up, dancing around with the O-Cedar in one hand, looking like a chick in a TV ad. She missed the bakery explosion, too, although their building is even closer to Zoltan's than Froger's.

Annie checks the answering machine, but there's a big red zero in the messages waiting window. That means nothing in itself, lots of people call without leaving a message, but—

Star-sixty-nine reports the last call at eight-forty last night. Annie dials it anyway, hoping against hope that somewhere outside the big room that looks like a Grand Central Station movie set he found a place to re-charge his phone. To him it might seem he last spoke to her yesterday. Or only minutes ago. *Time is funny here*, he said. She has dreamed of that call so many times it now almost seems like a dream itself, but she has never told anyone about it. Not Craig, not even her own mother, now almost ninety but alert and with a firmly held belief in the afterlife.

In the kitchen, the Village People advise that there is no need to feel down. There isn't, and she doesn't. She nevertheless holds the phone very tightly as the number she has star-sixty-nine-ed rings once, then twice. Annie stands in the living room with the phone to her ear and her free hand touching the brooch above her left breast, as if touching the brooch could still the pounding heart beneath it. Then the ringing stops and a recorded voice offers to sell her The *New York Times* at special bargain rates that will not be repeated.

COUPLE OF LOVERS ON A RED BACKGROUND

by Rebecca Makkai from *Brilliant Corners*

———————⚬———————

I've been calling him Bach so far, at least in my head, but now that he's started wearing my ex-husband's clothes and learned to work the coffeemaker, I feel it's time to call him Johann. I said it out loud once, when I needed to get him off the couch before the super came up, but I'm not sure I pronounced it right, *Germanic* enough, because he didn't respond—though I'm not sure I'd recognize *my* name, either, in the midst of someone screaming a foreign language. He got off the couch and went to the vacuum closet only because I practically carried him. No easy task, pushing someone so big and sweaty, even with the weight he's lost since he got here. I'd take him out for some real German food, but if there's one thing I've learned from the movies about caring for transplanted historical people, it's never to take them out in public among the taxis and police and department store mannequins.

I've kept the windows closed and the TV unplugged, but I did introduce him to the stereo so he'd have something to do every day while I'm gone. I'm proud of the way I did it: First, I dug my angel music box out of the Christmas decorations and played it for him. He seemed familiar with the concept, so I pointed back and forth between the angel box and the CD player, then put on some Handel. He was pleased, not at all scared, and now he's pushing buttons and changing discs like he was raised on Sony. At first I only let him have Baroque, but recently we've been moving up in history. He's fond of Mozart, unsurprisingly, but for some reason Tchaikovsky makes him giggle. When I played him "Dance of the Sugar-Plum Fairies," I thought he was going to wet the couch. Five minutes later he went to the piano and played the main part from memory, busting out laughing at certain notes. If such a thing is possible, he played it *sarcastically*. He has a laugh, incidentally, like you'd expect from a pot-smoking thirteen-year-old, whispered and high-pitched. At first, when I thought I was making this all up, I wondered if I'd borrowed that bit from the movie *Amadeus*. But on the phone the other day, my mother said, "Who's that laughing over there?" At least she thinks I'm dating again.

───────⋙───────

He doesn't seem to remember living in the piano. He never lifts the lid to look inside, which I would certainly do if I'd lived there ten days. The morning he came, I was in my sweats and playing his Minuet in G—the one you know if you ever took lessons, the first "real" piece you learned by a serious composer: DA-da-da-da-da-DA-da-da, et cetera. I was remembering that the day I first learned to play it was the same day my father, the journalist who wished he were an opera baritone, first took interest in my lessons. I was seven. He stood behind me and beat time on his palm. He even made up a little song for it, when I wasn't getting the rhythm right: "THIS is the way that BACH wrote it, THIS is the way that BACH wrote it, THIS is the merry, THIS is the merry, THIS is the merry tune!" I'd keep playing even though it panicked me, and I'd think of the picture from my cartoon book about Beethoven, the one where his father stood behind the piano with dollar signs in his eyes. I wasn't gifted enough that my father was thinking of money; maybe he wanted me to entertain at his dinner parties, or just to be better than *he* was. Treble clefs in his eyes.

I was remembering all this, playing the "Minuet in G" pretty damn well despite a couple glasses of wine, when I started to feel like something was stuck in my throat. Since my hands were busy playing, I didn't cover my mouth—just turned my head to the side and coughed something up. I think I passed out then, although I don't remember waking up. There's a chunk of time I can't account for.

The next day I heard scratching inside the piano. I figured, shit, I have mice again. I didn't want to open the lid and poke them out with the end of a mop. I didn't want them running panicked across the carpet, their terror feeding mine. When I couldn't stop screaming over the mouse I found in the sleeve of my coat the winter of fifth grade, my mother gave me the old "They're more scared of you" talk. I said, "I know, and that's the problem."

The piano's an old upright, a cheap Yamaha that David, my ex, bought used right out of college, before he even bought a couch. Only we're not divorced yet, just separated. So not my ex—my separatee. I thought, if mice eat out the insides, it's not the worst thing. An excuse to get something nicer. David fancied himself a great pianist, but he didn't have the ear for it, just the fingers. He never sprang for a good tuning, and now the thing is beyond repair. I wondered if our insurance would pay for a new one.

———————— ❧ ————————

The scratching kept on for almost two weeks, and every time I hit a note something would scurry around, hit against the strings. I stopped playing the piano. One morning I was sitting at my little glass table eating breakfast, getting my papers ready for the condo I was going to show, and the lid of the piano lifted up. I'm not a big screamer anymore, so I just sat there paralyzed, and out climbed a little troll. It was about two feet high, and it moved so fast I didn't even notice its clothes or hair. It ran straight into the side of the couch, then out into the middle of the floor, where it scampered in smaller and smaller circles. I held my folded newspaper in front of my legs like a shield, chased it into the vacuum closet and shut the door, then tried to put it out of my mind because I had twenty minutes to find a cab, get across town, and tell the Lindquists why they should invest three hundred thousand in a walkup condo with non-perpendicular hallways. I told myself I *had* to go because I was about two failures away from fired; I hadn't closed in three months. Maybe I also wanted an excuse to get the hell out of there.

"It's a beauty," I told the Lindquists, my voice on autopilot. "Very raw, very Brooklyn. And so close to street level! It's almost earthy!" They passed, said it just didn't feel like home. Mrs. Lindquist with those awful, crimson nails. By the time I was done, I was sure I imagined the whole thing. I reminded myself I'd been dehydrated lately, that I should drink more than just alcohol and coffee. But when I got home

I found my guest fully grown, just a little shorter than me. He'd let himself out of the closet and was sleeping on the couch.

———— ⤜ ————

I had no idea who he was at first Weird old clothes, but I'm not good at fashion history. All I could tell was old, grimy, European, a little too much lace at the cυ Ϳs for my taste. He doesn't have a wig as in his pictures, just ιessy, reddish, greasy hair. But after I stared at him for half an hour, he woκ ιϳ ηd walked to the piano and started to play. Just scales at first, like he was getting used to it, then he launched into a couple Inventions that drove me crazy in high school. So I looked up Bach online, and it's definitely him, the exact same fleshy cheeks, the same dark eyes pinched small between thick brows and heavy, sleepless bags.

I decided I should look respectable in the presence of a genius, so I started freshening my face every day in the taxi on the way home, not just on the way out. I bought razors and started shaving my legs again. I tidied the apartment, too; I cleaned out the freezer, all those big Ziplocs of David's chili, and I finally filled in the missing bulbs in the row above the bathroom sink. It was startling, to see my face so clearly there—loose skin on my eyelids that caught the green eye shadow in clumps, and my roots growing in gray-brown under the Honey Kissed. I'm only 38. Johann is supposed to be the one with white hair. I made an appointment for the spa.

I showed Johann soap and deodorant, and the other day while I was gone he finally changed out of that yellowish shirt and those disgusting pants. Now he's wearing David's gray flannel shirt and his old corduroys. He looks so normal, sometimes I glance up from my magazine and forget it's not just David sitting there, drinking his beer.

———— ⤜ ————

When I was ten years old, my father started the game "You Can't Get Out of the Car Until You've Named This Composer." He'd have hidden the cassette case throughout the drive, and he'd only pose the question as he pulled up to the curb where he was dropping me. I'd ignore his conversation for blocks, knowing what was coming and concentrating on my guess. My older brother had a practiced method of shouting the name of every major composer in rapid, random succession, a litany that started with "RavelRachmaninovSaintSaensBeethoven" and ended with "BuxtehudeChopinSchoenbergBernstein." I took the more methodical approach, at least establishing a general period before naming my probable suspects. Once, when the answer was Smetana, I sat there until I was half an hour late for eleventh grade English. I suppose he'd have been proud of me, identifying Bach so quickly.

Johann, of course, is remarkable at naming composers. Every time we put in a new disc, I'll say the name, loudly and clearly—"SCHU-BERT," for example—and he'll repeat it. I'm not sure if he can read the CD covers, or if he's used to a more gothic script.

———⋈———

He's been learning English. I suppose this shouldn't surprise me, when I consider that he *is* a great genius, and he has a good ear and so forth. The other day, I came home from an open house and he started pointing around the room, doing nouns. "Table," he said. "Piano." He must get this all from me. I've been talking constantly, the way you would with a baby or a dog, things like "Now I'm putting the milk in your coffee, mmm, that will taste delicious."

On my way out of the elevator the next morning, my super stopped me, bobbing her head and smiling. "Such piano you play! You are like concert! I had no idea of this!"

"Practice, practice, practice," I said. And what propelled me out the door and down the street was a mixture of relief that I'm not crazy and panic that there's a real human being who's not just going to vaporize. So calling a shrink is out, but at the same time calling anyone else is out, because they'll *think* I'm crazy. I find myself wishing the Ghostbusters were real.

So that night, I started telling Johann about my life. I figured, if I can't take this to a shrink, maybe *he* can be my shrink. All they do anyway is sit and listen. So I made us a nice meal for once, chicken with cream sauce and rosemary, and opened some expensive Riesling.

"Johann," I said, "I understand you had something like twenty children. Babies." I rocked my arms back and forth, and he smiled. "Not to bring up a touchy area, because I know half of them died, right? Dead?" He looked confused, but just as well. "But back then people dealt with things and moved on. It wasn't some life-halting devastation because it was the *norm*. No one went around wailing 'Oh, why me, why does God hate me?' And that's how I've always looked at things. David's mother dies and I think, okay, that's normal. Sad, yes, but everyone's mother dies. David doesn't see it that way. His mother dying threatens his whole world view, makes him question his religion. I say, so your whole vague, lapsed-Episcopal belief in God was based on your mother being alive? On nothing bad ever happening? This is the man whose clothes you're wearing. CLOTHES. So David says I was more upset when we miscarried last year than when his mother died. True, but really that was more the hormones. Johann, you would not believe how the chemicals can wash over you. Your wives never even had to deal with post-partum, did they? Just got pregnant again and squeezed out the next one."

He nodded, used his bread to sop up sauce, yawned. I don't know if nodding is something he learned from me, or if they did that in old Germany. He was looking very American right then, what with the haircut I gave him, and his learning to use the electric toothbrush. I gave him the removable brush head with the blue edging. I have the pink. And he's not that old, really, maybe forty. I looked him up again online to make sure I hadn't altered history, stealing him away like that in the middle of his life, but he still seems to have died at 65. I didn't learn much else new, except that he never liked pianos. Didn't think they'd last.

Which is all to say, he's not bad-looking. It makes you think. Technically he's a married man, but even more technically, his second wife died 300 years ago. And it's not as if I can go out on dates now and leave him alone, and I can't bring anyone back *here*. Then there's this: He's clearly very fertile, and any child of his would be a musical genius. His sons certainly were, back whenever, and his daughters might have been, given the chance. Maybe that's the reason this happened, so I can have his daughter and give her a decent shot at life.

The question, then, is how to seduce an eighteenth-century German. If I just show up in a nightgown, he'll think I'm some kind of harlot.

***

I did it by introducing jazz. We went chronologically, from my *African Rhythms* CD through Dixieland, and by the time we got through two bottles of wine and up to Coleman Hawkins, he was leaning close, murmuring things in German. I wasn't expecting much. I mean, every month in *Cosmo* they keep announcing some new sex position, as if for years people reproduced like Puritans and we're only now figuring out the pleasure aspect. But Johann, he knows exactly what he's doing.

***

I try not to talk on the phone in front of him, since he can't understand I'm not talking to *him*. He'll laugh when I laugh, try to stand in front of me, nod when he thinks I'm asking a question.

When I got in the cab the morning after our first night together, I turned on my cell for the first time in two days and found a message from David. "It's me," he said. I could picture him standing with the phone, his back to the smudgy window of his loft. "Wondering if my shoe polish is still there. In the hall closet. Call me. I miss you." I haven't known David to polish his shoes in the last ten years, so this meant he had a date. Or wanted me to think so.

I called his house, since he'd be at work. I talked to his machine. "Me," I said. "Wednesday morning. If you left any polish, it's probably gone. My friend moved some things in there, so I had to make space. My friend John. Nothing too serious, but he's staying awhile."

When the message ended, a prerecorded woman asked if I'd like to review my message. I did. Then I recorded over it. "Me. Sorry I took so long. Can't find the polish. It was old anyway, wasn't it? You should just buy some new. So. Good luck with whatever you need the shiny shoes for."

The cabby looked at me in the rearview and smiled. If he understood English, he probably approved of my benevolence.

———— ≈ ————

Johann is really into the jazz, especially blues. Funny, I'd have pegged him for a Bird fan, something more complicated. He still only speaks a few words of English, "coffee," "eat," "pajamas," "no," but he's memorized a number of blues lyrics. Across the dinner table most nights, between dinner and ice cream, he starts into something like "What Did I Do to Be So Black and Blue?" and he even does that low, gravely Satchmo voice.

> *No joys for me*
> *no company*
> *even ze mouse*
> *ren from my house*
> *all my life srough*
> *I've been soooooo*
> *bleck and blue.*

Only he's grinning while he sings it. I think he's proud of himself.

———— ≈ ————

When he plays from the Chopin book I got him, it sounds different than it should—sharper, less Romantic, I suppose—but then there's something wonderful about the way he plays fantastical music in this normal, rhythmic way as if it weren't Chopin at all, just Hanon warm-up exercises. It reminds me of a Chagall painting: Here are some people, floating above a town. Here is a cow on the roof. Here is the blanket sky, poked through with blinding stars. Does it strike you as unreasonable? But this is just the way my town looks at night. I took my easel into the street to paint my flying neighbors, to get the purple starlight right. Normal, normal. Nothing Romantic going on *here*.

———— ≈ ————

I gave him some staff paper the other day, thinking maybe he'd write something while he's here, but he just looked at it, said "Nein, nein," shook his head sadly. Maybe it's against the rules to compose here, to leave parts of his genius as evidence. Maybe he can leave his sperm, but not his handwriting.

My father used to make me and my brother compose, the same way he made us pick lottery numbers. He'd sit us down, have us close our eyes, tell us if we cleared our minds of every noise and picture, something would appear. It always did, but then we never won the lottery or composed a masterpiece. I feared it was because of my cheating, my inability to filter out random images. I'd almost be clear, and then: Gorilla! Airplane! Christmas! I want to ask Johann how he does it, how he can sit and just concentrate. How he can keep out everything that isn't sound—the fifty thousand colors of the world, the glare of the light bulb, the smell of something burning four stories below.

The longer he's here, the more I think I should learn some German. We could piece together a conversation then, between us.

My Brahms-bearded art professor, the one who introduced me to Chagall in the first place, would use a piano during his lectures. The class met in the small theater at the back of the fine arts building, the one used for student recitals. There was a Steinway on the little stage, and somehow he'd gotten a key to the lid. He loved to run from his projection screen to that piano, talking about "Colors are like notes, together they make chords." He probably thought he was being quirky.

"This is blue and green," he said, playing C and D together. "So similar they create tension. Now blue and yellow." A third. "Now blue and orange." A fourth.

Another time, he ran to the piano to explain a terrible Rococo painting, something with clouds and bosoms. "The whites in Boucher are like *this*," he said, and trilled high up, delicate and saccharine.

But I was never sure he knew what he was talking about. He lost my faith when we studied *Guernica* and he said there would never be a war on American soil in our lifetimes. No canvas of mangled, color-void bodies. No slaughtered bull, no spears, no pale-eyed crucifixion. It struck me as shockingly naïve for a smart man, very bag-over-the-head.

And he was wrong about colors, too. "They have no innate *meaning*, of course," he said the second week of class, "but they have *connotations* we all share, as a society and as humans, yes? Green keys us into nature, life, so we see it as soothing. Blue is sky, so we think dreamy, ethereal, and the same with white. Black is fear. For three million years we lived without electricity, no? There are good reasons we're afraid of the dark. Red, of course, we see blood. So violence, drama, excitement, passion."

And that's where I took exception, where I still do. For men, yes, maybe. But for any woman since the dawn of time, red means no baby this month. It means, for better or worse, the staining and unignorable absence of a baby.

I lied before; the sex isn't that good. I had low expectations, so I was thrilled he knew *anything*. But actually he's pretty stiff, non-creative. I've tried things a couple times, very normal things for our society, where he's pulled away from me, started talking fast in German, turned bright pink.

The last time he did it, I put my clothes back on and decided to ignore him for the rest of the day. I went to the window and opened the curtains. I wasn't thinking about it, but maybe on some level I did it to scare him. He stood there and looked down at the cars, saw all the buildings, saw for the first time how high we were. He didn't cry, but he looked like he wanted to. He stayed there a long time, shaking and mumbling. Then he closed the curtains and ran to the couch, ran bent over at the waist as if he were scared of falling. I'm surprised he never opened the curtains himself while I was at work. You'd think a genius would be more curious than that.

To calm him down, I got my big music encyclopedia off the shelf and showed him all the pictures in the Bach section. The house where he was born, the church in Leipzig, a portrait of his oldest son. He pointed at each and said things I couldn't understand, but they seemed to make him happy. He flipped backward a page to the Handel section and made some kind of joke. He giggled and giggled, so I just laughed along with him.

"Yep, that Handel," I said. "One funny guy."

When I put it back on the shelf, I got out my little Chagall book from the MOMA show a few years back.

"Here," I said, and I opened it to *The Fiddler*. "This is what I think of when you play Chopin. See how he's making music, floating there above the town? That's what you sound like, like there's nothing under your feet, but you don't even notice."

Bach squinted at the picture, pointed at the fiddler's face. "Grün," he said.

"Yes, it's green. I wouldn't make fun. You looked strange enough yourself when you were three feet tall."

I flipped to the one called *Birthday*, the one where a man floats above the red carpet, over a woman to kiss her—the one with the city window and the flowers and her little purse. The man has no arms. The next page was *Couple of Lovers on a Red Background*, where they're lying in the red, and they're red themselves, drowning in it, only they're not drowning really because up above is a huge blue pool where the real water is, where the blue man throws flowers and the fish-bird jumps down.

"These are pictures of love," I said. "LOVE." He put his hand on his heart. I'd taught him that one the week before. "Everyone in these pictures can float, because they're in love, or they're the fiddler on the roof, or just happy." I pointed out the window. "That's why we can stay up here so high. It doesn't seem possible, but it is. Twenty-seven stories up!" I flashed my fingers in two tens and a seven. "Because we're playing music and we're happy."

He crawled back to the window, his fingers digging into the carpet, then reached up and lifted just the corner of the curtain. I came up behind him, and together we watched the bus shed passengers twenty-seven stories down. Then he looked at me and pointed at the wristwatch I'd given him, the one David left behind because it wasn't digital.

"You want to know how long the building can hold up against gravity?" Although maybe it was something else. How long must he stay here, how many lifetimes have passed since his own, what time is it in Germany?

"Tock, tock, tock," he said.

I chose to answer the gravity question, because it was the only one I could. "A long time. LONG TIME. It won't fall down while you're here, at least."

Since that afternoon, when he sings the blues, it sounds like the *blues*.

> "*I'm so forlorn,*" he sings,
> "*life's just a sorn*
> *my heart is torn*
> *vhy vas I born*
> *Vhat did I dooooo*
> *to be so bleck . . . and blue?*"

He won't look out the window anymore, but it doesn't matter. He knows. Every siren he hears now, he looks at that curtain. I've never been in the blissful ignorance camp, but in this case maybe it was too much for one man to handle. I remember a couple years ago when David made us stop watching TV so we wouldn't see bad news. I couldn't understand how it worked for him, because for me it was worse. If we don't watch the news, I said, how do we know the city's not on fire? How do we know we're not the last ones alive? Since Johann's been here I've kept the TV off, but I'll turn on my radio when he's in the bathroom. If only to hear some stupid ad, because then at least I know we're all okay. Those shrill used-car jingles, to me they're the sound of safety. There's still money to be made, they say. There's still something left to buy.

He's been turning pale, and if I'm not mistaken he's getting smaller. You can see it around the eyes, the way they're sinking back into his face. The skin feels loose on his arms. He hardly leaves the couch anymore, and when he does—when he finally gets his courage and darts to the bathroom—it's with shaking legs and outstretched arms, like he's worried the floor will give way any moment. He's scratched the arms of the sofa to shreds.

Yesterday I played the piano to see if he would follow suit. I brought my big blue Gershwin book out of hiding and got through "A Foggy Day" with only three or four mistakes. I'm good, if a little rusty. At the end of high school I was even applying to conservatories, making tapes, and getting ready to go on auditions, when I realized that although I could play almost anything you put before me, and skillfully, I'd never gotten through a major piece without at least one mistake. I could play the whole *Pathetique* flawlessly, then a measure from the end I'd breathe a sigh of relief and wreck the last chord. And so I majored in finance.

"Maybe that's what you are," I said to Johann after I'd flubbed the last two measures. "Maybe you're my repressed ambition." Not likely, the way he sits with his mouth caving in, his glare darting between me and the window.

He sighed. "I'm vhite . . . in-side," he sang.

"You're white all over, Johann," I said. Though truth be told, he's looking a little gray.

———— ⊰ ————

I get the feeling his tock, tock, tock is running out. But if my test sticks are accurate I'm ovulating now, so I only need him to hold out a little longer. I'll buy him a fattening dinner tonight.

I had to leave him on the couch just now, lock the door, ride down in my loud, slow elevator to show the Lindquists their eighth and (God, let's hope) final apartment. He didn't look good at all when I left him there, so small and pale and curled up in the cushions.

"I have to make money," I told him. "Deutschmarks, right? You'd understand. I'm sure you wouldn't have plonked your Sundays away on half the organs in Germany if you didn't have twenty mouths to feed. I'll need to buy things. Piano lessons. For the baby."

And so I left him, and even if he's still there when I get back, I won't be surprised if he doesn't last the night. But I've never planned on his being in the picture, long-term. I don't actually want him to *raise* the baby. It'll be easy enough to explain why he's not around. "Oh, the baby's father is so busy," I'll say. "He's quite a famous man, and this would simply ruin his reputation. Believe me. Very. Famous."

Of course I could always call David and apologize, maybe make him think the baby's his somehow, and we could get back to our lives. It wouldn't be that hard, and I've grown used again to having some company. And I *am* sorry. It's really a good thing not everyone is like me, born expecting things to come unpasted, fall apart. And yes, yes, I can see now how David was up there playing his fiddle without a roof to stand on, how one day when his mother died he just looked down, lost his grip on the air, fell through the night. Maybe I'll call him from the cab, on the way back from downtown.

But before that I have to buy Johann dinner, something to hold him together. And before *that*, I'm sliding on my stilettos in this elevator, growing three inches even as I sink three hundred feet. I'm putting on lipstick to sell the Lindquists a place to live, a nice plot of air so high above the city the Indians didn't think to charge beads for it. Look how convenient, I'll say. And how stable. It'll last a few hundred years, if nothing knocks it down. I know you're going to love it.

FLYING AND FALLING

by Kuzhali Manickavel from *Shimmer*

M uhil was born during a legendary thunderstorm that uprooted every banana tree in the village and sent a legion of white crabs to die on the highway. She was wrinkled, ordinary, and unremarkable save for the fact that she had a spongy knob on each shoulder and she didn't cry. Her father Ilango peered at her and had a premonition of dark, heavy things.

"What's wrong with her?" he asked.

"Some babies don't cry," said the doctor.

"What's that on her shoulders?"

"They'll probably fall off."

When she was awake, Muhil seemed to be measuring the ceiling with her eyes, ticking off invisible numbers with her tiny fists and feet. When she slept, she reminded Ilango of a stone at the bottom of a river. She never made a sound. On the rare occasions that she cried, she shut her eyes and opened her mouth so wide that Ilango thought her jaw might snap.

When she could sit upright, Muhil started to rub her back against anything she could get next to—the wall, the side of the well, her mother's arm. Soon the skin on her back hung in saggy, red bags beneath her tiny shoulder blades.

"Do you know what happens to girls who rub their backs raw like that? Their backs fall off, that's what," said Ilango.

He took her to a doctor who peered at the folds of skin and tapped the knobs on her shoulder with a ballpoint pen.

"What's wrong with her?" asked Ilango.

"Nothing," said the doctor.

Soon people began to accost Ilango and his wife on the road and tell them stories of children that drank water from puddles and barked like wild dogs. These children had gone on to become doctors or lawyers in foreign countries. Surely Muhil would do the same. But a few months later, Muhil began to clamber onto small stools and throw herself to the ground. When stools were placed out of reach, Muhil began throwing herself off people's laps.

"Why are you doing this to me?" said Ilango. "No other child does this. I never did this to my father."

Muhil did not seem concerned. She kept tipping herself over any ledge she could find and Ilango stopped going out, because nobody could find anything heartening to say about children who seemed hell-bent on suicide so early in life.

———— ⊰ ————

A few nights later Ilango dreamed he was lying on the roof of his house, watching the afternoon sky. Even though the sun was out he could see clutches of green and orange stars blinking above him. He stretched out his hand and something circled down and landed on his palm. It was Muhil. Two tiny wings had sprouted from the knobs on her shoulders. They looked like dried leaves.

"So it's you!" said Ilango. "Those are very pretty wings you have."

Muhil looked up at him and bared her teeth; they were round and white.

"Why won't you talk to me," he asked. "Why won't you say anything?"

She stood up and began to walk across his palm, her wings rustling behind her like paper.

"Everyone thinks I'm a terrible father, because you keep trying to break your head open. I wish you would stop doing that."

Muhil teetered forward, the edges of her wings stabbing awkwardly at the sky. They reminded him of a dead tree.

"You will be the world's first flying doctor," mused Ilango. "Or flying lawyer. Or maybe you could do both. What do you think?"

Ilango watched as she tipped over the edge of his hand and spun out into the sky like a dying moth.

"That's all right," he said. "You can tell me later."

By the age of four, Muhil was crooked, stunted, and more wrinkled than she was at birth. When she wasn't skinning her back against something she was tipping herself off anything she could climb. Her very existence had become uncomfortable to anyone who saw her. Well-meaning neighbors and friends began bringing pamphlets and newspaper clippings of places that kept children who couldn't be kept.

One evening Ilango sat with her on the back porch. Muhil kept pedaling against his arm, her breath coming in tiny, silent puffs as she tried to throw herself over the edge.

"Why?" said Ilango. "Why are you doing this? Look at your face. You know what people will think? They'll think I'm beating you up."

Muhil kept pedaling against his arm, her head lurching to the side as she tried to break free.

"Fine," said Ilango. "Go on. Break your head open."

He loosened his grip and Muhil pitched forward. Her tiny back curled and something shifted beneath her shoulders. Instead of falling, Muhil hovered in midair like a tiny hummingbird. Ilango saw the entire world swing from her shoulders as green and orange stars dripped from the sky. Then she crashed to the ground and split her lip open.

Ilango reeled under an overwhelming sense of understanding and purpose. Everything suddenly made sense and fit perfectly. He wondered how he hadn't seen it before. He arranged pillows around the wooden cot and held Muhil at the very edge.

"Try that again, what you did on the porch."

Muhil tipped over and landed face down in the pillows.

"Again," said Ilango. "Roll your shoulders, curl your back."

He tried the cot, the porch, and the lower branches of the mango tree but nothing happened. He tried to catch her off-guard, pushing her off the bed when she was napping, but she still landed face down on the floor. He finally decided to take Muhil to the roof and his wife decided it was time to summon the police and all the neighbors. By the time Ilango was ready, a crowd of familiar heads and pointing fingers surged around his house.

"Ilango, put the girl down," called out his neighbor Pandian.

"Not yet."

"You're scaring her, Ilango, put her down."

"No."

"What? What did you say?"

"Not now, I need to try something."

Someone came from behind and grabbed Muhil from him. Ilango turned and saw her lurch against a tangle of arms, trying to throw herself over the edge.

Ilango spent the night in jail, staring at the floor. He held his hand out and thought, this is how she floated. Roll your shoulders. Curl your back. This is how it's done. The next morning he came home to a house that was silent and empty. Pandian appeared at the door with a tumbler of coffee.

"Are they with you?" asked Ilango.

"They're fine," said Pandian. "What will you do for food? Shall I bring you something?"

"She isn't coming back?"

"Not right now."

Ilango watched the shadows spill across the walls and ceiling. He listened for the sound of a small body hitting the floor somewhere or the rustle of wings but he couldn't hear anything.

"We'll try again, that's all," said Ilango. "We'll just try again."

A week later Muhil and his wife were back home. Pandian came over in the evenings to make sure everything was all right. He also made half-hearted attempts at inspirational speeches.

"We've all made mistakes in the past," he said. "Important to look forward. Don't worry."

"Why should I be worried?" said Ilango.

"You need to be a good husband and father now. You need to remember that Muhil is sick."

"She's not sick. What makes you think she's sick?"

"You have to be responsible."

"Fine."

"I'm serious."

"So am I."

After supper Ilango would watch as Muhil clambered onto the cot and tipped herself onto a pile of pillows below. He felt a rustling in his brain telling him of flying doctors or flying lawyers or maybe both.

Whichever she liked.

"We'll try again," said Ilango.

———— ❧ ————

A few nights later Ilango took Muhil to an abandoned bridge at the outskirts of the village.

"Roll your shoulders, curl your back," he chanted as he carried her. "Say it with me, roll your shoulders, curl your back."

He turned her chin to the sky and made her look at the stars and the tops of the trees.

"You can go up there if you like. You can see nests and birds sleeping. Maybe you can see our house."

When they reached the bridge he held her on the edge of the railing and looked down. It was darker than he had thought it would be.

"Don't go far," he said as he slowly loosened his grip. "And come back quickly, do you understand?"

Muhil teetered for a second on the railing. Then she tipped sideways into the darkness like a bundle of old clothes.

Ilango stretched his hand into the darkness and waited.

THE KING OF THE DJINN

by Benjamin Rosenbaum and David Ackert from *Realms of Fantasy*

Grinding and roaring, the sixteen-wheeler crested a great dune, and Musa rejoiced: there on the horizon, the Mediterranean glittered, blue as Heaven. "God is great!" he shouted as he shifted into second for the downgrade.

Each week, Musa made this trip, carrying a ton of devilish black carbonated soda from the bottling plant of El-Nasr to the decadent tongues of Cairo. And each week, when he reached the open road, his heart threw off its burdens.

In the town, the nights were empty and cold. He'd awaken again and again to the sudden emptiness of his house—his wife Suha dead, his son Jamal away at university. The days were full of packing and loading and tinkering, activity and worry. The men of the bottling plant were always asking Musa for blessings, for amulets, for the resolution of disputes. They'd found out, somehow, that he'd once studied Qur'an and Hadith in the great merkab in Cairo. Sometimes he even had the odd sense that they knew about his meetings with the King of the Djinn. He never knew what to say to them.

On the road, Musa was with God alone. He prayed without words as he drove, using only his breath, opening himself to God as the great bounty of the world came into focus. Every blinding white grain of sand reflected God's glory at Musa; the blue vault of the heavens was filled with God's breath. The roaring engine of the semi and the black ribbon of the highway testified to the great genius God had entrusted in man. Whenever Musa saw a camel or a goat or a date tree in the sand beyond the highway, it was full of life, full to bursting, and the life in it reached out into Musa's heart and whispered to him: *We are one.*

The King of the Djinn had been right. It was he who had told Musa to abandon the academy, that his soul was starving. Musa had given his inheritance to charity, dropped out of the merkab, and found this simple work. For forty years, he had devoted himself to the secret path of the breath. He slowed down enough for God to find him, and God took Musa in the palm of His hand and held him there. Even at Suha's death, God's love of Musa never wavered; Musa cried like a woman at her graveside, and God held him with strong arms and kept him safe from despair.

Now Musa could see tiny white flecks against the sea's blue. Whitecaps dancing. The road turned parallel to the shore.

As for the King of the Djinn: Musa was not sure, of course, that he really was the King of the Djinn. That was just a guess. He called himself "Gil."

But since 1952, when they had met in a café in the student quarter, Musa had become an old man, and Gil had not aged a day. Gil looked like a Persian, but he spoke a fluent and elegantly complex classical Arabic, the way no one had spoken it since the time of the Prophet. And in Gil's eyes, Musa saw the kind of fearlessness men had only when they were young and arrogant, or old and dying. Yet Gil possessed it all the time.

Given his instrumental role in turning Musa to the true knowledge of God, it was possible that Gil was an angel. But Gil did not act like an intimate of God's. Whenever he showed up, every few years, Gil would ask for Musa to talk of his discoveries, hanging hungrily on every word. It was the hunger of an unmarried youth asking about sex, or a poor man asking about luxury. There was something that kept Gil from embracing God's presence, from accepting God's love as Musa did. For this, Musa pitied him. Even so, Gil also had a majesty about him, an admirable depth and power. To call him just a Djinn seemed meager. Surely he was the King of the Djinn.

When Musa's thoughts turned to Gil like this, it was often a sign that he would be visiting soon. Musa's heart beat happily at the thought. If he had a friend in this world, with Suha gone, it was Gil.

The motor coughed a particularly agonized cough, and Musa looked quickly at the temperature gauge. It was in the red. Musa had no clock; he used the motor's periodic overheating to time his daily prayers. He pulled the truck off the road into a patch of sand packed down by the tracks of many tires.

Musa sloshed the remaining water in his canteen skeptically. He had drunk too much that morning; there was not enough for drinking and purification both. He clambered out of the cab and, in the shadow of the truck, did the ablutions with sand. Then he performed the prayers. How it lifted his heart, to be one with the millions of the faithful, all yearning toward the city where God had spoken to his best and final prophet. Thus had God completed the work of filling the world with his bounty: air to breathe, water to drink, food to eat, people to love, and finally the gentle and firm rules and the great poetry and wisdom of the Word of God.

His prayers done, his motor still smoking, Musa sat cross-legged in the shadow of the truck, on the sand, and allowed his soul to rise.

His soul ascended and saw the sand and the date palms, the ribbon of highway and the truck, the sea and cliffs beyond. It swept higher and he saw the fertile valley of the Nile and the teeming cities and the ships and cars and airplanes.

His soul descended into Cairo and flew through the streets, yearning for his only son Jamal. It was a Tuesday, when his son had no classes at the University. He would probably be watching soccer and drinking coffee at his favorite café.

Musa's soul entered the café. But there was no laughter, no shouting, and no urging on of players running after a ball. The men sat in silence. The room was choked in anger.

On the television, Zionists were committing their atrocities in the camps of Palestine. Tanks fired at young men. Bulldozers tore houses open. Old women, old men, and children ran bleeding through the devastated and smoking streets.

Musa's soul found Jamal sitting in the corner, his fist clenched around his coffee glass. Jamal was full of fury. *Why?* Jamal's heart cried. *How can we bear our weakness, how can we bear to see the innocents suffer!*

My son, Musa's soul called to him, *do not be taken by hopelessness. There are always evildoers in the world, as long as men are weak. Take heart, God is great—*

But Jamal's heart did not listen. It went on suffering and raging in its own misery and shame. *I sit here in Cairo,* it said, *studying engineering, while America buys bullets to kill the children of Palestine.*

While my father delivers America's soda pop! To earn the money with which I buy this coffee. We are all slaves!

Musa's soul was struck as if his son had kicked him. It flew out of the café and out of Cairo, and back into his body where it sat by the road.

Musa prayed that his son would not be swept away by hatred and bitterness. As he prayed, his heart galloped like a horse, and he was aware of the thousands of bottles of Pepsi sitting in their crates in his truck, and he prayed that his son would not despise him.

At the sound of a car stopping, Musa opened his eyes. There, in the glare of the desert sun beyond the shadow of the truck, was the King of the Djinn getting out of a Jeep.

Musa got quickly to his feet. He bowed deeply in greeting.

The King of the Djinn walked into the shadow of the truck and bowed back. He was wearing a European-style suit and carrying a briefcase. Beneath his calm smile Musa could feel a great, empty yearning.

"It is good to see you," Musa said as they shook hands. He resisted the urge to embrace the King of the Djinn.

"And you."

Musa's heart was still thundering from his encounter with his son, and he was dizzy and sweating from the heat. He looked at the smile of the creature in the suit, and all of a sudden he found himself asking the question that was always on his tongue, but which he had told himself he would never ask. And so stupidly—he had not inquired as to the health of the other, had not offered him water or coffee or apologized for his inability to provide proper hospitality, had not told or heard any stories, had exchanged neither compliments nor proverbs. His stupid tongue simply jumped up and asked rudely: "Are you a Djinn?" Then he clapped his hands to his mouth in horror.

Gil grinned. As if he approved of the question, was proud of Musa for asking it. He squinted and pursed his lips as if deciding how to answer.

"I don't know what I am," he said finally. "But that is the best proposal I have heard so far."

Musa stood transfixed with embarrassment. He coughed and tried to think of what to say to return the conversation to its proper course.

"And since I am, for lack of a better word, a Djinn," said Gil, "I should offer you wishes."

"Oh no!" said Musa. "I could not accept!"

"Musa," said Gil, "our encounters have been valuable to me over the years. You deserve at least one wish. Would you like it for yourself, or for your son?"

"For my son!" gulped Musa. *Old fool!* he shouted at himself silently. *You did not even refuse three times!* And yet he was so worried about Jamal.

"Very well," said Gil, smiling and handing Musa the briefcase. "Here is what your son wants most in the world."

A chill went through Musa's hands. He set the briefcase down in the sand and looked at the latches. They were shiny and brass.

"Well?" said Gil.

Musa reached out with shaking hands to open the latches.

Most of the contents of the briefcase were covered with a cloth of fine dark silk. But on top of the silk was a blue plastic booklet with a picture of an eagle, and western letters on it. An American passport. Musa opened it. There was his son's picture. He looked up at Gil, confused. Was this what Jamal wanted? To go to America? Musa did not know what to think. There would be dangers, temptations—but at the same time Jamal would learn much, and perhaps—

Gil's eyes were sad—though Musa thought, again, that the sadness was on the surface, like a mask; that beneath it was emptiness—and he gestured back to the briefcase.

Musa looked down again. He moved aside the black cloth.

The rest of the briefcase was filled with thick yellow cylinders of something that looked like clay, connected with electrical tape and wires.

"No!" shouted Musa. "No!"

With that passport, Jamal could go through the border at Taba, into Israel. He could go to the busiest café, the most crowded corner in Tel Aviv, and murder himself and a hundred Zionists—Zionists in baby carriages, Zionists in bridal gowns, Zionists with canes and false teeth—and join the Palestinian martyrs in their struggle.

But surely Jamal would never get through! He would be searched at the border. They would find the bomb, they would punish him! But the stillness in Gil's eyes told Musa that the King of the Djinn had granted far greater wishes, and that Jamal would not fail.

Musa prostrated himself at Gil's feet, burying his face in his hands. "No!" he cried. "Please! Please, sir—Gil—whatever you are—do not do this!"

"Musa, you have become complacent," Gil said. "You have a special gift, a special connection to God. But it is too easy for you. You drive your truck and have visions and take it for granted that it is enough. But God requires more. Sometimes God requires sacrifice."

Musa struggled to his feet, looked wildly around. "This isn't what God wants! Don't tell me God wants my only child martyred! To murder innocents along with the guilty, as the oppressors themselves do! Is that how the Prophet fought?"

"Musa," said Gil, and in his voice was an ancient, ancient cold, with ten thousand years of emptiness behind it, "there is nothing you can do about that. Here is what you can do."

Musa waited, watching Gil's bottomless, glittering eyes.

"Write an amulet," Gil said. "For the protection and redemption of your son's soul. If you think he is going into sin—write an amulet to protect him."

Musa wanted to protest more, to plead. But he found himself going to the cab of his truck and getting in, and taking his parchment and pens and ink out of the dashboard compartment. His tears mixed with the ink as he wrote the declaration of faith and he prayed, fervently, fervently. He no longer felt God's grace in every grain of sand. He felt as though God's grace was hidden at the end of a very long tunnel.

Gil came and took the amulet from him. "Thank you, Musa," he said, and walked to his Jeep and got in.

Musa started his motor. He would rush to Cairo, too, and talk to Jamal. He would persuade him of the wrongness of his actions. He released the clutch and eased onto the road as the Jeep pulled out ahead of him.

But Jamal would not listen. Musa could hear his arguments now. How else to strike at the powerful oppressor, he would say, but the only way we can? Could Musa say for certain he was wrong? *But not my son!* Musa's heart shouted. *God, God, not my only son!* Jamal would look at him with contempt. Driver of sodas.

The road began a long, steep downgrade. Musa took his foot off the gas, lightly tapped the brake as he followed. The Jeep sped on ahead.

Jamal would not listen. He would be gone, and Musa's life would be empty. If Jamal could only get through this period of youth and fiery blood, if he could only learn patience and humility, learn to trust God and endure injustice . . . but he would not have time. The briefcase in the Jeep ahead would see to that.

Help me, God, help me, Musa prayed, with all his heart.

Was it God? Or was it His Adversary? Or simply desperation? Something took Musa's foot off the brake and slammed it down onto the gas and held it there.

The truck groaned and shuddered as it surged down the downgrade. It gained on the Jeep.

The distance closed.

Gil looked back over his shoulder, and in that instant Musa realized he loved the King of the Djinn as a dog loves his master, and he slammed on the brake. But the inertia of a ton of Pepsi would not entertain such indecision. The wheels of the cab locked and skidded, the trailer behind slammed it forward, and the nose of the semi smashed into the Jeep, flipping it into the air. Musa was thrown into the wheel; his jaw snapped and blood fountained across the windshield. He felt the truck fishtail off the road, and then roll; he heard the sound of ten thousand shattering Pepsi bottles fill the desert.

Then it stopped.

Then came the sound of ten thousand bottles slowly reassembling themselves.

The droplets of blood swam slowly back through the air into Musa's veins.

The glass of the windshield reassembled, each piece flying silently, gracefully, back to meet its brothers, glinting in the sunlight. Behind them, the sky rolled back to its proper place above Musa.

The Jeep swung down out of the sky, kissed the cab of the truck, and moved forward onto the road. The trailer of the rig drew back and the cab settled down. Musa's foot left the brake and landed on the gas.

Musa had never known what a gift the gentle movement of time was, the succession of each moment in its turn, each moment a wide open field of freedom and of choice. He felt his heart beat backward, his breath move backward through his lungs. He wanted to shout, to cry, to escape the cab, but he could not: his limbs moved in their predetermined course as the Jeep and the truck crept backward up the hill. Slowly, time dragged its Musa puppet back through the seconds, until he was in his cab parked at the side of the road handing the amulet to Gil. Then it released him.

Gil gasped and spat into the sand. He was shaking. So was Musa. The King of the Djinn looked up at him with a wild, feral grin.

Musa gripped the wheel, his heart exploding in terror.

"You surprised me, Musa," Gil said. "I'm amazed. It's been a very long time since any of my collection surprised me." He looked out over the desert horizon. "I think I've had you on too loose a leash. Your talents make you too hard to control."

Musa watched this King of the Djinn in silent terror. This creature who played with time as a child plays with dolls. Was this Satan himself?

Gil glanced back and saw Musa's face, and for a moment the chill, benign mask of the King of the Djinn slipped, and Musa saw what was under it: desperate rage. Then Gil smiled coolly again.

"You're a fool, Musa. I'm not Time's master. I'm its victim."

He looked down at the amulet and stroked it once, gently. Then he slipped it into his pocket.

He threw the briefcase into the Jeep but did not get in. He stood and watched Musa. "Well," he said finally, "There's nothing you can do to save Jamal. And you won't see me again. So all your earthly attachments are gone now, Musa. You're free to find God." Gil pointed out into the empty desert. "He's that way."

Musa looked in the direction the Djinn had pointed.

God's presence was everywhere, in every grain of sand. It was the same huge, infinite, bountiful light.

But how could he have misjudged it before, to think it gentle? It was alien, inhuman, immense beyond reason. If every human was burned alive, if every creature on earth was swallowed in the fire, the Divine Presence would not blink.

Musa began to walk.

He walked until his throat was dry and his breathing shallow. Then, after a while, he was crawling. It was only a spiritual exercise.

The sand was hot against his cheek.

The Sahara was a vast white page, and Musa's body one tiny, bent black letter written on it. Seen from above, seen from very far away.

THE CITY AND THE MOON

by Deborah Schwartz from *The Kenyon Review*

It was in the year's shortest days, in the few spare moments before Molly would arrive home from work, that Asher filled out applications for graduate school. He did so furtively, in that premature night of early evening, feeling ridiculously too old, fearing Molly's logic. But he knew if he did not at least try, regret would stay with him like heartburn.

In early spring that one acceptance letter came. An enormous relief. But how should he break the news to Molly? Asher called his friend Leo, whom he had known since childhood.

"Take her out to dinner," Leo said. "Keep pouring the wine until she gets giggly."

"Do you think Molly gets giggly when she's drunk?"

"I think so," Leo said. "Don't all women get giggly when they're drunk?" The two friends thought about this for a moment, then Leo added, "Make sure it's a noisy restaurant."

That evening, Asher plied Molly with wine, and after the fifth glass, when her eyes looked misty and she had begun to hiccup, he placed the letter in front of her.

She smiled at first, thinking it a love poem, something sweetly adolescent and thoughtful. Then her eyes, which were having trouble focusing, grew dark. "You're doing *what*?"

"Please," Asher said. "Try to keep your voice down."

"I can't believe you did this. Behind my back."

Asher made a motion with his hand suggesting she lower her voice.

"Don't *shush* me." She was shrill with indignation. "This is serious. Does this mean you're quitting your job?"

Asher spoke to his dinner plate. "Not until May. I'm going to start taking classes early."

Asher had miscalculated with the wine. Molly was certainly not giggly. Her eyes were now rolling like loosed marbles. "This is *dishonest!*" she said. "*Dish-honesht!*" Her voice had reached an agonizing squeak. "You have breached a trust!"

Suddenly, Molly's head slumped. Asher threw some money on the table, shoved the acceptance letter into his pocket, then grabbed her under the arms. The clock was ticking. Coats in one arm, Molly like dead weight in the other, he hauled her back home. They made it as far as the fire hydrant outside their apartment before she began vomiting.

Asher quit his job in May to begin graduate school. Two weeks later, Molly was laid off. As summer blossomed, each long, bright day grew increasingly hotter. The temperatures were reaching record-breaking highs, and the light seemed unrelenting. The streets stunk of slow-cooking garbage. Heat filled Molly and Asher's apartment like latent anger. The couple could not touch each other even in sleep, the sheets sticking to their skin in the dark in the thick night air. Their days together became one long fight, the cry of the teakettle at boil.

Neither of them could have predicted that Molly would lose her job, but she blamed Asher for it just the same. Their dwindling finances made her feel paralyzed, suffocated. She blamed Asher for his lack of sympathy and for his disengagement. She would spend the hottest part of the afternoon in her underclothes, slumped on the couch, staring vacantly at their large television set. Asher was annoyed by Molly's extreme listlessness. He felt she was using her injured pride as an excuse to be angry and lazy and hurt. When he came home, he would try his best to keep his mind in the bubble of school. Their conversations were a series of non sequiturs dazed and flattened by the staggering heat.

Their old cat, Chester, was not unaffected by the weather. At fourteen years old and morbidly obese, the heat was more than he could bear. He left his steady spot at the foot of the bed for the dark corners of their closet. Molly panicked and placed trays of ice for him inside the closet. He rarely came out and took to urinating in their shoes. Molly moved the litter box and food bowl inside the closet, and placed their shoes at the foot of the bed.

With no income, they emptied their checking account, their savings account, cashed in bonds, Molly's IRA, Asher's coin collection. As August approached, they went grocery shopping and to the movies to cool off, carrying Chester with them in Asher's backpack. Everything cost money.

The air they breathed tasted stale. Sleep was not restful. One night, Molly ran a fever, and was overcome with relief to have the chills.

The heat broke during the first week of September. The entire city could breathe again. Molly and Asher met Leo for pizza. They sat by the open window and marveled at the breeze, at the flexibility of the cheese on the pizza. And for the first time in months, they were able to laugh.

The summer had been uncommonly hot, and in the temperate weeks that followed, Molly found another job, one which she did not like much, but one which kept her occupied and provided a paycheck. Chester came back out of the closet. By early October, the couple was wearing sweaters, and halfway through the month they had to retrieve their winter coats from the back of the closet. Asher began to study later, and Molly went with friends to a jewelry-making class. At night, when the heat from the clanking pipes was not enough, Chester slept between them, his loose, furry flesh spreading out like a pancake. Things had righted themselves. And then the deaths began.

The first call came from Molly's mother at seven in the morning. Molly's aunt Silvia had passed away during the night. Silvia had only been in her late sixties, but had been battling one type of cancer or another for the past decade. "She died at home, not in the hospital," Molly's mother said. "Everyone was with her. *Both* ex-husbands." Molly's mother sounded sober and alert. Today was Tuesday. Religious law required that Silvia be buried as soon as possible, but the family decided she would have preferred good attendance to strict adherence. The ceremony was set for noon on Sunday, Molly's mother picking them up because the couple did not have a car.

The sky was gray and the trees were prematurely bare, and even though the wind made the autumn day feel frozen, nearly one hundred people showed up for the funeral: relatives, friends, both ex-husbands, the temple sisterhood, and every last member of three separate Mahjong groups. Molly's mother snorted through her tears and remarked that if Silvia had been alive, she would have been very happy. She always loved a well-attended party.

When Asher and Molly arrived back home, the message light on the answering machine was blinking. It was Asher's uncle. Something had gone terribly wrong. His son Stanley's second child—a three-year-old—had died early that morning. They didn't know what it was, some kind of absurd virus that had come on suddenly. His uncle's voice cracked, then resumed. The funeral was on Tuesday. Could Asher please call the other cousins and tell them the news?

Stanley was only two years older than Asher. He was an observant man, slight and kind. Asher sat on the bed and put his hand on the phone. He looked down at his lap. Molly handed Asher the address book, then poured them each a glass of Scotch.

The funeral was upstate, and Leo lent them his car. He had known Stanley from childhood—their families had all lived on the same block. In grade school, the boys played baseball together. Sometimes they played cops and gangsters. But their favorite was astronauts. Once, Leo and Asher and Stanley all put a few of Leo's action figures in the oven, saying they were traveling to a distant star, a red giant. When they smelled burning plastic all the way from the den, Asher's stomach dropped. They threw the oven door open and an unnaturally black smoke billowed out. "Get out," Stanley said, and he put on a pair of oven mitts. He removed the melting figures from Asher's mother's oven, tossing them hissing and sizzling into the sink. Leo wailed as Stanley scraped the melted plastic from the bottom of the oven, and Asher stood still and dumbfounded, watching, unable to move, to thank Stanley, to console Leo.

Now Leo handed Asher his keys, saying it just didn't seem right that things like this should happen. He said going to the funeral would be the right thing to do, but the thought of Stanley's kid dying made him feel too low.

The child's funeral was much different than Aunt Silvia's. The men in the family carried the small pine box, lowering it themselves into the grave. The gravediggers stood by as the men piled up the soil until the hole was level with the ground. Thunder cracked and an icy rain fell. Their shoes and hands were caked with mud. They were dark wisps of men in the cold, gray air. Stanley's wife held an infant in her arms, and her other child clung to her skirt. Her face was empty and her lips were pursed. People rocked back and forth, wet, freezing, praying, their lips moving ardently with sounds that the wind stole, carried off across the vast crowded cemetery.

Molly grabbed Asher from under the elbow and squeezed him tight to her. For warmth. For comfort. They had no children. They had only Chester. And a small apartment in the city and several shoes filled with cat pee. They had a nice television set. They had at least one job between them. They had each other.

Molly and Asher drove around for forty-five minutes looking for a parking spot. They gave Leo his keys and sat with him for an hour and a half. They held glasses of Scotch in their hands, but didn't drink. The TV was on a low murmur. Finally, Leo said, "Two deaths in two weeks."

Asher looked up. "Maybe it's this cold front."

"Maybe it's something in the air," Molly said.

Leo smirked sadly. "Maybe someone put a whammy on you two." For as long as Asher had known Leo, he had been earnest and somber. He was a sensitive child, unusually frank and easily hurt. And even as an adult, he was the kind of guy who, when everyone had had a little too much to drink, might often find himself getting punched in the teeth. But he would never hit back. This was Leo.

Now the three of them sat on the couch with their un-drunk drinks while the TV went on soundlessly. Their insides felt like cold, wet socks. When Asher and Molly left, they took a cab the twelve blocks home, because they could not bear the damp, chilly walk.

They continued feeling this way all week long, until they got word Friday night that Molly's grandmother had had congestive heart failure. On Saturday, Esther's lungs collapsed and she had been put on a respirator. She sat there, propped up in the hospital bed, bloated and miserable. Her forever-black coiffure, which Molly and her sisters used to liken to a soufflé, had fallen and was bleeding purple against the pillow. There were bruises on Esther's arms and hands.

Molly's father slept in the chair by his mother's bedside. Molly's grandfather remained with the home healthcare aide because he was frail and increasingly demented, his thoughts swimming in blurred circles, crazed fish chasing their own fins. On Monday, Molly skipped her jewelry-making class to visit her grandmother, but arrived in the middle of a tussle. The aide had brought her grandfather for a visit, but he—stooped, loose-pants, once handsome—was pointing his finger at his wife and yelling, "This is not Esther. Where is my wife? Take this woman away and get me my wife." Both Molly's father and the home health care aide finally removed her grandfather from the room. Esther's eyes were wide and troubled and her mouth was full of tubing.

Molly came back to the hospital several days later. She made Asher come with her even though he had a paper due in two days. Molly's father was still in the chair. He looked worn. He was reading the entertainment section of the paper. They all talked to Esther, giving her updates on the lives of movie stars. Molly's mother came in with Chinese takeout. "They gave me six fortune cookies," she said. "*Six.*" Esther stared ahead, eyes full of trouble and confusion.

At night, the smell of heavy Chinese food and hospital cleaner remained in their skin. Molly burrowed into Asher for warmth. "It's so cold," she said. Asher held her until his shoulder fell asleep, then wriggled away to get an extra blanket. The pipes clanked violently. Chester joined them in the bed and half-licked, half-nibbled their hair. In the morning, he retched until he brought up an enormous hairball, a heterogeneous tangle of human and cat hairs. After lunch, Molly got the voicemail that her grandmother's lungs were full of fluid. She expired quietly the next night as the season's first snow fell.

At the funeral, the ground was slick with refrozen snow. One of Esther's oldest friends slipped and broke her hip on her way back to her car. While they waited for the ambulance, Leo gave Asher a look. His eyes showed amusement and sadness. But he said nothing.

The temperature continued to drop. The wind made their bones feel exposed, and their breath was forever visible like ghosts of words. Still, it got colder. The days came in identical grays. A ninety-year-old cousin of Asher's contracted pneumonia. Molly's grandfather, forlorn and now eternally befuddled, had stopped eating. One of Asher's professors had a brain hemorrhage. Each new week brought another death. Molly quit wearing black to work, for fear she would need the outfit for the next funeral.

Leo came over and they all ordered pizza. After dinner, Molly worked on her knitting. Asher picked up one of his theory books, and Leo sat with the cat in his lap. Chester whined until Leo patted him repeatedly on the rump.

When the cat began purring, Leo said, "This winter has been incredibly bleak."

"All these funerals." Asher said. "It's getting to be routine. They're drab and rote and mandatory. Like office parties."

Molly could see how unhappy Asher was. "It's easier that way," she said. "If you felt everything, the days would be impossible to get through." She wanted to go to the couch, take the book from his hands, lean into him, and feel calmed. But she could see he was in a distant mood. They had hardly fought recently, but it was because they were both too empty to fight. Molly made a sour face.

Leo spoke up as if to try to break the tension. "This old fart," he said, still patting the cat, "he better not get any funny ideas. In my mind, Asher, you are now permanently associated with the smell of cat pee. If Chester were to pass away, I wouldn't recognize you."

Asher was hardly responsive. Without looking up from his book, he said, "Don't even joke."

The news of Leo's death was sudden and unreal, the kind of news you laugh at after hearing, because it could only be a joke. And then you laugh again, more, like a cough, like a hiccup, repeated and uncontrollable, until maybe you are crying. And if indeed you are crying, you cry until your eyes are empty, and then you are numb and miserable and otherworldly. The morning of the funeral, Asher could not even move his limbs, they were so heavy. Molly dressed him, lugging him around, pulling at him. He was a rag doll run through the washing machine, food that had been chewed up and spit out.

Leo's mother wailed, tears almost freezing in the cold as they moved down her cheeks. Asher was dry and distant, as if he were hearing everything from a million miles away. As if he were listening through a tin can with a string attached, the kind of telephones he and Leo would make as children, pretending one of them was calling from the moon and the other from the Mother Ship. Asher was on the moon now. He was drifting. He could hardly hear the crying, the rabbi, the speeches people made after the casket was lowered, the wind consuming his ears.

Everyone had been thrown into space. Leo's death looked like a typical suicide, a mixing of too many Xanax and too much Scotch one cold night. And though everyone knew he had had a tendency for blue spells, for feeling low, for feeling too much, they would never have imagined such a cop-out. The pills, the slit wrists, the head in the oven, to hang yourself with an old sheet tied to a rafter. There was no note, no warning, no last words, and all Asher kept thinking when he could think in whole thoughts was that this was not like Leo, because it was, as an act, humorless and mediocre.

Their last conversation had been about cat pee, about old Chester, and how he made everything Asher owned smell of cat pee. *In my mind, you are associated with the smell of cat pee.* It was a code he could not break. The words looped in his head, forming questions. Addressed to Leo. Someone who could no longer answer them. Leo had bailed on him, the co-owner of the Mother Ship and half his childhood memories.

Before bed, Molly held Asher's hands and rubbed them. They were ice. She undressed him down to his boxer shorts and socks, then pulled him up onto the pillow. He had not been able to sleep the first few nights. Now, overtired, he spent the night cold, then terribly hot, trapped in a fine web of almost-sleep, dreaming with his eyes open, seeing shadows move across the room like ghosts, surfacing to find himself talking out loud, then falling back, sweaty-headed, into deeper rings of sleep.

The week after the funeral was better, and then the one after that. Asher was more placid. He took incompletes for all his classes. He sat at home and ate cereal in his underwear, watching the television with empty eyes, keeping it on always, like the rumble of family in the background. Molly left him alone during the day, unable to spare any more vacation days. Work kept her mind clear and occupied. She was thankful that she had remained in control of her facilities so far. At home, she tried to get Asher to eat hot soup, but he wanted only cereal, the kind with pictures of fruit and animals on the box and colorful marshmallows inside. Finally, he agreed to eat pizza again, though he ate it listlessly, as if it had no flavor.

That night, in some unnumbered hour of the nascent next day, a shadow swept across the room. It moved from the window down across the planks of wood floor, past the rug, and into the far corner by the dresser. A cloud may have passed across the moon, the light from which bled through the blinds of their bedroom window. But the shadow moved out from the corner of the room, making a slow circle around the rug, finally resting at the foot of the bed. Asher looked at Molly, whose face was pale and vacant with sleep. She had an arm draped around the enormous lump of fur that was Chester. Neither stirred. But the shadow was restless.

Asher strained his eyes at the formless, dark spot that seemed now almost perched on the edge of the bed. "Hello?" he whispered. "Is anybody there?"

He whispered so as not to startle Molly or the cat or the shadow. It appeared to be leaning in closer. Asher leaned in too, got up on all fours, moved nearer to the edge of the bed. The shadow seemed to turn slightly. "Who are you?" Asher said. "What do you want?"

The shadow moved back, almost stood, glided slowly but not entirely gracefully out of the room. It was headed for the kitchen. Asher, in his underclothes and stocking feet, followed close behind. The shadow stopped by the refrigerator. Asher opened the door, and in the dim light, he could make out the vaguest of features. A protrusion of a nose. The suggestion of a chin. He took the milk out and grabbed a bowl. Leo also liked the cereal with the fun-colored marshmallows.

Asher poured the cereal in the bowl, milk on top. He put down a spoon. They sat together at the table, Leo's vague shadowy hand moving down into the bowl, then up toward his mouth. Nothing moved.

"Are you eating the cereal or what?"

"I can't really eat anymore," Leo said. His voice was soft and reedy, like two thin voices at once, gauzy ribbons entwined, wind through the grass. "But it's nice to pretend."

"What are you doing here?" Asher watched Leo closely. "I mean, I'm glad to see you. But why are you here? After you did what you did."

Leo shifted in the chair, as if crossing his legs. "I had something I wanted to tell you," he said. He dipped his hand into the bowl again, raised it to his mouth. "I just loved this cereal," he said. "I liked the chocolate-flavored one too. But the fruity one is better."

"Something to tell me?" Hurt caught in Asher's throat.

"Yes, but I forget. Or, actually, I remember." He began to rock rhythmically back and forth, mumbling or chanting. "It's incredible, Asher," he continued. "I remember so much, I can hardly remember what I remember. It's become a bit of a problem." Something stirred. It was Chester. He was up, moving lopsidedly across the room. "Chester," Leo cooed, and the cat jumped up on the chair, circled, then lay down. Asher suspected the cat was trying to sit in Leo's lap, but it looked more like Leo had a cat stuck in his shadowy thighs.

Asher watched Leo move to pet the cat, which the two of them had taken in when they shared a dorm room in college. He said, "You left so suddenly. What happened?"

"Oh, yes," Leo said. "I have some old action figures at my mother's house that might be worth something. They're in good condition, but without their original boxes. Top shelf of the green bookcase in the basement."

"It was very unlike you."

"You can throw out or donate everything else. You can have the car too if you like."

"Did you do it on purpose?" Asher said. "*Cat pee?* Answer me."

"You know *Kaddish?* I've finally got it down pat. I don't even need to cheat off the transliteration. And I can see how each letter is connected in space." He went back to the cereal.

"Yes or no?"

"Listen to this: Leo, son of Gerald, son of Samuel, son of Meir, son of Avram."

"You're avoiding my question."

"Asher, please. You sound like my mother. Son of Yossel, son of Issur, son of Yankel . . . "

"It was a stupid thing to do."

"There's nothing I can do about it now."

"I'm angry at you. It was stupid and childish. You didn't even give me a chance to talk you out of it. And now look what you leave me with. This cat? Some action figures? A bowl of cereal? It was really rotten what you did."

"There are worse things to be left with."

"Why don't you just take Chester with you? Were you threatening that?"

"No."

"No what?"

"It's not his time yet."

Asher stood up and pushed Leo over. His hands kept going until they hit the back of the chair, which toppled over from the force. The cat fell too, shrieking and hissing. When Chester regained his bearings, he walked to the other side of the room where he gathered himself grumpily in a corner. Leo, more hazy now, stayed on the floor.

"You're such a fucking coward." Asher had his fists up.

"Now you're just being foolish."

Asher stopped. Crumbled at the edges. He sat down on the floor next to his friend, who was dead, who was fading, a faint, nebulous thing on the floor, because Asher had pushed him out of his chair, even though he was dead. "I told you what I came to tell you," Leo said. "Now Chester is mad at you. If you don't watch out, he'll pee in your shoes again."

Asher stood up, walked to the cat, and scooped him up. He turned back to Leo, who remained on the floor, sullen, translucent. Leo looked up at his friend and his cat and said, "Things just happen."

Leo's voice was so low now, it was hardly audible. He was fading back into simple shadows. He moved away, back toward the bedroom, and Asher followed him, cat in arms. In the bedroom, Leo was gone. Asher looked in the corners of the room, which were filled with the awkward blockiness of cold night air. Molly slept. She was turned to the other way now, facing the window. Her face was touched by the sallow glow from the city and the moon. He held their cat, his and Molly's, the cat Leo had found in a dumpster—Leo who let Asher take the cat with him when he moved in with Molly, Leo who held his old action figures so dear, Leo who was on the Mother Ship while Asher was on the moon, forced to discover new, uncharted territory. And here was Chester, cat, child of garbage, shoe pee-er, obese and needy. He shifted the cat to one arm as he crawled under the covers. Molly was warm but her nose was cold.

Leo had cried to see his action figures melted, smelling acrid and candle-like, pooling, ruining the bottom of the oven, hissing violently in the damp sink. And Asher had stood and watched Stanley, watched Leo, watched the tortured plastic figures move from the oven rack to the mitt to the sink. And Asher did nothing. But he took it all in. He saw everything, the melted plastic on the oven mitt, his mother coming home, screaming, the smack near the ear, himself scraping out the plastic from the cool oven with a butter knife, Leo hiding the remaining action figures away in a shoe box, on the green bookshelf in his mother's basement. Years later, they had heard a rattle in a dumpster near their dorm. Asher gave Leo a leg up, and he went in, looking for that small, starving kitten. They took it back to their room and cleaned it off and kept it secretly. And then Molly had fallen in love with the cat. Leo said, *No, don't worry about it. Take it with you.* Asher said, *But he's really yours.* And Leo said, laughing, *You'll be able to give Chester all the things that I couldn't.*

Asher placed the cat between himself and Molly, then he kissed her head and prayed for emptiness and for daylight and for sleep.

THE TWO-HEADED GIRL

by Paul G. Tremblay from *Five Chapters*

—————◆—————

1 I have to keep swinging an extra fifteen minutes before I can go downtown and to the Little Red Bookstore, because Mom wants to run the dishwasher and the blender tonight. I wonder if my time on the swing will generate enough extra juice for those appliances, or even if she's telling me the truth. I've been having a hard time with telling-truth or truth-telling.

Anne Frank is on my left again. I only ever get to see her in profile. Whenever I'm around a mirror she is always someone else. Today, she's the early-in-her-diary Anne, the same age as me. Anne spent most of my swinging afternoon pining for Peter, but now she wants to talk to Lies, her best friend before the war.

She says, "I feel so guilty, Lies. I wish I could take you into hiding with me."

I get this odd, stomach-knotty thrill and I pretend that she really knows me and she is really talking to me. But at the same time, I don't like it when she calls me Lies. I say, "I'm sorry, Anne, but I'm Veronica." The words come out louder than I intended. I'm not mad at her. I could never be mad at Anne. It's just hard to speak normally when on the downswing.

Anne moves on, talks about her parents and older sister, and then how much she dislikes that ungrateful dentist they took in.

"Nobody likes dentists," I say and I want her to laugh. She doesn't. I only hear dead leaves making their autumn sounds as they blow up against the neighbor's giant fence and our swing set and generator.

Mom sticks her only head out of the kitchen window and yells, "Looks like we need another fifteen minutes, sorry, honey. I promise I'll get Mr. Bob out here tomorrow to tune everything up."

This is not good news. My back hurts and my legs are numb already. She's promised me Mr. Bob every day for a week. She's made a lot of promises.

"Hi, Veronica." It's that little blonde boy from across the street. He's become part of my daily routine: when I come out, he hides in our thick bushes, sneaks along the perimeter of my neighbor's beanstalk-tall, wood plank fence, and then sits next to the swing set and generator.

"Hi, Jeffrey," I say. Anne is quiet. Jeffrey has a withered left arm. Both of us try not to stare at it.

He says, "Where's your dad?" His little kindergarten voice makes me smile even though I'm sick of that particular question.

"I don't know, Jeffrey, just like I didn't know yesterday, and the day before yesterday." I try not to be mean or curt with him. He's the only kid in town who talks to me.

Anne says, "My dad is hiding in the annex."

Jeffrey stays on my right, which is closer to my head. He only talks to me. I know it makes Anne lonely and sad, which makes me lonely and sad, just like her diary did. I don't remember what came first: me reading the diary or Anne making a regular rotation as my other head.

Jeffrey says, "You should ask your mom or somebody where he is."

I know Jeffrey doesn't realize what he's asking of me. I know people never realize how much their words hurt, sometimes almost as much as what isn't said.

I say what I always say. "I'll think about it."

"Can I ride on the swing?"

Anne is mumbling something under her breath. My heart breaks all over again. I say, "No, sorry, Jeffrey. I can't let you. You'd have to ask my mother." I find it easier to blame everything on Mom, even if it isn't fair.

Jeffrey mashes his fully developed right fist into his cheek, an overly dramatic but affective pantomime of I-never-get-to-do-anything-fun.

I say, "Do you want to walk downtown with me when I'm done?"

He nods.

"Go ask your parents first."

Jeffrey runs off. With his little legs pumping and back turned to me, I let myself stare at the flopping and mostly empty left arm of his thin, gray sweatshirt. He scoots onto his front lawn and past a sagging scarecrow, a decoration left out too long.

My legs tingle with pins and needles, and Anne is crying. I wish I could console her, but I can't. Now I'm thinking about the question I've always wanted to ask Anne, but never have because I'm a coward. I could ask her now, but it isn't the right time, or at least, that's what I tell myself. So we just keep swinging; a pendulum of her tears and me.

2 Jeffrey and I are downtown, playing a game on the cobblestones. I have to step on stones in a diagonal pattern. Jeffrey has to step on the darkest stones. I've seen him miss a few but I won't call him on it. I'll let him win.

Anne is gone and Medusa has taken her place. She is my least favorite head but not because she is a gorgon. I wish she was more gorgon-esque. Medusa is completely un-aggressive, head and eyes always turned down and she doesn't say boo. I feel bad for her, and I hate Athena for turning Medusa into a hideous monster because she had the audacity to be raped by Poseidon in Athena's temple. Athena was the one with the big-time jealousy and beauty issues, kind of like my mother. I used to try and talk to Medusa, to make her feel better about herself. I'd tell her that her physical or social appearance doesn't measure her worth and that her name means *sovereign female wisdom*, which I think is really cool for a name, so much cooler than my name which means *true image*. But she never says anything back, and when I talk her snakes tickle my neck with their forked tongues.

Jeffrey shouts, "I'm winning," even though he keeps falling off dark stones onto light stones. Balancing with only one arm must be difficult.

I say, "You're really good at this game."

It's getting dark and I know Mom will be mad at me for being so late, but I'm allowing myself to champion the petty act of defiance. We make it to the Little Red Bookstore with its clapboard walls, cathedral ceiling, and giant mahogany bookcases with the customer scaffolding planks jutting out at the higher levels. There are people everywhere. Customers occupy the plush reading chairs and couches, the planks, and the seven rolling stack-ladders. I hold Jeffrey's hand as we wade through the crowd toward the fiction section. No one notices us.

Jeffrey is as patient as he can be, but soon he's tugging at my arm and skirt, asking if we can find dinosaur books, then asking if we can go home. I need a stack-ladder to go after the books I want. They're still all taken. Even if I could get a ladder, I can't leave Jeffrey unattended and he can't climb the ladder and walk the bookcase scaffolding with me. So I grab a random book, something I've never heard of by someone I've never heard of, because I have to buy something. Then I walk Jeffrey to the kid section and to some dinosaur books. He sits on the ground with a pop-up book in his lap. He knows all the dinosaur names, even the complex ones with silent letters and ph's everywhere, and I've never understood why boys love the monsters that scare them so much. Above my heads, people climb in and out of the ladders and platforms and book stacks.

I say to Medusa, "I think they look like bees in a honeycomb." Medusa sighs and doesn't lift her head.

Jeffrey sounds out an armored dinosaur's name, *an-kie-low-saur-us*, ankylosaurus, then he stands and swings an imaginary tail at me.

I say to Medusa, "Come on. Tell me what you think. Something. Anything!"

Medusa's snakes stir, rubbing up against my neck. She says, "Unlike my sisters, I'm mortal."

Everyone in and above the stacks stops what they are doing and looks at us, looks at Medusa, who for once returns their stares. No one turns to stone, at least not against their will, and I know it's time for us to go. The customers are upset with us, likely because we're talking about mortality in a bookstore.

I brush a particularly frisky snake off my neck and I say, "Me, too," but enough time has passed so I'm not sure if Medusa knows I'm responding to what she said. Communication is so difficult sometimes.

We walk to the register and pay for the book I don't want.

3 It's dark when I get home. Mom is sitting at the kitchen table. She's dressed to go out even though she won't, wearing a tight candy-red top, the same red as her lipstick, with a black poodle skirt. Her black hair bobs at her shoulders. She could be my sister back from college

ready to tell me all she's learned about life and love as a woman, but she's not my sister.

There are two white, Irish-knit, turtleneck sweaters on her lap. On the counter, the blender is dirty with its plastic walls dripping something creamy. The dishwasher is in a loud rinse cycle. My dinner is on a plate, hidden under a crinkled, re-used piece of tinfoil.

Mom says, "You shouldn't keep Jeffrey out so late. He's only five years old. You know better than that." Her voice is naturally loud. She looks at me quick, like a jab, and she goes up the left side of one sweater with the scissors.

She's right, but I'm not going to acknowledge her rightness. Just like Mom won't acknowledge that my other head is Jeanne D'Arc. I say, "Jeffrey had a great time at the bookstore and his parents were fine with it." Suddenly not quite ready for an argument to start, I add, "Everything okay with the blender and dishwasher?"

Jeanne whispers a prayer, coving her face with my left hand, very pious and humble.

Mom says, "So far so good, thanks for asking. You're such a sweetheart." Mom goes up the right side of the other sweater. She works so very fast. "It's going to be cold out tomorrow, so I'm making you a nice, warm, and presentable sweater." She says presentable as if anyone will see me. Mom gets up and goes to her sewing machine next to the kitchen table. I wonder if Mom planned the sewing machine into this evening's allotment of electricity and then I'm worried that I didn't spend enough time on the swing today, and then I hate myself for being so trained.

I say, "What's for dinner?"

"Mushroom chicken, corn, rice pilaf. Go wash up first. And you are going to do your math and science homework tonight, Veronica. No excuses. I can't put off your exams any longer. They're due in the post in three days."

I mix truth with a lie. "I bought a book that I really want to read first."

"Tomorrow night is your book club and the next night you have to take the exams. You are going to do your homework tonight."

Mom is always so reasonable, and I hate it. Makes me feel like I'm the bad one for wanting to fight. I say, "I don't care," but not very loud.

I think Mom is going to let it slide, but then she breaks protocol by commenting on my other head.

"Why is there a boy on your shoulder?"

Jeanne crosses herself.

I don't know what to say. Other than when she's making two-headed clothing, Mom usually ignores my other head. I manage to say, "Real nice, Mom. She's Joan of Arc." I don't say her name in French because I don't want to remind Mom that she hasn't given me a French unit to work on in almost two weeks.

"I didn't say that to be mean, Veronica."

"Then why did you say it?"

She stares at me. "I won't let you start another fight with me over nothing," she says and turns on the sewing machine.

I throw myself into a chair and pick at my lukewarm dinner. I don't wait for Jeanne to say grace.

There's a spider fern hanging above Mom and the sewing machine, some of its leaves are browning. With the machine's vibrations, some leaves break off and fall onto Mom's head. She sews quickly and the result is a beautiful Irish-knit turtleneck sweater with two turtlenecks. No visible seams where two different sweaters come together. She is very talented and I hate her. Okay, I don't hate her but she makes me very angry without me being able to rationally explain why. Yesterday, I constructed an elaborate Cinderella fantasy where my father, a man I no longer remember, was driven off by my evil and shrewish mother. I suppose it's the only desertion scenario that doesn't hurt me.

I offer Jeanne some of my food but she is fasting. Now I feel guilty. I struggle to finish what's on my plate. I think about Jeffrey insisting that I ask Mom where my father is, or better yet, how come he doesn't see me if he really lives in the same town as us, but I know tonight is not the night for that conversation.

Mom says, "Try the sweater on, sweetie. Make sure it fits."

I pull the scratchy wool over our heads. Jeanne doesn't like it.

Mom tugs at the shoulders, waist, and sleeves, inspecting her work. She says, "This fits nice. Very nice. You look great." Mom is still at least six inches taller than me. I don't know if I'll ever catch up. Mom folds her arms over her thin chest, her defense and attack posture. Big smile, quite satisfied with herself, with what she's done for her daughter. It's a very intimidating look. One I don't know how to overcome.

She says, "Homework time. I'll check your answers when you're done."

I leave the kitchen with a full belly and empty of fight. As I walk into the living room and past the snarling fireplace, Jeanne closes her eyes and says, "*Allez!*" which means *Go!* I already feel bad about the food so I hurry away from the fire, but I trip and fall, my hands scraping on the brick landing in front of the fireplace. Jeanne spasms and twitches, trying to remove herself from my body and away from the fire, and I'm crying, but not because of the pain, and somehow this must be all Mom's fault too.

"Sorry!" I get up and dash up the stairs to my bedroom. My hands sting and I look at them. The palms are all scraped up and bloody.

Jeanne says, "It's only stigmata, but keep it secret. Go wash it off and don't tell your mother."

At least, that's what I think she says. My French is a little rusty.

4 Mr. Bob was my science teacher when I went to school. I don't miss school and the taunts and the stares and how incredibly lonely I could be in a lunchroom full of other people. Nor do I miss Mr. Bob, even though he's always been nice to me.

Mom and I are standing next to the swing set, watching Mr. Bob. Odd and misshapen tools that couldn't possibly fix anything fill Mr. Bob's fists and spill out of his tight, too-short, and paint-stained overalls.

My mother says, "Can you fix this?"

Mr. Bob says, "No sweat."

My other head is Marie Curie, child-aged, so no one recognizes her. She's very plain and I find that beautiful. Marie says something in Russian that sounds vaguely commiserative. Mom ignores this head.

Unprompted, Mr. Bob launches into an explanation of how the swing set works. Maybe he does know that I have young Madame Curie with me and he's trying to impress her. If so, that's really creepy.

Mr. Bob says, "This swing set is one big friction machine. Mounted on the horizontal bar above is an axle with circular plates, each plate turning and rubbing against pads when you swing, making an electrical charge. The prime conductors, your long brass pipes, follow the frame of the swing set. The ends of these conductors carry metallic combs with points bent toward the faces of the glass plates. The combs collect the charge, and the pipes bring the charge to the collector/generator and then to your house. Really it's very simple, but not very efficient."

Mom says, "Nothing Veronica's father did was very efficient."

I want to tell Marie Curie the obvious, that my father made this swing set, but he isn't here anymore and I don't know where he is but supposedly he's still in town, somewhere. I don't think Marie has learned English yet. The next time I go to the bookstore, I'll get her biography, and maybe some books on electricity and friction machines so I can fix this without any help.

Mr. Bob climbs a ladder to get at the axle. Tools drip and drop like a lazy rain. As much as I'd like the swing to be tuned up so it'll be more efficient, I don't want Mr. Bob touching any of it. The swing is my only connection to my father and I'm afraid Mr. Bob will ruin everything. Wanting to be random and unpredictable, but knowing differently I blurt out, "Where's my father?"

Mom folds her arms across her chest and says, "Why don't you go inside and wash up. Don't forget you're hosting the book club tonight and you haven't prepared any of the hors d'oeuvres."

I stare at Mom and I want to cry. Marie stares at Mr. Bob and clucks her tongue at his apparent incompetence. Marie says something in Russian that I think would translate as: *I'd like to see this contraption's schematic, you talentless monkey.*

Mom softens, and bends to whisper in my ear. She says, "We can talk about this later if you really want to. If you need to. But it's for the best, Veronica. Really. Go on, now. Set up for your book club."

5 My book club is here. Six women, ages ranging from Peg Dower's somehow rheumy thirty-six to Cleo Stanton-Meyer's health-club fifty-three. Our chairs and bodies make a circle, a book club Stonehenge, but with an end-table loaded with coffee, tea, water, chips, and spinach

dip, and biscotti at the center. Everyone has their dog-eared copy of *Mrs. Dalloway* by Virginia Woolf on their slack-clad laps.

Mom stays in the kitchen and doesn't participate in the discussions even though she reads all the books. She insists this is my *thing*. I hear the sewing machine turn on and off sporadically.

Bev Bentley, white-blonde and DD chest (Mom is so jealous), says, "Excuse me, but is that her, Veronica? Will we be able ask her questions?" Hands cover faces all over the circle. Peg and Cleo groan much like a crowd at a sporting event when something bad happens. Bev is the something bad happening. She asks me the same question every meeting. And every meeting I answer: "Sorry, Bev, she's not the author of this book." It is rather insulting for her to continually think that my other head is that simple or predictable, but I don't tell them my other head is Sylvia Plath. They should be able to figure that out on their own. Sylvia just smirks and takes it all in, burning Bev down with a look that could shame an entire culture.

Our discussion begins with Peg trying to compare Clarissa Dalloway to Catherine from *Wuthering Heights* but no one agrees with her. Sylvia laughs but it sounds sad. I redirect the discussion to the book's themes of insanity and suicide and reality and the critique of the social system. None of us says anything that's new or important, but it is still satisfying to discuss something that matters to us. Cleo wonders aloud how autobiographical this novel was for Woolf, and I wonder how hard Sylvia is biting her tongue or maybe she just doesn't care enough to join in. I'll need to keep me and her out of the kitchen and away from the oven.

Then book talk is over before everyone's teacups and coffee mugs are empty. And as usual, our talk deteriorates into town gossip.

"Darla has been sleeping with that new pharmacist."

"William Boyle?"

"He's the one."

"He must be ten years younger than Darla."

"Fifteen." ,

"And her divorce isn't even final yet."

They move on to discuss the high school gym teacher and his secret gay lover. As best as I can figure, this mysterious lover is more abstract ideal than reality. Sylvia is still disinterested. She's flipping through my copy of Mrs. *Dalloway* and doodling in the margins. And there's more of the who's-sleeping-with-who talk followed up with who's-not-sleeping-with-who talk, which includes Cleo's third husband's erectile dysfunction diagnosis and her daily countdown until he fills one of those blue pill prescriptions, likely to be handed out by the philandering pharmacist.

The sewing machine in the kitchen is quiet and has been for a while. Mom stopped sewing once the book discussion ended. I know Mom thinks this book-club-cum-gossip-session is a substitute for all the wonderful teenage conversations I don't have with other teenagers. I don't know if it is or not since I'm not having those teenage conversations with other teenagers. I generally don't mind the town dish as I do find it entertaining, but tonight it seems wrong, especially on the heels of Woolf's book. I mean, this was what she was railing against.

So inspired by Virginia to say something meaningful, or at the very least to yank everyone out of complacency, I say, "Does anyone know where my father lives?"

In the kitchen, the sewing machine roars to life, stitching its angry stitches. Sylvia whispers, "Atta, girl," into my ear. I look out into the newly silent Stonehenge of women. All of them here, all of them totems in my living room only because my mother asked them to be here. I love Mom and I hate her for the book club; not either/or but both at the same time.

The women, they shrug or shake their heads or say a weak *no*. Then they fill their plates with chips and biscotti. I know it's not fair to make them uncomfortable, but why should I always be the only one?

Our discussion slowly turns toward TV shows and movies, and then what book should we read next. Peg finds the book I didn't want to buy sitting unread on the fireplace mantel. She passes it around. Everyone claims to have heard about the book that no one has heard about. They mumble agreeable sentiments about it being challenging, something new, having buzz, and they decide, without asking me and before the book makes its way around the circle back to me, to make it our next book club selection. Sylvia thumbs through it and doesn't say anything.

Mom reappears from the kitchen with everyone's coat in her arms. Polite, light-pats-on-the-back hugs are passed back and forth, even when I insist upon handshakes, and then everyone leaves. I'm left with Sylvia, no answers to my father question, a mother pouting and sewing in the kitchen, loads of dishes and cups and trays to wash, and a book in my hands that I don't want to read.

6 I am up and out of the house before Mom wakes up. We haven't said anything to each other since the book club. Getting up and eating breakfast alone quickly becomes an hour on the swing set. It's cold and there's no way of knowing if Mr. Bob's tune-up did any good. The swing doesn't seem any different, or more efficient.

I really don't want to do this today. It's not helping that my other head is changing by the downswing, almost too many heads to keep up with. There's been Cleopatra, Bonnie Parker, Marsha Brady, Fay Wray, Emily Brontë, Cindy Lou Who, Janis Joplin, and even that vacuous snot Joan Rivers.

My heads never change this fast, and I hate it. I really wanted nothing more than to sit out here and talk with one of the heads, have someone help me decide what to do, or what to think. I don't know why finding my father is all of a sudden so important to me. Last week and pretty much all the weeks before that week, he was never more than a fleeting thought, a forgotten dream.

The swing coupled with my changing heads are making me dizzy, so I put my legs down, scraping my sneakers on the sand, digging an even deeper rut, and I stop swinging. Then I go and sit up against the neighbor's wooden fence with my head in my hands, trying to regain some level of equilibrium. Joan Rivers is yammering in my ear about my terrible clothes and iffy skin. The leaves I'm sitting on are cold and wet. I get up and walk.

I walk downtown to the cobblestones and the Little Red Bookstore and Joan Rivers becomes Lauren Bacall becomes Calpurnia becomes Scout becomes Boo Radley's mother, which is confusing. I stand outside with my hands cupped on the bookstore's bay window. The place is empty and I'd have the shelves to myself but I keep walking,

past the Little Red Grocery and Little Red Hardware and the Little
Red Candy Shoppe and the Little Red Bank, and out of the downtown
area and through the town square, and Boo Radley's mother becomes
Lucille Ball becomes Karen Silkwood becomes Mary Shelley becomes
Susan Faludi. I walk past the Little Red Library and the Little Red
Schoolhouse, which was where I dropped out during my sixth-grade
year. Tommy Gallahue showing up to school with a papier-mâché
second head was my last day of sixth grade. Susan Faludi becomes
Blanche DuBois becomes Alice in Wonderland. I walk past the town
high school and I walk past without any regrets. Alice becomes Rosa
Parks becomes Vivien Leigh. I walk through residential neighborhoods,
peeking over fences and into yards randomly, looking for the man I
don't remember, looking for the man I know I'll never find. Vivien
Leigh becomes a starving Ethiopian girl that I don't know but have seen
on commercials becomes Zelda becomes Flannery O'Connor. I don't
have a watch but it must be noon as the sun is directly over my head
and I'm very hungry, so I start walking back home, taking a different
route back, staying in the small neighborhoods, still looking through
fences and even inside a few mailboxes for what? I'm not sure. And
Flannery O'Connor becomes Oprah becomes Nancy Drew becomes
Maya Angelou becomes Shirley Temple becomes Eponine becomes
Little Orphan Annie becomes Amelia Earhart and I'm home.

My mother is on the swing. She's actually sitting on the swing that
apparently is not calibrated to precisely my weight. But she's not
really swinging. She's sitting, her legs folded under, her toes tickling
the rut in the sand, her face in her hands, and I can't be sure, but I
think she's crying. She's wearing an Irish-knit turtleneck sweater like
mine, but with only one turtleneck. Amelia Earhart becomes Shirley
Jackson becomes Hester Prynne. I'm hiding where Jeffrey usually
hides, in the thinning shrubbery next to our neighbor's fence. Then
Jeffrey runs out of his house, across the street, and to my mother. No
one has seen me yet. Jeffrey is talking with her. I guess, for him, it
doesn't matter who is swinging. I won't hold it against him. He's only
five. I wonder if he asks her the same questions he asks me. Mom
laughs then scoops up Jeffrey into her lap and they swing together.
Hester Prynne becomes the witch accusing Abigail, and I'm angry-

jealous, or jealous-angry, and maybe they're the same emotion, each just wearing something a little different. I walk out of the bushes and to the swing. Abigail doesn't say anything but just points with my left index finger.

Jeffrey says, "Hi, Veronica!" between giggles.

"Hi."

Mom stops the swing. She says, "Jeffrey you can swing by yourself, as long as you promise not to go too high. Promise?" If she was crying before, there is no sign of it now.

Jeffrey puffs out his chest, "I promise."

I want to ask how Jeffrey is going to manage this with his withered arm. But he hops right on the swing, tucks the left chain of the swing under his armpit, grabs the other chain with his good arm, and starts pumping. We watch him swing for a few minutes and Abigail has become someone else but I haven't bothered to look and see who it is.

Mom says, "We'll be right back, Jeffrey. I need to talk to Veronica for a bit. Keep pumping, kid." She puts a hand on my shoulder and guides me to the house. After a few paces, she says, "What?" like I've been staring at her expectantly, but I haven't. Then she says, "I need someone on that swing today. I need the juice to vacuum the floors later."

7 We're in the kitchen. I sit down. Mom stands and paces. She doesn't wait for me to say anything and starts right in with a simple declarative.

"You and I came home early one afternoon and I found more than the expected amount of heads in my bedroom."

I say, "How old was I?"

"One."

My other head is Mom. Mom when she was my age. Despite her pigtails, she manages older-Mom's fierce, intimidating look. I don't know what she's thinking, and I'm tired of trying to figure out who's thinking what.

I ask, "Who was he with?"

"Does it matter?" Mom doesn't waver, doesn't get all choked up or anything like that, not that I expected her to.

"I don't know if it matters, Mom. That's why I'm asking."

"The woman was the middle school science teacher that Mr. Bob replaced. She doesn't live in town anymore."

I imagine a woman who looks like Mr. Bob. She wears baggy clothes that have chemical stains and Bunsen burner singe marks. She has short, straight hair, mousy brown, wears thick glasses, and no makeup. Pretty in a smart way, maybe. I imagine Mom finding her in the bedroom with my father, who I can't describe in such physical detail, no matter how hard I try to conjure him.

Young-Mom doesn't say anything but just stares at her older self. Is this look of hers studied observation or soul-deep sadness?

"Did he leave after you caught him?"

"The very next morning."

"Did you tell him he had to leave?"

"No."

Young-Mom says, "Do you really need to know any more of this?" which I don't think is a very fair question. And it's not fair to be double-teamed by Mom like this, even though I know that I can't always blame everything on Mom. I fight the urge to tell the Young-Mom to shut up.

I say, "That's terrible. I'm sorry that happened, Mom. I really am."

"Thank you." Mom says it like she's accepting a throwaway compliment about her shoes. Young-Mom pouts. They are both so intimidating but I stand up and stutter-walk to Mom and give her a hug. She doesn't uncross her arms off her chest so the hug isn't soft and comfortable. I make contact mostly with the angles of her bones and the points of her elbows and the sweater wool scratches my face, but Mom does kiss the top of my head, twice. That's something, maybe even enough.

"Thanks again, sweetie."

I break the one-sided hug and say, "What did he look like?"

"You."

"Can I ask where he lives?"

Young-Mom sighs and shakes her head. Her pigtails tickle my neck, feeling eerily similar to Medusa's snakes, but I don't mind them as much.

"I thought I was ready to tell you, Veronica. But I'm not."

I want to ask if she knows who my other head is. I want to ask if she knows what it means. I want to ask if she knows that most days I dream about becoming her.

She continues, "It's not you anymore. I know you can handle it, now. But you'll just have to give me more time." Mom uncrosses her arms and looks around the kitchen, at the cluttered counter and the sewing machine, looking for something to do.

Young-Mom turns, whispers directly into my ear, "Are you happy, now?"

I unroll the neck of the sweater and pull it up over her mouth and nose. She doesn't stop me or say anything else.

I say, "Okay, Mom," but I don't know if it is okay and I don't know if I feel guilty or satisfied or sad or angry or scared. What I'm feeling no one has bothered to name or classify or dissect, or maybe this feeling has already been outed by somebody else and I just haven't stumbled across it and that seems likely but at the same time it doesn't, and then I think about all the books in my bedroom and the giant stacks of books in my Little Red Bookstore and I wonder if *it* is there or here or anywhere else other than inside me.

Mom says, "All right, back to work, then." She claps her hands and I feel my other head change but I won't look to see who it is yet. "Could you go and take over for Jeffrey on the swing? He's making me nervous. I appreciate it, honey. And don't forget about your big tests later."

8 It's windy and cold, the temperature dropping by the minute. Jeffrey stops swinging, but stays on the seat. "Do I have to stop now?"

"Yes, my mother wants me to take over."

He doesn't argue, but he hasn't moved off the seat either. He releases the swing chain that was tucked under his armpit. "You and your mom had a talk?"

"Yes, Jeffrey." I notice I'm standing in my Mom's pose, but I don't change it.

"Did you ask her about your dad?"

"I did."

"Did she tell you?"

"Tell me what?"

"Tell you where he is."

"No, not yet."

Jeffrey nods like he understands. Maybe he does. He says, "Maybe you should ask someone else."

"Like who?"

"Me?" He says it like a question, almost like he doesn't know who *me* is.

I play along. Anything to keep me off the swing for another few minutes. "Okay, Jeffrey. Do you know where my father is?"

He nearly shouts, "Yes."

My arms wrap tighter around my chest. This isn't fun anymore. "Then where is he?"

Jeffrey scoots off the swing and points behind him. He points at the neighbor's big wooden fence. "He lives there. Right next door."

That's impossible. Isn't it? Wouldn't I have seen him by now? I think about who lives there and I can't come up with anyone. Is that right? Has he been this close all along and I just haven't noticed, or haven't wanted to notice?

Jeffrey says, "I'm not lying, Veronica. I've seen him."

"I didn't say you were lying."

He says, "I think he's even out in the yard right now. Go and see."

I look at the fence, seven feet high, completely wrapping around the property. "How?"

"There's a knothole in the fence behind your bushes. You know, I usually hide in your bushes."

I snort, ready to charge. "Okay. Jeffrey, go home please."

He reacts like I hit him, and tears well up.

I soften. "You can come back over later, but I need to do this by myself."

Jeffrey nods, still fighting those tears, then sprints home, this time gripping the empty arm of his sweater. I walk to the bushes, to where Jeffrey hides, the same bushes I hid in earlier. There is a knothole in the fence, the size of a quarter, plenty big to see through. I should've seen this earlier, but I guess I wasn't looking for it.

I remember my second head. The turtleneck is still rolled over her nose and mouth. I roll it down and find Anne, again. Only this Anne

252

is older, older than me, even older than the one in her diary. Her skin has sores and is sallow and tight on her face, deepening and widening her already big eyes. Her hair has thinned and I see white scalp in too many places. This Anne doesn't ask any questions. This Anne isn't chatty. This is the Anne that no one dares imagine after reading her diary. I want to help her, take care of her somehow, and I think she senses this, because she points at the knothole with my left hand and nods. Before I look into the hole, I think, selfishly, that this might be the right Anne for the question I've always wanted to ask.

There's a man in the back yard. He's wearing jeans and a moth-worn, olive-green sweater, sleeves pushed up to his elbows. He's raking leaves with his back turned to me. When he stops raking, he walks over to a tire-swing tied to a thick branch of an oak tree. The branch has an axle and generator setup similar to my swing set, but no one is riding the tire-swing. There are rocks duct-taped to the bottom of the tire. He pushes the tire-swing a few times, to get the pendulum moving, then goes back to raking leaves. This man has two heads.

I wait and watch. He rakes and pushes, but he doesn't turn around so I can see either of his faces. His hair is brown and short on each head, and now I wish I never looked through the hole.

Anne says, "Why has he never contacted you? Why does he hide so close to home? Does he do this so he can see you when he wants? Or is he just being cruel, mocking you, mocking your mother?"

I want to stay crouched in this spot and let leaves and snow gather on me and never stop watching, but I do pull my eye away from the knot. Anne and I scan the length and height of the fence. I don't know the answer to Anne's questions and I know the likelihood is that I may never know.

I decide to ask Anne the question. I hope it doesn't seem callous or even cruel to her. I understand how it could be interpreted that way, but I hope she understands me and why I do what I do. I still hope.

I say, "Anne, in your last diary entry, you wrote something that . . . that I need to ask you about. This you in particular. Do you know what I mean by *this you*?"

"Yes."

"Do you still believe that people are really good at heart?"

Anne sighs and closes her eyes and it's terrible because it makes her look dead. She holds my left hand, the fingers suddenly and dangerously skinny, over her mouth and chin. She's thinking and I know she will give me an answer. But now that I've asked, the answer isn't as important to me as it was a few days ago, or even a few seconds ago. Because no matter what she says, I'll go back to my swing set and to feeding my house what it needs and I won't tell Mom that I know where he is and I'll take my tests tonight and try my best and help her with the dishes and then talk to her about *Mrs. Dalloway* and the women in my book club and maybe even convince Mom to become an official member. Because, maybe foolishly, I still hope.

But I'll sit in the bushes and wait as long as is necessary to hear what Anne has to say. I owe us that much.

THE FIRST SEVERAL HUNDRED YEARS FOLLOWING MY DEATH

by Shawn Vestal from *Tin House*

The food is excellent. The lines are never long. There's nothing to do with your hands. These are the first things I tell my son. Then we don't talk again for something like two hundred years.

The food is excellent, but nobody knows where it comes from. Your mother's Sunday dinner. A corn dog from the county fair. You eat from your own life only. You order from memory, as best you can. Your birthday cake, your wedding cake, your graduation barbecue. You give the cafeteria workers some coordinate, some connection, and out comes the tray. Your grandmother's pot roast. The double cheeseburger from the Lincoln Inn.

If you try to take a bite of someone else's food, it vanishes as your teeth descend.

In the cafeteria the workers call out the year at regular intervals. For a while, every time you go to eat you hear them shouting: "Twenty-five thirty-four! Twenty-five thirty-four!"

Until, before you know it: "Twenty-five thirty-five! Twenty-five thirty-five!"

Right now, as I tell this, it's 2613. There's a long way to go.

Your age at death becomes your age forever. Your body at death is your body forever—from scars to missing limbs to brain damage. In the cafeteria, people sit with others of their age and era—tables full of bald old men from my century, children from flu epidemics in the 1800s, young soldiers from every time. When you see mixed ages, it's

255

a family, and it usually means someone new has arrived and they've gathered in welcome.

I woke up here at forty-seven, a familiar arthritic throb in my hip. I couldn't think what came before. I beat almost everyone: my mother, my two brothers, my son, my daughter, my ex-wife, possible grandchildren, and Janet, the woman who lived in the apartment down the hall. Not counting my father, I went first out of all the people who mattered in my life. I never went to a single funeral that made me cry.

After my ex-wife, Brynne, arrived and spent fifty years or so here, we talked about that. How I left so much grieving behind. She told me it was just one more example of me getting away with something. She was still angry, after all that time.

"You never wanted to do the things everybody had to do," she said. "You're like a child."

"No one's life is all one way," I said.

"Or an impulsive monkey."

In my whole life I never felt anything but thwarted and blocked. Nobody ever understands you, not even here.

Here is something I wish I'd told my son and never have: There is no peace here. All the trappings of peace, yes, all the silence and emptiness, but those are just shells. If you want peace, you'll have to find it in the life you left behind.

You wake in a simple room of interlocking cinder blocks, painted gray. One chair, one cot, one window filled with opaque gray. You can't tell whether the gray is an outside air or the windowpane itself. You will never know. It is like morning, in half-light. A late morning after a dream.

When I woke up here, Dad came to see me first—he's the one who showed me out of my room and explained how the cafeteria works. He called me "buddy" and seemed maniacally happy about my arrival.

"Wasn't expecting *you* this quick," he said, and then he laughed so wide I could see the metal fillings in his back teeth.

He was nervous and a lot nicer than I was used to. I'm older than him here and that was strange. We stole looks at each other like kids at a dance. Pretty soon, my whole outlook about him changed. I'd always thought he was mean, but I started to see him as only young, too young to expect much from. I hoped maybe I could teach him a thing or two, but nothing like that ever grew up between us.

I don't know why, but he never told me about reliving. I found out about that on my own.

A few decades later, my daughter, Annie, arrived and I started going to see her. She was too young to die—breast cancer at fifty-one—but she's still older than me here. She seemed perfectly put together—neat black hair, beautiful dark eyes, a stillness under every movement. I felt proud of her, though I had no credit coming. We would get together and share a meal and I would try to give her advice about this place. I made a point of telling her about the reliving—how to control it, how to guide it.

"Now that it's gone," I said, "your life is the only thing you have left."

I told her how to concentrate in just the right way, to lock on to some detail or emotion from the moment in your life that you want to visit. Concentrate in the right way, I said, and the next thing you know, you're back in it. Back in it for as long as you want. Back in it to hunt for perfect moments. I told her to watch out for the bad times, though, how the bad times are always underneath even the happiest ones. I gave her the best advice I could. I was afraid she might be forgiving me the same way I had forgiven Dad—holding me 1 or 2 percent more blameless due to youth and ignorance.

"Try sports," I said, suggesting some avenues for reliving. "You always liked sports."

She was a nice woman, no thanks to me, so I didn't find out for years that she hadn't played a sport since she was twelve, that she never once attended a sporting event as an adult, and that she refused to let her son play football because she was scared he would get hurt.

I am in the swimming pool, bob-walking through the four-foot section, the water tugging against me as I try to speed up, and the pool is a chamber of sound, of children's cries and parents calling and everybody

257

shouting names, names, names, but none of them mine, and I sink underwater and open my eyes in the stinging blue. It's like shade under there, the legs like machine parts, moving without purpose against the pressure of silence.

It's hard to keep straight, but it goes something like this: My father died first, then me, then my mother, my ex-wife, my daughter, Janet from down the hall, my son.

Janet, the last woman in my life, the last chance at a real whatever, told me after she arrived that she didn't want to see me here. She was the first to turn. After I died, she'd started seeing a counselor. She said I had abused her emotionally.

"Emotional abuse is every bit as harmful as physical abuse," she said, nodding certainly. "Every bit."

"How would you know?" I said. "Even if I did abuse your emotions? Did I ever hit you? Did anyone ever hit you? Physical abuse is probably *a lot* worse."

This was fairly early in my death, and I hadn't yet begun to prize relationships.

She said, "You didn't love me enough. You didn't love me at all, maybe."

"I absolutely did," I said, which wasn't true, not like it was with my wife, who I loved so much at one point that I felt like it could have destroyed me. Janet and I wound up together over a shared interest in drinking, and the proximity of our apartments. I hadn't been aware that love was even hovering around our hemisphere. I had always thought that was the good part about us.

The food is excellent. The lines are never long. You eat from your own life only, which is too bad for people like my friend from the Middle Ages, who will never know the joy of ice cream or a corn dog.

But for me, the food is excellent.

You can order generally or specifically. It's fun to listen to the people around you as they order.

Hamburger, please. Any one from the Oh-So-Good Inn.

I'd like the prix fixe meal I had with my wife in Paris, 1961.

Easter ham and scalloped potatoes. Whenever.

Once he discovered the cafeteria, my son, Tyler, ate the same thing for years and years. This was long after he'd arrived, and we'd started seeing each other occasionally.

"Thanksgiving dinner!" he would say, like he didn't know how loud he was being. And then he would shovel it in while I talked. I would ask him if he remembered this or remembered that, and he would nod like he was keeping time to a song. He was old, old enough to be my father.

Here's what I should have told him, and what I still, for various reasons, have not: Now that it's gone, your life is the only thing you have left. Ransack it, top to bottom. Plunder that fucker. Find whatever you can in there, because it's all there is.

I am with Angela Jarvik in her bedroom and her parents are downstairs and we know that they never come up and she has her hand on me, over my jeans, and I have my hand on her, inside her jeans, and her mouth tastes like sweet metal and she groans and twists away. I am on my back in the sandy weeds outside the kegger, and Jennifer Luttin has me pinned, slides onto me, her kinky black hair brushing my face, and I feel an exquisite tightness beneath a flaming center, and when she leans forward to kiss me I taste beer and cigarettes and see a burst of white. I am in the apartment of a woman named Sandy, who I met over Christmas break in Boise, and she is whispering nastily in my ear while I'm just trying not to let it end too soon, and then I am on my knees on a hardwood floor at the foot of a bed, my face between the legs of my not-yet wife, Brynne, and my tongue aches, and then I am in the shower with a woman whose name I can't remember, I'm behind her and she's leaning forward, and she's saying the filthiest things and I get all twisted up inside and thrust into her as hard as I can, like I want to hurt her, but she slips forward and then I do too, ramming my leg against the cold-water spigot, which leaves a stupendous bruise, a bruise that I know I will have to lie to Brynne about and then keep straight in my head what the lie was in case it somehow comes up again, now that I'm careful about every story.

You know it when the people you love die. You become aware. I first visited Brynne right after she arrived. I took myself to her room and waited outside her door until she opened it. When she saw me she flinched.

Her hair was white and thin. You could see through to her scalp. Liver spots covered her arms, and her heavy breasts made a stomach inside her smock. She seemed somewhat like the woman I had once loved, but made-up in sloughing latex and sour talc. I wanted to tug at the skin of her neck. I wanted to peel away the folds above her eyebrows.

"How do you feel?" I asked.

"Strange," she said.

"Can I come in?"

"I don't think so."

She seemed confused. She had to be ninety.

"You know I'm Rex," I said.

"I know who you are," she said.

I hadn't seen her for eleven years before I died. Now all I wanted was to find something beautiful in her, something that could remind me of her knockout twenty-three-year-old self. Then I thought, not for the first time: *I am a purely horrible person.* Her eyes were wet with anger.

"Are the kids all right?" I asked.

"You got used to not knowing that," she said.

"Come on," I said. "I've been dead."

I died lucky. You could go in a coma or after dementia. Some people never get out of their cots and make it to the cafeteria. You could go young, without enough to relive. Because that's everything, the reliving, the hunt for perfect moments. The poor kids, the teenagers, the twenty-year-olds—you look at them and they're beautiful, you want to taste them. The younger kids run screaming through the cafeteria, playing tag, and you think at least they've found something to do and a way to make friends. The games of tag include kids from everywhere, from all times and places, African kids and Japanese kids and American kids and Bolivian kids. It is the only joy you ever see.

Sometimes you envy these children. Then you realize all they'll never be able to relive, all the food they never ate, the places they never went, the sex they never had, the Christmas mornings, the Easter Sundays.

I am sitting on the couch in my bathrobe, and Brynne is cross-legged on the floor, helping Tyler and Annie open their gifts. The odor of evergreen and coffee fills the room. Charlie Brown Christmas music. Tyler throws his new football and it hits Annie in the face, bouncing into her Barbie Beach House, and she begins to howl. Brynne says, "Tyler." And he says, "I didn't mean to," but I know he's lying, and a surge runs through me and I vibrate with fury that we can't just have a happy fucking Christmas morning, kisses and hugs and then some football, and not a house full of crying and the stink of dirty clothes and bad breath. Tyler picks up the ball and spikes it like one of those NFL showboats and it bounces onto the coffee table and knocks my cup to the ground. I pick him up by his arm and swat him three times hard on the butt, and I only hear him bawling a few seconds later, after I've put him down and something has evaporated inside my head. Brynne kneels there, one arm around each child. Looks at me without blinking. Packages wrapped in silver and red and green. Tyler cries louder than he needs to. Brynne keeps her eyes right on me. She hasn't blinked in forever.

Nobody tells you anything. No instruction sheet, no welcome wagon. You wake up on your cot. Your room is empty and pleasantly cool. Eventually you go out, where the balconies stretch in either direction, up and down, for farther than you can see. Across a gulf is another series of balconies, facing back, with precisely spaced doorways. At the bottom of the gulf is the cafeteria, filled with metal tables and chairs, welded to the painted gray concrete floor. Every few hundred yards is another food line. The food is excellent. The lines are never long.

My father was the first one to point this out. When he showed up at my door, he wanted to talk a lot, which seemed unusual. When we were growing up, he'd come home from work and the house would go silent for hours. Sometimes if he was watching TV and I started making too much noise, he would call out, "Shut it." If my mother was telling him a story, he'd say, "Edit yourself, Marie."

Now he wants to talk.

We go to the cafeteria, and we try to order meals together. We pick Sundays out of a hat and see what we get. Ham and scalloped potatoes. Roast beef with gravy. A lot of times we'll eat two in a row.

He asks me questions about my childhood, asks me didn't I think I was lucky to have the upbringing I did, wasn't our family one of the lucky ones, and because it's all over and doesn't matter, I say yes.

He always was an asshole, honestly. But he was a good provider. That was what Mom said, and once I became a father I thought that was what I was too. A good provider. The head of the household. Later, after I'd vanished and left the household headless, I tried hard to remind myself how much I'd hated it whenever Dad was in the house, how the air grew thick with tension, how we held our laughter under our breath. How happy I thought we'd be if he would just leave.

At the cafeteria, people gather by age—tables of snowy-haired, liver-spotted white people, tables of smiling, gabbing African children with protruding bellies. Kids race between the tables, squealing, and sometimes a crank will yell at them. You can recognize a killjoy in every language in the history of the world. Other children sit glumly by themselves, and they are a shattering sight, because you realize that the allure of tag, like everything, can last only so long.

My friend from the Middle Ages died old for his day: forty-three. He loves to hear about televisions and microwave ovens. Tells the damnedest stories about the plague years, about the exhilaration of every day. When things got depressing, he and his friends would go looking for Jews or lepers and beat them with clubs.

"The Black Death," he said, with an air of pride. "You knew you were alive. You knew the value of a day."

He slurped from his spoon, and his smile fell. "When my daughter got it, that was the worst. I'd have rather had it myself."

He looked around for eavesdroppers. We were sitting at the metal cafeteria tables. I was eating a corn dog from the Ada County Fair, 1976. He was eating his wife's mutton stew, with salt and bread, from the winter of 1335.

He held his spoon poised between bowl and mouth. One cube of greasy mutton. He whispered, "I'd have rather my wife had it. I would have given it to her if I could've."

I thought about how worried we'd been when Tyler had the flu as a baby. The chemical purity of the hospital.

The man's eyes turned bright. "Tell me again about your toilet," he said. "You would sit there and read magazines."

My son sometimes eats four meals in a row. The same thing, four times in a row. He walks up to the counter and yells, "Thanksgiving dinner!" He is shiny on top, with blotchy brown freckles on his scalp, and his cheeks have slumped into jowls.

One time I told him, as he worked a huge forkful of turkey and mashed potatoes into his mouth, "I thought about you kids on the holidays every year. I really did. That might be part of what I had coming, I guess. I'm not asking for any slack."

He chewed for fifteen seconds, then said, "Did you like cranberries, Roy?"

"Rex," I said. "Or you could call me Dad."

There is no peace here, and so you go looking in the life you left behind. You think it will be full of perfect moments—great days, great afternoons, great nights, a collection of moments that make up a shorter, more perfect life. First you relive all the sex, then you try the peak days—the weddings, the births of your children, the graduations. Then sports and hobbies, then work, then your kids' school plays. You remember something that seemed good and you go back to it.

But you find it hard to land in a single untroubled moment. Every second is crowded with life, with misery and anxiety that just won't be stomped down. Even the happiness can kill you. I went back for the birth of my son, and it shocked me how disfiguring it was, all that intensity, how it broke me open in a way that soared way beyond happiness.

The door at the Mirage lets in a slab of yellow light. A woman comes in, fortyish. Tattoo on a freckled bosom. Can't tell yet what it is. Smoker's laugh. I am at the bar, four hours in. It is cool and drunk. I am cool and drunk. I turn a pack of matches in my fingers, folding and unfolding the cover. I want to climb that woman. I light a cigarette and watch her, raising my eyebrows and holding out the pack, and she accepts. Janet. We tell our stories in the dark. The world is full of hope, and mistakes are easy to spot. We're at her apartment by 8:30. When I kneel to tug down her pilled satiny panties, I notice curly hairs escaping from the homeland between her legs, little strays on the pillowy inside of her thighs.

The first time I saw my son here, he seemed confused, like Brynne had. Then I relived a bunch of the old times with him, and my self-loathing became richer, developed shades and nuance. Even the safest-seeming times roiled with undertow. We played catch in the backyard, and I yelled at him for throwing wild. I taught him how to ride a bike. When he fell over and skinned his knee, I mocked him for crying. I wanted him to be tough.

And then, back here, I couldn't make myself go see him again for a long, long time.

I relived the first years of my marriage. Some days I relived morning to night, over and over again. Hardly any undertow.

Then I'd come back here, where I hate the way my ex-wife is now. I stopped seeing her for years after that first visit, but it didn't matter. I longed for the young her everywhere and the only way I could get her off my mind was to bury myself in diversionary reliving. I repeated a four-hour drunk at the Mirage with my buddies Kevin and Jayce thirteen times in a row. I went to a Foghat concert, Boise, 1972. One week I spent in Belize with my college girlfriend, mostly on a king bed with the balcony door open onto a perfect blue seam of sky and sea. The small, cocoa-colored man at the hotel's front desk smiled shyly at us whenever we passed. We did it in the shower, in a chair, with her leaning out over the balcony in the middle of the night. I held her from behind, felt her ribs in my hands.

Every time I came back here, I was ravenous. In the cafeteria, I ordered the Belize meals again—whole red snapper, pit-roasted pig, bottles of clear Belikin beer. I would sit there and eat slowly, watch the children at tag, and feel a tender ache in my balls and long for sunburn and the whispery feel of dried seawater on my skin.

After Brynne showed up here, we started seeing each other from time to time. She softened. I wondered when my children might appear. She told me about their lives. Tyler had lived alone in Denver, and almost never called. He worked on the maintenance crew at a junior college. Annie had married a guy who used her good credit to buy cars and a home, and then ruined it before she knew what was happening. Spent money like crazy. They had two children, a boy and a girl, and Annie decided to stay with him when they had to turn their house over to the bank and rent an apartment.

"Did they ever ask about me?" I asked her.

"All the time," she said.

"What'd you tell them?"

"I told them how we met. I told them about the day we got married. How handsome you were. How hard you worked. How no one could understand the way you just vanished. How you still loved them."

"Wow," I said. "I don't know what to say."

"How it was probably hard for you to live with what you'd done."

All I'd done, at first, was the usual rigmarole. Sleeping around. All that urgency about women. Your whole life concentrated into tiny waves and crests. We had a teary day when Brynne found out, a day I kept getting tugged into when I wasn't careful about reliving. She told me I didn't deserve to have a family anymore. The kids watched us fight like they were peering through a fence at barking dogs. I moved into a room downtown, and within a week she and the kids had moved to her mother's in Oregon.

I've spent years trying to figure out why I did what I did next. I didn't call the kids for eight months, and then, after fourteen minutes on the telephone, I didn't talk to them again for four years. They sent a few letters at first.

"How you probably hated yourself," she said. "And who could blame you?"

I am driving home from Twin Falls when the semi truck in front of me begins to change lanes and slides sideways on a patch of ice. It stretches out before me, then I hit the ice myself, and when the semi reaches the next dry patch it crashes onto its side, sparking off the freeway and into the snowy weed chaff alongside the road and into a power pole. I slide off, roll once, and come to rest. The world goes silent. Something cloudy in my head. Adrenaline racing. Trembling.

I think of the kids.

I think, *Okay, Rex.*

I open the door and step out and a surge of unbelievable whiteness passes through me, shoots out my eyes and fingertips, burns my hair crisp.

Then I woke up here. I always wanted to know more about it, see my funeral, see the days after, watch how my void took shape. Like Huck Finn at his funeral. But you don't get to do that.

Eventually, you give up on finding the shorter, more perfect life. You start hunting for a single great day. One day of peace. One day of still water, start to finish. Then, after a few years, you start to think: Okay, one great afternoon. One morning.

One great hour.

Ecstatic moments lose their thrill. The worst times start feeling attractive. Everything pressed to the edge, pulled into focus.

I stumbled across a day right after my wife had her miscarriage. It came between our kids, late in the pregnancy. A humid oppression over everything. Everywhere we looked, we saw babies—a mother carrying a red-faced girl in pink blankets, strollers crowding the sidewalks.

One day we were watching TV and a diaper commercial came on, with a peach-colored infant sitting on a white backdrop.

I said, "Jesus Christ. We ought to make a drinking game of it."

Brynne began to cry and wouldn't let me touch her.

Her tears didn't move me much. That's not the way I wish I had been, but I have to say it. Nothing felt important.

Later that night, after she'd gone to bed, I sat on our front steps. It was summer, the nights just cool, and as I sat there, a skinny gray and orange cat came into our yard and looked at me. The cat seemed hungry and shrill, alone, and it mewled at me. I looked away. The cat made the sound again, more keenly, with more ache, and then wandered off.

My eyes burned.

When I came back here, I developed an unbelievable longing for a cat, a desire to hold a cat in my lap or scratch one between the ears, and the emptiness of the days became defined by cat-less-ness.

Once, for what felt like a hundred years, I became obsessed with cigarettes. I found myself reliving ten minutes of smoking from 1977, perched on a stool at the Mirage Lounge, over and over again. It was like smoking thirty-seven cigarettes in a row and emerging with clear lungs. And then lying around and eating meals and longing for the cancerous bite of the smoke in your chest, yearning for it like you were yearning for the return of your one great love, and all you can feel the entire time is desire, which bleeds the reliving paler and paler with each turn. Sometimes you need to sleep for a long time afterward. It's really the only time you can sleep, when you've relived something exhausting, and when you return, sadness follows you around like a dog you want to kick, and so you sleep for a long, long time, until your hunger forces you awake.

My son died at ninety-three. He went in his sleep, which made me happy. I went right to his door. The sight of him shocked me. A distorted version of me—larger in every particular: head, hands, frame. And yet his whole body cramped down, hands gathered inward like claws. He looked like he was still dying.

"Tyler, it's your dad," I said, and he said, "Okay."

"You remember me, don't you?"

He worked his mouth for a second, and said, "You seem like someone."

He fixed his eyes on the wall somewhere behind me, and I left. For two hundred years or so I thought about that moment the most. You can drive yourself crazy. I don't know what made me go back, besides having enough time to think it over.

Tyler seemed the same when his door opened to me a second time. I went in and sat on the chair, and then he sat on the cot. He waited.

"I've been thinking about you a lot, Son. Thinking about you and me, and realizing how much I let you down. You and your sister. And your mother, of course."

He nodded absently. He sat forward in his chair, and his head bobbed.

"I know I wasn't much of a father. I know that. But I hope we can work back to something together. All of us. We're still a family, you know, no matter how much hurt we've suffered."

He cleared his throat, and seemed to wait for a few seconds to make sure I was done. I couldn't read anything in his face.

"I don't go in for a lot of talk," he said.

We sat in silence for what must have been an hour, until I said, "Are you hungry?" and he said, "I don't have any food."

"What about the cafeteria?"

He looked at me blankly. I became aware of the possibility that he had not yet left his room, after all these years. I walked to his door, then out to the balcony, and looked back at him. He sat unmoving for several moments, and then I said, "Come on."

He came uncertainly onto the balcony. Brittle on his feet. He looked carefully out and down into the chasm.

"What is this place?" he asked.

———⋘———

I had been dead for 326 years when I got an idea. We would have a family dinner. Me, Tyler, Brynne, and Annie. When I told Brynne, she said Annie would want to bring her husband. I'd never met him. And their kids. My grandchildren.

"And why not my parents?" she said.

"And mine?" I said.

Brynne made a face. She'd never liked my folks. She was from Boise people. Country-club types. Golfers. My dad milked cows for other men. We'd lived in Eden, didn't even have a post office.

"Look, if we're going to invite everybody, we can't go leaving out my family," I said.

"I don't see why not," Brynne said.

"Maybe I should invite one of my girlfriends," I said, and here's maybe one thing about me that's different now: I knew that was shitty the moment I said it. Used to be, when I said some shitty, mean thing, I justified it to myself for days and days, until I realized that it was shitty and told myself I'd never do it again. Now, I recognized it immediately. It was a hopeful sign. There's a long way to go.

I told my friend from the Middle Ages about my plan for a family dinner.

"That sounds awful," he said.

"Why?"

"I'm sick of this food. I'm sick of eating the same thing every day forever. I'm sick of old lamb. I'm sick of potatoes and mush cakes. You know what I did? I went back and ordered the gruel we ate during the winter of 1329, when we were damn near starving, and the soup had got rotten and it made us all so sick we almost died. I laid about in bed, shitting myself until I couldn't shit again. Days of that. I thought I was going to die. My wife crying all the time, begging God, this and that." He laughed. "We didn't know what we had then, is what it is. We had no idea what we had."

"I guess not."

"So here, I go up and order that rotten soup and eat it, and you know what happens?"

"What?"

"Nothing."

"That's good."

He looked at me in disgust, and spat a piece of bone into his bowl.

It's hard to get a group together. There's no way to communicate—if you want to see someone, the only thing to do is go and see them. So Brynne and I split up and went door-to-door. Brynne went to get her family. I went first to Tyler's.

"You want to have what kind of dinner?" he asked.

Tyler and I went to Annie's.

"I guess, if Tyler's coming," she said.

Tyler, Annie, and I went to see Annie's husband, Duff. He looked pretty good—he'd come here at fifty-eight. Heart attack.

Then Tyler, Annie, Duff, and I went to see Duff and Annie's kids. When I introduced myself, they had looks of uncertainty in their eyes. Like they'd forgotten the details, but remembered the general idea.

We all went to see my mother. She wept a little when I told her what we were doing.

"Oh, Rex," she said. "I always knew you were a good boy."

Then we went to see my dad.

"Sounds like a lot of noise and trouble, buddy," he said, and the words filled me with a painful nostalgia for childhood.

In the dining room, no one could agree on what to eat. There was nothing we could all share—nothing we'd all had together. Finally, everybody just had what they wanted. I sat by Annie and Duff, and we didn't say much. I ate a Thanksgiving dinner, the one when Brynne tried putting nuts in the stuffing. All together we took up four tables, and people kept walking by and looking at us. Sometimes they'd ask us what was going on.

"Family reunion," I told one of them.

The next one who asked, Duff said, "Beats me."

We ate for a while. At first, people talked. No one talked to me, but I could hear them talking to each other, catching up on their lives, sharing tips about the reliving. I listened to Duff and Annie laugh over family stories I'd never heard. Sometimes they would ask me a question, like I was someone they'd met on a train. Eventually, people stopped talking and started getting ready to leave. I heard some of my family making plans to get together later. Duff and Annie put their silverware across their trays and looked around.

I felt like it shouldn't be over, like I needed to keep this going. No one needs to rush off, I wanted to say. Couldn't we all just sit here and talk a little more?

But what I said was, "Isn't the food here great?"

Duff looked at me like I was insane.

That was when I realized. The food here is not excellent. That's just a lie. It's the same food, the same food, the same food forever.

Then you finally find it, and it's not even an hour.

For me, it lasts thirteen minutes and forty-seven seconds. I stand on a bridge and look into the Snake River Canyon. It's two weeks after Brynne kicked me out. I hear the wind-sound of planes. The air smells like sweet hay and cow shit. My mind hums with a pleasant emptiness. I light one cigarette off another and watch the butt tumble out of sight into the canyon below. I am entirely alone. The empty peace makes a sound that takes in everything.

RABBIT CATCHER OF KINGDOM COME

by Kellie Wells from *Fairy Tale Review*

One sudden spring, when trees and flowers, bamboozled by warmth, began budding in January, the prematurely honeyed air flatly refusing to chill again until late December, the town of Kingdom Come, Kansas, was beset by a plague of black-tailed jack rabbits that were not only many but jumbo, bigger than great danes they were, gargantuan rabbits, suspiciously well-fed, slavering over the zoysia, plump middles heaving, back feet long and brawny as a sailor's forearm and ears you could fan a fainting princess with. And not at all timid, never darting under privet or disappearing behind fences at the last minute, but glaring tauntingly at cats and hobbled crones, whom the town feared would be dragged away to an unspeakable end in the riparian thickets whence these strapping rabbits multiplied, their numbers seeming to double each week. They licked their paws and stroked their ears and whiskers while leveling a menacing eye and leering toothily at any passerby bold enough to look them in their flea-bitten mugs. They stood up on their whopping hoppers and waggled their ears, as though receiving a communiqué from jack rabbit HQ, the air crackling with animal electricity, and then they'd charge a neighbor's chihuahua, the javelin of their ears at a determined tilt, and the runt mutt would leap with a shriek through its doggy door. They hopped defiantly into busy intersections, and station wagons and pick-up trucks, afraid a collision with one of these sturdy lagomorphs would surely cause their vehicles to crumple like beer cans against an obdurate forehead, hit one another and rolled in ditches instead, coming to rest tires-up among the cattails. At night the rabbits drummed their feet so rhythmically the earth seemed to growl and the sleepless citizens of Kingdom Come locked and relocked their doors and windows until the thumping ceased at sunrise. The town was in a pickle, had a big-eared crisis on its hands, fast multiplying pestilence, cotton-tailed epizootic, and, well, it feared for its safety and solitude.

Which is why, when the man in the parti-colored coat appeared and claimed he could, for a nominal, one-time fee, rid the town of this nuisance forever, the drowsy burghers fell gratefully at his feet.

He pulled from his pied pocket the largest carrot anyone had ever seen; even Farmer Bauer, known county-wide for his prize-winning cucumbers the size of hockey sticks and potatoes that frequently resembled past presidents, was agog. And from this carrot, the man in the colorful coat whittled a fife, whose music the town was deaf to, though dogs howled and whimpered and shimmied under sofas when he blew.

This man, let us hereafter refer to him as Herr Pfeiffer, testing the irresistible pitch of the pipe, played a casual tune one night, strolling in the unseasonable and glistering warmth of the moonlight, and the ritual rumbling was replaced with a high-pitched keening that caused people to fill their kitchen sinks, eject ice from metal trays, and immerse their throbbing noodles in ice water.

The next day, Herr Pfeiffer began to silently ululate in earnest, and the wild-eyed rabbits were tugged, tail first, toward where he stood piping in the gazebo; a pyramid of resentful rabbits began to wriggle in front of him, the ground scarred with claw marks as they tried to resist the sonorous magnetism of Herr Pfeiffer's *Hasen*-song. This bushel of black-tailed jack rabbits writhed and kicked, heaped higher than a haystack, but when Herr Pfeiffer lowered his fife, they all went limp and began quietly to snore. The people of Kingdom Come couldn't bring themselves to witness the rumpus through locked windows and sliding glass doors, but they cautiously parted their drapes when the air gently thundered with the sound of sleeping rabbits, a welcome aestivation they hoped would last.

After a week, people began to emerge from their houses and children stole away at night to secretly stroke the silken feet of the rabbits as they slumbered, and occasionally one would snort and turn on its side and below it an ear or a paw would stir to life and wave weakly, yellow teeth chomping with dreams, and the children would gasp and back away, until the mound again snuffled in unison. Some rabbits slept with their eyes open, and beneath a full moon their eyeshine made the town blush, bathed it in a pink glow that stuck to the skin, causing adolescent boys, fearful of the hell they'd have to pay if ever they were spotted sporting girly hues, to stay indoors. They ate their meat extra well-done, never mind that it shrank to shoe leather, and they never let their tongue dart from its cave, even when Dr. Hildebrand wagged a depressor at them and told them to open wide. No pink no how.

The town council met to decide what was to be done with this big-as-a-boat-footed vermin now hypnotized in an unsightly jumble of tails and whiskers and ears and feet in the middle of town. Would the rabbits remain indefinitely under Herr Pfeiffer's spell and snore themselves senseless, dwindle to bone? And how long might that take? And were the townsfolk really obliged to pay the piper? He hadn't, after all, actually emancipated the town from its trammels, no siree bobcat! He'd only bewitched it into unconsciousness, and who knew how long that would hold? Surely the hypnotized rabbits would soon rouse from their stupor, perhaps mad with a ravenous hunger, and who could say what might be on the menu!

Herr Pfeiffer, sitting quietly at the back as the town's alarm rose in pitch, stood and asked to be recognized. His colorful coat was bejeweled with light kindled by the flickering fluorescence of the town hall and seemed to swarm with diamond-back beetles. "Esteemed elders and good people of Kingdom Come," began Herr Pfeiffer, "I am not in the business of slaughtering God's creatures, however vexatious their presence. I corral and subdue, I enchant—I have done as you asked, no longer does the rumble of your bane's feet keep you sleepless at night—but it is not for me to decide the ultimate fate of living things, would you, dear brethren whose knees audibly knock in the presence of God, not agree?" Here Herr Pfeiffer smoothed his hands along his coat and light glittered across the sunken cheeks of his anguished auditors.

"But if you insist. If you wish, in no uncertain terms, that these scapegraces be mortally dispatched, I am indeed able to provide this service. However, the cost of extermination is a good deal more, dear. In addition to the tender I will ask you to part with, you must be prepared to open your ears to a sound like no other. It is the sound of suffering and will infect your flesh like a virus, thickening your blood, burrowing in your most vital organs. It will become the caries that corrode the teeth that wake you with aching at night, the congested vessels of the eyes red with grief, the creeping spots on skin gone slack as a turkey's wattle with time. It is a fevered howling that will ring in your heart for the rest of your days and sound to you as though the Earth's soul is being throttled. You must ask yourselves: can your hearts, stalwart and true as you may believe them to be, afford it?"

The town council asked Herr Pfeiffer if he would kindly step out so that they might consider the merit of his . . . intriguing proposal. He tapped his heels and bowed, and a bedazzling train of light followed him as he took his leave. Widow Winkler said if you asked her, relying on Herr Pfeiffer a second time would be throwing good spinach after bad, and she for one hadn't a plug nickel to throw in any direction. (Widow Winkler lived from her departed husband's paltry pension. He'd been an itinerant Messiah, headlining in passion plays across the state—seasonal work but he was the best Christ in Kansas, could suffer and forgive at the drop of a hat, and so was handsomely compensated for each performance—but the Messiahs had only recently unionized and bargained for benefits when Herr Winkler died on the job, on the cross! He'd been devoted to his craft and felt he'd understand Christ's motivation better if just once he could be properly staked. As misfortune would have it, Herr Winkler was a bleeder, heretofore unbeknownst. Retirement funds had yet to accrue and life insurance (the whole notion of which was complicated by all those nightly resurrections, matinees on Sunday) had been dismissed on principle, so the other Christs of Kansas, who also yearned to bleed believably, donated a portion of their income to create a modest annuity for Wilhelmina Winkler, surviving spouse of Berthold Winkler, voted Greatest Jesus Since Jesus at their annual potluck and Most Likely to Raise the Dead.) Mayor Finsterwalder suggested they stipulate payment be remitted only after this plague was stamped out, the rabbits a fading chapter in the town's otherwise placid history. "But," asked Constable Schutzmann, "what about the sound of suffering Herr Pfeiffer warned against, a brutal music *that* would certainly be" (Constable Schutzmann, though a by-the-book beadle in every other regard, kept at home a three-legged marten he'd found wounded near his well and coddled back to health and trained to waltz, teaching her to hop rhythmically on one foot *one-two-three, one-two-three*, and clearly he nursed a secret affection for all velvety creatures, however unsettling their snarl, however monstrous their feet). "Ah, pfrrrt," spat Farmer Bauer. "We are no strangers to suffering! We all know well the shriek of a hog what has gotten downwind of his fate, do we not? Surely we'll not allow the brief bellowing of animal torment to stand in the way of our happiness?!" With this, a snort flew from his bulbous schnozzle—his woolly moustache shivered like the legs of a centipede and appeared as though it might scuttle off and leave his newly naked lip to fend for itself—and he folded sun-leathered arms across the bulging barrel of his chest. "These rabbits have it coming!" he boomed. And so it was decided: though there was still some disagreement, among the more pinch-fisted skinflints among them, over the exact monetary value of such a service, Herr Pfeiffer would be retained and asked to exterminate the waggle-eared menace and the feet they hopped in on.

Farmer Bauer reluctantly plunked gold pieces into Herr Pfeiffer's eager mitts (the only form of lucre he'd accept—paper currency, he said, so easily a stiff wind's hostage), said the rest would be proffered once services were rendered, and Herr Pfeiffer again clicked his heels and bowed solemnly then backed away until he found himself in sunlight, and he turned and strode forward, showily pumping his arm in the air like a drum major, marching to music he had yet to make. His coat exploded kaleidoscopically in the light, spangling the air, throwing disks of color everywhere, everywhere, and a train of jewels blazed brightly behind him. He turned his head once and grinned over his shoulder, and his unusually long eyelashes fluttered gracefully in a beckoning manner, like the undulating fingers of a sea anemone. Widow Winkler, eyes like boiled eggs, yelped and slapped at the beetles of light that scurried along her arms, then she grabbed the shoulder of Frau Kinderbein and said, "I see your Irmalinda floating in the candy-colored light, trailing close behind him. You must keep her near as shadow!" And Frau Kinderbein, whose marigolds had suffered more than once at the paws of Widow Winkler's snuffling mutt Schatz and whose daughter sometimes suffered from night terrors brought on by the manic midnight twittering of the widow's canary Petunia, shrugged off the crone's craggy hand, sniffed, and stormed off, her bosom raised to a bumptious altitude.

The rest of the frazzled citizenry of Kingdom Come headed straight home, gathered bread and jam and candles enough for a week, plugged their ears with dollops of wax, and stowed their families safely away in root cellars. Let the rabbit extraction commence!

The townspeople waited in dimness, held their heads in their hands and tried not to listen, silently played cards and whittled vague shapes from turnips, ate pickled okra and boysenberry preserves, fed their mewling cats condensed milk, taught their dogs, who whined barometrically and argued with their feet, to play dead.

After they'd been underground for three days, they began to feel like grubs or tubers, like the least shrew, smallest mammal in Kansas—they felt puny and too comfortable in darkness, so the close, dank quarters began to shrink, and the townspeople thought: surely the pox has been antidoted by now.

It is worth remarking that too often it is impatience or boredom that persuades us to step foot into the lion's yawning maw—with the passing of time comes accidental daring—but the minute our britches catch on the barb of an incisor, we awaken to the delusion, turn tail, and gallop in the direction of our sensible cowardice.

So it was in Kingdom Come on this the day that would later and forever demand atonement. Just as parents and grandparents, restless offspring and orphaned cousins, filed toward the steps, tunneling a pinkie into an ear to free it from silence, preparing to periscope their heads above ground for confirmation that the plague had been piped into oblivion, suddenly family cats tossed back their mangy heads and began to bay like wolves beneath a swollen moon, *ahroooor!* The dogs, nobody's dupe, could see that such behavior was a sign the world was soon to end, soon to crumble like a day-old biscuit beneath the crack of doom, and they tried to outwit the apocalypse by falling stiffly onto their sides, thud, good dog, good dead dog! Big-fisted toddlers clutched wooden alphabet blocks so tightly their skin gave and their hands bled, as if they'd been bitten by feral words in the act of forming (to this day a ghostly branding on the palms of Kansas children remains faintly visible, even beneath the impetigo that scabs the skin in spring; however, the letters change each year, capital *H* one year, lowercase *e* the next, then a faint *l*—*Help? Hell? Hello? He lives?*—as though their hands were trying to tell them something, ouija them a bulletin from the world beyond hands, perhaps warn, snailishly, of the coming of evil—or the coming of good, equally disruptive, who can say?). And so families returned to their bunkers, huddled together, while hamsters and mice and gerbils all ran themselves ragged on squeaking wheels, nearly reduced themselves to a rundle of butter, and awaited the all-clear of daylight that rewards the night shift, vampires and owls and astronomers and fireflies, with sunny and dreamless sleep.

Once settled on cots and benches, the final hand of hearts dealt, the townspeople too heard the sound, felt it in the roots of their teeth, as it increased in pitch and volume, a concatenated shriek so piercing, sharp as an awl, that eardrums shattered, like crystal beneath the pressure of a tenor shrilly trilling a lofted note, and blood trickled from their ears, but still they could hear. Children began to hiccup and whimper and parents held damp tea towels to their paling cheeks. And then they found themselves on their feet, standing without meaning to, stumbling dreamily, wakeful somnambulists, pulled forward, up the steps, into the afternoon—they squinted against the dazzle of day—into the sound that seemed to empty their hearts of blood, sap them of all volition, into the soul-curdling caterwaul that sounded to the pious folk of Kingdom Come as though God Himself were being lashed, the world's skin peeled from muscle, flesh sheared from bone, the sound of gore dripping, dripping, ichor thinning to a rivulet, the hollow thum-thump of life on the ebb. They walked, eyes at half-mast, arms a-dangle, limp as slain geese, and they stopped when they reached the river, where their magnetized eyes remained riveted and unblinking, burning with sight, as one bedeviled rabbit after another pitched itself, screaming, off the banks and into the rushing water, paws peddling for purchase in the air, bodies dashed against rocks, necks snapped by the force of the current that churned with the spring thaw, and the rabbits' quivering ectoplasm, translucent but pink as a tongue, rose slowly into the air like gluey bubbles, gelatinous vapor, wafted overhead, clouding the sky with an oily glow, then burst, the town blanketed in ooze, a viscous rain: the rosy slime of a slaughtered soul! Off in the distance, beneath the sun's mid-afternoon glare, the spellbound burghers saw a winking brilliance on the shoals, like a mirror splashed with light, and when their eyes adapted to the brightness they could make out Herr Pfeiffer's pipe raised in the air, the man at the other end reminding them of Dr. Jekyll guzzling his fateful elixir straight from the alembic tipped to his lips. The townspeople frantically swabbed the goo of extermination from their limbs, and all at once children and dogs fell to the ground, eyeballs shuddering beneath the lids as if recording a seismic shift, as if a-twitch with a shattering dream, which is how they would later think of it, the wickedest dream they could ever recall having, an experience not of God's still-watered, green-pastured, and be-tuliped kingdom, a dream that beggared even the most tormented imagination, and parents opened their mouths and tried to swallow the sound, gulp it down and drown it in their gullets, choking on air polluted with suffering. This malignant yawp, it cannot properly be described; it harrowed to the quick the halting spirits of the sorrowful citizens of Kingdom Come, Kansas, who never again fished in the river, who never again whittled a carrot, waltzed in the moonlight, nursed a wounded animal, whose weddings hereafter were somber as wakes, who never again heard the sound of children singing or weeping or calling their dogs (though the taproot buried beneath these burgeoning *never agains* is yet to be revealed, all in good time!).

The river boiled with the bodies of rabbits.

The true name of the piper, they later discovered, was Herr Dr. Dr. Edelhans Hasenfänger, once world-renowned musicologist and zoologist, of the Hameln Hasenfängers, a name that mysteriously appeared one day on the town registry in a variegated ink that bled across the thatched fibers of the parchment in such a way as to make it seem botanical, rhizomes creeping in all directions, a name (like that of that other notorious subterranean scoundrel) never uttered in polite company.

It cannot be said that Kingdom Come returned to normal once the rabbits had rattled their last jack-rabbity breath, had met their misguided maker, but the town fell in step again with its former rhythm and the townsfolk choused themselves into believing they'd surmounted the worst of their tribulations. Until.

Until that day when house dogs, those crystal gazers, began burrowing under davenports (Mayor Finsterwalder's Irish wolfhound Hedwig schlepping his prized Biedermeier daybed on her back from the parlor into the dining room as she tried to creep toward invisibility) and cats hid in haylofts where they let mice scurry past them, unpawed. The mice were not especially grateful for the amnesty because, well, mice are as fond of routine as the next rodent. Lassitude caused them to thin nearly to extinction for they did not feel they could crumb-gather or invade the corn-rick in good conscience with no claws snapping at their tails to give them fleet-footed purpose.

On that day, Herr Pfeiffer appeared again at a council meeting "to settle unsettled accounts." As he strode into the hall in his light-spangled mantle, seeming for all the world like a spreading fire, the townspeople felt the heat on their cheeks and parted to let this conflagration pass, stepping wide for fear they too might combust. Herr Pfeiffer asked to be recognized and Brother Angsthase yielded the lectern and stepped down from the dais. Later, when the town would attempt to reconstruct Herr Pfeiffer's appearance so that they might offer a bounty for his capture, they would each recollect the features of his face differently, would in fact reconstruct him in their own image (gutless god-wannabes all of us)—face round as a skillet with eyes like dull stones; aquiline nose above fat lips garish as poppies; teeth blue-green as oxidized copper and a monkish baldness—and they'd forget the mesmerism of his motley coat and the bewitching pitch of his piping.

"Your town has been purged of its pestilence," said Herr Pfeiffer, "and I have returned to collect my due. If you would be so good as to remit my quittance and square the score, I will gladly quit *you* and be on my way." He bowed and tossed his hat to the mayor.

Each alderman searched the bewildered eyes of the next for some guidance, some cue, and the hat passed quickly from hand to hand.

Herr Pfeiffer stepped down and returned to the center aisle and the hat came round to him, sagging with booty. He smiled, clicked his heels, glanced inside the hat, then a lupine grimace darkened his face. When council members recounted this later, they would say he bared blinding teeth that glistened like daggers and his eyes yellowed with animal rage, but he said nothing, and his silence rang inside them like a clapper in a bell, making their bones hum and their hearts skip, their livers clang, their souls clamor to be free of that four-flushing flesh that would soon turn to dust and settle on armoires and sconces only to be swept into the bin with yesterday's rubbish, sorriest of sorry fates (pragmatic, if fickle, souls always look for an escape hatch when the end inches closer)! Inside the hat were candy wrappers, pencils, plug nickels, balls of lint, marbles, four-penny nails, assorted flints, last week's raffle tickets, willow buds, but nary a gemstone or drop of gold, a hatful of the nothing Nothing carries in its pocket. No one drew a breath or twitched so much as a toe.

"S-s-see here," stammered Mayor Finsterwalder at last, "the rabbits have gone, there's no arguing that. But so too has our felicity, the sweet sanctity we once enjoyed—fled, owing in no small measure to that . . . that diabolical song we cannot shake from our ears, a lamentation we strongly suspect is infernal in origin, and he who p-p-p-pays the devil will be in debt for eternity!" sputtered the mayor, miscalculating the breath necessary to propel reticent indignation, the last word scarcely a whisper.

A chilly stillness settled again on the room, inside of which Herr Pfeiffer's coat seemed to blaze anew and the fire flashed in the shrinking pupils of the onlookers, their irises emptying of color, welling up with heat.

"And what if," asked Herr Pfeiffer with a mouth that did not move, "it was . . . God who murdered the scourge? Isn't extermination always God's purview, his bailiwick, prerogative, his Reason for Being? What if it is God to whom you owe your fitful sleep? He is surely indemnified and you can be certain He will collect." A half-grin propped up one side of his mouth. "You cannot outrun the Constable, dear thimbleriggers, cannot stiff the piper for long. Consider yourself in arrears!" Herr Pfeiffer blazed out of the room, and each person he passed fell to his knees and grasped at the trailing smoke, fingering the air for forgiveness.

A week passed and there was no further peep from the piper. The aldermen's ears felt mauled by Herr Pfeiffer's last clapperclawing, so no one uttered a word about the threats the town fervently hoped were idle as disrepair, indolent as a capsized velocipede with a badly bent wheel. Those Kingdom Comers secretly given to occult imaginings in the yearning privacy of long and moonless nights wished he'd been spirited away by a vigorous wind to an inhospitable continent remote as the stars and prayed that a techni-colored coat fueled by a grudge was not a reliable means of conveyance.

Even the most stubborn mortal funk is tamed by Time, taught to bear up under the yoke of mortality like all God's oxen, so after a fortnight, the people dared to think that perhaps Herr Pfeiffer's bite fell short of his bellow and they allowed themselves at last to sink like the dead into the soft ticking of their mattresses at night. So dog-weary were the sleep-deprived brethren of Kingdom Come, Kansas, that no bodies stirred from their stupor when the animals began to pace. Not even the yowling and hissing, the stamping of hooves, could rouse the snorting sleepers from this deliciously leaden embrace of Morpheus, whose tenderness they'd sought in vain, like mooning schoolgirls, for months.

It is natural to grope for metaphor, sentiment twice removed, in moments of guarded contentment. To say simply the town at last slept soundly is, for those who set store by the sorcery of words, to further court the endless ills that flesh is heir to—calamity is warded off by being eternally anticipated, the devil too. Tranquility, as any comfortable basset hound can tell you, must always dissemble, masquerade as irreversible woe, lest it jinx its own wobble-wheeled future. (Lunita Betelheim, who didn't believe in shouldering debt, sobbed for an hour every afternoon promptly at three o'clock to pay down the dejection we come into the world owing and to invest in a retirement free of all but the most trifling miseries; she believed five months of sobbing immunized her against the death of a loved one, three weeks for a prolonged illness, two months unrequited adoration, one month garden-variety abjection; such were Lunita's mathematics of preventative mourning.) But even the artful dodge of language or gesture, little more, let us be frank, than a parlor trick, cannot save us in the end. And this is how God can be certain He is God: His legerdemain relies less on the distance of sense than the intimacy of sound; His is a thundering melody of wrath and repentance, which is to say a song understood by all, the song we arrive in our bodies bleating. And so it was that the good and decent people of Kingdom Come, Kansas, came to doubt the inoculating power of piety: fat lot of good their devotion had done them! See if it isn't so.

———— ❧ ————

In Kingdom Come there was a girl, who shall henceforth be referred to as (. . . Wall Will Woe Wallow . . .) *Willow*! (Lithe as a . . . !) Willow Himmelfarb, a child born big as a camel's hump, big as a fable, so big she broke the stork's bill, delaying delivery of other infants, which caused the mothers to hiss at her and rub their beleaguered loins when they passed her, wombs whose phantom pains of labor persisted for years and caused the women to cry out each day at the stroke of their child's birth. In fact this is how the town, who'd always mistrusted the tilt of the sun and whose bodies' collective electricity caused clocks and watches to spin so fast folks feared they'd live their whole lives in less than a day, began to tell time: Gisela Schadenfrau 11 A.M., Malvina Marquart shortly before supper in the evening, Rapunzel Peabody and Elfriede Kinderbein a minute to midnight.

And with each passing year the blue expanse between Willow and the outer heavens grew smaller. The community waited for the day she'd exchange a chaplet of clover for that of clouds. In that year of the piper, Willow was ten years old but could already stare the stateliest stallion in the eye (though she generally steered wide of livestock for fear they might claim her as one of their own). And on that particular night, the night of the stony sleep, Willow, like all the children of Kingdom Come, felt herself rise from her bed and float into the midnight air (Elfriede and Rapunzel's synchronized howls peeling behind her), and it was such a lovely and alien sensation this weightlessness that she felt no fear, thought God had come to rescue her at last, free her from the anvil of her earthly form, slip that ponderous noose from her neck. Once outside her house, with no ceiling to stymie her, Willow thought she'd drift quickly toward Canicula and, fond admirer that she was of both dogs and remote locales, she suffered no regret, but then she thought of her brother Ogden, imagined him grounded at home with only her parents for company, and she felt her soul kedged across the prairie, her body an anchor; her feet began to drag, then her knees, her belly, her chin, until she found herself face down in buffalo grass. She rolled on her back and saw animal eyes blinking around her. She wished she could muster fear, but she knew buzzards and badgers, coyotes and foxes, even the occasional mountain lion and vagrant bear would scatter once they could see she was no tidy morsel (two autumns ago a black bear had been spotted on a bitter night curled at the feet of the statue of Mendelsohn Paddletrap, who in 1883 invented the tornado harness, a honking contraption that could lasso a twister, rope the energy round the ankles, and with that force momentarily tamed, he would loose it again on the ground to conjure his heart's fondest longing: a coop full of the most pluckily prinked bantams—feathered to the nines—you could ever hope to fancy and that laid not only the best-tasting eggs this side of capital P Paradise but produced chicken milk to boot! Which, it turns out, is ambrosia to bears, more enticing than all the honey in Bear Heaven). Above Willow, children wafted in the air with unspeakable grace, fluid as eels, but then the moon illumined their bodies and in their nightclothes they reminded her of the seeds of a milkweed parachuting toward fertilization. *Everything is more something else than itself*, thought Willow. Willow, who usually felt fettered by history (always a short man's story by her measure), thought then about Amelia Earhart, corn-fed Kansas girl like her, Meely her sister called her, who constructed a track on her father's tool shed, greased it with lard, drove a wooden box off the edge, hung suspended in time and space like a lost planet, fell to the earth, and said, "One day I'll disappear in the clouds, Pidge, you watch." (Everyone who grows up in Kansas has a yen to be airborne sooner or later, if only to glimpse where God hides His unimaginable form, that fat carcass. Many a prairied Kansan, landlocked and starved for altitude and love, tall trees and tender music, has had a bone to pick with Herr Dr. Dr. G-o-double-crucifix.) Willow thought it was not tragic but a dream fulfilled that Amelia Earhart lifted into the sky one day and never returned. *Willow Airheart*, thought Willow, air the element in which her empty heart naturally thrived. Then she thought this: *It's always thin women who disappear.*

And suddenly there was Ogden swimming in the sky overhead, clutching the feet of a sleeping girl who bobbed in the air in front of him, Irmalinda Kinderbein. Ogden who prayed at the foot of Willow's bed and smuggled into her room at night ginger snaps and peppernuts her mother hid from her. "Ogden, Oggie!" she called. He waved to her with his feet. So Willow, who now felt to herself more weighted with flesh than ever, picked herself up and followed the floating children deeper into the night.

Willow followed them until her feet ached and she was sure they had reached what her parents called "the ragged edge of Christendom"; beyond the windbreak planted to halt the raging dust that, back in the day, had stormed the lungs of every breathing thing; beyond the forest she was warned never to trespass lest she awaken the wild omnivorous one-eared cows that were afraid of mirrors and goats but who chewed children like grass and spit up baskets woven from hair and bones and teeth; to a clearing in the trees, and there the children began to flutter to the ground, lit by the throbbing moon, looking like blank slips of paper. Now Willow could hear the rhythmic croaking of the pipe that sounded like the whirring of June cicadas as they slid from their skins. She walked through the sleepy children lying on the ground, careful not to step on their outstretched hands, and searched them for her brother, Oggie with his nose dusted with freckles and his button mouth that mumbled in sleep. She pulled up short when she saw dagger-toed boots, be-tasseled at the knee, gleaming with lanolin and lampblack, tapping the ground, and there standing among the slumbering kindergarten was Herr Pfeiffer, who held in his hands a panpipe. Willow, who had been Kingdom Come Olfactory Champion three years running and who this year would compete at state, having identified with a single sniff the secret ingredients in Mrs. Sigismund's Schwarzwälder Kirschtorte (half a thimble of red currant schnapps and a dash of rosewater) and in Mr. Zwiebel's patented moisturizer that the prunier elders sopped up like bread and couldn't get enough of (suet), could smell the hazelnuts and clove and marzipan of this lebkuchen pipe and marveled at how the instrument never grew smaller though he bit off a nibble with each blow. Actually, this made Willow a little sad because it reminded her of her own body: no matter what you did to it—you could slather it with schmalz and dangle choice cuts beneath the snouts of the most ravenous wolves—it defied reduction, and the more you tried to contain it, the more it erupted in every direction. And Willow found the idea of regenerative food in a world plagued by unending starvation, mouths forever agape and bellies taut with hunger (everyone in Kingdom Come seemed reasonably well-fed, but she'd read books and knew there were people thinning everywhere, thinning, thinning as she slept), she found that troubling, one of those paradoxes God bullies mortals with, all the miserable hangdog Jobs of the world, the people who bleed and ache and dwindle and swoon and get back up again and offer Him their chin. *The faithful, those* patsies, thought Willow. *God is a prowling alley cat and we are the wounded mice he bats around until the everyday terror of living makes our hearts skid to a stop.* Ogden, heart sore, had sobbed when the rabbits disappeared, he their one true ardent admirer, and since then, it is safe to say, Willow and God had been on the outs.

The piper stopped playing when he saw Willow and grinned the thinnest of grins. As though he were fiery daylight and she a spelunker just emerged from deep in the belly of a cave, she had to squint to look at him, and then her eyes adjusted to the sight and she could see now his coat rippling around him, teeming with life, undulating, tidal. The lively coat (*hmph, no mere grogram for this dandified bugler,* thought Willow, eyes again narrowed, hands squeezed into fists, trying telepathically to tame the piper and his tumultuous ulster), it was a whirling cosmos under glass and hung in such a way as to remind Willow of a droplet of water about to fall from the spigot. She saw and could somehow identify all the animals tangled together in the terrarium of the coat: single-celled wrigglers and chiggers and night snakes and chihuahuan ravens and spotted skunks and banded sculpins and fatmucket mussels and meadowlarks and sicklefin chubs and boxelder bugs and silver-haired bats and pocket mice and mooneyes and bobcats and bobolinks and black-tailed prairie dogs and mule deer and mud daubers and piping plovers, of course, and in the middle of it all, looking stunned and logy as stowaway immigrants who just stepped woozily out of steerage onto foreign shores: those capacious jack rabbits! It seemed as though the animals were trapped beneath glass; they pawed and pecked and gnawed but the edge of the universe of the coat would not give, would not even admit to being the edge, and the animals, wild as anyone without a discernible planet beneath her feet would be, searched anxiously for cover. Willow looked into the piper's eyes and could see something writhing there as well, and she feared for the animals, she feared for the children, she feared for dear Oggie her brother. *All God's children, and he's come to claim them!* she thought. *Such is not the Kingdom of Heaven.* Oggie had told Willow that life began with her—big girl that she was, biggest in Kingdom Come and beyond, biggest in Kansas, a state *full* of ample maidens—she could give it and take it away, and she wished now she had believed him, but, always mistaken for a lumbering boy when she was a tyke and her hair was bobbed at the nape, she wasn't one to readily volunteer for the breeches part. *That fraud piper's no match for you,* he'd said, *Godding about like he is. Your movements are sometimes a mystery and your heart's big as Kansas and you'd never let any innocent come to harm!* But she hadn't saved the rabbits. *Even the surliest of God's creatures deserve affection,* pleaded Oggie. He'd thought the rabbits could be reformed with just a little lettuce, a spacious warren, and true love. But she was no redeemer, those rabbits weren't her invention, who was she to try to save another when she herself was lost? Just try finding the wee needle of her soul in that husky haystack of flesh!

The sound the pipe now emitted was the insomniac humming of those strapping rabbits, and the children sprang to, stiffly, like stepped-on rakes, then their bodies quaked in spasm, jerked and whirled and thrashed about with their eyes still sealed, and Willow thought with a start, *Totentanz!* There'd been an epidemic of dancing in neighboring towns, and many stories floated among the children of Kingdom Come about the spastic fandango of the soon-to-be-dead, which is why you'd never catch Willow Himmelfarb waltzing in the moonlight, or even swinging her hips by the light of the porch, and when Willow saw her parents fox-trotting in the kitchen after supper, she went outside, hid behind the buffaloberry bush, and threw stones at the window until her father came out to investigate, sure it was the Spitzbübisch twins from next door up to their usual hijinks, and her mother continued clearing the table, returning the corn relish and rind pickle and buttermilk to the icebox.

The humming increased in pitch and fervor and tiny tulips blossomed on the arms and legs and faces of the children, their skin a field of flowers, beautiful, beautiful! followed by a calyx of proud flesh stemming their spread; geraniums bloomed red as a fresh wound from open mouths, and the children's small bodies perspired to such a degree they looked rain-soaked, and Willow, who could not get her leaden legs to budge an inch, reached out toward Oggie. She was a zeppelin cumbered by sandbags, yearning to rise with the rest, and she knew she'd never get off the ground. Oggie reeled and grinned but wouldn't open his eyes, and she could see in the slant of his smile that he was hoping to meet up again with those walloping rabbits who'd met an unseemly end in Kingdom Come, Kansas.

And then the piping stopped, though the children continued to twitch and leap. The piper called out their names.

Eva, William, Ludmilla, and Hans! Heinrich and Albert and Ulrich and Alice! As the names were called, children flew up into the air and spiraled toward the moon like full balloons whose throats are suddenly unthrottled, looping like a whirligig higher into the ether until there was only a faint twinkling in the stratosphere. In another county, a man with a telescope would report spying a "passel of dying stars in the night sky, all with the faces of startled children." Willow's eyes followed the path of the rising children: fallen flesh on the way to becoming again incorruptible air, *God's changelings*, she thought. *He sucks the spirit out of us at birth and leaves behind this residue of flesh, pilfers the marrow, and discards the ransacked bone.* She looked down at her own fat feet, feet that kept the cobbler occupied. *There is no such thing as a human being.*

Ursula, Josephine, Irmalinda, and Ogden! Willow cried out and saw Oggie open his eyes, two doleful blooms amidst the garden of his face. And Willow could see his final thought as a boy: *Why ever would God remain on Earth, feet so firmly planted in the soil, weighty shrub, while faithful children were rocketing toward Heaven?* She would not tell her parents how he looked, his mouth widening in terror as his feet left the ground. She would not tell her parents she could see sorrow in the way his eyes flickered then dimmed as he looked at her, eyes that had never known sadness.

The piper's coat now churned angrily about him, a cyclone he conducted with his piping from the calm of the eye, and Willow had to shield her face from the stinging rubble he kicked up, then he blew on his pipe a final note, the rabbits bared their teeth and flattened their ears aerodynamically, braced for velocity, and the piper and his pendant universe disappeared in the dust, *haboosh!*

Willow wobbled on her hammy stems.

She found herself nose to nose with a vole as she awoke beneath the rising sun. When she opened her mouth to yawn, the vole tried to run, then sank its feet into the ground, but the wind of her inhalation lifted it into her mouth, and she coughed when it flew down her throat, vague irritant; the vole, who until now had only ever dreamt of flying, went sailing into the next county: Willow had grown in the night. Actually she felt as she always had and so didn't know if she'd enlarged or the world had shrunk, as the world has a habit of doing, but she figured either way the guilt was hers.

She stood up, lifted a nest of speckled eggs out of the cleft of a craggy oak, ate it, and wept. She had always been a prisoner of her own appetite.

She remembered an upsetting story she'd read once of an unwavering paradise, stubborn in its immutability, a land of more-than-plenty, hemorrhaging milk and honey, oozing with bounty; where trees were heavy year-round with toothsome fruits that didn't know how to rot; a comely land free of the eyesore of humpbacked crones and whiskered spinsters; free of catastrophic dogs and pugilist gods who blacken your eye so they can forgive you the sin of being a spirit who has the gall to gussy itself up in flesh (of all the hare-brained solutions!); a land free of fatal children; where barnstorming monks take sudden flight, the unfailing sun warming their tonsured noggins, and wheel about on the zephyr of all the unheeded pre-paradise orisons they'd ever uttered, tempted out of the sky only when the abbot paddles the creamy saddle of a chosen maiden—*thwap!*—until it glows so scarlet it can be spotted from the moon, and the monks see the beacon and steer themselves back toward the runway where their very own bare-bottomed nuns with bums in need of reddening await them; a place where pigs politely roast themselves, crackling stuck with knives and forks, and trot across the table on charred hooves ready to be carved; where geese ascend and soar near to the sun, self-broiling, then drop from the sky and fly into the gaping mouths of the zaftig and eternally peckish, cooked animals just so much more relaxed and accommodating than wild ones inclined to snarl and balk at the fate of meat, the destiny of fueling human industry, the labor of meat-making for example (no matter how generously you stuff the gullets of human beings, the next day there they are again, drooling and famished as if never fed, no magically multiplying fishes or loaves ever enough, cursed with hunger till the day they die, cursed!). *What a sad bunch of insatiable greedy-guts*, thought Willow, *making the world vanish a mouthful at a time*, she herself the worst offender, hungry, hungry, ceaselessly hungry.

As Willow wiped the sleep from her eyes, which now loomed in the sky, she imagined, like two gluttonous moons, she noticed tiny limbs scattered on the ground, bodies neatly butchered, arms and tongues and legs and eyeballs, fingers and ears, brains and hearts, strewn everywhere as if to fertilize the clearing, and she picked up an arm and held it between her fingers. It was bloodless and rubbery with the weensiest fingernails, like a doll's arm. But it wasn't a doll's arm. She gathered all the parts she could find into the aching marsupium of her mouth, some of them still trembling with reflex, and she cradled her weighted muzzle in her hands. *Life begins, life begins, life begins with* me, she sang. She stood towering, and the air she noticed was so thin, her head felt like a helium balloon making a break for the heavens, drifting ever farther from her. The hard ground beneath her feet, miles and miles away now, rose up quickly and walloped her in the face.

———✥———

That morning, the town awoke to find itself purged of children. The women who wailed at the birth-hour fell silent, and time stumbled forward without anyone noting its passage. The phantom pains that would soon stab them, their fingers, their belly, their heart, an aching for which there was no suitable thunder, would be the weight of their child's face in their hands, an arthritic longing that would quickly gnarl their grasp. Now the sound of stifled sorrow was the music to which people stepped in Kingdom Come, eyes always searching the night sky or the banks of the river for some sign of *Matilda and Ephraim, Ezekiel and Hannah* . . . There were those who said the children, so suggestible, had surely followed the rabbits into the river, had wanted to see where the river would lead the unwanted, but no bodies were found on the rocks and dragging the river yielded only the usual detritus, milk bottles and boxing gloves and birdcages and saxophones and cowboy boots and bear traps and kitchen sinks and rocks some folks thought the water had whittled into the winsome visage of the Blessed Virgin (not that these Lutherans ever paid the Virgin much heed—a virgin who appears in a bowl of wheatina or cries blood on holy days, always making a spectacle of herself that one, snort). Others said perhaps the children had misplaced their innocence—it had gone down gurgling with the last accursed rabbit—and now were fearful of their own end so had left to seek out the seductive gloom of the Transylvania they had secretly read about in their closets at night and the immortalizing incisors of those merrily ex-sanguinated Undead. And there were the devout and hopeful (though famished hope always fades when unfed) who were convinced the children had traveled into the howling wilderness and were crusading with wayfaring Flagellants, spreading the Word between yelps: God *ow* God *ow* God *ow* God. Still others believed the children, who had all been feverish the night before, contracted a wandering disease that afflicts only the small-footed and were somewhere on the plains wading barefoot through prairie grass, walking themselves to death. This theory gathered the most momentum among the townsfolk for a time because the one memento the children had left behind was their shoes, pairs of which could be found sitting empty throughout the town, in the sorghum field, beneath a linden tree, in a hayloft, the gazebo, because the children, raised right, hadn't wanted to soil Death's immaculate lodgings and so had politely removed them and left them at the door. Of course it was alarming to think the portal to eternity could open beneath anyone's feet, even the blameless feet of infants, at any moment. But behind this speculation was the unspoken conviction that it was Herr Pfeiffer who was the source of their blue ruin, and that's when joyful noise was officially outlawed in Kansas, even songbirds verboten, and birds remapped their migrations around the flatlands, flying hundreds of miles out of their way, because of course rare is the bird who can abide a soundless sky or a morning awakened by silence. Even crows, those nattering gossips, like a melodious sunrise.

Few people recall that the sky over Kingdom Come was once yellow with canaries. After the children disappeared, canary hunters picked them out of the air one by one, and now nothing sings in Kansas. Widow Winkler tried to muzzle her sweet Petunia, who was known to whistle all of *Waldszenen* with little encouragement, and hid her in the cellar, but canary trackers eventually sniffed her out and forced their way into the widow's house, armed with a bow the size of a swallowtail butterfly and a quiver of wee arrows they slung over their thumbs, and between two fingers the town fletcher, Kingdom Come King of the Popinjay, held the arbalest, and with index finger and thumb carefully nocked then shot an arrow (whose flights were fletched with the feathers of other slain canaries) into Petunia's terrified heart. She was frantically warbling the beginning of "The Bird Prophet," trying to forestall her own fate, when the arrow struck her, and the marksman wept when she fell to the ground. Not long after, Widow Winkler herself gave up the ghost, the only thing aside from Petunia and Schatz she'd been halfheartedly clinging to for years, Petunia lying on the pillow next to her, the tiny arrow lodged in her breast as though she were little more than a cocktail sausage spindled on a toothpick.

When the blood rains began, a week after the children disappeared, Kingdom Comers knew better than to believe what the scientists were saying, which was that the raindrops had merely collided with iron oxide on the way down, consumptive steel mills having coughed the red dust into the atmosphere. Parents, however, were wise to the ways of a carnivorous universe and they knew they were being rained on by their own children, that it was their children's blood that ran down their cheeks, and they put out mason jars in which to collect it, but the next day the jars were always empty, no residue of red rain remaining on the glass. Some people stayed up all night watching the jars, waiting to see the blood vanish, daring it to disappear in their presence, their own blood! But blood's a born mesmerist, and it waited for the eyelids to droop with fatigue, then allakhazam: there blink gone, like everything in the world. Most people believed God was not dead, despite the headlines, but even the formerly pious decided all the same to wash their hands of Him and to store the rack-a-bones of their souls at His house. After the rain had fallen, the town appearing mauled, people would find a ribbon or pair of glasses, a sock, a necklace, that belonged to one of their children, and the church, long deserted and waiting to be razed by God's notorious pugnacity, was converted into a reliquary, where all these items were stored. The shoes they lined up neatly beneath the pews. Parents now spent their days compiling lists of regrets, page upon page, an entry for each day in the child's life they were sorry they would miss, and they placed their book of documented mourning into their children's shoes, hoping these too might disappear, might fly up and out of the world. Of course many things vanish from this world without a moment's warning—prosperity, sanity, umbrellas, love—but not sorrow, never sorrow: sorrow always wears thin its welcome.

The town resented having a witness to an abduction but no earthly solution to the crime, especially a witness who'd suspiciously doubled in size, swelling to decidedly unfeminine proportions overnight, and it showed Willow its back. People whispered that Willow was a wicked species of kobold with a dash of ravenous giant in her genes and that she had crawled out of a cave when she was born and chosen this town to menace because it boasted more children than most, a fertile town Kingdom Come. *Always suspected that one would be nothing but trouble,* they said, *body like that.* Some said they knew for a fact she ate children, swallowed them whole like aspirin—*Just look at her! No pork cutlet ever made a body grow like* that!—and if you cut open her stomach, you'd find them all there waiting to be extracted, poor little tumors, clutching their cold feet. Other people said they saw her dancing at night under a gibbous moon, skin blue as a plum, trying to persuade it to flaunt its full belly every quarter, tempt it to wax and wax like her. Willow grew and grew, big as the Alps, into the sky, beheaded by clouds, ruptured the sky over Kingdom Come, consorting with birds, and people said she was taking up space that should have been inhabited by children. Sometimes they bit her sturdy ankles and she let them. No one ever again mentioned those infernal rabbits infested with misery.

Willow, no grumbler, took it on her sizable chin like a champ. She had known what it was like to be the object of the boundless adoration of a small boy, a wondrous thing. It was only fair, she thought, that she should know too what it is like to be loathed, to be thought an abominable cannibal demon. Her parents bore the shame of being the only parents whose child survived the fateful piping, and her mother spent her days baking custard pies and cherry cobblers and apple slump, basting briskets, simmering succotash, whipping up griddlecakes for breakfast, canning rhubarb and peaches, all for the other parents, who promptly tossed every grubgift she brought them into the trash or left it sitting on the stoop for the fattened foxes and lonesome dogs kicked to the curb. They'd eat nary a morsel prepared by the mother of evil, let them waste to bone first!

At night, while her parents sat in a darkened parlor, Willow lay on her back and tried to stitch the stars together in the image of Oggie, and she thought to herself that the sky was as good a guardian as any, certainly more able than humans, who are so fallible it's always merely a matter of time before they make a mess of all they touch. The universe will one day stop to rest its weary remains and then give up, thought Willow, refuse to be provoked into being again, by a big bang or a seamstress mole with an endless skein of thread or a week of Godly labor or a dismembered deity whose parts are itching to be reanimated in the shape of mountains and rivers, because humans will have finally and irreversibly swapped love for war, life for death, and bloodied the planet but good, caused it to hemorrhage beyond all stanching.

———— ⌁ ————

The last sound Kingdom Come ever heard was the sound of the earth shuddering as Willow Himmelfarb walked into the river and the murmur of the water as it parted around her legs, which stood stalwart as silos, then she sat down and her body dammed the river, and the townspeople slept for the first time since their children had disappeared, slept in their children's beds. There wasn't enough river for Willow to drown herself—there wasn't enough water in all of Kansas for that—but the water rose and rose around her and flooded the land, swallowing prairie and crops and automobiles and barns and threshers and finally houses, cleansing the town of its heartache, the parents of the lost children gushing forth out of bedroom windows, bobbing in the escaped river beside coffee pots and overcoats and lampshades and adding machines and pitchforks and sneakers and tubas and yo-yos and incomplete sets of encyclopedias, singing, singing, singing, singing, happily abducted by water.

for Alena Kathleen Wilson

SERIALS

by Katie Williams from *American Short Fiction*

———————⊱⊰———————

S o . . . Mr. Briggs, my pre-calc teacher, has decided to become a serial
killer. It's not like he's announced it or anything, but with so many
people becoming serial killers these days,[2] a smart girl learns to read the
signs. Like how when Mr. Briggs gives us silent work time, whereas he used
to sit at his desk reading back issues of *The Atlantic Monthly* and sipping
out of a mug with the words *Bald Is Beautiful* printed on its side, now he
points to each of us with the tip of his mechanical pencil and then writes
things in a notebook hidden in his lap. Or how, yesterday, he bent over my
desk and said, "Nice," and I was supposed to think he was referring to my
equations, but really I saw him sizing up the meatiness of my arms. Then,
he asked my best friend Maryellen Swiswanski if it was true that she still
lived in the two-story powder blue house on the corner of Oak and Grove,
and if the lock on her porch door was broken like it appeared to be when
you peeked over the fence in the backyard. Mr. Briggs even offered her ten
extra credit points if she promised to leave her bedroom window open at
night. But what really clinches it is how he came in yesterday wearing a
new pair of glasses with round lenses and slim wire rims. The serial-killer-
with-delicate-glasses-and-a-cold-stare look has been very popular as of
late; today's killer doesn't go in much for the untucked shirt, bowie knife
look anymore. That went out of style last spring.[3]

Maybe I shouldn't worry about Mr. Briggs. It's not like this is the first time
I've had a serial killer for a teacher. My freshman year French instructor,
Mme. Rambeau, liked to sever the hands of grocery store bagboys. But at
least her victims weren't us, her students. Except for Brian Ott, of course,
who got an unfortunate after-school job at the Carrotorium—the health
food store attached to the mall. Brian kept telling us how he was safe from

---

2. Bernard Trott, "If Dahmer Could See Us Now," *The New York Times Magazine*, 1 September 5,
2004, 41. Greta Salsburg, "A Time to Kill," *Harper's Magazine*, August 2004, 63.
3. Camille Dire, "Murder Is the New Black: The Return of the Turtleneck," *Vogue*, March 2007, 101.

Mme. Rambeau because the Carrotorium didn't count as your typical grocery store. "Everything's organic," he reminded us, as though the simple presence of flaxseed supplements would save him from a handless death. Mme. Rambeau got him around winter break, whether for being a bagboy or for his terrible verb conjugations, *je ne suis pas sure.*

And then sophomore year, there was Mr. Wesson, my photography teacher, who—if you can believe it—actually got busted for serial killing. He was playing it fast and loose, having his students develop prints of his crime scenes.[4] We all knew that it was only a matter of time before Kelly Mint would tell her parents on him. Lots of kids' parents wouldn't have cared. For instance, my parents would have said something like: "You have to grow up sometime, Stacey."

But Mr. and Mrs. Mint are very serious about Kelly's education. She spends Saturday afternoons filling out SAT practice tests, and has private tutors in both Latin *and* Japanese. So, you can imagine how the Mints felt when they discovered that their daughter's class time was being used to promote her teacher's photographic talents instead of her own. After all, attaching a photography portfolio to one's college application shows personality *and* sensitivity—that extra oomph the Ivies are really looking for these days.

The Mints scheduled a special meeting with Principal Scott. And quicker than you could say "multiple victims," Mrs. Prentice, the school guidance counselor, had gathered the entire Intro to Photo class in her office. She asked us if we'd noticed anything unusual about Mr. Wesson's classes. A couple kids said, "Nope," but then some other kids told the truth, and after that pretty much everyone was confessing all at once.

Kelly Mint stood in the back of the office, staring politely at the tops of her slip-on sneakers. She didn't say a word, but everyone had already figured out who the snitch was. Some kids still give her a hard time about tattling, but I don't think she did anything wrong. Serial killing *is* illegal, after all. It's like downloading free music from the Internet; just because a lot of people do it doesn't make it right. Besides, Isaac (my boyfriend—we've been together since Homecoming) told me that Mr. Wesson made about a million bucks selling his story rights to CBS. The

4. Joseph Bunting, "Local Teacher Assigns Gallery of Death," *Petoskey News-Review*, November 23, 2006.

miniseries is coming out next fall.[5] I wonder who'll play me. I've got my fingers crossed for Miley Cyrus.

The shocking thing about Mr. Briggs is that most teachers who serial-kill work hard to keep their professional and private lives separate.[6] See, us high school students, especially us girls, already have to contend with about a million non-teacher serial killers who've decided that we're their ideal victim demographic.[7] I blame all those slasher films from the '80s that make us look so perky and screamy to kill. That's Hollywood, people. It's all silicone implants and Karo syrup; trust me. Murdering high school girls is not as glamorous as it is in the movies. And now that Mr. Briggs has gone serial, I'm supposed to worry about being sliced and diced while simultaneously learning the finer points of the quadratic formula? Come on!

Of course, there are steps a teenager can take to lower her chances of becoming a serial killer victim. That's why, on Saturday morning, Isaac, Maryellen, and I get up early and go to one of those free classes they offer at the YMCA. First thing after we sit down, the instructor, a bouncy woman named Betsy (who we call Bouncing Betsy, or B.B. for short), makes us sign a statement pledging that we aren't serial killers ourselves. Sometimes serial killers sneak into the class, she explains, to try to find the best victims. Naturally, this news makes Isaac, Maryellen, and me take a closer look around at our classmates. Some seem pretty suspicious; like, one woman is wearing a zip-up velour jumpsuit, and another guy has on a pair of latex gloves that go all the way up to his elbows. But everyone signs the form, so, I guess, no problem.

Once we're cleared, B.B. goes over the basics: Being pretty, large-breasted, and/or chipper are the top risk factors for girls (which puts Maryellen in danger on three counts). Belonging to the football team, driving a sports car, or boasting to your friends about the sex you had last night are dangerous behaviors if you're a boy. Being both mean and popular is a perilous combination for either gender, as those teenagers are viewed as "having it coming to them," especially by the growing number

5. Internet Movie Database, "Under the Black Light: The Petoskey Photo Murders," www.imdb.com/title/tt0373889/?fr=c2l0ZT1kZnxE_;fc=5;ft=20;fm=1.
6. Seth Zone, "Ten Tips to Kill on Your Off-Hours—And Five Reasons You Should!" *Maxim*, June 2005, 72.
7. Seth, Zone, "Ten Signs She's Worth Killing—And Five Warnings She's Not!" *Maxim*, June 2005, 71.

of high school students who are experimenting with serial killing. But being unpopular and misunderstood is equally unsafe, especially if you're unpopular and misunderstood in a poetic sort of way. Say you wear a scarf twined romantically around your neck or draw pen sketches of ravens on your inner arm during class. According to B.B., you'd better stop drawing those birds if you know what's good for you.

B.B. also reviews the obvious rules, which everybody already knows about.[8] Like don't help a man with a cast who's struggling to unlock the back of his big, white, windowless van. Never, ever go camping. And, if you accept an invitation to a home-cooked meal, you may as well just jump into the cooking pot yourself and save your host the trouble.

"Remember," B.B. says, "you can't tell who's a serial killer and who's not just by looking at them."

"And, even if you ask them," she continues, "they may not be entirely honest with you. They might say something like, 'That was just a phase I went through during college.' Or, 'I only murder accountants.' The rule I live by (and I mean *live* by): Assume everyone serial kills, until proven innocent."

"How can you prove someone's innocent of being a serial killer?" Isaac asks without raising his hand.

"Well . . ." B.B. answers, bouncing on her heels. "I guess the only sure way is if they turn out to be a victim."

"So, we can only trust murdered people?"

"At least then you know you're safe," she says.

Maryellen and I agree that the YMCA class didn't teach us anything new. Isaac says that he learned to stop bragging to the guys in the locker room about our sex life. I sock him in the arm, even though I know he's only kidding. Isaac and I haven't had sex yet, and besides, he changes into his gym clothes in the back seat of his car, not the locker room, to keep the guys from teasing him about his oddly colored chest hair.

In pre-calculus class on Monday, I keep silently repeating the tips that B.B. taught us, hoping that maybe one of them will save me from Mr. Briggs. Isaac, Maryellen, and I are supposed to be figuring out problem twenty-

8. Emmet County Safety Commission, "Don't Be a Statistic. Be Safe," Pamphlet No. 34, 2007.

four, but our graphs keep coming out crooked as a result of shaky hands. Maryellen is especially scared, because of that deal Mr. Briggs offered with the extra credit and her window. She says she'll take her B-minus, thank you very much. Isaac tells her not to worry, that he thinks that Mr. Briggs's comments are just subterfuge, and that really the teacher has been staring at me much more than he has at Maryellen. I shoot Isaac a look like, *Hey! Thanks a whole lot!* But, he doesn't seem to catch it.

Just then, a voice behind us murmurs, "What are you three discussing with such . . . vigor?"

The way Mr. Briggs pauses before saying the word *vigor*, I just know that he has *The Silence of the Lambs* in his DVD player at home. Maryellen yelps. Isaac grabs her hand. None of us knows how long he's been listening. I think we all simultaneously realize how stupid we've been, talking about Mr. Briggs in his very own pre-calculus class. I remember that that was one of the tips B.B. gave us: Don't discuss how someone is a serial killer within his or her earshot. He or she may find it threatening.

Neither Isaac nor Maryellen is answering Mr. Briggs's question, and he's just standing there, staring at us . . . or . . . me, actually. So, I blurt out, "Vectors! We were talking about how vectors are, uh, interesting."

"In-*te*-resting," Mr. Briggs repeats. He studies me for a moment and then reaches up and removes his glasses. He extracts a handkerchief from his jacket pocket and begins to rub the lenses, gently but fastidiously. The three of us watch him, all quiet, while he cleans. After what seems like an hour, he puts his glasses back on, his eyes growing small behind the lenses. "What an interesting girl *you* are, Stacey. Just as interesting as any vector." And, he's smiling at me with the kind of smile you can only get when you have a secret. Finally, he glances over at Isaac and Maryellen. "Back to work," he says and strides away.

"Walk me home from band practice," I beg Isaac.

Isaac pauses and then says, "We can all walk home together," including Maryellen in his gaze.

I can barely sit still in Government class. It's more stressful than the time I tried out for the school musical, when the accompanist played "I'm Gonna Wash That Man Right Outta My Hair" two keys higher than the one I'd practiced it in. I seriously consider going to the nurse's office and calling my mom to come pick me up, but she has a report due at work today, and besides she never believes me when I claim to be sick. And if I tell her the truth about the situation, she'll only say, "Stacey, you're going away to college next year. It's about time you learned how to be more resourceful."

And, wouldn't you just know it? All Mrs. Yonks wants to talk about in class is serial killer legislation. She's wearing the pink cardigan she always wears, the one that smells like cat food, and she's holding up a news magazine for us to look at. On its cover is a drawing of Patrick Henry wielding a bloody knife under the caption *Give Me Liberty or Give Me Serial Death.*[9] [Patrick Henry said "Give me liberty or give me death."]

"Serial killing is an exciting political issue," Mrs. Yonks tells us, "with no clear ideological divide by party lines."

She talks about a bill being debated right now in the Senate that will bar people from holding public office if they have a serial killing conviction on their record.[10] And how, during the debate about this bill, one of the senators accused another of ideological inconsistency, since this other senator was both pro-choice and anti-serial killer.[11]

"What do you guys think about that?" Mrs. Yonks asks us. "Can someone believe in both the right of abortion and the rights of a serial killer victim?"

"This is what happens when you don't allow prayer in the schools," says Eugene Hart, who is very religious and always says that no matter what the question is.

Kelly Mint raises her hand. "Isn't the goal of our penal system rehabilitation and, once time has been served, full acceptance back into society?"

"Very astute, Kelly!" Mrs. Yonks says.

"*Penal* system," someone repeats, and the whole class giggles, except for Kelly Mint. And me who, even if I sucked up a whole tank of laughing gas, couldn't force so much as a chuckle.

9. R. L. Midgen, "Give Me Murder or Give Me Death," *TIME* magazine, February 25, 2008, 52.
10. John Aiken and Heather Gurgany, "Bill Will Ban Serial Politicians," *The New York Times,* February 24, 2008.
11. Heather Gurgany, "Grossman Chides Haupt, Dems Say 'Out of Bounds,'" The New York Times, February 28, 2008.

In the shuffle after band practice, I lose sight of Maryellen and Isaac. And, when I go to our usual meeting place at the drinking fountains by the choir room, they aren't there either. I finally find them back near the band lockers whispering to each other. They stop when they see me, like they don't want me know what they've been talking about. Probably which Emily Dickinson poem they'll read at my funeral.

"Guess we should get walking!" Isaac says in a hearty voice that I've never heard him use before.

We leave the school building, and it's this great, sunny day outside. Honestly, I'd much rather be murdered on a rainy day than a sunny day. At least then I could say to myself: Oh, well! Guess I don't have to bother with galoshes anymore!

As we walk, I keep looking over my shoulder and am relieved that I don't see Mr. Briggs following us. My relief turns quickly into annoyance, though, when I notice how Maryellen is walking in the middle with Isaac and me on either side of her. Shouldn't I, the potential target, be in the middle for, like, basic safety reasons? I swear, just because she has C cups, Maryellen thinks every serial killer is out to get her.

No one is talking, so I say, "Sometimes I think it'd be nice to live in the olden times, before the serial killer epidemic."

"Can you even imagine?" Maryellen asks, hugging her chest to her . . . well, chest.

"My grandma called them 'the good, old days,'" I go on. "But then again, my grandpa was a serial killer, and she always supported him in his avocation."

"Sure, living pre-serial killers sounds nice on the surface," Isaac says, "but you're not thinking about all the modern conveniences you'd have to do without, like electricity and penicillin."

"I guess you have to give up something to get something," I answer, and Maryellen shoots Isaac a meaningful look that I don't understand.

I understand it two blocks later, though, when we come to the entrance for my subdivision, Winding Hills, and Isaac and Maryellen don't follow me in.

"Guess we'll see you later," Isaac says, waving a little wave.

"What? You guys aren't going to walk me to my house? It's only two blocks away!"

They both stare at me. Maryellen twists a strand of her hair slowly around her finger. I think about how even though she's always complaining that she's at high risk for being a serial killer victim, *she's* the one who dyes her hair blonde every month. *She's* the one who fastens the buckles on those little schoolgirl kilts.[12] And I guess, my emotions are a couple of steps faster than my brain, because right then I feel how much I hate her without knowing exactly why.

"There's something we have to tell you," Maryellen says to me in a voice that all of a sudden isn't the littlest bit ditzy anymore.

Isaac opens his mouth to speak, but Maryellen silences him with a hand on his chest. Her other hand is still twirling her hair.

"Isaac and I have decided that we're going to start dating, which means (I'm sure you've already figured out) that he's going to have to *stop* dating you." She takes her hand from Isaac's chest and snakes it around his middle. "And, since Isaac's *my* boyfriend now, it's his responsibility to walk *me* to *my* front door."

"Isaac?" I ask, hoping he'll say that they're only joking, like the time he joked about telling the guys in the locker room that we'd had sex. And then, it hits me that he and Maryellen have probably already *had* sex, in the locker room or in the back seat of his car, her fingers curled through his oddly colored chest hair.

Isaac kind of gulps and stammers, "It's true, Stacey. And like Maryellen said, it's my responsibility to walk her home now."

"This is really bad timing," I tell Isaac. I refuse to look at Maryellen for a myriad of reasons besides the tears skating down my cheeks.

"I'm sorry, Stacey, but these things choose us." Isaac shuffles his feet. "I want you to know that I don't hold any grudges against you and that I sincerely hope you'll make it home without being serial-killed."

Maryellen makes a little coughing noise, which I figure is their secret signal to go, because they both turn then and walk away, their arms cast around each other's backs. I can feel the anger welling up inside of me. It is like the anger of every victim of every serial killer since the beginning of time.

"Oh, yeah?" I yell after them. "Well, I hope, on the way home, that you two *do* get killed by a legion of serial killers!" Isaac glances back at me. Maryellen doesn't turn around. "Legion!" I shout. "Serial!"

I'm so mad that I don't even look where I'm going, but just march into Winding Hills, which is how I end up smacking into Mr. Briggs and landing on the sidewalk at his feet.

12. Skotskie Curtis, "Dress for Survival," *Seventeen*, October 2007, 41.

"Stacey, how nice to *run into* you," Mr. Briggs quips, stroking his shiny butcher knife in the exact same way I'd seen him stroke his graphing calculator about a million times.

I scramble backward on my hands and feet. Mr. Briggs walks after me lazily.

"I knew you were a serial killer," I tell him.

"You always were one of my most *apt pupils*."

"Apt this!" I say, punning like B.B. taught us. With that, I try to kick him. But he flicks my foot away, and I end up back on my ass.

"I have a question for you, Stacey." Mr. Briggs towers over me, the sunlight hitting his glasses so that I can't see his eyes.

"What?" I ask, looking around wildly for someone, anyone, to help me.

There's a woman across the street walking a runny-eyed cocker spaniel. She pauses and gives us a nasty look. "The neighborhood watch has regulations about this kind of thing," she yells, shaking her fist. "Come on, Skippie!" She jerks on the leash, pulling her dog after her, muttering, "Mommy's going to give them a piece of her mind at next month's meeting, Skippie. Oh, yes, she is."[13]

Mr. Briggs isn't listening to the neighbor woman, though. Instead, he's holding his knife at all kinds of different angles, like he's trying to decide where to cut me first.

"You said you had a question for me?" I remind him.

He pauses in his pretend cutting. "Right you are. Listen carefully, because I'm only going to ask you once. And, if you answer correctly, I'll let you go." He takes in a big breath, and then says, "If Train A leaves the station, heading north at a rate of 65 miles per hour, at the same time Train B leaves a station 200 miles away, heading south at a rate of 80 miles per hour, how long until the two trains meet?"

"Mr. Briggs!" I get to my feet. "My boyfriend just dumped me for my best friend who has dyed blonde hair and C-cup breasts. If you think I have the capacity to do advanced math right now, you're crazy!"

Mr. Briggs glares at me then gets distracted by his reflection in his knife. Finally, he says, "Yes, Stacey. That *is* how long it will take for the trains to meet. You may go now."

....

13. Winding Hills Neighborhood Association, "Winding Hills Neighborhood 'Good Neighbor' Rules and Suggestions," Pamphlet No. 1, 2007–2008.

I don't argue, just dart around him and walk off in the direction of Skippie the runny-eyed cocker spaniel.

"Oh, Stacey," Mr. Briggs calls out after me.

"Yeah?" I turn around. He's standing just where I left him, using his handkerchief to polish his knife.

"The serial killer moniker I've chosen is The Mathematician. If you happen to give any interviews about our *encounter*, I'd be grateful if you mentioned it. I'm trying to cultivate good word of mouth."

"Sure, Mr. Briggs." I raise a hand. "See you in class on Monday."

"You may want to study as if there were going to be a pop quiz on vectors." He winks. "Don't tell the other students I told you so."

EPILOGUE:

I get an A on my vector quiz. And, the rest of high school goes okay, too. After the interview I give to the school paper,[14] word gets around about The Mathematician, and everyone starts studying math really hard, since they want to make sure they can answer the killer's question. Come spring, our school ends up with the highest standardized math scores in the state, and Mr. Briggs is awarded a Golden Apple Teaching award for having inspired us all so much.[15]

And even though I decide not to be friends with Isaac or Maryellen anymore after that fateful walk home from school, I'm still polite to them. I say "hi" when I pass them in the halls and all that. And, boy, am I glad I decided not to hold a grudge against Isaac when Maryellen murders him after prom. It turns out that Maryellen is a serial killer whose victims are boys with oddly colored chest hair.[16] No one had any idea. I guess I should've remembered what B.B. taught us: anyone could be a serial killer, even my best friend. But then again, sometimes a girl needs a break from worrying she's going to be murdered all the time.

....

14. Kelly Mint, "One + One = Alive: Senior Figures Her Way out of Serial Death," *Petoskey High School Herald*, March 6, 2008.

15. Phillip Briggs, "Fear as a Teaching Tool," *National Journal of Pedagogy* 37, (June 2008): 38.

16. Kelly Mint, "They Grow Purple; She Sees Red—A Student Profile," *Petoskey High School Yearbook*, 2007–2008.

CONTRIBUTORS

David Ackert has published two short stories, one in *Fantasy & Science Fiction* and the other ("King of the Djinn") in *Realms of Fantasy*. Both were coauthored with Benjamin Rosenbaum. When he isn't writing, he's acting on television shows such as *CSI: Miami, Bones, The Unit,* and *Monk,* as well as films like *Maryam, Suckers* and *The Line.* He is currently producing a documentary film entitled *Voices of Uganda.* David lives in Los Angeles with his wife, Rebecca.

Ramona Ausubel is from Santa Fe, New Mexico. She has an MFA from the University of California, Irvine where she served as editor for *Faultline Journal of Art & Literature.* Her work has appeared in *One Story,* the *Green Mountains Review,* the *Orange Coast Review* and *pax americana.* This year her work was included in the Best American Short Stories list of *Distinguished Stories* and twice in the Best American Nonrequired Reading's *Notable* list.She is finishing a novel and a collection of stories and starting a book of essays about what it means to people all over to contemplate starting a family at this moment on the planet, a project which took her around the world in 2009.

Peter S. Beagle was born in New York in April 1939. He studied at the University of Pittsburgh and graduated with a degree in creative writing in 1959. Beagle's first novel *A Fine and Private Place* (1960) has long been a cult classic. It was followed by the non-fiction travelogue *I See by My Outfit* in 1965, and by his best-known work, the modern fantasy classic *The Last Unicorn* in 1968. Beagle's other books include novels *The Folk of the Air, The Innkeeper's Song,* and *Tamsin;* collections *The Fantasy Worlds of Peter S. Beagle, The Rhinoceros Who Quoted Nietzsche, Giant Bones, The Line Between, Strange Roads, We Never Talked About My Brother;* several non-fiction books; and a number of screenplays and teleplays.

Ryan Boudinot is the author of *The Littlest Hitler* (Counterpoint, 2006) and *Misconception* (Grove Atlantic/Black Cat, 2009). His work has appeared in *McSweeney's, The Best American Nonrequired Reading,* and elsewhere. He blogs about film at therumpus.net and teaches at Goddard College's MFA program in Port Townsend, Washington.

Will Clarke is the author of *Lord Vishnu's Love Handles* (Simon & Schuster 2005) and *The Worthy* (Simon & Schuster 2006)—both were selected as the *New York Times* Editors' Choice in 2006. Clarke was also named "The Hot Pop Prophet" by *Rolling Stone* magazine as part of their annual "Hot List." "The Pentecostal Home for Flying Children" also appeared as part of the Simon & Schuster superhero fiction anthology, *Who Can Save Us Now?* edited by Owen King and John McNally in June 2008.

Martin Cozza's fiction has appeared in *The Missouri Review, Columbia, The Massachusetts Review, Carolina Quarterly*, and elsewhere. He is a graduate of the Iowa Writers' Workshop and lives in Minneapolis with his wife, son, and daughters. He is working on a novel for children.

Jeffrey Ford's first published story, "The Casket," appeared in John Gardner's magazine MSS in 1981, and since then his work has appeared in numerous magazines and anthologies, and has won the Nebula, Fountain, Edgar Allen Poe, and World Fantasy Awards. He is the author of seven novels and three short story collections, including, most recently, *The Shadow Year* and *The Drowned Life*. He is a professor of writing and literature at Brookdale Community College in New Jersey, and he has been an instructor at the Clarion Workshop.

Chris Gavaler's short fiction has appeared in over two dozen national journals, including *Prairie Schooner, Shenandoah*, and *Witness*. He earned an MFA at the University of Virginia in 2006 and now teaches writing at Washington and Lee University in Lexington, VA, where he lives with his wife and children.

Thomas Glave is the author of the fiction collections *Whose Song? and Other Stories* and *The Torturer's Wife*, and the essay collection *Words to Our*

Now: Imagination and Dissent (winner of a 2005 Lambda Literary Award). He is the editor of the anthology *Our Caribbean: A Gathering of Lesbian and Gay Writing from the Antilles* (winner of a 2008 Lambda Literary Award). A founding member of the Jamaica Forum for Lesbians, All-Sexuals, and Gays (J-FLAG), Glave was 2008–09 Martin Luther King, Jr. Visiting Professor in the Program in Writing and Humanistic Studies at MIT. He teaches in the English department at SUNY Binghamton.

Lisa Goldstein has published thirteen novels, two under the pseudonym Isabel Glass. Her novel *The Red Magician* won the American Book Award for Best Paperback. She has also published a short story collection, *Travellers in Magic*, and many short stories. Her novels and short stories have been finalists for the Hugo, Nebula, and World Fantasy awards. She has worked as a proofreader, library aide, bookseller, and reviewer, and she lives in Oakland, California, with her husband and their cute dog Spark.

Laura Kasischke has published four novels, two novels for young adults, and seven collections of poetry. Her newest novel is *In a Perfect World* (Harper Perennial, 2009), an apocalyptic tale of the near future. She lives in Chelsea, Michigan, with her husband and son.

John Kessel co-directs the creative writing program at North Carolina State University in Raleigh. A winner of the Nebula Award, the Theodore Sturgeon Award, the Locus Poll, and Tiptree award, his books include *Good News from Outer Space*, *Corrupting Dr. Nice*, and *The Pure Product*. With James Patrick Kelly, he co-edited *Feeling Very Strange: The Slipstream Anthology*, *Rewired: The Post-Cyberpunk Anthology*, and *The Secret History of Science Fiction*.

His collection *The Baum Plan for Financial Independence and Other Stories* was published by Small Beer Press in April 2008.

Stephen King has published stories in such venues as *Startling Mystery Stories*, *Fantasy & Science Fiction*, and *The New Yorker*. He is the author of over thirty novels, including *Carrie*, *The Shining*, *Salem's Lot*, *Christine*, *The Stand*, *Misery*, *The Green Mile*, *From a Buick 8*, *Lisey's Story*, *Blaze*, *Duma Key*, and *Under the Dome*. His stories have been collected in such books as *Night Shift, Skeleton Crew, Four Past Midnight, Nightmares & Dreamscapes, Everything's Eventual,* and *Just After Sunset*. He has written the nonfiction books *Danse Macabre* and *On Writing*, and he has been a guest editor of *Best American Short Stories*.

Rebecca Makkai's fiction has appeared in both *The Best American Short Stories 2009* and *2008*, and in journals including *New England Review, The Threepenny Review,* and *Shenandoah*. She lives near Chicago.

Kuzhali Manickavel's debut collection *Insects Are Just Like You And Me Except Some of Them Have Wings* is available from Blaft Publications Pvt. Ltd. Her work can also be found at *Subtropics, Per Contra,* and *The Café Irreal*. Born and raised in Canada, she now lives in a small temple town on the coast of South India.

Benjamin Rosenbaum lives near Basel, Switzerland, with his wife Esther and his children, Aviva and Noah. His stories have appeared in *Harper's, Fantasy & Science Fiction, Asimov's, McSweeney's, Strange Horizons,* and *Nature,* have been nominated for the Hugo, Nebula, World Fantasy, BSFA, and Sturgeon Awards, and have been translated into 14 languages; also, he has it on good authority that he is fancier than Noah's elbow. His first collection "The Ant King and Other Stories" is available from Small Beer Press. More at http://www.benjaminrosenbaum.com.

Deborah Schwartz has published stories in the *Kenyon Review, Gulf Coast,* and *Arts & Letters: Journal of Contemporary Culture,* winning first prize in their 2004 short story competition. She has found herself employed by a September 11th commemorative gallery, a sculpting resin manufacturer, a Holocaust museum, and an affordable housing developer. Presently, she lives in Brooklyn with her husband and her giant ego.

Paul Tremblay is the author of the novel *The Little Sleep* and the short fiction collection *Compositions for the Young and Old*. He has served as fiction editor of *CHIZINE* and as co-editor of *Fantasy Magazine,* and was also the co-editor (with Sean Wallace) of the *Fantasy, Bandersnatch,* and *Phantom* anthologies. Paul is currently a juror for the Shirley Jackson Awards as well. His website is www.paultremblay.net.

Shawn Vestal's stories have appeared in *Tin House, McSweeney's, The Southern Review, Quarterly West*, and other journals. A graduate of the Eastern Washington University MFA program, he lives in Spokane, Washington, with his wife and son.

Kellie Wells's collection of short fiction *Compression Scars* won the Flannery O'Connor Prize in 2001. *Skin*, a novel, was published in 2006, by the University of Nebraska Press, in their Flyover Fiction Series. She teaches in the MFA program at Washington University, in St. Louis.

Katie Williams attended the University of Michigan and the University of Texas in Austin, where she was a Michener Fellow in Creative Writing. Her short stories have appeared in a handful of journals, and her first novel, *The Space Between Trees*, will be released by Chronicle Books this spring. The story "Serials" is currently being adapted into a full-length feature film by Divisadero Pictures. Katie would like to offer her thanks to the MacDowell Colony and Yaddo, where she wrote this story.

RECOMMENDED READING

The editors would like to call special attention to
the following stories published in 2008:

"Run! Run!"
by Jim Aikin
Fantasy & Science Fiction,
September 2008

"The Lagerstatte"
by Laird Barron
The Del Rey Book of Science
Fiction and Fantasy,
edited by Ellen Datlow

"Within the City of the Swan"
by Aliette de Bodard
Shimmer,
The Art Issue 2008

"What the Redmond
Men Found"
by Matthew David Brozik
Zahir, Summer 2008

"The Loa and the Gaping Jaw" by
Brendan Byrne
Flurb, a Webzine of
Astonishing Tales,
Fall–Winter 2008

"Jimmy"
by Pat Cadigan
The Del Rey Book of Science
Fiction and Fantasy,
edited by Ellen Datlow

"Poor Little Egg-Boy
Hatched in a Shul"
by Nathan Englander
McSweeney's, Issue 28

"Drone"
by Gemma Files
Not One of Us, Issue 39

"All the Little Gods We Are"
by John Grant
Clockwork Phoenix: Tales
of Beauty and Strangeness,
edited by Mike Allen

"The Difficulties of Evolution"
by Karen Heuler
Weird Tales,
July–Aug 2008

"The Hand of the Devil
on a String"
by M. K. Hobson
Shimmer,
Spring 2008

"The Last Dead"
by Drew Johnson
Virginia Quarterly Review,
Winter 2008

"Far and Wee"
by Kathe Koja
Weird Tales,
November–December 2008

"Litany"
by Rand B. Lee
Fantasy & Science Fiction,
June 2008

"We Love Deena"
by Alice Sola Kim
Strange Horizons,
February 11, 2008

"But Wait! There's More!"
by Richard Mueller
Fantasy & Science Fiction,
August 2008

"The Glazers"
by Joyce Carol Oates
American Short Fiction,
Winter–Spring 2008

"On the Banks of the
River of Heaven"
by Richard Parks
Realms of Fantasy, April 2008

"The Joined"
by Helen Phillips
Mississippi Review,
Spring 2008

"The Small Door"
by Holly Phillips
Fantasy Magazine,
May 19, 2008

"Creature"
by Ramsey Shehadeh
Weird Tales,
March–April 2008

"Detours on the Way to Nothing"
by Rachel Swirsky
Weird Tales,
March–April 2008

"The Body Autumnal"
by Lisa Wells
Ecotone,
Spring 2008

"A Different Country"
by Wayne Wightman
Fantasy & Science Fiction,
December 2008

"Two Tales"
by Imants Zicdonis
Fairy Tale Review,
White Issue

PUBLICATIONS
RECEIVED

In addition to online sources and printed materials sought out by the guest
editor and series editor, the following websites, journals, and anthologies
sent their publications to Best American Fantasy for consideration.

ALASKA QUARTERLY REVIEW
University of Alaska, Anchorage
3211 Providence Drive
Anchorage, AK 99508
www.uaa.alaska.edu/aqr/

AMERICAN SHORT FICTION
P.O. Box 301209
Austin, TX 78703
www.americanshortfiction.org/

Backward CITY REVIEW
PO Box 41317
Greensboro, NC 27404
homepage.mac.com/
languageismycopilot/
backwardscitydotnet/home.html

BLACK GATE
New Epoch Press
815 Oak Street
St. Charles, IL 60174
www.blackgate.com

BLACK WARRIOR REVIEW
University of Alabama
Box 862936
Tuscaloosa, AL 35486
blackwarrior.webdelsol.com

BRIAR CLIFF REVIEW
Briar Cliff University
3303 Rebecca Street
P.O. Box 2100
Sioux City, IA 51104
www.briarcliff.edu/bcreview

CALYX
P.O. Box B
Corvallis, OR 97339-0539
www.calyxpress.org

CHELSEA
P.O. Box 773
Cooper Station
New York, NY 01276-0773
www.chelseamag.org

CRAZYHORSE
Department of English
College of Charleston
66 George Street
Charleston, SC 29424
crazyhorse.cofc.edu/

ECOTONE
Creative Writing Department
University of North Carolina
Wilmington
601 South College Road
Wilmington, NC 28403-3297
www.ecotonejournal.com

ELECTRIC VELOCIPEDE
P.O. Box 5014
Summerset, NJ 08873
www.electricvelocipede.com

FAIRY TALE REVIEW
Department of English
University of Alabama
Tuskaloosa, AL 35487
www.fairytalereview.com

FANTASY & SCIENCE FICTION
P.O. Box 3447
Hoboken, NJ 07030
www.fandsfmag.com

FICTION
Department of English
City College of New York
Convent Avenue at 138th Street
New York, NY 10031
www.fictioninc.com

THE GEORGIA REVIEW
The University of Georgia
Athens, GA 30602-9009
www.uga.edu/garev

GLIMMER TRAIN
1211 NW Glisan, Suite 207
Portland, OR 97209-3054
www.glimmertrain.com

HAWAII REVIEW
Kuykendall 402
1733 Donaghho Road
Honolulu, HI 96822
www.english.hawaii.edu/journals/
journals.html

KALEIDOTROPE
P.O. Box 25
Carle Place, NY 11514
www.kaleidotrope.net/

THE KENYON REVIEW
Kenyon College
104 College Drive
Gambier, OH 43022-9623
www.kenyonreview.org

LADY CHURCHILL'S
ROSEBUD WRISTLET
176 Prospect Avenue
Northampton, MA 01060
www.lcrw.net/lcrw/

MERIDIAN
University of Virginia
P.O. Box 400145
Charlottesville, VA 22904-4145
readmeridian.org/

MISSISSIPPI REVIEW
University of Southern Mississippi
118 College Drive, #5144
Hattiesburg, MS 39406-0001
www.mississippireview.com

NEW ENGLAND REVIEW
Middlebury College
Middlebury, VT 05753
www.middlebury.edu/~nereview

NEW GENRE
P.O. Box 270092
West Hartford, CT 06127
www.new-genre.com

THE NEW YORKER
4 Times Square
New York, NY 10036-6592
www.newyorker.com

NINTH LETTER
University of Illinois at
Urbana-Champaign
234 English Building
608 South Wright Street
Urbana, IL 61801
www.ninthletter.com

NORTH CAROLINA
LITERARY REVIEW
East Carolina University
Department of English
2201 Bate Building
Greenville, NC 27858-4353
www.ecu.edu/nclr

NOT ONE OF US
12 Curtis Road
Natick, MA 01760
not-one-of-us.com

ON SPEC
P.O. Box 4727
Edmonton, AB
Canada T6E 5G6
www.onspec.ca

ONE STORY
P.O. Box 150618
Brooklyn, NY 11215
one-story.com

PARADOX
P.O. Box 22897
Brooklyn, NY 11202-2897
www.paradoxmag.com

PHANTOM
9710 Traville Gateway Drive, #234
Rockville, MD 20850

PORCUPINE
P.O. Box 259
Cedarburg, WI 53012
www.porcupineliteraryarts.com

REDIVIDER
Emerson College
120 Broylston Street
Boston, MA 02116
www.redividerjournal.org/

ROSEBUD
N3310 Asje Road
Cambridge, WI 53523
www.rsbd.net/

SHENANDOAH
Mattingly House / 2 Lee Avenue
Washington and Lee University
Lexington, VA 24450-2116
shenandoah.wlu.edu/

SHIMMER
P.O. Box 58591
Salt Lake City, UT 84158-0591
www.shimmerzine.com

SOU'WESTER
Department of English
Box 1438
Southern Illinois
University, Edwardsville
Edwardsville, IL 62026-1438
www.siue.edu/ENGLISH/SW/

THE SOUTHERN REVIEW
Old President's House
Louisiana State University
Baton Rouge, LA 70803
www.lsu.edu/tsr/

TESSERACT BOOKS
P.O. Box 1714
Calgary, Alberta
Canada T2P 2L7
www.edgewebsite.com

TIN HOUSE
P.O. Box 10500
Portland, OR 97296-0500
www.tinhouse.com

WEIRD TALES
9710 Traville Gateway Drive #234
Rockville, MD 20850-7408
www.weirdtales.net/

ZAHIR
315 South Coast Highway 101
Suite U8
Encinitas, CA 92024
www.zahirtales.com

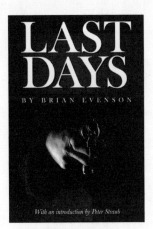